GIRLS OF FLIGHT CITY

GIRLS OF FLIGHT CITY

INSPIRED BY TRUE EVENTS, A NOVEL OF WWII, THE ROYAL AIR FORCE, AND TEXAS

LORRAINE HEATH

THORNDIKE PRESS
A part of Gale, a Cengage Company

**LIBRARY OF CONGRESS CIP DATA ON FILE.
CATALOGUING IN PUBLICATION FOR THIS BOOK
IS AVAILABLE FROM THE LIBRARY OF CONGRESS.**

ISBN-13: 979-8-8857-8042-1 (hardcover alk. paper)

Published in 2022 by arrangement with William Morrow Paperback, an imprint of HarperCollins Publishers.

Printed in Mexico
Print Number : 1   Print Year : 2022

In memory of all those courageous souls
whose final rest is
far from home
To those they loved
To those who loved them

If I should die, think only this of me:
That there's some corner of a
foreign field
That is for ever England.
— From "The Soldier" by Rupert Brooke

PROLOGUE

Leaning heavily on her cane, she walked slowly along the meandering path toward the specially designated portion of the Oaklawn Memorial Cemetery as she had for nearly eighty years. Her steps were smaller, and a twinge of pain in her knees and hips accompanied each one. She doubted she had another year left in her — which was the reason she was now regaling her great-granddaughters with the stories.

Having shared them with her daughters and their daughters over the years, she knew full well they could relate the tales to this latest generation with a great deal of accuracy, but as long as she was able, she believed it important they hear them from someone who had been there. Someone who had fallen in love during those early months. Someone who had spoken, laughed, and danced with these twenty-two men.

They'd been boys really. Most of the young Brits who had come to learn how to pilot an aircraft had been. Eighteen, nineteen, twenty. Some a little older. For many, it had been the first time they'd ever crossed an ocean. Certainly, fewer than a handful had ever traveled to the United States before, much less visited Texas.

They'd brought with them their lovely accents, which had caused anyone who had ever worn a skirt to sigh and fall a little bit in love with them for that alone.

Arriving on the train, they'd been filled with enthusiasm, determination, daunting responsibility, and perhaps a little fear. How could they not have experienced some fear when the world had been in such turmoil, and they'd known that, when they finished their training and returned to England, they would be battling not only for their lives but for the very existence of a nation, a world, democracy?

Although these twenty-two never returned home, they'd been no less brave or noble. She'd vowed they'd never be forgotten, never abandoned.

Finally, she reached the monument that Lord Halifax, British ambassador to the United States, had dedicated in 1942 when he'd visited this small section that honored the fallen of his homeland. Nearby, a Union Jack fluttered in the slight breeze. The saplings she'd long ago planted were towering oaks now, providing shade and protection from the harshness of the Texas sun as she passed beneath their boughs and came to a halt at the first gray granite headstone. So profound in its simplicity, with his service number, rank, and name inscribed above *Royal Air Force.* Below was carved his date of death, his age, and the epitaph provided by his family:

HE FLIES NOW AMONG THE ANGELS.

After all these years, still the tears came. Along with a flood of memories. As though it were yesterday, she recalled the afternoon he'd arrived and more.

She remembered the beginning of it all . . .

CHAPTER 1

In the skies above North Texas
Sunday, March 9, 1941

It had been dubbed the dance of death.

The aerial stunt was Jessie Lovelace's favorite because of the precision required to align the double wings of the Jenny so that they overlapped and hovered between those of the biplane flying alongside hers. It demanded a great deal of trust in the other pilot's skill as they both cruised over the airdrome in tandem at a predetermined altitude and speed. It also necessitated an exorbitant amount of concentration not to crash into the other aircraft, sending both barreling toward earth, where the fliers might not only fail to survive but could take with them a few of the gathered spectators who had each paid a dollar to be thrilled by the daring exploits of the two women aviators.

Focusing on the task made it impossible

to drift into thoughts regarding the men in her life who had recently betrayed her.

Her brother, who'd gone off to fight in a war that wasn't theirs to fight. "It will be," he'd said. "Eventually Hitler will come for us, especially if England falls."

Their father, who'd died unexpectedly in his sleep three days after Christmas. He hadn't left any instructions or made any arrangements regarding his half of the flight school he'd established with his brother following their return home after flying planes for the army during the last war with Germany. As a result, Uncle Joe wanted to abandon the business, sell the whole kit and kaboodle, and find employment elsewhere.

Her boyfriend — a term that had worked when she and Luke Caldwell were in high school, but now that she was twenty-four seemed juvenile. However, when she'd mentioned that little tidbit to him, he'd grinned and said, *"Fiancée* works. Or *wife."* Since her dad's passing, Luke had been pushing for them to marry. Even her mom was dropping not-so-subtle hints that it was long past time Jessie became a homemaker. Try as she might, however, Jessie couldn't envision finding satisfaction in the before-sunup-to-after-sundown life of a rancher's wife.

The truth was, she resented her brother for finding a way out of Terrence, resented even more that his flight skills had made his escape possible. Her ability to handle an aircraft was equal to his, but the only aviation avenues she'd had any luck securing were crop dusting and barnstorming, neither providing consistent employment, sufficient income, or the more fulfilling life she craved. Occasionally she gave flying lessons at the Lovelace School of Aviation, but she was growing weary of constantly searching for work, being forced to take the odd job where she could find it, and feeling like she'd gone into a stall, unable to regain lift.

As she neared Annette Gibson's airplane, she took a deep cleansing breath and cleared her mind of everything except the matter at hand, focusing completely on lining up her wingtips between Annette's, then slowly, carefully, easing closer until the edges intersected slightly, stopping just shy of making contact with the struts bracing the upper and lower wings.

As they sailed along together, she experienced a rush of pleasure. She might not always be in control of her life, but she was in control of this baby, her father's Curtiss Jenny, which he'd purchased nearly twenty years earlier as the start to his business.

After passing over the crowd, she and Annette peeled away from each other, going into a ballet of loops and rolls. Then another dash over the gathering, coming in so low that people ducked — even though they were in no danger of being hit by the wheels. Annette carried on to land, but Jessie wasn't quite done yet. She considered being a daredevil in the sky to be an art form, taking a wide blue canvas and painting images over it that those who viewed the creation, no matter how briefly, would never forget. Although recently she'd begun losing her enthusiasm for barnstorming. People were less impressed with stunts and more interested in witnessing a fiery catastrophe. Still, she was determined to give them a show that would take their breath away.

She opened the throttle and pushed the stick forward, using gravity to accelerate. When she was satisfied with the momentum she'd gained, she pulled back on the stick, lifting the nose until the aircraft was practically standing on its tail, and then continuing over until she was flying upside down. After several seconds, she rolled upright and soared a good distance away from the fallow field. Banking wide and heading back, she determined she'd allowed plenty of room for landing. The Jenny wasn't without its design flaws, one of them being its absence of brakes. Once her wheels touched the ground, she reduced the throttle and taxied toward her destination. When she was close enough, she cut off the mixture control to stop the engine, coasted to a stop, and shut off the mags.

She removed her tinted goggles and leather helmet, then combed her fingers through her mahogany curls. While in high school, she'd chopped off her shoulder-length waves as a tribute to Amelia Earhart, after her idol had made her first solo transatlantic flight. She'd always wanted to be as much like the intrepid female pilot as possible — except for the going missing part. She'd mourned for days after hearing the news on the radio, and still held out hope that they would find the beloved aviatrix on an island somewhere in the Pacific.

Jessie climbed out of the cockpit and hit the ground. A gaggle of youngsters immediately surrounded her, several excitedly waving a leaflet advertising the airshow and asking her to sign it. She answered their shouted questions, giving extra attention to the girls, assuring them they, too, could touch the clouds. When she'd applied her signature to the last handbill and the chil-

17

dren had wandered off, she turned to find Annette waiting for her.

"That was fun," her fellow aviatrix said. She'd met Annette at an airshow a few years earlier. They'd gone to instructor training school together, both getting certified to teach others how to fly. "It's good to have you back."

"It's good to be back." She hadn't done any stunt work since her father had passed. When she was six, he'd flown her into the skies, and she'd fallen madly in love, not only with the sensation of flight but with the vast and different world that surrounded her. Sweeping from horizon to horizon, the colors seemed brighter, the possibilities endless, and the freedom from earthly constraints seductive. After that, nothing could keep her on the ground if she had a chance to soar among the clouds. While she'd taken the Jenny up several times since December, she hadn't participated in an airshow. It had been difficult enough performing after her brother had left, because they'd always been a team. While she did a lot of maneuvers solo, some were better with a partner, especially when mimicking a dogfight.

"I know I'm no substitute for Jack," Annette said.

"You held your own."

"How's he doing?"

"Exhausted, I imagine. He's not writing as much, what with all the bombing going on over there. It's like the Germans are trying to sink the island." She made it a point to attend the movies at least once a week, simply to see the latest newsreels. She read the newspapers voraciously and listened to the radio whenever she could, hoping to catch some news about the war — preferably when her mother wasn't around, because any reports on the devastation taking place across the ocean upset her. "It's terrifying. Have to admire the Brits for not surrendering, though. I want it all to stop, and I'm not in the middle of it."

"I'm glad we're not. I voted for Roosevelt because he promised we wouldn't get into the war."

At that moment, the organizer of the show walked up. "Here you are, ladies." He handed them each fifty dollars. "We'll be in Oklahoma City next weekend. Hope to see you there." He ambled away, passing out flyers about the upcoming airshow as he went.

"I'm going to fuel up and head home," Jessie said. She held out her hand. "Thanks again, Annette. I appreciate that you took

19

the risk of doing the Dance of Death with me."

"I live for the thrills, and that particular maneuver never fails to get my heart to pumping. Maybe I'll see you in Oklahoma."

"Don't see why not."

Following a slow descent through the fluffy cumulus, Jessie leveled out, increased speed, and took satisfaction in the smooth roar of the engine as the wind whipped past her in the open cockpit. Below, the Jenny's shadow glided over the terrain she knew as well as she did her instruments panel. To her left, cornstalks rustled in the breeze. She made extra money dusting those fields and others, flying in low to better reduce any potential drifting of the powdered lead arsenate. To her right, on the other side of the narrow paved road ribboning east and west, which she'd driven numerous times into Dallas, was the start of the Caldwell Ranch. Six thousand barbed-wire-enclosed acres that were home to Angus cattle and a pretty pinto mare named Buttercup she sometimes rode.

She soared over the ancient oak tree where she'd played hide-and-seek with her brother, received her first kiss from Luke, and later agreed to wear his suede varsity football jacket to symbolize they were officially going steady. Continuing on, she flew over the creek where she'd caught her first catfish, still swam on hot summer afternoons, and had dared to skinny-dip one moonless night with Luke.

Nearing the heart of Terrence, she saw the depot that had been built in 1873 to accommodate the arrival of the Texas and Pacific railroad tracks along this stretch of North Texas. A few miles beyond lay her father's airfield.

As it came into view, her chest tightened with the memories of all the times he'd stood there, watching, waiting. She couldn't help but feel he was still observing — with his arms crossed over his lanky frame and a wide smile on his weathered face — as she brought the Jenny in for a smooth and easy landing. Flying was a passion they'd shared, and she missed him more than she thought it possible to miss a person.

After seeing her father's beloved plane safely stored in the hangar, Jessie climbed onto the Indian Scout, her pride and joy, which provided the closest experience to flying she'd found when on the ground. Once on the road, with the motorcycle purring beneath her and the wind rushing past, she began mentally preparing herself to be

21

as cheerful as possible when she walked into the Victorian-style house where she lived with her mother and younger sister, Kitty. Upon her arrival, she parked her motorcycle in the drive, shut it down, and climbed off. Trixie, Jack's black lab, bounded around the corner of the house and dropped to a sit in front of her, tail wagging, tongue lolling out. Reaching down, she gave her brother's dog an affectionate rubbing over her head, shoulders, and back. "Hey, girl, you been keeping watch?"

After she straightened, Trixie dashed off. No doubt there were squirrels to chase.

Jessie headed up the cobblestone walk of the white house with the blue trim that had been built at the edge of town by her grandfather near the end of the last century. Leaping over the three steps to the porch, with its bench swing on one side and two wooden rockers on the other, she pulled on the screen door, pushed open the oak door, and stepped into the foyer, which still somehow managed to carry the lingering scents of those she loved who were no longer there. The overpowering rose perfume that had always enveloped her grandmother and anyone she hugged. The sage fragrance of the Brilliantine her grandfather had used to make his silver hair shine. The menthol scent of the Aqua Velva aftershave her father had used religiously after she'd given him a bottle for Christmas a few years ago.

Then she noted the scent of stale tobacco that belonged to Uncle Joe and always announced his arrival. She wouldn't recognize him without a fat cigar clenched between his teeth. Because the smell was so pungent, she knew he'd visited sometime that afternoon, was possibly still around.

"Jessie?" her mother called from the front room.

Peering in through the open doorway to her left, Jessie saw her mother, with a brow that had been far too furrowed during the past year and her slender hands knitted together in her lap, sitting on the sofa. Squinting as he blew out the smoke from his cigar, Uncle Joe — a heftier version of her father, dark-eyed and dark-haired — stood beside the fireplace that was used only a few times each winter. "Hello," she greeted them.

"How was the airshow?" her mother asked, but something was wrong with her voice, as though she was delivering bad news, and Jessie realized the furrows in her brow were running a little deeper and her knuckles pushing against her skin had gone white. Her first thought was that a disaster had befallen Jack, but her mom's eyes weren't red or swollen, so her upset no doubt had something to do with their company.

With a desperate need to protect her, Jessie stepped fully into the room. "We had a good crowd. What brings you by, Uncle Joe? I get the feeling you're not here just to make sure we're doing okay."

Her mother patted the cushion beside her. "Why don't you sit down?"

She crossed her arms over her chest. "I'm good standing."

"Think I'll sit." Uncle Joe went to a small table where a half-empty bottle of her dad's Kentucky bourbon waited for a man who would never again take pleasure from sipping it in the evening, a man who would have chided her for not considering it half full. "At the worst of times, Jess, still look for the positive." It took everything within her not to scream when her uncle carelessly splashed some into a crystal tumbler. It was stupid to hold on to the liquor when Jim Lovelace had always offered it to anyone who walked into the house.

Then Uncle Joe dropped unceremoniously into her father's recliner and her gut tightened, because it seemed incredibly wrong

24

for anyone to sit in a chair that over the years had reshaped itself to mold comfortably around the man who had passed on his love of flying to her. Afraid she might grab her uncle's shirtfront and yank him out of the chair or snatch the bourbon-filled glass from his hand, she marched over to the sofa, eased onto the wide arm, and forced herself to wait.

Her uncle took a slow sip and then leaned forward, managing to clasp the glass with both hands, his cigar wedged between two fingers. She'd never known him to look so nervous. "I was just explaining to your mama that the town has an interest in buying the airfield."

Her stomach felt like she was sitting in a plane that had suddenly lost all power and gone into a free fall. "Your share, you mean. How would that work?" Being in partnership with another person, she could understand . . . but with a town?

He shook his head. "They want the whole thing."

"Half of it is ours." Specifically, her mother's, but since the moment Dad had first taken her into the skies, Jessie had developed an attachment for the airfield, considered it hers as much as anyone's.

"Your mama's, yes. But she's open to selling her portion, too."

"No." The word had come out harsher and more defiant than she'd intended. She'd never been shy about standing her ground. No doubt it stemmed from growing up with a twin brother who never let her forget he'd been born twenty-two minutes ahead of her. They'd always challenged each other. And as far as she was concerned, the matter regarding the airfield wasn't open for debate. As though her body had forgotten how to work, she lurched up and over to the fireplace, standing where he had been, and gave a pointed look at the woman who had birthed her, raised her, loved her. Pouring all her conviction into her tone, she declared steadily, "It's not what Dad would have wanted."

"Jessie, honey, I can't run an airfield."

"But I can." Suddenly it seemed imperative that she not lose this last link with her father, that she keep his legacy safe and under her protection until Jack returned. "We could purchase Uncle Joe's share. Buy him out."

"Where are we going to get that kind of money?"

"A loan. We're descendants of one of the original families, homesteaders. Surely the bank will give us a loan."

Her mother's head leaned slightly to the side, as though the weight of what she had to say made it unable to remain upright and steady. "They'd want collateral."

"The house. The flight school."

She shook her head. "We were fortunate that my parents left us this place. The school doesn't bring in a lot of money, Jessie. It's the reason your dad traveled around selling airplane parts. I shudder at the thought of having a loan to pay off, of owing anyone anything. Besides, you'll be getting married soon and don't want to saddle Luke with debt. And once you're his wife, you won't have time for the school."

Only recently beginning to ease away from years of suffering through a depression, everyone was extremely cautious, not fully ready to accept that better times were on the horizon. Her mother was correct, though. Luke wouldn't want the debt or her working. But she was also wrong, because Jessie couldn't see herself getting married anytime soon. She looked earnestly at her uncle. "I can manage the airfield and the school. You could go do whatever it is you want to do, and I'll send your share of earnings every month."

After finishing off the bourbon, he set the glass aside. Maybe he required the fortifica-

27

tion to break her heart. "I need the lump sum, Jess."

Not want, not prefer. But need. Without the school, what was she going to do? Her dream was to become an airline pilot, but only one woman — Helen Richey — had ever been hired for the position. She'd been denied membership in the pilots' union and seldom allowed to fly. Eventually she resigned. Still, Jessie yearned to apply, to see if attitudes had changed, but she didn't yet have enough experience to make an impression. Maybe she could teach elsewhere. But worse, she envisioned the school her father had loved bulldozed down, returned to a field for growing crops or a home for cattle. "What is the town going to do with it?"

"They've been yammering for a couple of years now about wanting to have an airport. We have the land, the hangar, an office building. It's a start."

"Dad would hate this."

"Jim was considering it."

"No, he wasn't." He would have said something to her if he was.

Uncle Joe shoved his cigar in his mouth. The end of it was dried ash. She couldn't even see a red ember glow any longer. Without him puffing on it, it had sizzled and died, a bit like her hopes and aspirations at the moment. "Managing a business is hard work, keeping it going. The stress and responsibility — especially with Jack not here to help — was taking a toll." He gave a negligent shrug. "Obviously."

"Don't you put his death on Jack."

"I'm just saying that we were struggling, and Jim was starting to feel the pressure of it."

How much of that struggle was her uncle's fault, a result of his lack of ambition? *Don't go there, Jessie. It was no one's fault. Dad went to sleep, and the angels came.*

But if her father had mentioned the struggle, she could have done more to lessen his burdens. Guilt gnawed at her. She should have known. Somehow.

"I was helping, doing what I could." What they would allow her to do. Packing the parachutes, helping to keep the planes running, giving flight lessons. Granted, there didn't seem to be as many people signing up lately, but business always dropped off in winter. It should start picking up anytime now.

"You were. No question. But Jack was good at getting out and drumming up business. Gift of gab that boy has, like his pa. However, all that is beside the point. I have a family to provide for. I need to find greener pastures and selling the airfield and school will help. It's on the agenda to be discussed at the town hall meeting Tuesday." He rose to his feet. "I came by to let your mama know. If they approve buying, I'm selling. I wanted to make sure she was good with selling her share, too, because they want the whole thing or nothing at all."

Her mother looked small and mortified sitting there as her green eyes, the same shade as Jessie's, met her gaze imploringly. "We can use the money."

Her mother had never been particularly invested in the flight school or worked outside the home. As far as she was concerned, her job was to turn their house into a home. She excelled at it. Her father had always handled the finances. Her mom hadn't bothered to disguise her surprise when she discovered how very little had been set aside for a rainy day, most of it no doubt going back into the business. Jessie could hardly blame her now for wanting some security. "If it happens, I'll take care of telling Jack."

Even if he was able to resign from the Royal Air Force, was willing to, he couldn't come home. He'd broken the law when he'd gone over, violated the Neutrality Acts, which prevented a person from serving in another country's military. In a town this small, no one did anything without people eventually learning about it, and he'd made the mistake of confiding in a girl he'd been seeing at the time, hadn't felt right about breaking things off without telling her the truth about his plans. After he'd left, she'd cried on a good many shoulders, too upset to keep her word of never telling a soul about his secret adventure. Some folks didn't approve of what he'd done. If he returned home and they alerted the authorities, he could be arrested and sent to prison — for following his conscience. "We don't want him worrying or thinking he could have done something to change the outcome."

All his efforts needed to remain focused on staying alive.

March 10, 1941

Dear Mama, Jess, and Kitty Kat,
   You'll be relieved to know I haven't seen much action since I was transferred to this all-American Eagle Squadron. Escorting convoys through the North Sea is boring as all get-out. Although they're keeping us busy when we're on the ground. Been interviewed for newspapers, magazines, and the radio. The other day they had a camera crew out here filming us for a newsreel. Think its purpose is to recruit more American fliers, so you might see me at the movies when all is said and done.

Love,
Jack

P.S. Give Trixie a treat and tell her it's from me.

CHAPTER 2

Tuesday, March 11, 1941

Jessie arrived late to the meeting on Tuesday evening. Ironically, she'd been delayed taking a potential student on a tour around the airfield, showing him the airplanes used for training and explaining a little bit about the curriculum. If the worst happened tonight, maybe she could give private lessons, talk the town council into leasing her a section of the airfield and a portion of the hangar.

As soon as she rushed into the city hall's small meeting room, Rhonda Monroe — a striking redhead seated near the back and obviously keeping an eye out for her — frantically waved her arm. Muttering her excuses, Jessie edged her way past knees that knocked the backs of her legs until she reached the empty chair and dropped into it.

Rhonda leaned over and whispered, "You haven't missed anything important. They've been discussing how some school districts are adding a twelfth grade. Should ours do the same?"

"Why do students need another year of school?"

Rhonda did an exaggerated eye roll. "Because the school board is made up of sadists?"

Jessie fought not to laugh. Rhonda had hated school, although she was as sharp as a tack and seldom had to study — which had come in handy, since she held the school record for most days playing hooky.

"Your curls are getting unruly. You need to come see me." A stylist at the Cutting Up Hair Salon, Rhonda kept her vibrant red strands tamed, currently turned under in a wave that rested along her shoulders. When she had a date, she opted for more of a Rita Hayworth look.

"Too much going on. Maybe once all this mess is settled, I'll come in for a trim."

"And you could use a bit of color. I've got a new shade of lipstick that would look great on you." Like a magician, she pulled a tube from her purse and extended it toward Jessie. No doubt responsible for keeping Max Factor in business, Rhonda never went anywhere without makeup and knew how to apply it, so she always looked as gorgeous as any actress sauntering on the big screen. She gave lessons in applying makeup, which Jessie failed every time, content to pretty up with a swipe of lipstick — which Rhonda always declared was the wrong shade for Jessie's complexion. Not that Jessie cared. When it came to style, they couldn't be more opposite, but they'd forged a friendship in grammar school that had remained unbroken and deepened through the years.

"No thanks," Jessie said.

"If you're here to make a statement, you should wear lipstick."

The woman sitting in front of Jessie abruptly turned around, impatience brimming in her tight features, and delivered a clipped "Shh" with a glare that never failed to quiet the congregation when she delivered it from her seat at the church organ.

Rhonda bent forward. "Miss Harding, I love your hat. Gives your profile a movie-star quality."

The organist blushed and patted her nape, her fingers touching strands that had been yanked up and secured in a tight knot. "Thank you, Rhonda."

She faced forward, but her fingers continued to flutter at the edge of the hat. Jessie directed a silent laugh her friend's way — one she gave her often because of her gift

35

for diffusing situations. She wished Rhonda had been there Sunday to help make her uncle see reason. Now she caught sight of him sitting in the front row, beside a farmer who was arguing that he needed his boy in the fields, not in the classroom for another year. A rising cacophony of agreement began filling the room.

"All right, all right, we're going to table the school year discussion for now," Buddy Baker, mayor and owner of the only car dealership in town, said with a banging of his gavel on a wooden block. "Obviously the majority of you good folks aren't ready for such a change, so let's move on to the most important reason we're gathered here tonight — the airport we've been considering."

"*You've* been considering it, Buddy," Mr. Thomaston said. "We've got Love Field a little over an hour from here. Don't see that another one is needed so close."

"Then get yourself some bifocals, Larry. More and more people are flying. We could offer a place for smaller, private planes to touch down. Not to mention acquiring government contracts for various things like mail delivery. After Jim Lovelace's passing — may he rest in peace —"

Jessie wished she hadn't come. Hearing a

36

reference to her father like that . . . her eyes started burning. Rhonda reached over, cradled her hand, and squeezed gently.

"— his brother, Joe, is wanting to sell their airfield and it would provide a good start for us, and with a bit of improvement —"

"How much?" somebody yelled.

"Forty thousand to start."

The objections came swiftly and loudly, a couple of men even standing, jabbing their fists toward the ceiling.

"Town ain't got that kind of money!"

"You're off your rocker, Buddy!"

"We need a new mayor."

Jessie felt a measure of hope that her uncle's schemes were going to fall through, that she might have some time to put a strategy in place that would allow her to purchase his share. That she could keep the airfield.

Mr. Baker was out of his chair, pounding his gavel like he was hammering a spike into a railroad tie. "Settle down, settle down! Hear me out!"

Reluctantly, people quieted and retook their seats. Mr. Baker remained on his feet, slowly looking out over the room, assessing the crowd, as though he was preparing to sell them an automobile that they neither needed nor wanted. "Granted, we will have to sell bonds." A groan echoed through the room, and he held up a hand. "I said, hear me out." He looked at his fellow council members. Each nodded. He gave a final jerk of his head and somehow managed to meet and hold the gaze of each person in the room.

Jessie felt like he was on the verge of talking to her personally and that wasn't good. She suspected a few were already reaching for their pocketbooks to purchase whatever he wanted them to before he uttered another word.

"This isn't common knowledge," he said quietly, intimately, "but Roosevelt has given permission for the British to start training pilots for the Royal Air Force at civilian schools over here, and they are interested in using our little airfield."

As the room exploded with speculation, Jessie scooted up to the edge of her seat. She hadn't missed the fact that he already considered the airfield as belonging to the town.

"Brits?" Rhonda whispered excitedly. "They're so suave, so debonair. Cary Grant. Leslie Howard. Laurence Olivier." She pressed a hand above her breast. "Heathcliff. This is one British invasion I'll welcome with open arms."

"I don't want any foreigners here," Miss Harding declared, twisting around in her seat. "Can't trust them."

For all the blood rushing between her ears, Jessie barely heard what those around her were saying. Had her uncle known about this development? Surely not . . . but now that they knew . . . what did any of this mean?

The gavel was once again making its presence known, banging away. "Quiet! Quiet!"

The voices went silent, but chairs were creaking as people continued to shift with unease or excitement or anticipation. Jessie sat there as though she were a statue, barely breathing, striving to think it through, to figure out how it would affect everything.

"Thank you," Mr. Baker stated succinctly. "We'll have to invest some, but the Brits will work in conjunction with the army to make most of the improvements needed. When all is said and done, we'll be paid for the use of the airfield." He held up a finger. "But here's where it gets interesting. It'll bring jobs and business to the town. I'm telling you, this here is an opportunity for us to prosper after these long years of struggling. Love Field started out as a training facility during the last war and look where it is today."

"Don't like it," Mr. Gunder said. "Don't like the idea of foreigners coming to our town."

Miss Harding began bobbing her head in agreement.

"They won't all be foreigners," Mr. Baker said. "The civilians working the place will be Americans."

"Never liked the Brits," Mr. Penn said. "Lost my leg to them in the last war."

Mr. Baker glared at the speaker. "The Germans were responsible for taking your leg when they tossed a grenade into your trench."

"Still, I was fighting to help the Brits. Don't know that we should be helping them again. It's America first. Roosevelt said so. Hitler ain't gonna like it."

"Which is the reason we're not going to tell him."

"I agree with Buddy," Mr. Johnson, president of the largest bank in town, said. "This is an opportunity for us to grow. Afterward, I assume we'd convert the airfield into an airport."

"That's right," Mr. Baker said. "I'll donate twenty-five hundred dollars toward what's needed."

After that announcement, chaos ensued, with people offering support and voicing

40

objections, amounts being shouted out. It all made Jessie dizzy, especially as she saw the prospects of her family keeping the airfield slipping away. Somewhat resentfully, she had to admit it was a good opportunity for the town.

"What do you think?" Rhonda asked.

"It would be a chance to help the Brits, to have a role in the war effort." She'd resented that Jack had been able to go off and fight in combat, to make a difference, while she'd been forced to stay behind, feeling impotent and lacking in a purpose that mattered. She wanted to make a difference as well, and being part of this British program was her chance. She might have as little impact as a pebble thrown into an ocean. It wouldn't alter the tide, but it would still create ripples and those ripples might change the course of some flotsam they encountered. Somewhere, something or someone would be affected, she hoped in a way that altered the outcome positively. But she also experienced disappointment in herself as a spark of excitement threatened to turn into a blaze of want as she began to consider the opportunities that would bring advantages her way. "They'll need flight instructors. I'm right here. Certified. Why wouldn't they hire me?"

She'd still be working at the airfield, teaching. But on a larger stage. When the war came to an end — surely it would soon — she might be able to leverage all the hours flying she'd amass and the experience she'd gain into a career with an airline. Standing, she shouted over the cacophony, "Any idea how many they want to train?"

Somehow Mr. Baker heard her, looked at her. "Hundreds."

She sank back into the chair. Keeping her voice low, she said to Rhonda, "If we're helping the Brits, how could they imprison Jack for doing the same thing? Maybe he could come home after the war."

If she was training RAF pilots, providing a cadre of men skilled enough to watch his back, she might be able to ensure he survived to come home.

Within fifteen minutes, they had twelve thousand dollars in donated funds and had approved the selling of bonds. When the meeting was adjourned, some people dashed up to the front to discuss the matter further with the council, while others were heading for the door. Jessie jumped to her feet and jostled her way through those departing until she was able to step in front of her uncle and prevent his escape. "Did you know about this plan involving the Brits?"

The guilt mirrored in his eyes gave her the answer before he voiced it. "Buddy may have mentioned something about it."

"You didn't think you needed to share that information with Mama and me? They could lease the school from us directly."

He slowly shook his head. "I need out, Jessie, away from this town, away from living beneath my brother's shadow. You understand what it's like."

To know Jack had always been given more responsibility, that if he were here now people would listen to what he said, would respect his opinion. That if her father had left a will — a small uneasy part of her didn't want to consider that he would have designated his portion of the airfield go to Jack, to only Jack. That he'd seen her as a hobbyist, not as someone who could make a living piloting a plane. That he'd humored her when she'd shared her dreams with him but hadn't really taken her seriously. Otherwise, why wouldn't he have confided his worries, his struggles, his fears? His consideration of selling the school?

Someone bumped into her on his way to the door, apologized without stopping. But it was enough to bring her back to herself, to stop the doubts from circling around. Shaking her head, she repeated what she'd told him Sunday. "He wouldn't have wanted this."

"Then he shouldn't have goddamned died."

Anger and frustration slithered through his voice, just before he spun on his heel and stormed out. For the first time, her heart went out to him. He wasn't doing any of this out of spite. He was floundering, struggling to find his place as much as she was striving to find hers.

She was clinging to the airfield and school because they provided a tangible connection to her father. Uncle Joe needed to shed himself of it for a similar reason: it was a yoke that tied him to the older brother he was desperate to break free of. He was right. She did understand.

So much of what she'd accomplished had been tied up with Jack's accomplishments. When he'd left, she was suddenly flying solo, her copilot having bailed out. She'd been angry, experienced guilt for being mad at him. While she'd always been close to her father, during the months since Jack's departure, their bond had deepened, strengthened.

Now her dad was gone, and she was struggling to hold the plane — her life — steady. This latest development wasn't helping, but she couldn't blame Uncle Joe for wanting to forge his own path.

She simply had to figure out how to forge hers.

May 15, 1941

Dear Jess,

We got relocated to ——, otherwise known as Hell's Corner. Today, finally, I was back in a dogfight. The excitement, the thrill, the terror of pitting my skills against another pilot's. All those mock dogfights you and I did when we were barnstorming prepared me for this.

Don't tell Mama or Kitty, but I got a little too close for comfort to a Messerschmitt. Swear I could see the bastard piloting it smile at me. He gave me a run for my money, but I finally got him. Strange thing. As I watched him going down in flames, I kept hoping he'd bail. Seems wrong to respect the enemy, but he'd put up a good fight.

Miss having you around to talk to, especially after I land, and my nerves are wired so tight. I head to a local pub for a pint and always take a moment to glance around to see if you're there. I can share thoughts and feelings with you I can't share with anyone else. I wish you were here, but you'd be pissed all the time that they wouldn't let you fly into combat. Their loss, I say.

Cheerio!
Jack

P.S. Give Trixie a treat and tell her it's from me.

loss, I say.

Cheerio!

Jack

P.S. Give Trixie a treat and tell her it's from
me.

CHAPTER 3

Terrence, Texas
Tuesday, June 3, 1941

Swooping down from the heavens in a
recently acquired Stearman — a bright blue
biplane with yellow wings — Jessie saw the
locomotive in the distance chugging away
and knew it had recently departed from the
Terrence depot. She also knew at least two
of the passengers had disembarked. She
could almost hear the rattle of the old
wooden platform as their bootheels hit it
with a nearly ominous vibration. Retired
Major Dave Barstow, the man the army had
chosen to operate the flight school, would
have welcomed the Royal Air Force officers
before taking them for a tour of the facili-
ties.

After the town hall meeting that had
intensified the crumbling of her once-secure
world, everything had happened incredibly
swiftly, at a dizzying pace. Within forty-eight

hours, bonds had been issued and the money needed to purchase the airfield had been raised. In a demonstration of forgiveness, she'd accompanied her mother and uncle to the meeting, where they'd signed over the family treasure. Immediately afterward, her mother's brow wasn't as deeply furrowed, and Jessie wondered what burdens she hadn't shared. By the end of the week, Uncle Joe had moved his family to Austin, where he'd taken a position at Mueller Airport.

Nearing her destination, she barely recognized the airfield where she had spent a good deal of her life. On the once-familiar landscape had been built a mess hall, canteen, recreation hall with a screened-in wide porch on all sides, dispensary, two barracks, and a second steel hangar. An extension that housed additional offices and more classrooms had been added to the building where students received ground school instruction. Construction had begun on a control tower and another hangar.

After bringing the aircraft in for a perfect landing on the grass field and shutting it down, she removed her helmet and goggles, climbed onto the wing, and leapt to the ground. The chief mechanic who had been at the airfield since its inception ambled over to her. "Nobody lands as pretty as you, Jess."

"Thanks, Billy. Listen, she started running rough in cruise but improved after I shut down the left mag. Would you check the ignition?"

"Sure thing." Narrowing his gaze, he glanced over his shoulder at Barstow and two other men she assumed to be the RAF officers, all standing near the newest hangar, apparently lost in conversation. "That new fella's been showing the Brits around."

That new fella was hardly new. He'd been hard at work getting things ready for well over two months. "I take it you met them, then."

"Yep. He's been introducing 'em to everyone."

"What do you think?"

He looked back at her, shook his head. "Fere'ners. Talk funny."

She chuckled softly. Billy Collins had never ventured far, preferring the known to the unknown. "We knew that already, Billy. Other than that, what was your impression?"

"Seemed all right, I guess. Serious fellas."

"Where they come from, things are pretty serious right now."

"I reckon." Jutting out his chin, he took a

50

step closer, as though to impart a secret. "Ain't right what they done to you."

Barstow hadn't hired her to be a flight instructor. When she'd confronted him about it, he'd said, "I'm not certain military men would take a woman as a flight instructor seriously."

She'd responded with, "I'm fairly certain they'd prefer it to being shot out of the sky. I've taught men before with no problem." Her retort hadn't earned her any points with him.

"These aren't a bunch of hobbyists coming in for an occasional lesson when they have time. It's going to be grueling, long days of getting them up to speed as quickly as possible."

"I can handle the work and the cadets." But she'd had no success convincing him she was qualified to take on the task effectively. She should have been prepared for his skepticism. When she'd gone to take the test to get her license, she'd learned not everyone believed a woman belonged in a cockpit. The man who'd given her the flight test had sneered at her and not bothered to hide his disgruntlement at the end when he'd had to make the notation that she'd passed. But she'd worked so damned hard to be able to fly that she hadn't cared. She'd merely barked out a triumphant laugh, slapped him on his shoulder, and thanked him.

"At least they gave me a position here, Billy." While it wasn't the one she wanted, it was something.

"But it was your pa's place. They should have respected that, honored your previous role here."

She glanced around. "Hardly looks like it anymore, though, does it? I suppose it's a reminder that nothing stays the same."

"It's a reminder there's a war on," he grumbled. "Some don't like having that."

She had been getting a few more narrowed eyes lately — it had started shortly after Jack had left and his secret had been spilled — but she'd definitely noticed an increase in disapproving glares since the airfield had changed hands. Maybe her uncle had high-tailed it out of town so quickly because he'd experienced some confrontations. Men were more likely to voice their objections openly, whereas women — at least those in Terrence — tended to do it with whispers behind backs. "I can't concern myself with petty grievances. We've got a job to do here and need to do it the best way we can."

With a brusque nod indicating he was ready to get to work, he patted the fuselage.

"I'll get this lady decked out, ready to dance before the rest of them Brits show up next week."

The first class of fifty cadets were scheduled to arrive Sunday to begin an intensive five-month course that would see them earning their wings. Every five weeks another class of fifty would arrive. Eventually they would have two hundred students in various stages of training. "Thanks, Billy. It'll make that new fella happy."

He grinned broadly, indicating she hadn't offended him by not wanting to get bogged down with gossip. With a purpose to her stride, she headed toward the hangar to put away her gear and, if she was honest, take a gander at the new arrivals. They wore gray suits — the material appeared to be wool — with white shirts and black ties. Wool. In Texas. In June. Apparently, someone had failed to explain Texas weather to them, although she suspected their clothing was the last thing with which they were concerned. The somberness they projected indicated they were well aware of the weight they carried on their shoulders.

She didn't have to see them in uniform to know which one was in charge. Despite leaning on a cane, he gave the appearance of standing at attention, ready to inspect the troops with a steady gaze that was assessing her, just as she was him.

As she neared, Barstow motioned her over. "Miss Lovelace, I'd like you to meet the commanding officer and chief flying instructor, Wing Commander Royce Ballinger."

So she'd guessed right, regarding who was tasked with managing the operation of the school and monitoring the relationship between the civilian operators and the RAF students. He removed his hat to reveal black hair clipped short. He had the bluest eyes, the shade of azure she saw from the cockpit when flying above the clouds late in the afternoon. But they were haunted, and she didn't want to contemplate the horrors he might have witnessed. These men had left a war — or at least she'd thought they had. To see them now made her realize they might have brought a good bit of it with them. He looked to be on the far side of thirty, but the creases and strain in his features told her he'd already lived a lifetime. She stuck out her hand. "Wing Commander."

He blinked, hesitated, as though he'd never before seen a hand. Likely, he'd never had a woman offer her hand in the same forthright manner as a man. According to a film on etiquette she'd been forced to watch in high school, a lady wasn't supposed to shake hands with a gentleman, but Jessie recognized she was in a man's world, and had no intention of being demure about it, not when she'd overcome so many obstacles to get where she was, not when she still had to convince Barstow she was equal to a man when it came to flying.

Finally, his palm met hers, his fingers closed around hers. He had a good hand, large, strong, solid. One that could control a plane when things got rough. "Miss Lovelace."

"And this is the chief ground instructor, Squadron Leader Peter Smythson," Barstow continued.

"Miss Lovelace, it is indeed a pleasure." He offered her a warm smile, not nearly as somber as his counterpart, as he shook her hand.

"Squadron Leader."

"Miss Lovelace is our other female Link Trainer operator."

The Link Trainer was basically a cockpit inside a blue-painted plywood box that allowed a student to experience a simulated night flight. But Barstow's introduction of her made her want to shriek. Why had he felt the need to use the gender modifier?

55

Did he think the Brits couldn't determine she was a woman?

"Until the students arrive and are using the Link, she's helping out by taking the ships the army delivers on test runs."

Ballinger nodded in the direction from which she'd come. "That landing was well done."

Any other time, she might have viewed his words as a compliment, but she had the uneasy sense he was patronizing her, that, like Barstow, he wouldn't consider her flight instructor material because she had breasts. Or maybe she was too sensitive after two months of dealing with Barstow's attempt to keep flying a good ole boys' club. He was near her father in age, but not nearly as enlightened. However, she didn't want to get off on the wrong foot with these fellas. While Barstow managed the civilian aspect of the school, the Brits were paying for it and would oversee the cadets and have some influence on the training to ensure they were getting their money's worth. It was going to be a delicate balance of control and power until they determined how everyone was going to work together in this unique endeavor. Impressing the new arrivals was to her benefit. "Appreciate the assessment. On another matter, I'm not sure if you're aware the Stearman is equipped with a Gosport System for communication." Words traveling through the rubber tube, which had a funnel at one end and earpieces at the other, were often garbled. "Since it allows for only the instructor to speak to the student, you might want to ask the army to issue you a two-way communication system that the mechanics can install."

"A gosport device is standard for the aircraft used during the initial training phase, Miss Lovelace," Barstow said succinctly, clearly irritated she'd brought up the subject after discussing it with him a month earlier. He'd declared her worrying for nothing. "Students are supposed to be listening, not carrying on conversation."

"I'm aware, but it could prove a hindrance for trainees who aren't familiar with the slow thick drawls of some of the instructors. Once in the cockpit, they won't have the opportunity to ask for clarification."

"I've had no trouble teaching with a gosport," Barstow said.

"Still, I don't know that Miss Lovelace's suggestion should be dismissed out of hand," Ballinger said. "I've discovered we may, in fact, have some communication challenges. For example, you use the term *landing gear* for what we refer to as *undercar-*

riages." He gave her a slight nod. "Smythson and I will certainly give your notion some consideration, Miss Lovelace."

"Thank you." She was pleasantly surprised by his willingness, since Barstow summarily rejected any recommendation she had for improvement.

"It's your money," he said now, rather petulantly.

"Yes, it is, rather, isn't it," Ballinger stated.

"We should probably get going," Barstow said, an undercurrent of impatience in his tone, as though he didn't want her charming these men. If she'd held any favor with him at all, she'd probably just lost it. "Ballinger, you'll be staying with Miss Lovelace's family until you can make other arrangements. Smythson, I secured you a room at Mrs. Wilcox's. Miss Lovelace, if you want to store your gear, we'll wait for you in the parking area."

"Yes, sir." She dashed into the hangar and darted through to the storage room, where she hung up her chute and stored her goggles and helmet in her designated locker. By the time she got outside, she discovered they hadn't made much progress, Ballinger's limp, his favoring his right leg, slowing them down. Easily catching up with them, she could see the strain in the set of his jaw, and sympathy swelled within her. Barstow was explaining how they needed to keep an eye out for rattlers, the occasional coyote, and escaped cows. It wasn't unusual to see the last wandering through the town square.

Smythson dropped back to walk beside her.

"Did y'all have a good trip over?" she asked, determined to do her part to make them feel welcome.

He smiled at her. "You really do say *y'all* over here."

"We do, cowboy."

His inviting laughter rumbled out of him. Lord have mercy, the ladies were going to be charmed by this one. Even Miss Harding, who still wasn't pleased about having foreigners in town, was likely to relax in his presence and serve him some of her famous buttermilk chocolate cake.

"We didn't get torpedoed," he said lightly, as though the possibility of it happening might not have weighed heavily on him during their journey across the Atlantic, "so we considered it a success."

"It had to be a bit unnerving, though, knowing German U-boats were patrolling in those waters."

He sobered. "We tried not to think about

59

it. Although to be honest, I didn't sleep soundly the entire way over, always wondering if a wolf pack was near, and lacking confidence that we'd have success against it. But my worries were for naught."

He said the last as though discovering an apple wasn't rotten as assumed. The Battle of the Atlantic, as Churchill referred to it, presented a real danger, and she had to admire these men, as well as the ones who would soon follow, for taking the risks involved in getting here. The war was so far away. Most people in town gave it very little thought.

"The train ride down from Canada had to be less threatening," she said, hoping to shake off the reminder of the worst aspect of their journey.

His smile returned. "It was indeed. Everyone was warm and welcoming, and it gave us an opportunity to see some of your country. We spent a few days in Washington, D.C., meeting with the RAF delegation established there and learning more about what is expected of us in our roles at the BFTS." The British Flying Training School. Six civilian schools across the South had been converted for training British pilots. "We had an opportunity for a bit of sightseeing while we were there. I'm hoping for a

60

chance to see a tad more of your country while we're assigned here."

"You're a little over an hour away from Dallas and beyond that is Fort Worth" — she pointed to the west — "and you'll find some interesting places there."

"Perhaps you can offer some suggestions."

"I'd be happy to." Maybe she could gather some information to put in the recreation hall. Surely the cadets might want to tour the sights as well.

They reached the parking area, and Barstow directed them toward his car.

"I'll meet y'all at the house," Jessie assured them. Giving a quick wave, which only Smythson returned, she climbed on her motorcycle and headed up the road. Smythson was certainly a talker, a charmer, a bit of a flirt. Ballinger seemed more the dark and brooding type for whom Rhonda was searching.

After reaching the old homestead, she pulled into the drive, parked her Scout, and strolled to the edge of the street. A couple of minutes later Barstow drew to a stop, and Ballinger clambered out, carrying a kit bag and coat.

"I'll see you tomorrow, Miss Lovelace," Smythson said, moving from the rear seat to the front, stopping with a hand on the door.

"Call me Jessie."

"Short for Jessica?"

"Yes."

He gave her a warm smile and a wink. "One of my favorite names."

With a light laugh, she figured any woman's name was his favorite. He ducked inside and Barstow drove off. She turned to Ballinger, who was studying her as though unfamiliar with the sound she'd made. She kept her smile in place and her tone easy. "Is he always such a flirt?"

"He appears to be. I'm afraid I don't know him that well. We met only after being given this assignment."

She wanted to ask what his opinion of Barstow was, but figured it wouldn't do her any favors to give the impression she wasn't particularly fond of her boss. Although she suspected some of her bias was because he was serving in the role her father would have filled if he hadn't died. That reminder brought with it the usual sharp pang. Refusing to give in to the melancholy, she focused on doing what she could to help the Brit feel comfortable with his new surroundings. "You can see a portion of the town square from here. Anything you might need you can probably find in one of the shops circling it."

"Doesn't look to be too bad of a stroll."

"You might feel differently come July and August. Come on. This way."

"I — uh."

Having taken only a step, she turned back to him. He looked incredibly uncomfortable. "Barstow mentioned your father's passing. My condolences."

So much for trying to shore up her defenses, but she needed to acknowledge his kindness. "Thank you. It's been almost six months, and I'm still not used to it."

"I'm not sure one ever does get used to loss. He also mentioned your father owned the airfield."

"He did. He and his brother. The town bought it after he died. He'd have approved of it being used to train pilots for the RAF."

"He taught you to fly, I assume?"

For the first time since his death, as the memories came to her, they didn't feel like an assault. They were more like a gentle breeze stirring leaves. "He did, yes."

"The sky isn't biased. Barstow doesn't seem to be of the same persuasion."

She wasn't expecting his words or the way he studied her as though daring her to contradict him. "Noticed that, did you?"

"It's a bit hard to miss."

"He's under a lot of pressure." She glanced toward the house. "Mama's expecting us to be on time for dinner."

"Righto. We should probably make haste then."

She ambled slowly up the walk, noting how he gripped the silver handle of his cane. "I know it's none of my business but were you wounded in action?"

"Just a little mishap during an enemy encounter. Nothing to worry over. I'm on the mend now and should be fully to rights soon."

She didn't like the thought of his having been hurt but doubted he'd appreciate her offering a hand as they ascended the three steps to the porch. Before she could reach for the screen door to pull it open, he was doing it for her. "Thank you."

Because of the heat, the main door was open. She stepped over the threshold into the hallway, keenly aware of him following. "Mama!"

Quick footsteps echoed over the hardwood floor as her mother and sister hurried out of the kitchen and through the dining room to greet them. Jessie and Kitty had inherited their mom's golden-brown hair with its hints of red. Her green eyes glittered with warmth as she wiped her hands quickly on her apron. "Wing Commander, welcome. We've been anticipating your arrival."

"Thank you, Mrs. Lovelace. It's good to be here at last."

"Dot, please. You must call me Dot. This is my younger daughter, Kitty."

"A pleasure."

Kitty gave a little laugh. At sixteen, it seemed she was always laughing. "You sound like Errol Flynn."

Kitty had fallen in love with the actor when they'd gone to see *The Adventures of Robin Hood* a few years earlier. But she was wrong. With a deeper, smoother voice, he sounded much better than Errol Flynn. He also seemed at a loss for words. Was he blushing or was the heat starting to get to him? She liked the idea he might be a blusher.

"I appreciate your billeting me until I can make other arrangements."

"It's no problem at all," her mother said. "Stay as long as you need. Now, Kitty and I are going to finish getting supper ready. Jessie, show him upstairs to Jack's room."

As they rushed off, it suddenly occurred to Jessie that he should be staying with Mrs. Wilcox, because her house had no stairs. Against her will, her gaze drifted to the cane.

"It's quite all right, Miss Lovelace. I can navigate stairs."

Going up, they passed an array of family photos hanging on the wall that documented their lives, from her parents' wedding to their children as babies and high school graduates. At the landing, she crossed over into the bedroom on the left. He followed her in. The room still carried the fragrance of Old Spice that her brother had always slathered over his jaw. She shouldn't get sentimental about the smell or her memories of how she'd razzed him when he'd first started shaving. She waved her arm around. "Here you go. Just make yourself at home."

"I noticed a lad in the photographs along the stairs. Is Jack your brother?"

"My twin, actually. Mama thought our names should at least begin with the same letter, so Jack and Jessica. I'm just grateful she didn't decide to go with Jack and Jill."

His lips moved slightly as though he might smile, but instead he glanced at the shelf lined with baseball and football trophies. "It seems he's quite the athlete. Is he off at university?"

"He's in the service."

He gave his attention back to her, such

somberness in those blue eyes. "A pilot, I'd wager."

She smiled. "Yes, as a matter of fact." She considered telling him the details of Jack's involvement in the war — he certainly wouldn't object — but something stopped her. "If you'll excuse me, I need to change clothes. Make yourself comfortable. No jacket or tie at dinner. It's too damn hot."

She headed for the door, stopped just before crossing the threshold, and turned back to face him. "Jack left most of his clothes here. You're close in size." Six feet, which put him half a foot taller than she was. "You can probably find a cooler pair of trousers that'll fit. As a matter of fact, make use of any of his clothes. They're better suited to the Texas weather than what you're wearing now and will probably be out of style before he needs them again."

"I appreciate the generosity."

"You can head downstairs whenever you're ready."

In her bedroom, across from his, she chose a softly shaded peach dress with a tucked-in waist, a flaring skirt, and short puffy sleeves. Taking one last look in the mirror, she headed into the hallway and came up short at the sight of Ballinger stepping out of Jack's room. He'd changed into a pair of gray cotton trousers that fit perfectly. His jacket and tie were gone. Only one button on his shirt was undone and the cuffs were secured. She'd give him a week before those sleeves went above his elbow.

"Cooler?" she asked.

"Considerably, yes."

"Based on the smells coming up, I'd say supper is ready." She didn't wait for his acknowledgment but simply headed down, aware of his following.

When her feet hit the first floor, her mother popped out of the dining room. "Oh, good. I was about to call for you. Come on, let's get seated."

Leaving the place at the head of the table — where her father had sat — empty, they offered Ballinger the chair opposite hers. Kitty wiggled into the one beside Jessie's. Her mother parked herself at the end near the door to the kitchen. They began passing bowls and platters around until everyone had beef tips, potatoes, green beans, and corn bread spread out over her mother's finest china, with its ring of blue flowers around the edge of the delicate dishes normally reserved for Thanksgiving and Christmas dinners.

"It's been a while since I've had a man at my table," her mother said. "Do eat up,

Wing Commander."

"No need to be so formal, especially after the warm welcome. Royce will suffice." He glanced at each of them. "For all of you."

"I've never known anyone called Royce before," Kitty said.

"It's a name that's been in my family since one of my ancestors first donned armor."

Her sister's eyes widened. "Was he a knight?"

"He was indeed."

"Then you come from a long line of warriors," her mother said. "How is this latest war really going?"

The Brit froze as though he were a deer that suddenly sensed the hunter had him within his sights, his finger on the trigger. He cleared his throat. "We've been advised not to discuss the war, either Britain's involvement in it or America's lack of."

"I imagine you were. People around here tend to ignore what's going on, but Jack left last summer to join the RAF, so I try to keep up with how things are going. And he's certainly not going to share the truth of what's happening over there with me in his letters."

Royce narrowed his gaze at Jessie before looking back at her mother. "Your son's a member of the Eagle Squadron?"

69

"I believe so. Jessie keeps up with those details better than I do."

His gaze came back to her for confirmation. "He fought with a British squadron during the Blitz, but when they formed the all-American unit, he was transferred to it," she explained.

"So how bad is it?" Mama asked.

Those blue eyes focused on her mother, and Jessie knew he was going to lie. If not outright, he was at least going to paint a rosier picture of the situation. "He's no doubt flying a Spitfire. An incredible aircraft. We suffer fewer casualties with it. But this recent training partnership will give us so many more pilots that it will reduce the risk for everyone. Unfortunately, he's not receiving food in this abundance, and I'm rather certain he's missing your delicious cooking, Mrs. Lovelace. It's all quite tasty."

Her mom's eyes began misting over. "I should get us some more corn bread." Quickly she rose and went into the kitchen.

Jessie shoved back her chair and stood. "Excuse me. I'm going to see if she needs some help."

In the kitchen, she wrapped her arms around her mother, where she stood at the sink, quietly weeping. "It's all right, Mama. Jack is going to be okay."

She shook her head. "I went through this during the last war, with your dad, when he was over there. It's much harder when it's your son. I keep seeing him as a little boy and I just want one more hug."

"And you're going to get it. I made him swear he'd come home."

Her mother gave a little laugh. "You were always the bossier one."

Jessie loosened her hold, stepped back. "So you know he's gonna do what I tell him."

As she swiped at the tears drying on her cheeks, she nodded toward the door. "Do you see how skinny he is?"

Slender, yes, but not skinny. "He looks solid to me. You don't need to be fattening him up. Otherwise, he won't be able to fit into a cockpit." Little brought this woman more joy than feeding people.

"I just hope he was wrong, and Jack is getting enough to eat," she muttered as she headed back to the dining room.

If Royce or Kitty noticed they returned to the table without additional corn bread, neither said anything. They steadfastly avoided any mention of war after that, although Kitty peppered him with questions about England, declaring she was going to visit someday.

71

When all the forks and knives had gone silent, he looked over at her mother. "It was a wonderful meal, Mrs. Lovelace. Thank you."

"Dot."

He nodded, and Jessie doubted he was ever going to call her mother Dot.

"While we finish up in here," Mama said, "why don't you make yourself comfortable in the front room?"

"I'm more than happy to help with the tidying up."

"I appreciate that, but for tonight you're a guest and you've had a long journey. Relax."

"Come with me," Jessie said, "and I'll pour you a glass of Dad's Kentucky bourbon." She didn't know why she welcomed him having some when Uncle Joe's helping himself to it had irritated her so much. Perhaps because she knew her dad would have offered it, would have wanted the Brit to feel welcome.

She led him into the front room, said, "Make yourself comfortable," and continued on to the small table in the corner. She lifted the bottle —

"Why didn't you tell me your brother was in the RAF?" he asked quietly, solemnly. He sounded disappointed she'd let pass the opportunity to explain when they were in

Jack's bedroom. He was also standing right behind her, so close she was aware of his fragrance — a hint of earth and spice.

Turning, she met his somber gaze. "Because I don't like to think about it. And voicing it makes me think about it, and then I start to imagine him in the sky, being shot at, maneuvering to avoid being hit. I can almost experience his heart pounding, his skin growing clammy, his breath coming faster. If I think about it long enough, then I envision him not getting out of the way."

Then Uncle Joe's words about living in his brother's shadow came rushing back to her. "And I guess if I'm honest, I didn't want your opinion of me influenced by my brother's actions."

He gave a slow nod, studying her intently as though striving to decipher the true measure of her words. "Duly noted. Two fingers."

She blinked. "Pardon?"

He held up two fingers horizontally. "I'll have two fingers' worth of the bourbon."

She gave a little laugh. "Right." And turned back to her task.

After she saw him settled into an armchair — she couldn't bring herself to offer him her father's recliner — she returned to the dining room to help with the final clearing of the table. "Kitty, I know it's your turn to wash the dishes, but I have plans for tomorrow night. Switch with me."

Her sister grinned. "Plans with Luke?"

"Who else?"

"I don't know why you don't go ahead and marry that boy," her mother said. "You shouldn't feel a need to put your life on hold to see after me. I'm adjusting to my new circumstances, and I'm anxious to have grandbabies."

Jessie's world, her view of herself, tilted precariously, throwing her off balance, unable to respond as her mother carted a stack of dishes through the swinging door into the kitchen. She hadn't put her life on hold. While she had yet to reach her ultimate goal, she'd been working toward achieving it.

Sometime later, standing at the kitchen sink, she took her time washing the dishes, looking out the window into the backyard at the tire hanging by a rope from the sturdy branch of a towering oak tree. She and Jack had spent many an hour swinging on that tire. A good number of her memories involved him. He'd been there with her from the beginning, and it was odd not to have him about. She should have gotten accustomed to his absence by now but kept expecting him to sneak up on her just to hear her screech or to tap on her bedroom door to ask her opinion about some girl he'd suddenly become interested in.

Her mother had never hounded him about getting married but, like so many of her friends, she measured a woman's success, her worth, by her marriage and ultimately by the children she produced. However, never before had she made Jessie feel like she wasn't doing anything with her life. As for going ahead and marrying *that boy* —

While she and Luke had been extremely compatible in high school, lately it seemed they were at odds more often than in agreement. He didn't agree with some choices she'd made, and she didn't agree with his not agreeing with the choices she'd made. Now she was uncertain as to whether her mother supported her choices. It seemed everywhere she turned, she was having to fight for what she wanted — even with the people she loved.

CHAPTER 4

Kitty enjoyed listening to Royce talk, liked the way he pronounced his words with a poetic refinement that was easy on the ears. He and Mama were discussing their shared interest in mystery novels, especially those written by Agatha Christie and Sir Arthur Conan Doyle. Kitty almost asked if he'd ever read Nancy Drew, her favorite, but suspected he hadn't. She wished she knew more about planes in order to impress him, but she had never possessed the same enthusiasm for aviation as her siblings. Certainly, she enjoyed the occasional flight but had no desire to learn how to handle the controls. Her interests ran more toward homemaking. And she loved collecting and organizing mementos in her scrapbook. She especially liked the postcards of quaint villages and landmarks that Jack sent her.

At that very moment, she was sitting cross-legged on the floor, gluing onto the cream-colored paper the article announcing the arrival of the RAF officers she'd clipped from that morning's issue of the *Terrence Tribune.* The write-up had reported that one of the officers would be staying with her family.

She'd shown Royce an article with the headline *The British Are Coming!* that had appeared shortly after the town council announced the airfield would be part of the British training program. Royce had smiled at that. He had a nice smile, but she was left with the impression he wasn't used to turning up the corners of his mouth. He'd even looked a little guilty, as though it was wrong to do such a thing. A heavy sadness hung over him, like the thick fog sometimes creeping in from the creek. It could be seen, but not touched.

Mama was sitting on the sofa, her fingers flying as she knitted a pair of socks for the Terrence War Relief Society — which she'd formed and become president of a few months ago — to ship abroad for the soldiers, along with the clothing she collected for those left with little after a bombing. She'd knitted a thick woolen scarf for Jack to take with him to England. "It's colder over there from what I hear," she'd told him.

Mama hadn't cried when they'd seen him

77

off at the station last July, but after the train was on its way, she'd released huge, gasping sobs as Dad's arms had gone around her and tucked her in close. Dad had always had something to say, but that afternoon he'd been silent, and his ominous hush had scared her more than Mama's crying. And it had all made Kitty realize Jack was headed into real danger. Jessie had taken her hand and squeezed it. "Let's go get some ice cream." They all had, but mostly they'd watched it melt.

Now here was this man who came from the country where Jack was living, and she had so many questions for him, but it was rude to interrupt. She wanted to know if he knew Princess Elizabeth. Kitty had listened to the princess's speech to the children who'd left Great Britain in order to remain safe from all the bombing. It had made her feel better about Jack's being over there, had made her believe he'd done the right thing. Although it certainly hadn't seemed right at the time, when he'd walked into the living room that quiet Sunday evening and announced solemnly, "I'm going to England to join the RAF."

Mama, sitting in her usual spot on the sofa, had gasped. Jessie's mouth had dropped open, her eyes had widened. She and Jack confided everything in each other, and sometimes Kitty was jealous of their closeness, but he'd apparently not shared that little bit of news with his twin. She'd known a war was going on in Europe, but it wasn't their war.

Dad had shoved himself out of his upholstered recliner. "You sure as hell are not."

"You can't stop me, Dad. I'm twenty-three."

"Living under my roof."

He'd given a little shrug. "I'll be moving out." Moving across an ocean.

"There is nothing glamorous or glorious about war. You do not want to go, son."

"No, I don't *want* to, but I have to. France has surrendered. If Britain falls . . . This madman has to be stopped. Sooner or later, we're going to have to get involved."

"When we get involved, you can fight then."

"I prefer sooner. I've heard the Brits are welcoming American fliers."

"Joining the RAF will be a violation of the Neutrality Acts. You could lose your citizenship. You might never be able to come home."

He'd swallowed, nodded. "I know, Dad. But you taught me that doing the right thing isn't always easy, and sometimes you pay a price for it, but you still do what's right. I can't not go when I know there's a chance that I could make a small difference. I'm a hell of a pilot. You know it's true because you taught me that, too."

Dad had lowered his gaze to the floor. "Goddamn it."

Kitty had widened her eyes in alarm, because her father never used profanity. But seeing the relief on Jack's face, she'd known he had won, had proven his point. Then her brother had looked over at their mother. "I'm sorry, Mama."

She had gotten up, walked across the room, and wrapped her arms around him. "We love you, and while we're going to worry, we're still proud of you."

A week later, Jack had headed to Canada.

Kitty didn't understand exactly why they wanted Americans interested in joining the RAF to go through Canada, but then, a lot was happening in the world that didn't make one lick of sense to her. She'd certainly never expected to have a Brit sitting in their living room.

A knock rattled the screen door.

"I'll get it." Kitty jumped to her feet. It was probably her best friend, Fran Gaines. She sometimes came over in the evening, and she was excited about the Brits coming to Terrence, wanted to meet them. But when she got to the door, she found two older ladies, wearing their Sunday best and hats decorated with far too many flowers. She shoved open the screen door. "Evening, Mrs. Johnson, Mrs. Berg."

"Hello, Kitty," Mrs. Johnson said loudly. One of the most prominent ladies in town, president of the Ladies' Auxiliary Club, she spoke with a slow drawl, her volume always turned up. "Is your company here?"

"Yes, ma'am."

"We'd love to meet him."

Kitty wasn't quite certain he was going to love meeting them. They had a way of taking over a situation. Still, she pushed the screen door open wider. "Come on in."

CHAPTER 5

As she was finishing up in the kitchen, Jessie heard Mrs. Johnson's booming voice announcing her arrival. The woman had been a Dallas socialite when she'd married a young man with ambitions who'd soon become president of the Terrence Bank and Trust. Townsfolk were intimidated by her, in awe of her, or held her in high esteem. Jessie admired her. She knew how to get things done.

After setting up a tray with some refreshments for their guests — Mrs. Johnson seldom went anywhere without Mrs. Berg at her side — she made her way to the living room. Introductions had been made and the two ladies were already happily ensconced on the couch near the chair in which Royce was sitting.

"Would anyone care for some lemonade?" Jessie asked.

"Ah, you're such a dear. I'm incredibly

parched, thank you," Mrs. Johnson said.

After giving everyone a glass, including Royce, although she suspected he'd have preferred two more fingers of bourbon, Jessie made herself comfortable on the floor beside Kitty. Her sister's scrapbook was closed — she didn't share its contents with just anyone, but Jessie figured she'd shown at least the portion that dealt with the Brits to Royce. Her sister was a historian at heart and had started keeping her first scrapbook when she was seven. She'd be entering her final year of high school in September and had already been selected to serve as editor of the school newspaper.

"Wing Commander," Mrs. Johnson began, "as I was saying, Mrs. Berg and I wanted to welcome you on behalf of the Ladies' Auxiliary Club. It's not often we get foreigners in these parts, and it's rather exciting to have you in our midst."

Jessie wouldn't have used the term *exciting* but also knew that some in the town took a somewhat celebratory stance on having the Brits come over. Several ladies were anticipating the arrival of eligible men. Once a gal had dated every fella with whom she'd gone to high school, the pickings got a little slim.

"Our members have expressed an incredible amount of interest in you and your country," Mrs. Johnson continued enthusiastically. "Lou Lou — Mrs. Berg — and I were hoping we could entice you into addressing our group during an upcoming luncheon."

He looked uncomfortable as he shifted in his chair, appearing to be searching for words. "I appreciate the welcome." He cleared his throat. "And the offer to speak to your ladies. However, we have a lot of work to accomplish and I'm not certain I'll have time for such . . . undertakings."

For some reason, his tone seemed more appropriate for the word *nonsense.* Jessie couldn't imagine he was particularly happy about this development or the realization that some didn't truly grasp the importance of their mission in coming here. But she knew Mrs. Johnson well enough to know she was even less happy at that moment. Shaped very much like the prow of a ship, she had a way of slicing through objections as easily as a ship sailed through calm waters.

"I thought you might be hesitant, Royce. May I call you Royce? Not as much of a mouthful as Wing Commander."

"Yes, certainly."

"Well, Royce, you see some folks in the

area aren't quite comfortable with the British walking among us. Not to mention those who believe we shouldn't have any involvement at all in the war. Poor Dot, with her relief efforts, doesn't get nearly the donations that she should."

"It's getting better, Daphne," her mother said, perhaps a bit too curtly. She'd been incredibly disappointed when she'd set up her War Relief Society that so few had taken an interest in participating. However, the lack of support hadn't deterred her from pouring herself into the endeavor and doing what she could to aid the country her son now fought for.

"But still, in my mind, it's simply that people don't really know the British, don't have a connection to them. I have some neighbors who have never ventured beyond the Texas border. Whereas I've been to London and found its citizens to be quite charming. Your speaking would put a face to a country, as it were, and would certainly assist with developing a relationship of mutual appreciation. Don't you think?"

Whenever she ended her discourse with those three little words, she was really saying, "You wouldn't dare disagree with me, would you?"

Royce released a sigh that might as well

have been the raising of a white flag. "You may have a point. I'll have to get approval from my superiors."

"Splendid. I knew we could come to an agreement."

If they didn't give approval, Jessie suspected Mrs. Johnson would be phoning them. Or sending a telegram or speaking with the American ambassador. Or even the prime minister himself. The woman was truly a force of nature when she set her mind to something.

"Lou Lou and I also were considering arranging a dance to welcome your soldiers over."

"Airmen," Jessie and Royce said at the same time. He looked at her, his grin still small, but his eyes dancing with mirth.

"They're not referred to as soldiers," Jessie clarified. "They're airmen."

"Oh, well, isn't it wonderful to learn something new? Would your superiors have a problem with us arranging a dance?"

"No, ma'am, I'm certain they wouldn't."

"A dance would be swell," Kitty said. Boys were all she and her friends ever talked about anymore, and Jessie knew they were eager for the arrival of the cadets. Kitty was always lamenting the lack of enough boys to go around, and had never had a date or even attended a school dance.

"Perhaps you could assist with the decorations," Mrs. Johnson said. "And help us spread the word."

"I'd like that," Kitty said, smiling brightly.

"Wonderful." Mrs. Johnson looked at Royce. "I assume your men will have some time off."

"They'll work until noon on Saturdays and then be off until Monday morning."

"We'll arrange something that works with that schedule, then. We won't keep you any longer. You're no doubt tired from your travels. But it was lovely to meet you, and we look forward to a deeper association."

As she rose, everyone else came to their feet.

"I'll see you out," Jessie said and followed the ladies through the foyer onto the porch, letting the screen door slap closed behind her.

"You tell Jack hello from us the next time you write him," Mrs. Johnson said.

"I'll be doing that tonight, so I certainly will. Y'all take care."

After watching them drive off, she opened the screen door slightly, reached in, and turned off the porch light to reduce the number of moths and june bugs flying around. Then she dropped onto the bench swing. With the window behind her open, the din of the conversation inside created a pleasing, muted background for her thoughts, but she was acutely aware of Jack's absent voice tonight. A slight breeze danced over her skin. She always enjoyed ending her nights out here. Trixie leapt onto the porch and curled up against her feet. "I know, girl. I miss him, too."

For some reason, tonight the constant hollowness that had formed in her chest when Jack left seemed more expansive, deeper. Maybe because the Brits were here. They brought the war a little closer to home. Put faces to a country, as Mrs. Johnson had said.

Or maybe the hollowness had more to do with her mother's earlier comment. She couldn't bring herself to ask her remaining parent if she truly thought Jessie's life had been placed in a holding pattern. Looking back, she could see now that it had always been her father who had recognized and celebrated her accomplishments. Her mother had smiled, but there had been no real exuberance behind it. Probably because she saw each achievement as a possible delay in acquiring grandchildren. It was odd to suddenly feel like a stranger in her own home. She'd always thought her mother was the glue holding the family together, but perhaps it had been her father. He'd understood her so well.

The screen door squeaked as it opened. Royce crossed over to the white wooden railing, leaned his hips and cane against it, and crossed his arms over his chest. Even without the porch light, she knew his gaze was focused on her with a directness he no doubt used when in the air, to gauge his surroundings. "I very much doubt Mrs. Johnson is going to take no for an answer."

He was apparently very skilled at judging people. "No, she won't."

As though suddenly aware of an idle hand, Trixie got up and ambled over to Royce. He bent over and began petting her, rubbing behind her ears. "Hello, there."

Jessie had always had a soft spot for those who treated animals kindly, and Royce's actions had obviously been natural. "That's Trixie, Jack's dog."

"Hello, Trixie. I imagine you miss him, don't you, old girl?"

She wondered who he missed, who was back in England waiting for his return. "Do you have a dog waiting for you back home?"

He chuckled softly. "No, I've never really had a proper place for a pet."

"A wife, a sweetheart, someone special?"

"No. I don't."

A depth of sadness had woven itself through his voice, and she considered asking him about it but decided against prying. They weren't friends, would merely be working together toward a common goal, sharing the same purpose. "Thank you for earlier, for not giving my mother the reality of the situation over there."

While he continued to spoil Trixie, he directed his attention back to her. "I gave her the reality, just not all of it."

"It was kind of you to spare her the worst of it, then. Jack does the same. His letters to her and Kitty always read as though he's simply over there for sightseeing. He's a little more candid with me, made me swear never to let them read what he writes to me." She gnawed her lower lip. "Where's Hell's Corner?"

He gave Trixie a final affectionate pat and straightened. "Southern Kent — Dover and the area around it. It's the nearest point to France. Since the Luftwaffe can get to it quickly, without using up a lot of fuel, it weathers the brunt of their attacks. Is that where your brother is serving?"

She nodded. "The censors removed any mention of his exact location but left in his reference to Hell's Corner, so I wasn't quite sure where he was."

90

"Knowing precisely where he is probably wouldn't bring you any measure of comfort, and we strive not to reveal our strengths and weaknesses."

"Is that where you were wounded?" He looked toward town, and she was afraid he was now reliving the memories. "I'm sorry. I shouldn't have asked."

"Yes." His voice was low, hoarse, as though he'd pushed the word out. He looked at her. "Yes, Hell's Corner has a habit of collecting casualties. I was one of the more fortunate ones. I was serving with the 601. We suffered a lot of losses, I'm afraid. But there were also men who went untouched. We shall hope your brother is one of them."

"He's a good pilot. I'd never admit it to his face, but he is a little better than I am."

His grin was edging toward being a full one, although she suspected he thought she was exaggerating her skills. "How long have you flown?" he asked.

"I was six the first time Dad took me up. Eight when he turned the controls over to me. I should have been terrified at the responsibility. Instead, I was determined not to let him down for placing that much faith in me. And the thrill of being able to go where I wanted to go . . . I'd never felt anything like it. I was sixteen when I got my private pilot's license."

He angled his head, arched a brow. "I'm impressed. You've been at it a good deal longer than I have."

"When did you start flying?"

"Not until the summer of thirty-two. I was all of twenty-two. Young and reckless. Some mates and I wanted to fly and had the smashing idea of joining a civilian corps of the Royal Auxiliary Air Force. We were trained with the understanding that we would fly for the RAF if war came. Which it did."

She couldn't imagine him young or reckless. Nor had she realized he was only thirty-one. She'd have put him nearer to forty. War no doubt aged a person. "You must be a skilled pilot to have moved up so quickly. If you were in the army, you'd be a lieutenant colonel."

"You know your ranks."

"Dad fought in the Great War. Although he seldom spoke of it, he still managed to give me an appreciation for all things military. What do you think they'll call this war?"

"The last, I hope."

She not only hoped the same but wished it would end soon. Before they were even finished training their first course of cadets.

Wouldn't it be lovely for them if it just turned out to be a trip to another country?

"You should also be aware," he continued, "that my rank has more to do with my family's exalted position in society. Unlike with your military, in ours, promotions seldom come about because of merit — or at least that's the way it's always been, although it does seem to be changing toward recognizing accomplishment rather than the fortunes of birth. I'm for it; I'm of the opinion we will acquire better leaders."

"Still, you must have proven yourself or they wouldn't have given you such an important job here."

"They had to do something with me. Presently my leg is damned useless in a cockpit." His anger and frustration were evident in his tone.

"It's not permanent damage, then?"

"The doctors don't think so." His gaze shifted again toward the town.

"It must be odd to see lights at night." Jack had written about the blackouts.

"It is, rather. I'd forgotten how . . . enticing it can all appear."

She couldn't imagine the total darkness, how depressing and frightening it would be. Why the hell did some want to be conquerors? "Most of the businesses are closed now,

93

but would you like to walk through the area?"

"Yes, I believe I would."

After getting out of the swing, she called through the window, "We're going for a walk."

The pounding footsteps sounded just before Kitty shoved open the screen door with an eagerness similar to Trixie's. "Can I come?"

"Of course."

Kitty charged through and leapt off the porch. "Come on, Trixie."

The dog loped after her. Jessie wandered down the steps and waited until Royce made his way to the path leading to the sidewalk. Intentionally, she kept her pace slow and even, very much aware of his cane hitting the cobblestones. "Let me know when we need to head back."

"The stroll will do me good."

"Are you in much pain?"

"Less every day."

Hardly an answer. She glanced over at him. "What is it you Brits say? Stiff upper lip? Is that what you're demonstrating here?"

"Chaps have endured worse."

"How were you injured?"

He sighed as they turned up the sidewalk,

94

the distant streetlights faintly illuminating the way, creating a mystical atmosphere. "Out over the Channel, too focused on shooting my target to notice his mate coming for me. The one I took down had barely hit the water before I was forced to evade the second. We got into it. Took a bit of maneuvering to get in behind him, but he ended up in the drink as well. Wasn't until I landed back at the airfield that I realized his strafing bullets had gone through the fuselage and I'd taken a couple in the leg and hip."

He said it all as though reciting from his logbook, as though he hadn't been terrified, hadn't thought for a single moment that death might have been bearing down on him. If he was anything at all like Jack, he was undoubtedly frustrated to have been in the action but grounded now. "You mentioned the Spitfire at supper. Is that what you flew?"

"And will fly again if I have any say in the matter."

"I've heard a Messerschmitt doesn't go down without a fight."

"And we give it the fight it's looking for."

"I'll just bet you do. But I've read the Messerschmitt is better at climbing and diving."

95

"Ah, but the Spit has a lovely Rolls-Royce Merlin engine and the ability to make tighter turns. However, I would argue the advantages between the two are minimal and it is the skill of the pilot that matters the most. A talented aviator can compensate for anything lacking in an aircraft."

It was odd to be talking aviation with someone other than her father or brother. Luke had never even gone up in an airplane, preferring instead to keep his boots securely on solid ground. Whenever she talked flying, he nodded and murmured a few sounds to indicate he was listening, but she suspected he used the time to drift into thoughts about cattle feed or fence repairs. "I've read wonderful things about the Spitfire's maneuverability and speed. I'm a little envious."

"When the war is over, come to England and I'll take you up."

His offer sounded sincere, but more, it held the tone of inevitability. The war would end, and he would be around to again soar through the skies there. Jack's letters contained the same optimism. He would always survive to fight another day. She supposed all those who found themselves in the heat of battle had to cling to the hope of being spared. Otherwise, how could they find the courage to face the dangers?

Kitty skipped back to them, Trixie on her heels. "Royce, do you have movie theaters in England?"

He grinned. "We do indeed."

Kitty's smile was brighter than a full moon. "Do you like going to movies?"

"I do. Although I haven't been to a cinema in a while."

"Maybe we can go sometime."

Jessie's heart gave a little lurch. While it might have been an innocent suggestion, she couldn't help but fear that her sister was falling a little bit in love with the airman.

"I'll keep your invitation in mind, but I doubt I'll have much time for the pictures."

They passed the movie theater and Mona's Dress Boutique, where the more prominent ladies in town shopped. Kitty came to a stop in front of Delaney's Drugstore, closed up for the night. "I work here," she announced. "Behind the soda counter. If you stop by, I'll make you a Coca-Cola float with extra ice cream."

He shook his head. "I'm afraid I don't know quite what that is, but it sounds wonderful, especially the extra ice cream bit. The lads are going to get rather spoiled with the abundance of offerings here."

"Do you think they're afraid to come?"

"I think they're excited about the prospect of seeing a bit of the world and making new friends."

"Are you going to let them take girls out?"

"I very much doubt we'd be able to stop them from taking an interest in getting to know the lasses around here, but you have to remember, Kitty, they aren't staying. When they leave, a good many of them . . . won't have the opportunity to come back to visit."

He was sugarcoating for Kitty the same way he'd done for their mother, trying to soften the realities of war. They wouldn't have a chance to come back because they wouldn't survive.

"Will you?" her sister asked. "Will you come back to visit?"

"That's difficult to say at the moment."

Nothing in life was ever guaranteed, but war seemed to bring it into sharper focus. The future was always uncertain. How many people had made plans and not lived long enough to see them through?

They crossed the street to the town square, a small tree-lined park with a white wooden gazebo in the center of it. Although the trees created deep shadows beneath the branches, enough light poured from the streetlamps and the store signs that Kitty was able to locate a small twig, pick it up, and toss it toward one of several benches resting along the edges of the green where flower beds flourished. Trixie rushed off to retrieve it.

While Kitty waited, Jessie and Royce continued on. Across the street from the far end of the square, the Cowboy Grill was still open, the muted din of the customers inside the café spilling out into the night.

"I'd forgotten how innocent the young can be," he said quietly, his cane steadily tapping in rhythm with their steps.

"I'm afraid she, like the Ladies' Auxiliary Club, has romantic notions about foreigners coming to town."

"Nothing romantic about war."

"But you've been in the middle of it, and we haven't. Certainly, we know it's happening but haven't experienced it. It's hard to grasp the realities of it."

"I shall hope you're not forced to."

"Do you wish we were over there?"

They took several steps in silence before he finally said, "My opinion on the matter is probably best kept to myself."

"So maybe you're a little bitter that we're not?"

Another several steps in silence but she

99

could sense it thickening and the tension radiating from him.

He emitted a strangled sound like a growl that he was striving to swallow. "Do you know Churchill approached your government about the possibility of training our pilots more than a year ago? However, Roosevelt worried that providing any assistance at all would ruin his chance at reelection. Of course, once the election was over, they reconsidered our request, but we lost months of preparedness — and that cost lives." His cane hit the ground with more force, punctuating his words. "Adding insult to injury, we're not allowed to travel directly to the United States. We have to come in through Canada and resign from the RAF before being given our visas, so we can board the train. We can't wear our uniforms except at the airfield for fear someone takes offense that we're here. We are to be as subtle and unobtrusive as possible. Slip in quietly, do what is required of us, and slip out. God forbid Hitler decides the U.S. is offering aid and comfort and might come for you lot. Or that our presence is an indication you Yanks might step up and join the fight."

She had no response to his anger. He released a deep, shuddering breath. "Yes, I suppose I am somewhat bitter. I apologize for the outburst."

While she hadn't expected such an honest and heated diatribe, she didn't blame him for it. "Bet it felt good to get all of that off your chest, though."

His quick burst of laughter carried an echo of surprise in it. "Yes, it did, rather." He looked at her, his grin small but still managing to transform his features, so he appeared younger, and she could almost envision how he might have looked in his youth before he carried the weight of war on his shoulders. "However, you were undeserving of my tirade. You've a brother in harm's way."

"He thinks eventually we will join the fight."

"Perhaps it'll all end before you have to."

"You don't believe that."

"No, I don't." He looked up. "But it is a lovely night. It's been a while since I've been able to enjoy the peacefulness of an evening without the worry of sirens going off. Yet the serenity is marred somewhat by the guilt that I am here instead of there."

"What you're doing here will make a difference."

"I shall cling to that hope. I should probably make my way back to the residence now."

The strain in his voice told her that he was experiencing discomfort if not outright pain. "Kitty! We're heading home."

The journey back was a bit slower. He'd probably pushed himself more than he should have. When they neared the house, he said quietly, "I do appreciate the aid your country is now giving us, and I especially appreciate your family's hospitality."

Once they were inside, they discovered her mother had already retired. Kitty grabbed her scrapbook and headed upstairs.

"I'll turn in as well," Royce said.

"Barstow is coming by for you in the morning, isn't he?"

"At half eight."

Four? Her face must have registered her struggle to figure out his meaning, because he said, "Eight thirty."

His earlier expression made sense now and with a little more thought she would have gotten there. "I'll be gone by then, but if you ever want to risk riding on the back of my motorcycle, I'll give you a lift." What was she saying? He'd risked being shot out of the sky.

He seemed amused, as though he'd had

the same thought. "I'll keep your offer in mind."

A polite way of saying it would be entirely inappropriate, possibly awkward, for them to be zooming about, spooned together on her Scout. "You might have noticed a container of talcum powder on the stand beside the bed."

"I did, yes."

"Sprinkle it on the sheets before you climb in. It'll help to keep you cool as you fall asleep."

"Thank you. Good night."

"Pleasant dreams." Even as she said it, she wondered, with all he'd seen and experienced, if he was even capable of having them. She went to the back door, opened it, and called for Trixie. The lab scrambled up the steps and into the small room just off the kitchen, which was used for storage. She settled onto her mound of blankets. Jessie gave her a final pat before locking up, turning out the lights, and heading to bed.

A few hours later, something woke her. She wasn't quite certain what it had been. Squinting at her alarm clock, with the moonlight and streetlights spilling in through the lacy curtains, she was barely able to make out the time as being a few minutes after two. Crawling out of bed, she

103

crept to the door, opened it, and saw the one to Jack's room was ajar. Listening intently, she could detect no sounds coming from anywhere down the hallway — or from elsewhere in this old house that creaked with any sort of movement at all. She heard only the quiet.

After retreating into her room, she walked to the window and gazed out. The darkened silhouette of a man stood in the front yard, a tiny red glow from what she assumed was a cigarette periodically arcing toward him and disappearing for a bit. She very much doubted it was pleasant dreams that had sent Royce out there. She considered joining him, offering him company, but in the end, she returned to bed and stared at the ceiling, feeling a weight of responsibility she'd not expected. The war was never far from her thoughts, but suddenly it was striving to take up residence in her soul.

June 3, 1941

Dear Jess:

With my squadron's transfer it took longer for your letter with the unexpected news to get to me. I can't believe they sold our airfield!

And yet, I was hit with a sense of relief at being set free. You and me, Jess, it would have kept us in Terrence — if I was able to get back. But now, the sky's the limit (pun intended). I think it's harder on you because you're there. And you were always closer to Dad. You were his favorite, admit it. You know it to be true.

He and I were too much alike, always butting heads. Sometimes I think that's part of what drove me to come over here. I needed to get away from his influence, needed to feel like I was making my own decisions, the ones that were right for me. Maybe in time, you'll see this development as a good thing and have a similar realization.

Although they censored most of your letter regarding what they were going to do with the airfield, I have a pretty good idea based on what I've heard through the grapevine here. I'm glad you're sticking around to help them out. You're a damn good pilot (please burn this letter so I can deny ever admitting that).

Figure —— will already be there by the time you get this letter. Anxious to hear how it went.

Miss you, Sis.

Your older, and thus wiser, brother,

Jack

P.S. Don't forget to give Trixie a treat and tell her it's from me.

CHAPTER 6

Wednesday, June 4, 1941

That morning, after taking the Stearman she'd flown the evening before out for a test to ensure all was running smoothly after Billy worked his magic, Jessie headed to the hangar to store her gear. Three flight instructors were leaning against the side of the building, smoking. She didn't know them well, had exchanged only a handful of conversations with them since they'd arrived last week, each from a different part of the country. She gave them a quick nod as she ambled past them.

"Is Ballinger going to see that you get what you want after you spent the night with him?"

She froze in her tracks. Doug Forester hadn't bothered to disguise his innuendo. Slowly, so slowly that the air around her didn't even stir, she pivoted back around. He was giving her the hard glare that she'd caught directed her way more than once since he arrived. She didn't know what she'd done to offend him. He wasn't much older than she was but seemed to walk around with a chip on his shoulder. "I beg your pardon?"

"Heard you wanted to be a flight instructor. Figured you'd take advantage of the time he was at your place to butter him up." He sounded thoroughly disgusted with her. She vaguely wondered what his reaction might have been if Royce had arrived on the back of her motorcycle with his arms around her. While she'd briefly experienced concerns that Jack in the RAF would cause Royce to view her more favorably, she'd certainly never entertained the notion that anyone here would see her taking advantage of his staying with her family. The army had approached her mother regarding the arrangement, probably because of her past association with the airfield.

"Why would you care?"

"Dames don't belong in the cockpit."

"My licenses say different." In addition to her private license, she had a commercial one. She turned —

"Your brother's fighting for the wrong side."

Swinging back around, she narrowed her

eyes and took a quick step toward him that had him rearing his head back. Where was he getting all his information? Although since her brother's decision was common knowledge in town, his exploits reported a couple of times in the *Terrence Tribune,* Forester could have heard it anywhere. "He couldn't fight for us, since we're not involved in the war yet."

He adjusted his stance. "The Brits are going to lose. He's going to die for nothing."

He wasn't going to die. The Brits weren't going to lose. Her hands began flexing into fists. Was he suggesting Jack should fight for Germany? "They seem to be holding their own."

"It's just a matter of time before they surrender. The Germans have air superiority. The Messerschmitt —"

"Isn't without its flaws, but if you believe England hasn't a chance of winning, what are you doing here?"

"Getting paid. It's a job."

Everything she'd ever done in her life had been spurred by her passions. She couldn't imagine being so lackadaisical when referring to something that occupied most of her day. She hadn't been impressed when she'd first met Forester, and was less so now. "Are you going to convey that pessimism to the trainees?"

He shrugged. "I'll teach them what they need to know, but I'm not giving extra time to them." He looked toward the area where she'd just landed. "They can't win."

Anger was seething within her, boiling up. She looked past him to his two buddies, who were occupied looking down and grinding out their cigarette butts. "Do y'all feel the same?"

"Hard to say," one of them answered.

"Actually, it's pretty easy to say yes or no. We're here to make a difference, to give them the skills to be victorious in the skies. To help prevent their country from being invaded."

"We're just teaching them to fly," Forester said. "We're not saving them."

She shoved him with enough force to send him staggering back. She did want to save them, to try at least. She'd do it if she wasn't being paid. All her years of flying, all her hours of practicing rolls and loops, turns and dives. Learning what an aircraft was capable of, how to maneuver it . . . She had moments when she believed it had all been for this. She couldn't fight in the air, but that didn't mean she couldn't do her part to see that the battle was taken to the enemy. Germany under Hitler was the enemy — invader, terrorizer — and this guy was acting as though it was little more than a football rivalry. That nothing more was at stake than numbers on a scoreboard. Not lives, not a way of life, not democracy and freedom.

He'd caught himself and braced his legs apart as though preparing to take another blow. She certainly wanted to deliver one, harder and more forceful. "My brother's efforts on behalf of England aren't for nothing. What we're doing here isn't for nothing. If you believe it is, maybe you ought to quit."

Spinning on her heel, she strode into the hangar, put away her gear, and then marched with purpose to the wooden building where the Link Trainers were set up. When she reached her destination, she opened the door, welcoming the cold air washing over her. The sensitivity of the equipment required a cool environment, so it was housed in the only structure at the airfield with air-conditioning.

"Uh-oh. I'd say someone is fit to be tied," Rhonda said, leaning back in her chair behind the table housing the controls that operated a Link Trainer. She'd given up hairstyling at a chance to spend more time in the company of the Brits and believed what she could accomplish here was a worthwhile endeavor. She wore a khaki skirt and shirt, and a tie a shade darker. While they weren't military, it was still important to look the part.

"I ran into Doug Forester. He thinks we're just wasting our time here." Her breaths were coming fast and furious. She needed to calm them, needed to calm herself. His attitude toward the war and the training was much more infuriating than the stupid personal goading he'd initially engaged in.

"He strikes me as an idiot and someone who never does anything for the benefit of others."

Jessie walked to a metal closet, retrieved clothing that matched Rhonda's, and began to change out of her coveralls.

"Might want to be quick," Rhonda said.

"No one ever bothers us in here."

"Ballinger and Barstow already stopped by this morning."

Tucking her shirt into the waistband of her skirt, Jessie glanced over. "They did?"

"Yep." Rhonda tapped her long fingernails, polished a bright red to match her lipstick, on the tabletop. "Ballinger seemed disappointed you weren't here."

Jessie turned her attention to the mirror hanging inside the cabinet door and began working on knotting her tie. The rosiness in her cheeks was a result of her anger with Forester, not any delight she'd unexpectedly derived from Rhonda's words. "I very much doubt that."

"Did you give Doug what for?"

Jessie was more than happy to return to that topic. "I suggested he quit." Satisfied with the symmetry of her clothing, she closed the door and swung around. "I guess I expected everyone working here to be committed to a purpose greater than themselves. We can have an impact, an effect on the outcome of this war."

"It's more personal for you than it is for a lot of people. Unfortunately."

She walked over to her table, turned the chair behind it so it faced Rhonda, and sat. "It's more than my encounter with Forester that has me upset. He just lit the flame of the firecracker."

"I figured there was more to it."

Nearly eighteen years of friendship meant they were open books to each other. There wasn't anything they couldn't share. Leaning forward, placing her elbows on her thighs, she clasped her hands tightly. "Last night . . . Mama told me I shouldn't keep my life on hold for her."

Rhonda's eyes widened. "I wasn't under

113

the impression you were. What was she referring to?"

"She wants grandbabies, and until I marry Luke, she doesn't think I'm doing anything worthwhile."

"Well, that's certainly not true."

"I've never been able to really talk with her about my love of flying. It was always Dad and me going to the airshows, flipping through *Popular Aviation,* discussing the articles, photos, and planes, and working side by side on our aircraft model kits." Then he'd help her hang the finished models from her bedroom ceiling. They were all still there. "I've felt so untethered since he died, and with Jack gone . . . it's like swimming upstream against the current. Last night, Mama said it so casually, like it was a fact of life, and now I'm wondering if she didn't fight to keep the airfield because she places no value on anything I've been working toward. If she thought selling it would push me into marriage. I don't think she comprehends what I want to do with my life."

"I don't have a lot of experience dealing with mothers." Hers had run off with a traveling brush salesman when Rhonda was in first grade. It had helped to cement their friendship, because Jessie had offered sym-

114

pathy, even though at the time she hadn't really understood the situation and what everything meant. "But maybe your mom, like so many others, believes marriage is the only path to fulfillment for a woman. She didn't mean to come across as insensitive to your dreams."

"I know you're right. Still, her words were like a slap in the face."

Rhonda tapped her nails several times. "Considering her attitude, maybe it's time we revisited our plan to move in together."

They'd decided last summer to rent a house. Then Jack had made his surprise announcement about going overseas, and Jessie hadn't felt right about moving out so soon after Jack did, had felt like she'd be abandoning her mom. Then with her dad's passing . . . She could see now that she'd cast aside her independence.

"Honestly," Rhonda continued, "I'm really getting tired of dealing with my father's censure whenever I have a date and stay out later than he thinks any respectable woman should." As a preacher, he had extremely high expectations regarding his daughter's conduct. He'd no doubt be appalled to learn she had taken to drinking beer before she was of age. "If we're ever going to do this, we need to do it before everyone they've hired to work here has taken all the rental properties. They've got people coming from all over the country. There's at least a million people moving into town."

"Not quite that many." By the time they were at full capacity with students and aircraft, more than a hundred families would have moved to the area. "But you're right. If we're going to do it, we should do it now. How about Saturday morning we check out what's available?"

Rhonda grinned. "I have someplace in mind already. A cute little house on Chestnut Street. I was getting desperate, searching for something I could afford on my own. We could go look at it when we get off work."

"Okay, let's do it." Until last night, she would have felt guilty leaving her mom — but she'd already begun feeling hemmed in.

"I'm really looking forward to having my own place. Maybe it's because of Dad's job, but he sees everyone as a sinner in need of redemption. Which makes it really hard on me, being a sinner." Rhonda wasn't quite the bad girl she painted herself out to be.

The door suddenly opened, and heat swarmed in as Peter walked through decked out in a dark blue uniform. They must have stored the clothing they'd wear at the flight

116

school in their office the day before. "Ladies, how are you doing this fine morning?"

Jessie rose briskly to her feet. It seemed required when he appeared so official. She almost saluted. She did lie, although after talking with Rhonda she felt somewhat better. "Good."

Rhonda came out of her chair in a sinuous move that would have made Hedy Lamarr jealous. "I'm more than good at being a little bit bad. You?"

He smiled warmly but ignored the innuendo. "Adjusting to a rather quiet day. Ballinger wondered if he might have a word with you both in his office when you have a minute."

"He's welcome to have as many words as he likes. And so are you."

Peter laughed freely and exuberantly. "I'll keep that in mind, Miss Monroe. Perhaps you could make an appearance in, say, ten minutes?"

"We'll be there," Jessie said.

"Very good." He winked. "See you then."

As soon as the door was closed behind him, Rhonda sank into her chair. "Good Lord, he is drop-dead gorgeous, more so than I recalled from meeting him yesterday. What is it about a man in uniform that makes it such a challenge for me to think straight?"

"The sight of any man makes it hard for you to think straight."

Rhonda chuckled low. "Especially when he has such kissable lips."

Jessie gave her an indulgent smile. "Rhonda, I know what you're thinking, but he's not going to have time to get involved with you."

"They'll be here for months, Jess. Are you seriously telling me they aren't going to want some company and comfort while they're here? They're men. Even if they're working seven days a week — which I'm betting they won't — they'll need to relax every now and then. Why can't Peter relax with me? Besides, why shouldn't we get to know them? They're part of the community while they're here. I'd bet money Mrs. Johnson is already trying to figure out how to get them to come talk to her Ladies' Auxiliary Club."

After grinning and rolling her eyes, Jessie admitted, "Yes, she came over last night, but that's different from dating them. Don't get me wrong, Rhonda, I like Peter, but he is something of a flirt. A charming one, but still a flirt."

"So am I. Makes us perfect for each other."

118

Jessie's scoff that echoed around them held affection from all the years they'd spent whispering about boys. "Thought you wanted dark and brooding. That would be Royce." Even as she said it, her stomach knotted up as though preparing for a blow. What did she care if her friend went with him?

"Changed my mind. Decided it would be too much work. I just want to have some fun, and Peter strikes me as someone who knows how to show a girl a good time."

"He's not going to be here forever."

"You know me, Jess. I'm not looking for forever."

"He could have a girl back home."

"I very much doubt it. Royce, though, probably does. He's all serious, wears a cloak of responsibility. While it's sweet of you to worry about me, I can take care of myself. Let's go see what he wants."

Outside, they walked up the paved path that led to the offices and classrooms building. The area was a beehive of activity with some men heading toward the planes or hangars. Others were inspecting the aircraft. Construction continued on the tower and the additional hangar. So much remained to be done in preparation for the cadets' arrival. Curriculums hammered out, flight

119

paths determined, maps marked.

They reached their destination, went inside, and strode down the hallway, past the classrooms, where students would learn the basics of flight, navigation, meteorology, and the myriad things one needed to know to become skilled at flying.

The door to Barstow's office was closed, the one to the Brits' open. Rhonda rapped on the doorjamb of the spartan office with its two desks, a long worktable, and several chairs. Both men came to their feet from behind their respective desks. Royce had changed into his uniform as well, which fit him much better than the suit, leaving no doubt as to the breadth of his shoulders. He wasn't skinny as her mom had indicated, but trim. After seeing him in uniform, Rhonda was probably going to shift her interest to him. Jessie suddenly realized how incredibly insulting it was that they weren't allowed to wear their uniforms in town. It wasn't as if anyone wouldn't immediately recognize them as members of the RAF as soon as they spoke. Royce had every right to be annoyed with the ridiculous rules governing their presence while here.

"Come in, ladies," Royce said. "We're grateful you could find time to join us. Please have a seat."

Rhonda and Jessie settled into chairs in front of his desk. He retook his, leaned forward slightly in earnestness, his forearms on the desk, his hands clasped. He cleared his throat. "First, to be perfectly clear, we appreciate the role you'll undertake to ensure our lads are properly trained. What you're doing is generally done by men, so I recognize it might be a bit of a challenge."

"We're up to the task," Jessie reassured him.

"I'm not doubting your abilities but rather the cadets' attitudes, which might require some adjustment. If any cause you problems or fail to take your directions seriously, do let us know and we'll set the matter to rights."

"We appreciate the offer, but we'd do better handling things ourselves."

"Possibly, but if you encounter difficulties, don't hesitate to call on us."

"Sounds fair," Rhonda said. "We're grateful for the support."

"I assure you that it's here should you require it. This next bit is going to be somewhat awkward but needs to be addressed. Ladies, we must insist you not fraternize with the cadets."

Rhonda scoffed and rolled her eyes. "Shouldn't you have Mrs. Winder in here?"

Mrs. Winder was the airfield secretary and was fifty if she was a day.

"She won't be teaching these lads how to pilot a plane. You will. We can't have you becoming emotionally involved with a chap to the extent you might grant him a favorable review of which he is not deserving. Squadron Leader Smythson and I will be relying upon you to be objective in your assessments regarding each cadet's mastery of the subjects and skills required for success as well as his suitability as a pilot."

Although Jessie understood his concerns, she was disappointed he felt a need to voice them. She gave a curt nod. "We're fully aware of our responsibilities to these young men. We understand their lives are at stake and don't want them to die any more than you do. Trust me, getting tangled up with any of these fellas is the last thing we plan to do." She looked at Rhonda. "Right?"

Rhonda's gaze darted to Peter before she returned her attention to Royce. "I swear I have no interest whatsoever in fraternizing with any cadet."

"Good. We thought it best to be clear upfront so we're not working at cross-purposes." He stood, and everyone else followed his lead. "As I said, we appreciate your coming by."

122

"Anytime," Rhonda said, although her gaze was focused on Peter. He didn't wink or give her a seductive smile, as though in this room he was all business.

"Mind how you go," Royce said.

Jessie smiled, not exactly sure what he meant.

As soon as they were in the hallway, Rhonda nudged her shoulder. "I think dark and brooding has an interest in you."

Trying not to be flattered by the thought, Jessie offered up a horrified expression. "Don't be ridiculous."

"His eyes never strayed from you."

"I think it's a requirement of military men to have that penetrating stare."

"So you noticed."

"No, I . . . I was just paying a great deal of attention to everything he was saying, which was probably more than you were doing. Besides, he may have been a little more comfortable focusing on me after last night —"

"What happened last night? What haven't you told me?"

"Nothing. But we talked, you know, like civilized people do. Anyway, I have a boyfriend." That word again sounded like something spouted on a grammar school playground.

"How can you be so sure Luke's the right one when you've never kissed anyone else?"

Stumbling to a stop, she stared at her friend, whom she sometimes fought not to judge for giving away her kisses so freely. "You want to get involved with a Brit, get involved, but don't drag me along. You might be content to be an LT operator, but I want to take them up into the sky. I need to figure out a way to maneuver myself into that position when they start hiring more instructors. Step one is having absolutely no interest in getting entangled with any British flier — novice or experienced."

Rhonda held up her hands, palms out. "All right. Forget I said anything. I was probably wrong. It was about the star quarterback I thought had a crush on you in high school."

Jessie spun around and shoved on the door, carrying quickly through to the outside, where the sun warmed her, not certain why she'd suddenly grown chilled. But Rhonda hadn't been wrong about the star quarterback. "Maybe our sharing a place isn't such a good idea."

No matter how fast she walked, she'd never been able to outpace the tall redhead with her long legs. "Oh, come on, Jess. If you're going to live with someone, who better than the person who knows all your secrets . . . and how to keep them."

CHAPTER 7

Kitty had just placed a root beer float on the counter in front of Mr. Peterson — a retired lawyer who came in every afternoon at two o'clock on the dot for "his usual" — when she heard the rumbling coming from overhead, like the sky was breaking apart.

She wasn't the only one to rush out onto the sidewalk. People were climbing out of their stopped automobiles. Mothers were cradling their bawling babies close. Wide-eyed children were clutching their mamas' skirts. Balls weren't bouncing and jacks previously tossed on the sidewalk beneath the shade of the oak trees that circled the town square were forgotten, no longer being snatched up. Everyone was craning their necks to gaze up at the cloudless blue sky and the sun glinting off the visible objects.

She was hit with a sense of wonder and awe. Planes, so many planes. Maybe two dozen. Like giant birds with blue bodies and bright yellow wings. She didn't know what kind of aircraft they were, but Jessie would know. She knew them all.

"They headed to your dad's place?" Mr. Peterson asked, standing beside her.

She had to shake off the momentary twinge of sadness. He wasn't here, and it wasn't his place any longer, but sometimes people forgot both facts. He'd love seeing all these planes, although hopefully he was — from above rather than below like her.

"Probably." She knew they were expecting more planes to arrive from the army. Fighting not to cover her ears at the deafening growl as they came directly overhead, blocking out the sun, casting shadows over the town, she wondered if the skies over England were always echoing a deep thundering that was at once terrifying and hopeful.

"What a beautiful sight," Mr. Peterson said.

Only if they were friendly. She didn't want to think about Jack having to face that many planes, engaging in battle with them.

Then they were gone, their roar fading in the distance, and the sky was clear with nothing but light blue once again spreading to the horizon, and yet she would never forget the sight of those planes or their growl or the vibrations reverberating all around as though the very power of those machines had traveled straight through her.

"It was incredible," Kitty said during dinner that evening. "How many were there?"

"Two dozen," Jessie said. "But only half of them stayed. The rest flew the extra pilots back home."

"Oh, I never thought about what happens to the people who deliver the planes. Did you see them, Mama?"

"I did. I was working in the garden when I heard them."

"I think the whole town saw them," Jessie said. "Cars and trucks stopped on the side of the road. People got out and started walking across the field. A couple of men got in the way as some pilots were trying to land. Royce, you might want to discuss with Barstow building a fence around the airfield. Unfortunately, not everyone has common sense. Some folks might show up to watch the cadets practicing."

"That's a splendid idea. I'll have a chat with him about it tomorrow."

Kitty had never known a man to talk so little during dinner. Her father and Jack had always dominated the conversation. Jessie was skilled at inserting herself into the discussion, offering her opinion or down-

128

right arguing with them. Mama had always simply smiled, like watching a play and enjoying it. Kitty had been a little intimidated but imagined her father now, grinning fondly as she rattled on about aircraft, of all things. "They were different from the planes I've seen you fly, Jessie. They had only one level of wings."

"They weren't biplanes. They're Vultee trainers. The flight instructors will use them for the second phase of training, because that particular aircraft is a little more complicated to operate."

Kitty looked across at Royce. "Are there that many planes in the skies over England?"

His smile was somewhat sad. "Sometimes more."

"I didn't like all the noise they made."

"It's better to hear them coming than to be taken by surprise, at least from our perspective. Although we have radar stations to keep watch, so we usually know they're coming before we hear them."

"Airplanes are so pretty. It doesn't seem right for them to be used to hurt people."

"That's because they shouldn't be. But then, it would be rather nice if no one wanted to hurt anyone, wouldn't it?"

Suddenly feeling sad, she just nodded. They ate in silence for several minutes, and

Kitty became aware of a tension building in her sister. Finally, Jessie said, "I was going to mention this later, but no reason to wait. Before coming home, I took a gander at a house over on Chestnut. Rhonda and I are going to lease it."

"For what?" Kitty asked.

Her sister's laugh was soft, maybe a little self-conscious. "To live in."

"But you live here."

Jessie darted a glance at their mother. "Rhonda and I talked about moving in together last year, but, well, when Jack left —"

"You worried about me," Mama said.

"It didn't seem right for us both to go. Then with Dad suddenly being gone . . . But last night you indicated you'd adjusted to their absences, so I decided it's now or never."

"Lord knows you're old enough to have your own place, but maybe you should discuss this with Luke before making a final decision. He might have other ideas about where you should live."

"I'll mention it to him tonight, but he's not going to change my mind. The house is furnished, unoccupied, and we'll move in Saturday."

"You're certainly not letting any grass

130

grow under your feet or leaving any room for adjustments."

"We wanted to get settled before things get really busy." She looked across at Royce. "The landlord mentioned another house for rent a couple of streets over, on Pecan. Fully furnished. I don't know if it's what you're looking for. Two bedrooms."

"Thank you. Smythson and I will have a look at it."

"You're welcome to stay here, Royce," Mama said, and Kitty hoped he would. She liked having him around. He made her miss Jack and Dad a little less. "Your fellow officer could move in as well, take Jessie's room."

"Thank you, Mrs. Lovelace. It's a kind offer, but I don't want to overstay my welcome. We'd always planned to have our own accommodations, and our hours are likely to become somewhat erratic as the training gets fully underway."

Kitty couldn't help but be a little disappointed.

"Well, Kitty, if we're going to have two empty bedrooms soon, I wonder how you'd feel about us taking in a cadet or two on an occasional Saturday night?"

"What do you mean?"

"The War Relief Society met this after-

131

noon, and we discussed the possibility that these young men, being so far from family and the familiar, might get homesick and appreciate the opportunity to spend the night in a home rather than the barracks. We decided to make a list of those willing to take them in for a night, have it posted in the recreation hall, and let them sign up. That is, if you think it's a good idea, Royce."

"I think it's a marvelous idea, and they'd enjoy it very much. You're incredibly homely, Mrs. Lovelace."

With a gasp, Kitty stared at him in horror. "Why would you say something so mean?"

He looked confused, like her words made no sense.

"Kitty, darling," Mama began.

"No, you're beautiful. Why would he say you're not? Even if he thought it, it's rude to say it."

"Ah," Royce murmured slowly, "seems I may have blundered. In Britain, *homely* means friendly, domestic. Your mum is welcoming and has a way about her of making someone feel comfortable. I was complimenting her. I take it by your reaction that here, it means unattractive."

Kitty nodded. "It sure does."

"I shall jot that down for the lads. I'm making a list, you see, of all the things in

American English that mean something different in the King's English, so they'll know what not to say while they're over here."

The idea of the list fascinated Kitty. "What is on your list?"

"Gasoline. We call it petrol. Cookies we refer to as biscuits."

"What else?"

"Well, there's —" He stopped, studied her. "Right. Well, I really can't think of anything else off the top of my head."

"Can I see your list when you're finished with it? Maybe we could have it published in the newspaper so none of us say the wrong things."

"I'll certainly give it some consideration."

He complimented her mother on her flower beds and from there the conversation easily flowed into his love of English gardens, in particular his *mum's.* When they finished supper, Jessie helped Kitty clear things away before going upstairs to prepare for her date. Kitty didn't dawdle when it came to washing, drying, and putting away the dishes. She wanted to spend more time with Royce, especially since he wasn't going to be living there for much longer.

When she joined him in the living room, she invited him to play checkers. She'd barely gotten the board set up on a table near the window when a knock sounded at the door. "I'll get it."

She wasn't surprised to see Luke.

"Hey, Little Bit," he said as she pushed back the screen door. Well over six feet, he'd been a great quarterback because he'd been able to see over so many of the players and throw a pass right into the arms of a runner. When he wasn't wearing a helmet, he wore a cowboy hat, which he removed as she led him into the living room.

While her mom began the introductions, Kitty hurried up the stairs to let Jessie know her future husband had arrived.

CHAPTER 8

Jessie had just finished dabbing Chanel no. 5 behind each ear when she heard the pounding of footsteps, quickly followed by Kitty's shouting through her door, "Luke's here!"

"Thanks. I'll be down in a minute." Looking in her mirror, she gave a little twirl and watched the skirt of her lime-colored dress flare. The heeled shoes weren't as comfortable as her boots, but they made her calves look good. Luke was a leg man. She didn't bother with a purse, because he would be purchasing the ten-cent admission tickets and her mother wouldn't lock the door if Jessie was still out, even if she went to bed before Jessie returned home. She supposed a lot of people considered Terrence to be a sleepy little town, but the police chief never complained about the lack of crime.

She headed down. As she neared the family room, she heard Luke's deep voice, one well suited to hollering at cowhands, and her mother's. When she walked in, the cowboy standing in the center of the room, tapping his straw Stetson against his firm thigh, gave her a wide grin. "Hello, darlin'."

Quickly crossing over to her, he took her hand, leaned in, and grazed a kiss over her cheek. Royce, who'd been sitting across from Kitty at the small table by the window, had immediately come to his feet when she entered the room. "You've met —" she asked.

"Yep," Luke answered briskly.

It was a silly question. Her mother, sitting on the couch knitting, would have made the introductions.

"Royce and I are playing checkers," Kitty piped up. "Only he calls it draughts. Isn't that funny?"

"Kitty, dear, don't make fun of our guest," Mama admonished.

"I'm not. I was just saying. I wasn't making fun." She looked at Royce imploringly.

"I know," he said with a wink and a warm smile. "It's something else for me to add to my list."

The kindness he bestowed on her sister seemed to come natural to him, and Jessie wondered if he had any sisters. Young ones, like Kitty, whom he might be missing. Had

136

she not asked more questions of him last night because she'd feared getting to know him, of liking him too much?

"We're going to be late," Luke said.

Snapping her attention back to him, she was very much aware of the odd look he was giving her, as though he was suddenly facing a contentious bull or a difficult math problem. She slipped her arm around his. "Right. Let's go."

Once outside, he directed her toward his truck, parked on the street in front of the house.

"It's close enough we could walk." She wasn't certain why she'd told him what he already knew.

"If we tarry much longer, we're going to miss the beginning of the movie. Besides, cowboys never walk anywhere. You know that. We either drive or ride a horse." He settled her into the truck, loped around it, and climbed into the driver's side. "So what's this fella do?" he asked, starting the engine.

"He's the commanding officer. He'll oversee the Brits, the training —"

"Thought you had another fella for that." He put the truck in gear, and they trundled up the road.

"Barstow?" She'd complained to Luke

137

about him until his eyes had glassed over and he'd suggested she quit working at the airfield. "He manages the operation of the school. It's a little confusing. I don't think they've really figured it out yet."

"But *this guy* is your boss?"

She was fairly certain by his emphasis that he was referring to Royce — and that he'd taken an immediate dislike to him. "I suppose, although I guess they all are, really. What difference does it make?"

"Just trying to understand his place."

He seemed to be saying a lot more than his words were implying. Was he jealous? Why was she suddenly feeling guilty? Because she'd taken a late-night walk with the Brit? Before things got awkward, she decided a detour of topic was needed. "Rhonda and I are going to lease a house on Chestnut."

"Do tell. What made you decide to do that?"

"We've been thinking about it for a while."

Taking her hand, he pressed her fingers to his lips and gave her a sideways glance. "I've got a house you can live in."

"It's a little far from the airfield." Half an hour as opposed to ten minutes.

"I wasn't thinking you'd still be working after we got married."

Her stomach quivered. Her detour had led them straight into awkward. At some point, they really needed to sit down and discuss expectations, but she wasn't in the mood for a confrontation now. "I've made a commitment to the school."

"For how long?"

"Until they don't need me anymore, I guess." He abruptly released her hand as though he wasn't pleased with her answer. "Anyway, we'll be moving in on Saturday."

"You gonna need help? Need the truck to haul your stuff over?"

"No, it comes furnished. I'm just going to pack up the essential things to start with. But I'm excited about it. It'll be good to be on my own, to have more freedom, to not feel so . . . hemmed in."

He darted a quick glance over at her before returning his attention to the street. "I didn't realize you were feeling that way."

"Neither did I. Not really." Not until she'd stepped into the house they were going to lease and breathed it in. "Things have been a little strained with Mama lately. I think putting a little distance between us will help."

"Yep, parents can be a little overbearing, even when they don't mean to be. It's the reason I built myself a little place away from

139

the big house." *The big house* was how he'd always referred to the large two-story white house in which had resided at one time or another the patriarch from every generation since the first Caldwell had planted his roots in the area. "Still, a lot of responsibility being out on your own."

She gave her head a little shake. "My job comes with a lot of responsibility."

Going around the corner, he pulled into a small parking area behind the cinema. "Any idea what this *Citizen Kane* is about?"

She shouldn't have been surprised he ignored her comment. They seldom spoke about her job at the airfield. She'd go out to the ranch, and he'd saddle up Buttercup for her and they'd ride over the land that would eventually be divided among him and his three sisters. But he never had any interest in going up in an airplane with her, of getting a taste of her world. He knew the sky from looking up at it, not from being in it, from soaring through it. Tonight, it really struck home and bothered her. Maybe because she'd spent too much of last night talking with another pilot, someone with whom she had so much in common.

"I don't understand why he said *Rosebud* while he was dying," Luke said later as they headed toward his truck with his arm slung around her shoulders.

After watching the newsreels of bombings, people scurrying about and searching through rubble, German tanks, and the realities of war, she always found it difficult to concentrate on the beginning of the movie. To sit in a theater, safe and secure munching on buttered popcorn, seemed obscene. She'd nearly missed Charles Foster Kane's utterance with his last breath. "I think the sled represented the only time in his life when he was truly happy."

"That'd be sad. If the happiest time in your life was when you were a kid." Pulling her in closer as they neared his truck, he pressed a kiss to the top of her head. "Mine's right now, being with you."

He did have a way of winning her over, and her earlier thoughts about their differences seemed trivial. Smiling, she tilted up her face and took his mouth with an earnestness that had him stopping in the poorly lit parking lot and circling his arms around her, which resulted in a few catcalls and whistles from those who were also heading to their vehicles. But it was all done good-naturedly. Not a single person in Terrence didn't know she and Luke were an item, didn't expect wedding bells to ring for them. Maybe that was part of the problem, why she was beginning to feel on edge, combative with her mother. Everyone else's expectations suddenly didn't seem to align with hers.

Drawing back, he pressed his forehead against hers. "Want to go back to my place for a while? I'll be more than willing to make it a *happy* time for you."

She squeezed her eyes shut, hating to disappoint him, knowing the hard hug she gave him wasn't going to soften her words. "I can't. The first class of cadets arrives Sunday. I still have so much to do to get ready for them."

Within her arms, he stiffened, dropped his head back, and sighed heavily. "I don't know why you have to be involved in this program."

"Because Jack's not here to do it." Although even if he was, she'd still want to be an instructor. She enjoyed witnessing a student's thrill the first time she turned the controls over to one. It was scary for a trainee, but equally breathtaking. Being restricted to teaching on the LT, she was going to miss sharing that satisfaction of accomplishment.

Luke released his hold on her completely. "I don't understand that either, Jess. It's not *our* war, and he's fighting for a piece of land that he never set foot on until he went over there."

"So we're not even supposed to help?"

"Not when *our* government tells us to stay out of it."

Holding up her hands, she took two steps back. "Did you object to your father giving us five hundred acres to use as an auxiliary field?" The land was located to the north of the airfield. A farmer, Mr. Robson, had given them three hundred acres to the south. Once all the students arrived, they'd need the fields to handle the additional air traffic.

"He didn't *give* it. He's leasing it. It was a business decision. But, yes, I had my doubts as to whether we should have done it."

"The government endorses what we're doing here. Hell, they're providing the planes and much of the equipment."

"Again, the Brits are paying for all of it — through the Lend-Lease Act. We're sending mixed messages to the Germans. It looks like we're no longer neutral."

"I don't want to do this again, Luke." They'd argued ad nauseam about it when Jack had left, each of them holding firm in their conviction of what was right. Since then, they'd avoided any discussion of what

143

was happening across the Atlantic, but it was getting harder and harder to ignore the horror of what they were seeing and reading about. And more difficult to ignore the impact of their differences, and what their individual beliefs said about each of them. "We agreed to disagree and leave it at that. I'm going to walk home."

"No, you're not. Get in the truck."

His curt tone did nothing to appease her rising temper. "I need to walk."

"Get. In. The. Truck."

"No." As she stormed forward, she heard his low growl, followed by his bootheels hitting the sidewalk two seconds after she reached it. She'd never been able to outdistance his long legs. She also knew that the gentleman in him wouldn't let her go home unescorted. At least he had the wisdom to not say anything.

She struggled to understand his position and the chasm her decision had created between them. Their silence grew thick and uncomfortable. She remembered a time when she'd drawn solace from his nearness, even when they didn't talk. Now she just wanted to be free of his disapproval. They hadn't always agreed on everything. He preferred her hair long, thought her motorcycle was too dangerous, and avoided airshows. She didn't like it when he participated in rodeos, but she still went and watched him perform.

When she reached the house, she marched up the walk, stopped just shy of the steps, and faced him, her heart squeezing at the sight of him, with one hand tucked into a back pocket of his jeans, his lean hip jutting out slightly, a stance she'd seen him take a thousand times. "Thanks for the movie."

"Sorry I ruined the night."

She shook her head. "I think that's on both of us. Or maybe it's the fault of the war. I know you're not alone in your beliefs and sentiments."

He gave her the lopsided, one-corner-hitched-higher-than-the-other grin that had stolen her heart when they were in high school. "Neither are you. I'll see you, Jess."

He began striding away.

"Luke?" When he stopped, she rushed over to him, wound her arms around his neck, and planted her mouth on his, taking great comfort in his arms tightening around her, drawing her in close. It wasn't the most passionate kiss they'd ever shared, but it was steady and sure. When she drew back, she cradled her palm against his strong jaw. "I'm not angry at you." Saddened, disappointed. "I'm just mad at everything . . .

145

and scared."

"I know, darlin', but Jack's gonna be okay."

Her throat threatened to knot up with the gentleness of his tone.

He nodded toward the house. "I'll wait until you're inside."

Maybe that was the reason she'd dashed after him, because he'd never before left until she was safely inside, and it had seemed so wrong to watch him walk away, as though if he did, everything between them would irrevocably change and he'd never come back. Sometimes she felt like she was walking on a tightwire where their relationship was concerned, and lately she was beginning to wonder if she should just let herself fall off — for both their sakes.

When she was standing in the entryway with the door locked behind her, she heard a rattling in the kitchen. It was nearing ten thirty, a little past the time for her mom to be stirring about, and yet she was grateful she was. Jessie needed to smooth things out there as well, needed confirmation that her mother was okay with her moving out. But if she wasn't, Jessie had come to understand that she needed to leave, needed space to figure out what she really wanted to do with her life. She headed through the dining room and into the kitchen. "Mama, I'm glad you're still —"

She froze at the sight of the man standing by the stove in pants and a white shirt with a couple of buttons not secured and the sleeves rolled up. "Uh, sorry, Royce. I thought you were Mama."

"I was having trouble sleeping. So bloody quiet around here. London was never this quiet, even before the war. I thought some warm milk might help. Would you care for some?"

"In this heat?" Following a grimace, she smiled and arched a brow. "How about a beer instead?"

"That does sound better. But only if you'll join me."

"That was the plan." She opened the fridge and grabbed two bottles.

"How was the film?" he asked.

"Sad. A little depressing, really. Have you seen *Citizen Kane*?" She opened a drawer, found the bottle opener, and popped the top off each bottle.

"No, although I do think I saw my first authentic cowboy tonight. Is Mr. Caldwell a cowboy?"

"He is. Rides horses, herds cattle." She handed him a bottle. "Shall we sit on the porch? It's cooler out there."

On their way out, she turned on the light in the dining room, so when they stepped onto the porch, it was illuminated by the pale glow easing through the window. She sat in a rocker. The other one released a low, soulful creak as Royce settled in.

Trixie appeared and nestled her head on his lap. Jessie almost envied the dog when Royce's large hand landed comfortingly on Trixie and his long fingers scratched behind her ear. "Have you and your young man been together long?"

She smiled at the quaint expression. Her young man. As though Royce was so old at thirty-one. "We started dating our last year in high school. I was sixteen. Gosh, as old as Kitty is now, come to think of it."

"He seems like a nice chap."

"He's a good guy, decent, hardworking, would give you the shirt off his back if you needed it. We don't quite agree on the war, but it can't last forever, can it?"

"Good Lord, I hope not."

And then she and Luke could settle back into the familiar, without the god-awful rift hanging between them, constantly threatening to ruin their time together. Although it was more than that. It was what he wanted in a wife, what she desired as a woman. "I have to apologize for the awkwardness during dinner. I should have waited until later to tell Mama about my decision to move out."

"You shouldn't apologize for carrying on as you would if company wasn't underfoot. It's the reason I declined your mum's kind invitation to remain. There's always a bit of a strain with guests about — under the best of circumstances. When family matters need to be addressed, the situation becomes all the harder, I think. I take it you and Mr. Caldwell are engaged then."

She took a sip of beer, wondering why it suddenly seemed bitter. "Not officially." Not even unofficially. Shaking her head, she closed her eyes briefly. "Certainly, there's been no announcement. Still, everyone expects us to get married." But sometimes, especially lately, she felt like Dad's recliner, reshaping over the years to ensure a comfortable fit for someone else. She suddenly realized she was the one expected to do all the adjusting, all the changing. "He's a good catch. I'd be a fool to toss him back. It's complicated."

"Most relationships are."

Feeling disloyal discussing Luke with him, she opted to change the subject. "What did you do before the RAF?"

"I was a solicitor. A lawyer."

149

She trailed a single finger up and down her bottle, gathering up the dew that had formed. "I can see you as a lawyer. Have you always been so serious?"

"My father" — he shook his head — "both my parents were quite strict, with high expectations regarding behavior. Any sort of frivolity was frowned upon. However, I did have a bit of a wild streak when I was younger. Led me to flying."

She couldn't imagine him wild and carefree. "What was England like, before the war?"

"Where to even begin? England is full of history. From Stonehenge to Hadrian's Wall and all the castles in between. You could spend a couple of weeks in London alone, and not see everything of importance. But it's the people, I think, that make a country. We, Brits, are a stoic, determined lot. Working with these lads, you'll get a better sense of England than you would if you visited one of her many museums. Just as I'm getting a better sense of America. I've always detected an uneasy alliance between our two countries, ever since your chaps tossed perfectly good tea into a harbor."

She smiled brightly. "I suppose that did create some friction."

"A bit, yes. To be honest, we've received a

150

much warmer welcome than I anticipated. I feel quite rotten about unintentionally insulting your mother during dinner. She is anything but unattractive."

"I doubt she was insulted, and if she was, your explanation appeased her." She took another sip of her beer. "So what was the word you didn't want to share with Kitty?"

"Oh, Lord." He glanced off toward town, the light filtering through the window capturing his strong profile. "I probably shouldn't even share it with you."

"Something inappropriate then, possibly naughty? I'm a big girl. Not easily shocked or offended."

"Right, then. Rubber."

Her cheeks warmed with embarrassment. Obviously, she wasn't quite as sophisticated as she'd assumed. "As in condom?"

"As in eraser."

Her eyes widened. "You call an eraser a rubber? That could be humiliating if you asked for one in a store."

"Yes, it was."

He sounded thoroughly mortified, and it took everything within her not to laugh. "If it happened here, you won't be able to show your face in town."

"It happened while we were in Washington. I received quite the disgusted look from

151

the salesclerk."

"I'll just bet. But did you get your erasers?"

"Eventually, yes."

She was glad he'd been up, and they'd had some time to sit out here with a beer. Hope was filling her again. She hadn't realized how remnants of her argument with Luke had lingered. They each drank their beer quietly for a while, looking in the direction of town, where streetlights glowed in the distance.

Then he was tapping his long fingers against the brown glass. She was very much aware of his studying her as the silence eased in around them, interrupted occasionally by the chirping of the crickets, a faint bark, and the distant rumble of a car. She shouldn't enjoy sitting out here with him as much as she did. "Are you going to speak at the Ladies' Auxiliary luncheon?"

He sighed. "Unfortunately, my superiors are encouraging it. They think more visibility will be good for morale and relations."

"As a lawyer, I'd think you'd be good at speaking in front of people."

"I don't mind speaking. However, I'm not convinced it's the best use of my time."

"As you're no doubt discovering, there's

not much entertainment in this town. People get excited at the arrival of aircraft. Although it was probably the sheer number more than anything."

"We've had too much excitement the past couple of years. I like the quiet here."

"Even though it keeps you awake?"

"Even then. Although now I should probably be able to fall asleep." He held up his empty bottle as he got to his feet, leaning on his cane. "Thank you for the beer . . . and the company. I should abed now."

"See you in the morning."

She didn't stay out long before giving Trixie an affectionate pat and leading her inside. After locking up and turning out the lights, Jessie went up the stairs and into her bedroom. A few minutes later, she lay in her bed, staring at the ceiling, wondering why she felt more comfortable talking with Royce than with Luke. Maybe because she and Royce had a common goal, one they'd begin working to reach in earnest when the cadets arrived on Sunday. Everything would change then, although she wasn't convinced it hadn't already.

CHAPTER 9

"Kitty! Hurry! We're going to be late!" Fran called up the stairs.

In her bedroom, Kitty dragged her brush through her hair one last time before snatching up the banner she and Fran had created last night. It had helped to distract her from the fact that Jessie and Royce had moved out yesterday afternoon. Their respective houses were only a few blocks away, within walking distance, and both had told her she could visit anytime, but it had been odd not to have either of them around as darkness had settled in. She'd wanted to go see Royce because she had a thousand questions about the cadets arriving today, but Mama had discouraged her, saying he probably needed some time to himself. Although he wouldn't be alone since he was living with the other RAF officer.

But not getting to talk with him hadn't

dimmed her enthusiasm for welcoming the latest arrivals. With renewed excitement thrumming through her, she dashed down the stairs to where Fran was waiting. Her smile was as large as Kitty's as they hugged each other and gave a little squeal.

"I can't believe they're almost here," Fran said.

"I know." The cadets' arrival had been the big headline in that morning's edition of the *Terrence Tribune*. Having recently decided she wanted to document everything that had to do with the Brits, she'd clipped the article for her scrapbook.

"We really need to go," Fran said, grabbing Kitty's hand.

"One second." Kitty hurried down the hallway toward the largest bedroom. "Mama, are you ready?"

"Just about! You girls go on."

Not needing to be told twice, she and Fran were out the door and walking as quickly as possible toward the depot. Running wasn't an option, because they were each wearing their Sunday best and didn't need to break a heel on the way. By the time they reached the platform, it was already crowded. Kitty figured most of the town was here. The article had encouraged people to make the newcomers feel welcome.

155

"I knew we wouldn't get a good spot," Fran lamented. "They're not going to see our sign."

"Yes, they will. Come on." Grabbing Fran's hand, Kitty wended her way between people until she reached her destination near the front of the platform, where the two officers waited in their suits. "Good morning."

The Brits turned to her. "Hello, Kitty. What a pleasant surprise to see you here," Royce said.

"We wouldn't miss it. This is my best friend, Fran."

"Hello, Fran. Allow me to introduce Squadron Leader Smythson to you both."

"Hi," Kitty said, while Fran smiled and blushed. "Bet you weren't expecting the whole town to turn out."

"We were quite taken aback to see so many here."

"We want the cadets to feel right at home." Mrs. Johnson and Mrs. Berg had set up a table with cookies and lemonade. Children were scampering around. Kitty saw Mr. Peterson in the crowd.

"That's very kind of everyone," Royce said.

"Want to see what we made?" Kitty asked, but before he could answer, she and Fran unrolled the banner with WELCOME written on it, along with a drawing of the British flag. She'd borrowed a book from the library to make sure she got it exactly right.

"The lads will certainly like and appreciate your sign."

A train whistle sounded in the distance. Fran's squeal was accompanied by a little hop, but Kitty fought to give the appearance of calm. She and Fran held their banner high as the train chugged into the station and came to a screeching, thundering halt.

Passengers began to disembark. The cadets were easy to spot. They were all wearing the same gray suits that the officers wore. They also held canvas bags that probably had all their possessions tucked inside. Some had pipes in their mouths. She'd never seen anyone smoke a pipe before. A few looked like they should still be in high school, didn't appear to be much older than she was. Many seemed wary, unsure of how to respond as people converged on them. She saw a number of stunned, lost expressions. She couldn't imagine how confusing it would be to arrive in a never-before-visited town. The Terrence municipal band was playing "San Antonio Rose," and Kitty wondered briefly if there was an English song they'd rather hear.

But then she and Fran dropped their banner and were moving forward, welcoming the arriving airmen as Royce fought to corral the cadets toward the waiting bus.

"Welcome to Terrence. We're so glad to have you," she said brightly, as she shook each young man's hand. So many. They came in all sizes, tall and short. But thin, so thin, every one of them, and each had haunted eyes, no matter the shade, but there was an excitement in them as well. Their accents varied. She couldn't make out exactly what some were saying. She thought they were thanking her or maybe just saying hello. It was all confusing to her and had to be doubly so for them.

Reaching out, she took the next hand and pumped it enthusiastically. "Welcome to Terrence."

"And you are?"

No one else had bothered to ask. She liked that he did, liked the way he studied her as though he found her interesting. "Kitty. Kitty Lovelace."

"Hello, Kitty Lovelace. I'd heard Texas had the most beautiful girls. You've proven the rumor correct."

Her heart gave a little stammer, and her toes wanted to curl. No one had ever called

158

her beautiful. Oh, she knew she wasn't plain, but a boy had never voiced it. She didn't know how to respond but thought she would happily listen to him speak all day with that lovely accent. He had eyes the shade of Christmas fudge. Swallowing, she tried to regain her bearings, not wanting to come across as totally inexperienced when it came to boys, even though she'd yet to have a date. "What's your name?"

His smile was mesmerizing. "Harrison, but my mates call me Harry."

"Welcome, Harrison. I hope you like it here."

"I already do." He leaned in slightly. "Call me Harry."

She was pretty sure she was blushing. "Harry."

"Cadet!" Royce shouted, and Harry glanced over his shoulder.

"I'd best be off," he said. He winked at her. "But I'll see you around, Kitty."

Then he was gone, and she stood there for several long minutes, wondering if she would indeed see him again. Maybe he'd come into the drugstore, and she could fix him a soda fountain drink.

"Aren't they wonderful?"

She jerked her attention to Fran, who was smiling brightly, and she realized the bus was heading up the road and the townsfolk were wandering away. "Yes, they are."

"I love the way they talk. How long will they be here?"

"Five months." They started walking.

"And Jessie gets to train them? She's so lucky."

Kitty considered asking Fran if Harry had wanted to know her name but wasn't certain she really cared to know the answer. She liked thinking that maybe he'd been friendly with only her. None of the boys at school ever gave her much attention. She found she liked being singled out. She wanted to get to know all the cadets, couldn't wait for the dance Mrs. Johnson had promised to arrange. Life was finally getting interesting.

June 10, 1941

Dear Kitty Kat,

It doesn't matter where I am in London when I'm visiting, it seems I can see the dome of St. Paul's. After the worst night of the Blitz, they say Churchill wept when he saw the dome still standing through the murky haze. Here is a postcard for your scrapbook so you'll know what it looks like.

Glad you got that soda fountain job at Delaney's that you wanted. When I come home, you can make me a Coke float with an extra scoop of ice cream.

Running out of space here so I'll sign off. Miss you. Give Trixie a treat.

Love,
Brother

161

CHAPTER 10

Friday, June 13, 1941
Approaching the airfield in a Stearman, Jessie smiled at the two flags — Old Glory and the Union Jack — fluttering in the breeze near the main buildings. Symbolic in their simplicity. Two countries working together. A joint enterprise.

Since the cadets had arrived, they'd been in the classroom learning the basics. Monday they would begin training in a Stearman as well as in the Link. She'd spent the week taking final runs with the biplanes to ensure they were operating as well as possible.

She circled the airfield before beginning her descent. A plane suddenly swooped in front of her. Swearing viciously and pulling back slightly on the stick to arrest her descent, she shoved the throttle ahead, then threw the stick right and pushed the right rudder pedal to quickly go into a turn. She barely missed making contact. Her heart was hammering as she glanced out the side of the cockpit just in time to see the other aircraft bounce on the far side of a white square — a recent addition to the field. She released another blistering cavalcade of curses.

One of the newer instructors, Mark Lawson, seemed to prefer fun and games to work. Tuesday afternoon, when the official hours were over, he'd painted the target on the landing field and begun challenging other instructors to land, aiming for their wheels to touch down smack dab in the middle of it. Then they'd make bets as to whether a pilot would hit it perfectly. They'd also started a pot. To take a go at the target required dropping a dollar in the huge pickle jar. The first pilot to hit the target squarely in its center would receive the contents of the jar. No landing yet had been declared a direct hit. It was the stupidest exhibition of men striving to outdo one another and prove themselves strong and tough that Jessie had ever seen. To make matters worse, they timed their little reckless contest so they were showboating for the cadets as they were leaving class and making their way to the barracks. They'd end up wandering over to see what all the boisterousness was about.

While circling back around, she saw Doug Forester climb out of the cockpit. He was the numbskull who had nearly collided with her, probably hadn't even seen her because he'd been so focused on that little white spot rather than paying attention to what was happening around him. If not for her actions, they'd have lost two planes and possibly two pilots.

She came in for her landing and scrambled to the ground.

"That was almost a hell of a disaster," Billy said as he approached.

"Damn sure was." She was still trembling when she caught sight of Forester, laughing, being patted on the back like flying was a joke. With her rage simmering, she marched over and punched him in the shoulder hard enough to send him staggering back two steps.

Jutting out his chin, he glared at her. "What the hell?"

"I had the right of way, you idiot. Your negligence almost caused us to crash."

"Wouldn't have been my fault."

That was his argument? She glanced around. "Y'all saw what happened, right?"

No one said anything, but a couple of the guys shuffled their feet, some cleared their throats, none dared to meet her gaze.

"You're just upset because you know you couldn't land anywhere close to the spot," Forester said.

"Playing games isn't what I'm paid to do."

"We're practicing landing."

"Are you admitting you haven't even mastered that basic maneuver and require practice?" He turned so red she thought his cheeks might explode, but she recognized the heat of hatred in his eyes. She'd once seen it in a bull before he charged. She gave him no chance to respond. "You're wasting time, putting wear and tear on the aircraft because you're bored" — she jerked her head toward where the cadets had gathered a short distance away — "and feel a need to show off or display your manliness or prove something. I don't know. It's childish, whatever it is, but pay some goddamn attention to other aircraft in the area." Turning on her heel, she began storming back toward the hangar, the parachute she had yet to remove hitting against her backside with each angry step.

Rhonda was leaning against the steel wall, her arms crossed over her chest. "What happened?"

"Idiot came across in front of me."

"So why aren't you competing with them?"

"They're all hat and no cattle. It's not worth the time or effort."

Rhonda nodded. "They didn't invite you."

"The Brits are paying for the gasoline. It's a poor use of the resources."

"We're paying fifty dollars a month in rent. Sure would be nice to have that big jar stuffed with bucks. Can you land on that spot?"

Swinging around, Jessie watched as a plane came in low, but not low enough soon enough. It touched down, overshooting the mark. "Probably."

"Good enough for me." She held up a dollar. "I'll even pay your entry fee."

"I'm not going to play their juvenile games."

Another attempt was made, the wheels hitting too far to the right, the aircraft nearly hitting the crowd of idiotic instructors — whooping, hollering, and jeering — giving the observing cadets the impression that an airplane was a toy rather than something that deserved respect and awe.

Another flier came close to the mark, but as her grandfather had often said, close counted only in horseshoes and flinging shit with a shovel. Lawson, in commiseration,

166

clapped the shoulder of the failed pilot. The boys' club. The anger ratcheting through her could fuel a plane.

"Oh, for Pete's sake." It would feel good to hit that spot. Might even put a stop to all this nonsense.

As she started striding toward the plane she'd just taken for a ride, she heard Rhonda call out, "Hey, fellas! I've got five dollars that says Jessie hits that spot. Who wants to take me up on it?"

Nothing like pressure to add to the excitement. She'd always done better when more was at stake. By the time she reached the plane, a ground crewman was waiting for her. "Hey, Mike."

One of the men who'd been working here before its purpose shifted, he grinned encouragingly at her. "You held out longer than I thought you would."

"Let's fire this baby up." After doing her preflight inspection, she climbed into the cockpit with the parachute strapped to her, hanging down low enough to sit on, so it provided a bit of a cushion against the hard seat. She did her cockpit check and then gave Mike a thumbs-up.

He began cranking the propeller, filling the air with the high-pitched whine, and soon the propeller was spinning. He stepped

167

back and yelled, "Contact!"

She turned on a mag, taking satisfaction as she always did with the roar of the engine coming to life. She hoped to never stop experiencing the thrill of the power and potential of an aircraft. Finishing the starting procedure, she taxied forward, constantly checking her surroundings and position, finally turning so she was facing the wind. When she was certain all was clear, she gunned the throttle and took off.

She made a wide circle around the airfield before coming in low and fast — buzzing — over the other flight instructors, knowing she shouldn't but taking pleasure from some of them ducking. Another circle. Another pass, low and slower, mentally marking her target. A final circuit before lining up her landing. When the wheels touched the earth, she knew she'd hit the spot even before she saw Rhonda laughing, jumping, and waving her arms. She bumped along, applying the brakes, slowing down, coming to a stop. Mike was grinning like Orville Wright had just arrived to shake his hand.

She was on the verge of cutting off the engine when Rhonda ran up and clambered onto the wing. "They think it was a fluke. They're refusing to pay up."

Jessie groaned. "What rotten skunks." She

didn't think for a minute that if one of the men had spot landed, his skills would have been doubted. "Double or nothing."

"Make damned sure it's not nothing," Rhonda said before scrambling down.

Jessie took off, made one wide circuit around the airfield, and came in for the landing, having mentally marked her guide-posts during her first attempt. The challenge was that a pilot couldn't see over the front of the airplane, so she had to position herself based on what she could see when she looked over the sides of the plane. When the wheels hit, she was fairly confident she'd made her target. This time when she rolled to a stop, she turned off the engine, clambered out of the cockpit, and hopped down.

Mike was still grinning. "Don't think even Jack could have done that twice in a row."

"I've got great depth perception."

"You've got skill, little lady. Don't let that jackass Barstow convince you otherwise."

"I don't know what you're talking about." She'd never believed in publicly bad-mouthing someone and certainly hadn't mentioned to anyone at the airfield other than Rhonda that she and Barstow were at odds.

"Ground crews hear things."

She might have said something else, but

Rhonda was suddenly in front of her, gleeful and joyful, holding wads of five-dollar bills and hugging the jar.

"That was so much fun," Rhonda said. "I've never seen so many jaws drop at once."

"One of them should have done it before now. They weren't taking it seriously. They were just goofing off, setting a bad example for the cadets." She started to walk toward the hangar. Out of the corner of her eye, she saw Royce and Peter standing a short distance away from where the cadets had gathered. Shit. She wondered how much of the spectacle they'd seen. Peter said something. Royce nodded, but his gaze was homed in on her.

Turning to Rhonda, she took hold of the jar. "Let me have it. You earned enough with your private bet. You don't need this."

"What are you going to do?"

"Just give it here."

Rhonda released her hold. Jessie marched up to Royce and thrust the jar at him. "To help pay for the *petrol* our antics used."

Giving her a slight smile, mirth dancing in his eyes, he took the offering. Peter looked like he was going to burst out laughing.

She'd taken only a couple of steps away when Royce called out, "Miss Lovelace?"

Stopping, she faced him. Holding the jar

170

now, Peter was ushering the cadets back toward the barracks. The instructors had dispersed as well.

Royce studied her for a minute, as though striving to take a measurement. "That was incredibly impressive."

She shrugged. "I've done some barnstorming. A lot of the stunts require precision, so I've gotten good at lining things up."

"Why haven't you pursued being a flight instructor?"

"Who says I haven't?"

He seemed taken aback. "Are you certified to teach?"

She gave a long, slow nod.

"Did you apply to teach here?"

She released a quick burst of air. "Barstow doesn't believe women can be taken seriously when teaching from a cockpit."

"I see. Why didn't you mention this during one of our conversations? Did you think I'd agree with his assessment?"

Maybe she did. Maybe she worried that if he knew, if others knew he knew, they would view her accomplishment of becoming an instructor as undeserving, a result of charming him, like Forester had implied. "It's between me and Barstow, and I'll find a way to prove myself and prove him wrong. I

171

don't need you pulling rank or strings or influencing him on my behalf."

"That's admirable."

She smiled impishly. "Some would say stubborn."

His chuckle was low, humor laced. "You are that. Carry on then. Mind how you go."

"What does *that* mean?"

"It's simply a way to say goodbye or take care. A little like 'Y'all come back now.' The first time someone said that to me, I actually went back into the store to see what the fellow needed."

She laughed lightly. "It never occurred to me that would be confusing. Something else for your list."

"Precisely. Take care, Jessie."

She didn't know why she was reluctant to leave. Somewhere Forester was probably watching and counting the minutes they were together. Giving Royce a curt nod, she headed for the hangar to store her gear, wishing he hadn't seen her engage in such a childish display of needing to prove herself. It was danged embarrassing. Her father would have been disappointed. *Stay above the fray, prove yourself with your actions.*

On the other hand, she had proven herself with her actions and wished she'd seen those dropped jaws.

June 14, 1941

Dear Jess,

The 601! Ballinger was with the legendary Millionaires' Squadron? People considered those flyboys to be a joke. Sons of the nobility and the well-to-do simply playing at being pilots. Their training sessions included lavish parties. But when the Luftwaffe first came over, those men proved themselves to be valiant and skilled, made a name for themselves. Your fella is recognized as an ace with eighteen kills to his credit. Heard during his last mission, his Spittie was so shot up, no one can figure out how he managed to get it home and land — half the controls weren't working, and he couldn't get the wheels down. It was definitely a bumpy landing.

Glad to know he was discreet in what he shared with Mama. I don't want her worrying about me any more than she already is. Still feel guilty for not coming home for Dad's funeral but was afraid I wouldn't be able to get back over here. Also didn't think it would do Mama any favors if the Feds showed up to arrest her son.

Jerry is keeping us busy. Get those pilots

trained. We need them.

Love,
Jack

P.S. Give Trixie a treat and tell her it's from me.

CHAPTER 11

Delaney's had always been a gathering place for high school students, so Kitty wasn't surprised when the cadets migrated to the drugstore after they were finished with their morning exercises. Earlier while taking a break, she'd been sitting on a bench beneath an oak at the town square when she'd seen them marching into town, double file, whistling a tune. Excitement had thrummed through her, and she'd rushed in to share the news with Fran, who also worked behind the soda counter on Saturday. They'd watched at the window until the Brits had reached the town square, where they'd come to a stop and one of the fellas in the lead had shouted an order. Then they'd all dispersed, some heading toward the drugstore.

Now almost a dozen cadets were at the counter, keeping her and Fran hopping, get-

175

ting them Coca-Cola and ice cream floats. It was fun watching them take their first sip of the fountain drink. Some enjoyed it, while others wrinkled their noses. Apparently, it was a new experience for them, and a few couldn't decide if they liked it. She couldn't imagine.

While disappointed they weren't in uniform, she was still absolutely fascinated by them. It was more than their accents and the way they phrased things. There was a magical quality to the way they spoke. Some were shy, didn't seem quite comfortable with the way things were here. Most were in awe that they could order anything they wanted and a considerable amount of it would be placed in front of them.

She heard the bell above the door jingle. It was constantly ringing as people departed and others arrived. All the activity reminded her of being on a merry-go-round that never came to a stop. She wondered if Mr. Delaney would take it down until the RAF was no longer being trained here. He stayed in the pharmacy but would pop out now and then to make sure everything was going all right. He'd spend some time talking with the cadets before wandering back to his dominion.

"Can you get the guy at the end of the

counter?" Fran called out.

Since only the two of them were working, Kitty knew who she was asking. Turning, she came up short, her heart increasing its tempo. It was *him*. Harry. He was turned sideways, wedged in between two other cadets, talking to one of them. He looked even more handsome than she remembered. His hair, clipped short, was a sandy blond. Then he turned and smiled.

She melted. Never before had anyone directed such a bright, enthusiastic smile her way. Oh, she'd received lots of smiles before, even the fellas standing at the counter this afternoon had grinned at her, some a little bashfully, some a little sweetly, but none had contained such an abundance of gladness. Like she was someone special. She could hardly recall that she'd had a purpose in coming to him.

"Hi." She wondered why she sounded breathless, as if she'd run over here.

"Hello, luv." His brow furrowed slightly. "You were one of the girls at the train depot." One of the girls? That was disappointing. She wanted to be *the* girl at the train depot. "I'm Harrison, but my mates call me Harry. Who are you?"

He hadn't even remembered her name or that he'd told her all that before. She'd been silly to think he would. "Kitty."

"Well, hello, Kitty. Aren't you a looker?"

She thawed a little bit with the compliment, even though she knew she shouldn't have her head turned so easily. "What would you like?"

"Maybe a stroll through the park across the street."

She did wish his charm didn't seem so practiced. "I can't. I'm working. What can I get you to eat or drink?"

He studied her for a long minute. "Surprise me. Something with ice cream. I'm mad for ice cream." He winked at her.

She hurried to the middle of the counter, faced the mirror that ran the length of the wall, and started to dip out the vanilla ice cream for a root beer float.

"He flirts with everyone, you know."

Looking in the mirror, she could see a cadet leaning partially on the counter, supporting himself on his elbows. Dark-haired, he had the most beautiful eyes, although she couldn't decide if they were gray or just a very, very light blue.

After dumping the ice cream into a tall glass, she added root beer and turned around. "I'd sorta figured that out."

She carried the float to the end of the counter and set it in front of Harry.

He winked at her again. "Thanks, luv."

"That'll be eight cents."

He pouted. "Are you going to charge me, sweetheart?"

"I have to."

He reached into his pocket and brought out some coins. "Which would that be?"

Gingerly, failing at not touching him, she took a nickel and three pennies. "Thanks. Let me know if you need anything else." She looked at the fellas on either side of him. "Anyone need anything?"

They simply shook their heads. She wandered back to where blue eyes sat. "Can I get you something?"

"Another Coca-Cola."

She took his glass, put it in the bin to be washed, and grabbed a clean glass. Mr. Delaney was a stickler for not reusing dishes when people wanted a second helping. She filled the glass and set it in front of him. He slid a nickel toward her. She slid it back. "This one is on me."

"That's kind of you."

"I'm Kitty. What's your name?"

"Will."

She darted a glance toward the end of the counter. "How well do you know him?"

He grinned. His smile wasn't as bright as Harry's but it was more sincere. "Who?

179

Harrison-but-my-mates-call-me-Harry?" A quick burst of laughter escaped before she could stop it, but it made the blue of Will's eyes twinkle as though her reaction had pleased him. "He's all right, just thinks he's more important than he is. How old are you, Kitty?"

"I'll be seventeen in October." Sixteen suddenly sounded young, with all these fellas around. But she'd be graduating next May. Class of 1942. "How old are you?"

"Eighteen."

She glanced up and down the counter. "Is everyone about that age?"

"Most. Some are older. Not many."

She hadn't expected them to be so close to her in age. She wondered if she might be able to invite them to a high school dance.

"Miss?"

She looked at the blond-haired fella signaling to her. "I'll be right back."

By the time she was finished preparing a hot fudge sundae, Will was gone, but he'd left the nickel beside his glass. Apparently, he hadn't wanted her paying for his beverage. She wondered when Mrs. Johnson was going to get around to arranging a dance. She very much wanted an opportunity to dance with these fellas — almost more than she wanted to breathe.

The afternoon sped by. Six o'clock arrived before she knew it, and Mr. Delaney was shooing everyone out and locking the door. She and Fran cleaned everything up before beginning their trek home. A few of the cadets were wandering around the square, and she was tempted to speak with them, but knew Mama was waiting on her for supper.

"They're all so fascinating," Fran said. "So much more interesting than the boys at school."

"I felt the same way. They're not that much older than we are."

"One of them mentioned that they have open post Wednesday evening. I think that's what they call it when they have time off, because he said some of them are going to the cinema." Fran gave her a mischievous sideways glance. "I think we should go to the movies Wednesday."

With a grin, Kitty nodded. "I agree."

"But let's not tell our mamas the cadets are going to be there. Mine doesn't want me spending time with the Brits. She doesn't trust them, because they're not from around here."

"That's ridiculous. They're just like us." Except for the more interesting part.

Fran shrugged before veering off to go up

181

the street to her house. When Kitty reached hers, she was still bouncing with energy from the frantic afternoon and excited about their plans for going to the movie theater. The table was already set for two. It was so strange for it to be just her and Mama every night. "I'm home!"

Carrying a platter of pork chops and a bowl of greens, Mama swept through the swinging door. "Wonderful. Sit down. Everything is ready."

Once they were settled, she asked, "How were things at the drugstore?"

"Busy. A lot of the cadets came in. Do you know when Mrs. Johnson is going to arrange the dance that she mentioned?"

Mama went still for a couple of seconds before returning to cutting into her pork chop. "I don't. I know she invited you to help with it, but you can't go to it."

Feeling like she'd tumbled off one of Luke's ponies, Kitty stared at her mother. "Why not?"

"Because you don't need to get involved with those boys. They're too old for you."

She shook her head. "No, they're not. I met several today who were eighteen or nineteen. I even met one who was seventeen. He had to get his mother to sign a letter saying he could enlist. They're like the

182

boys at school."

"No, Kitty, they're not. They're more worldly and experienced. And because they are preparing to go to war, they are more inclined to cram as much of life as they can into whatever time they think they have, and I believe that could result in you getting hurt."

"But you seemed to enjoy having Royce here."

"Well, you are most certainly not going to be getting involved with *him*."

Of course not. He was ancient. "What about the cadets you'll invite to stay here? Am I not supposed to talk with them or play checkers with them?"

"I've rethought that, and I don't believe we're going to have any stay here, except maybe during the holidays."

"I don't understand."

Mama set down her utensils, placed her elbows on the table, and clasped her hands together as though on the verge of praying for strength . . . or maybe forgiveness. "When I took the notebook to the airfield so the cadets could begin to sign up if they were interested in staying in a home, I had an opportunity to visit with several of them."

"Then you know they're nice."

She gave Kitty a direct look, serious and

uncompromising, the one she used before laying down an edict or announcing a punishment for misbehavior, not that Kitty had ever been on the receiving end of it, but Jack certainly had. Even Jessie had on occasion. "I do, but I also know they are not appropriate company for a girl as innocent as you."

Her mother must have met Harrison-but-my-mates-call-me-Harry. She wouldn't have liked him at all. "That's not fair."

"Maybe after you graduate."

"They might not even still be here."

"Unfortunately, Kitty, I don't see this war ending anytime soon. So you'll have plenty of opportunity to grow up before spending any time in the company of those fellas."

Kitty couldn't believe this. She wondered if her mother had been talking with Fran's. "You let Jessie go steady when she was sixteen."

"With a boy her own age, who came with the same experiences. One I'd known since he wore diapers. I don't want you getting involved with those British boys."

"I won't get involved. I just want to visit with them, get to know them. Dance with them. Please?"

"You can greet them at the depot, talk with them at the soda fountain. But I have

184

to say no to the dance."

Kitty shoved her plate away, jumped to her feet, and darted up to her room. She didn't know what to do with her anger. She'd never done anything she wasn't supposed to. But that was about to change.

CHAPTER 12

Monday, June 16, 1941

Sitting at her table behind the controls, Jessie watched as Rhonda peered into a small mirror, slowly applied bright vermilion lipstick, and then smacked her lips together twice. "That's the third time you've done that in less than twenty minutes."

Rhonda dropped her mirror and lipstick tube into her purse before meeting Jessie's gaze. "The cadets will be here any minute for their introduction to the Link Trainer. I want to look my best."

The rumble of an engine reverberated around them. The first cadet was being taken on his maiden voyage and the knowledge caused an ache in Jessie's chest because she wasn't doing the taking. The students had been split into two groups, with half in the classroom and half getting practical experience, either via plane or Link. In the afternoon, the groups would switch.

"You could use some color," Rhonda said. "I have a shade that's not quite as bold if you'd like to borrow it."

Jessie knew her friend was striving to divert her focus from what was happening above, a place she desperately wanted to be. "Thanks, but I don't want to distract the trainees from where they need to direct their attention."

Rhonda got up, slinked over, and perched on the edge of the table. "They want us to distract. It's the reason Barstow hired women."

Jessie furrowed her brow. "Who told you that?"

"No one. But it makes sense. The LT isn't nearly as exciting as an actual cockpit. They have a minimum number of hours they're required to spend in the LT, but they can do extra if they want. The more time they devote to practicing, the better prepared they'll be. That's where we come in, providing enticing scenery to make certain they're enthusiastic about spending time here."

"They shouldn't require any incentive. It's the safest environment for learning how to fly by instrument."

"How many men do you know who care about being safe? You date a fella who thinks it's fun to straddle the back of a cantankerous bull until he's thrown off. These Brits are no different. If you weren't attractive, Barstow probably would have hired you to be a flight instructor — like you wanted."

Rhonda might be correct regarding the reason they were chosen to operate the LT, but Jessie very much doubted it was the reason she wasn't presently strapped into an aircraft. "Sitting behind these tables is like teaching in front of a blackboard or in a chemistry lab, and he sees teaching in a classroom as a perfectly acceptable occupation for women. But from a cockpit . . . he doesn't believe a man will take instruction from a woman."

"Well, if any of those cadets don't show me respect, I'm going to give them a ride in that simulator that will make them bring up their breakfast. You could do the same from a cockpit."

"And I would. I just don't think I'd have to. At least rarely. When Dad was alive and I taught men how to fly, they just wanted to learn. They didn't care who was teaching them. I explained that to Barstow, but he thinks military men are different."

"All men think they're different, but it's been my experience they're pretty much all the same." She tilted her head. "Are you sure you don't want some lipstick?"

The door opened. Rhonda quickly straightened as Peter strode in, six cadets decked out in their blue uniforms following in a straight line behind him, serious-faced, although Jessie noticed that a few gazes landed appreciatively on Rhonda, who had moved in front of her table and was standing with a hand resting on one jutted-out hip, no doubt striving to make her point as to why they'd been hired as LT operators. Rhonda believed in using her figure to its full advantage, while Jessie preferred it have no impact at all on anything she wanted to do in life.

"Ladies," Peter said, and she swore she heard Rhonda emit a little sigh. "I've brought you a few cadets to start. Thought I might stay around for a bit to see how it goes, if you don't mind."

"Why would we mind?" Rhonda asked. "You're always welcome, sir. Gentlemen, if you'll gather around, we'll introduce you to the Link Trainer, LT for short. Or Ellie, as I prefer to call her. She'll take you on a ride you won't soon forget."

A few hesitant laughs sounded, and Jessie wondered how long it would be before they'd all feel comfortable here, and how long before they'd all fallen in love with her daring friend. Rhonda took three over to the LT she would control, and Jessie took the others to the blue box with its yellow wings and tail that was her domain. It sat atop a pedestal housing pumps and bellows that she controlled to create pitches and turns, as rough as a bucking bronco, that the pilot should counter with the tools at his disposal. She opened the door and stepped back so the cadets could peer inside. "When you use the rudder and stick, the wings and tail move. Not that you'll be able to see it, but I will. When I close you up, you'll be in darkness except for the lights of the instrument panel and the dim light off to the side. It'll be like flying at night or in foggy English weather." That got her a few grins. "Limited visibility. You have to learn to trust the instruments to guide you. Who wants to go first?"

They looked at one another. Two of them didn't appear to be shaving yet. The third one had peach fuzz on his upper lip. Peach fuzz finally raised his hand. "I'll give it a go."

"And you are?"

"Geoffrey Moreland."

"All right, Mr. Moreland, I'm going to make it easy this first time. You're going to taxi, lift off, fly straight for about ten miles, then turn around, come back to where you

190

started, and land. I'm not going to do anything dastardly like have a storm come up or put you in a stall. A smooth flight all the way." Reaching inside, she pulled out a headset. "You'll put this on, and I'll wear one as well so we can communicate. Any questions?"

"I don't think so, ma'am."

"Climb in."

After he was settled, she took him on a tour of the instruments. He should have learned something about them during the last week, but she decided a quick refresher was a good idea. Then she lowered the canopy, shut the door, and enclosed him in near darkness. Ushering the others to one side of the room, she took her place at her table. Attached to a metal arm was a small triangle component referred to as a crab that traveled over the glass covering the table and marked the pilot's movements in red on a sheet of glass beneath which was a map. Rhonda's cadet was already in flight, while she was guiding him, watching the crab moving over her table. Standing behind her, Peter looked on.

"All right," Jessie told Geoffrey Moreland, "you're cleared for takeoff."

Ignoring the actual takeoffs sounding beyond the building, she focused on the

191

blue box that housed him, the way it tilted up and then evened out. He was only at fifty feet. "You leveled out a little low. Take her up to two thousand feet."

The crab began jerking back and forth. "Hold her steady. You're wobbling."

"I can't —"

She heard his breath, harsh and heavy. "Mr. Moreland, it's all an illusion. In reality, you're not even three feet off the ground."

"It's dark."

"You have the lights on the instruments panel?"

"Yes."

"Take a deep breath."

"I can't. I can't breathe in here."

Suddenly he was banging on the wood. She shut off the LT as the door sprung open and he spilled out, falling to the floor, pale and clammy, his hair plastered to his head. Grabbing her metal trash can, she vaulted across and shoved it against his chest as he started to heave between *crikey*s and apologies. The other cadets began murmuring. She might have even heard a snicker, but she glared over her shoulder with such intensity that they all immediately went still and silent. And Barstow didn't think she could remain in command in a cockpit.

Peter crouched beside her, watching, patiently waiting; she preferred the Brit when he was serious and concerned. "Could it be something you ate not agreeing with you, cadet?"

"No, sir." He set the basket aside, pulled a handkerchief from his pocket, and wiped at his mouth. "Sorry, ma'am. I was suffocating. It's so bloody small in there, and hot, and dark. I couldn't breathe."

"Here," Rhonda said, bending down and handing him a glass of water. She'd stopped her training session, her cadet standing beside the blue box and looking on.

"Thank you, ma'am."

"Cockpits are generally small," Jessie said, "but the darkness inside the simulator can be unnerving and make it a bit claustrophobic. Don't look around. Just focus on the instruments."

"I can't. I can't go back in there. I'll just have to fly during the day."

"I'm sure that'll be fine." Relief washed over his features. "I doubt the Germans fly at night."

And there was the defeat. "They do fly at night. Every night. For months."

She knew that, of course. "On nights when there is no moon, or the weather suddenly gets extremely bad, you can't always see the

193

ground or the water if you're over the Channel. You have to rely on your instruments. The Link is safe. Nothing is going to happen to you in there, even if you misread your altitude or misgauge your tilt or mess up your flight pattern. You learn in there how to compensate and adjust, so when you're in an actual plane and something goes wrong, reading and understanding what the instruments are indicating can save you."

He shook his head. "I can't do it. I can't learn to fly in the dark."

"So, you're telling me the Germans can do something you can't?"

Averting his gaze, he appeared stricken, embarrassed, unsure. She'd been hoping for anger and determination. "They had to master one of those things?"

She didn't know if they did or not, had no idea what sort of training they had. "If they're flying at night, they're relying on their instruments and had to learn that skill. You could do a couple of sessions without being closed in, but eventually you'll have to do it in the near dark. It's the best way for us to determine if you're using the instruments."

"Bloody hell. Flying at night gives me an advantage, doesn't it? I could better take

194

the war to them, I suppose."

She gave him a reassuring smile. "It's what I'd do."

He dragged a hand through his damp hair. "Afraid the heat was getting to me as well."

"It can get hot in there," Jessie said to Peter.

"They could remove their jackets and shirts," Rhonda said.

Peter jerked his gaze up to her. "The jackets perhaps, but not the shirts. Not with ladies about."

She shrugged. "We're not schoolgirls. Besides, men around here are known to toss their shirts aside when they're working."

He twisted around on the balls of his feet. "What was your experience, Mr. Brightwell?"

"It was rather muggy in there, sir."

"Very well." He stood. "Gentlemen, you're welcome to strip down to your undershirts before you go in."

"If it's all right, sir, I'd rather be done for the day than risk another upset. Still a bit shaky as it were," Moreland said.

"Stay to observe. All right, who's next?"

"I'll give it a go," a young man said, walking over in his undershirt.

"Is that wool?" Jessie asked.

Before he could respond, Rhonda said,

"No wonder they got hot. They'll swelter in there. Not to mention the heat rash. I'm surprised you're not already dealing with that. The wool undergarments have to go. I'm not having them pass out on me."

"Our men do not pass out," Peter said, clearly offended.

Rhonda took a step toward him. She was nearly as tall as he was. "Tell you what, sir. Why don't you go inside Ellie for ten minutes, let me put you through your paces, and we'll see if you feel the same?"

Jessie wasn't completely certain that the heat in the room wasn't a result of the way those two seemed to be daring the other to look away.

Peter blinked first. "These men will stay attired as they are, for today anyway. We'll see about getting them clothing better suited to the temperature."

"Bathing trunks would work."

"That would be entirely inappropriate. I was thinking more along the lines of their flight suits. Since this is, after all, simulated flight."

She smiled. "You're taking all the fun out of this, sir. However, if you change your mind and want a ride, you let me know." Before he could respond, she was sauntering toward the table, a crooked finger wav-

196

ing her cadet over. "Mr. Brightwell, let me show you how you did."

Jessie had a feeling her friend was tying Peter Smythson up in knots and enjoying herself a little too much while doing it.

CHAPTER 13

Wednesday, June 18, 1941

Standing outside the theater, simply waiting, Kitty was as nervous as a long-tailed cat in a room full of rocking chairs. Her mother hadn't objected to her going to the movies with Fran, but then, she probably didn't know that the cadets were going as well.

"I don't understand," Kitty said for the hundredth time to Fran. "She wanted to ensure that the cadets feel welcome, and then she decides *I* can't make them feel welcome. It's so unfair."

"I think my mom is afraid I'll fall in love and move away." Fran grinned slyly. "It would be kinda exciting and fun. I don't want to spend my whole life here."

Kitty couldn't imagine moving away, living somewhere else. She couldn't even imagine living in a different house. She loved Terrence and the people, wanted to

198

share that with the cadets, wanted them to see how wonderful it was here.

Suddenly she heard whistling in the distance and her heart sped up. She did wish the fliers would be quieter, would sneak into town so Mama wouldn't hear about them.

Fran squeezed her arm and whispered, "They're almost here."

Then they were visible, marching up the street. They followed the same routine they had Saturday afternoon, stopping in front of the town square before swarming toward the theater. Their voices echoed their excitement. Four of them spotted her and Fran and came over.

" 'Ello, luvs."

"Fancy seeing you here."

"This is a jolly nice surprise."

Kitty wanted to say something, but her tongue was all tied up. She'd met them at the drugstore but suddenly couldn't remember their names. But then, she was having a tough time remembering her own.

"Are you here to watch the film?" one asked.

"We are!" Fran said, the words sounding as though they'd burst from her, and Kitty wondered if Fran was as nervous as she was.

"Want to sit with us?" another asked. He'd ordered chili on Saturday.

199

She didn't know how they'd sit with all four of them, but still she nodded.

"Jolly good." Chili slung his arm around her shoulders, pulled her in close, and steered her toward the ticket window. For a brief agonizing moment of worry, she wondered if Mama was right about them being too old for her. She'd never been this close to a boy, had never felt like a possession — or a trophy. It was a strange sensation. Glancing over her shoulder, she saw Fran grinning and walking between two of the cadets, the third trailing behind.

When she turned back, she nearly ran into Will. He was standing there studying her as Chili brought her to a stop to wait in line to get their tickets. She gave him a shy smile and a quiet hello, which he probably couldn't hear over all the various conversations going on.

"You know she's only fourteen, right, mate?" he said.

Chili jerked just before his hold on her loosened and he looked down at her. "Are you?"

She didn't know what to say, didn't react at all as crazy thoughts scrambled through her mind. Was she supposed to lie? Why had Will? Had he forgotten what she'd told him on Saturday?

Chili slid his arm away from her, regret in his eyes. "Sorry, luv. You're too young a bird for me."

Then he was gone, cutting into the front of the line. She looked back at Will. He was holding up two tickets. "You're not too young for me. Want to sit together?"

She took a step nearer. "I'm not fourteen."

"I remember. Seventeen in October."

"Why did you lie?"

"Less trouble than fighting him over you."

She had a funny feeling in her stomach, like butterflies fluttering around. "Would you have fought him?"

"Nah, I would have just moped about, wishing you were sitting with me." He made her smile, and he seemed nice, but she didn't want to be alone with him or leave Fran alone with the others.

"Can my friend come with us? We have our tickets already."

"The more the merrier."

She hurried to Fran, standing in line with the fellas who'd been with Chili, and grabbed her hand. "Come on."

She heard Will say, "I have an extra ticket." Then he was introducing them to Antony Ashby.

Inside the theater, they found seats together near the back. Will sat on one side of her, Fran on the other. Antony was on the other side of Fran.

"Why are you called Kitty?" Will asked. "Do you fancy cats?"

She smiled. "No, my real name is Kathryn. My brother used to call me Kat, and I hated it, so he started calling me Kitty. It kinda stuck."

"I like it."

"Is Will short for William?"

He grinned. "Yeah. Nothing interesting about my name at all."

Still, she said, "I like it." And his grin got wider, brighter.

It became very quiet when the newsreel started up. Although they weren't touching, she was aware of Will stiffening beside her, going incredibly still. She was glad when it was over and the film started. Partway through the movie, she glanced over to find Will's gaze on her. "You're not watching the movie."

"You're more interesting," he said.

"I bet that's something Harry would say."

He looked back at the screen, and she studied him. She liked his profile, a strong jaw and sharp lines that reminded her of the care her grandfather had taken to whittle her toys, as though Will's features had been created with such meticulous at-

202

tention. After a while, he shifted his gaze back to her. "You're not watching the movie."

"You're more interesting."

He grinned, and she smiled.

Afterward, he and Antony walked Fran home and then stayed with Kitty until she reached the edge of her front yard. "I have to say goodbye here."

After saying it was nice to meet her, Antony wandered away, but Will stayed. "Thanks for sitting with me, Kitty."

"Maybe I'll see you at the drugstore."

"Count on it."

Then he was striding away, hands in his pockets. He reached Antony and they carried on. Her mother was right. Some were too old for her, but not all of them. Not Will.

CHAPTER 14

Tuesday, June 24, 1941

He lasted eight minutes.

With a sigh, Jessie shut down the controls as Geoffrey Moreland stumbled out of the blue box, bent over, braced his hands on his knees, and took great gulping breaths. At least he wasn't taking a second look at his last meal. She had to admire his tenacity. Tonight was the third time he'd asked her to discreetly meet him following supper. While all his fellow cadets were relaxing, playing cards, listening to music, or reading books, he was striving to overcome his fear of tight spaces, of being closed in. She was beginning to wonder if he also feared the dark.

She was concerned he would make it through the primary training, but when he moved to basic and the Vultee, with its canopied cockpit, he was going to suffer the claustrophobia he'd managed to avoid in the Stearman's open cockpit. Although if she was correct about the dark, he was unlikely to make it through his first night flight.

Straightening, he looked at her rather sheepishly, his smile wry, but she didn't miss the disappointment reflected in his eyes. "I can't do it."

"You lasted a minute longer than you did last night."

He gave a little scoff. "Don't tell my mates that. They'll make something rude out of it."

She smiled gently. "This is just between us."

The students had begun rotating in two at a time, one for each Link, so they could study while waiting their turn. Neither did they come every day for a session, so Moreland had experienced only one other scheduled session with her. After it had gone no better than the first, even wearing the cooler flight suit, he'd approached her about meeting him at night when no one else would be around to see his failure.

"Let's work with the instruments for a while without closing you in." He'd be expected to do around eight hours of instrument flying before he completed primary.

He'd use the instruments more during basic.

He gave a nod, and they spent another half an hour together before calling it a night. It was growing dark as he, hunched somewhat dejectedly, made his way to the canteen and she headed for her motorcycle. It was a moonless night, the sort where instruments could prove critical to a successful flight. She wished she had some advice to help him overcome his struggles.

Taking grim satisfaction in the revving of her engine, she started her journey up the dirt path, surprised to see a figure sauntering toward the road. His jacket, hooked on a finger, was draped over his shoulder, down his back. His shirtsleeves were rolled up past his elbows. His cane steadied his walk. She pulled to a stop beside him and cut the engine. "Royce, are you walking home?"

At her approach, he'd come to a halt. "I am, yes. Do the leg some good."

"Isn't Barstow still giving you a ride?"

"He is, but he and Smythson left earlier. I had some other matters to attend to. What kept you here so late?"

She wasn't surprised that he wouldn't leave a task to languish on his desk overnight. He struck her as someone with a great deal of self-discipline. When he was fully recovered from his wound, she'd like to see him in flight, suspected he exercised as much restraint in a cockpit, never once doing what he ought not. Had he ever buzzed a control tower or a small town or a girl's house? In high school, when Jack had an interest in a girl, he'd fly in low over her house, usually inciting anger from her father because of the loud noise that would reverberate around them with the plane so close. But she'd known girls who had lived to be buzzed by Jack Lovelace. Had any done the same for Royce Ballinger? She would have bet money he wouldn't have done it as often as her brother, and it would have meant something special when he did.

"Did Peter tell you about the incident last week with the LT?"

"Where Moreland panicked? Yes."

"He didn't have a better reaction during his second attempt. He asked me for some extra time to work to conquer it. We've been meeting in the evening."

"Not developing an affection for this young man, are you?"

She crossed her arms over her chest. "I was hoping we'd get married before he shipped back to England. I figured getting him to the point where I could buck him around in the Link like he's riding a wild

207

stallion would definitely have him proposing."

Royce seemed to take great interest in studying his shoes, and she thought he'd bent his head so she wouldn't see his smile. It gave her a spark of joy to think she might have broken through his serious facade. Clearing his throat, he looked up. "Perhaps you're showing favoritism because he's having such a rough go of it."

"I'd do it for any of them."

"Yes, I think you probably would. Is everything else going well?"

"Seems to be. From your end, how is it going?" Their paths seldom crossed at the school.

"Few adjustments needed here and there. To be expected. You might be interested to learn the army rejected our request for the two-way communication system. But I've sent to England for them."

"I'm sorry you're having to jump through hoops."

"It'll be worth it for improved communication."

"Speaking of communication, Mama mentioned you impressed the ladies when you spoke at their Auxiliary Club on Saturday." Not being a member of the club, Jessie hadn't attended, but her mother had.

Afterward, a couple of women had asked how they could assist with her war relief efforts, and she couldn't help but believe Royce's talk had made a difference.

"They were quite lovely. I even avoided going into a tirade."

"Maybe you shouldn't have."

"My superiors wouldn't have appreciated my coming across as an angry Brit. Nor would it have done my countrymen any favors. The other night I was having dinner at the café and overheard some grumblings about our presence. So it means a great deal that you and your family made us feel so welcome."

"Some people around here are set in their ways. I wouldn't take it personally."

"Oh, I shan't." He tapped his cane. "I should let you carry on home now."

She smiled. "Climb on. It'll be a cozy fit, but it beats walking. Unless you don't trust me."

"I'm not certain there's anyone I trust more."

They studied each other for what seemed an eternity but couldn't have been longer than a couple of heartbeats. Then he nodded, and she held her breath as he settled in behind her. She twisted around slightly. "You might want to hang on to me. I tend to go fast."

One arm circled around her waist, strength and power evident in its firm hold. She could feel the heat of his chest barely grazing her back. Glancing the other way, she saw his hand gripping his hat and cane resting on his thigh. He'd put his jacket back on.

"Take yourself home," he said, his breath warm against her ear. "I'll walk from there."

She turned on the ignition, revved the engine a couple of times, and shot forward, taking satisfaction in his grasp on her tightening. Detecting the road ahead was free of traffic, she barely slowed down as she leaned into the turn. She was tempted to holler like a banshee.

The rush of the wind dancing through her hair, the rumble of the engine between her thighs, and the power at her fingertips always brightened her mood — almost as much as flight. She'd occasionally given Rhonda or Kitty a ride, but she'd never before shared the experience with a man. It was intoxicating, to be held, to experience such closeness.

She pulled into her drive and shut off her bike. His arm eased away only slightly, until his hand — large and solid — cradled her waist. She didn't know why they were both still sitting there, so still. She knew only that she wasn't quite ready to be without his steadying presence.

"I should have dropped you off at your place," she finally forced out. "Save you the walk."

"I would have walked over here anyway to see you home safely."

"Not much danger in this town."

"Doesn't change what I would have done." His voice was a pleasing rumble in the night, giving her the courage to admit one of her fears.

She twisted around until she could see him, partially limned by the porch light. "I don't think Moreland is going to make it. He's trying so hard, but I'm afraid whatever is scaring him in the Link is going to eventually scare him in the cockpit."

"They're not all going to succeed, Jessie. It's better to cull them than make them fodder for the Luftwaffe." Seeming to suddenly realize he was still holding her, he released her and slid off the back of the motorcycle, standing, leaning on his cane. "Riding that is almost like flying."

Dismounting, she faced him and smiled. "Almost."

"Well, I'd best get on."

"How do you do it? How do you not care?"

"What makes you think I don't?"

"You're just so reserved. I guess I thought you weren't affected by any of this."

"I'm not certain it serves any purpose to let on when it does." He glanced up at the dark heavens sprinkled with stars. "But there are nights when I can't sleep for the caring."

"Is that when you stand in the front yard and smoke a cigarette?"

His gaze came back to her. "Saw that, did you?"

"That first night." When he'd seemed lonely, forlorn, solitary.

"It was a nightmare then, I'm afraid. I can't recall a single dream before the war, but now they're so vivid they weigh on me as heavily as Jacob Marley's chains. That night, my Spitfire was ablaze, and I couldn't bail out."

Her stomach tightened as though it had been lassoed and yanked. "Were you ever caught in a fire?"

"No, but I had friends who were. Or at least I saw their kites engulfed, didn't see them parachute out. Assume the worst. Ghastly way to go." He shook his head. "You'll have the nightmares now."

"Jack wrote that you're something of a legend, an ace." She'd received the letter only that afternoon, after taking a break from the airfield before returning for her rendezvous with Moreland.

Royce laughed as though incredibly amused. "Did he now?"

"You have eighteen kills."

"That's such a bloody awful thing to keep track of, isn't it?" He reached into his pocket and pulled out a package of Camels. "Do you smoke?"

"No."

He lit one up, then blew the smoke up and away from her. "Cigs remind me of better times, lounging about with my mates."

She could almost hear him finishing with "Now they'll remind me of you." Where had that thought come from? She should go in, pour herself a sip of her father's bourbon. She'd brought it with her, to have on hand when she needed a bolster. Or to save for Jack's return. The thought of anyone just guzzling it down had been unbearable. For a moment, she considered inviting him in for a drink. Her dad would have liked him, admired him. Royce would have returned the sentiments. "Do you miss being over there?"

"With every breath." He dropped the

213

cigarette, crushed it beneath the sole of his shoe. "All right, then. Sleep well, flygirl."

She laughed lightly but wasn't certain any other nickname would have pleased her more. "Good night, flyboy."

His grin was only a quick flash of white, but it made her smile.

"I'll wait here until you're safely inside, shall I?" he said.

"The only thing that's going to get me out here are the mosquitoes." They weren't nearly as abundant here as along the coast. Still, she headed for the house, gave a little wave at the door, and slipped inside.

"So I *was* right about the wing commander having an interest in you," Rhonda said from the sofa, glass of white wine in hand.

Guilt slammed into Jessie, along with a jolt of embarrassment that probably had her turning as red as Rhonda's hair. "What were you doing? Spying on me?"

"It's hard to miss your arrival on that thing, but when you didn't come in, I just peeked out to see if you were okay and saw you weren't alone."

Jessie slung her keys on the table, and in a bit of a pique, dropped onto the corner of the couch. "He needed a ride. It was all innocent." Except for the reassurance she found being in his company.

"You know losing your virginity to a guy doesn't obligate you to marry him."

Jessie glowered at her friend. One of the secrets Rhonda knew was that Jessie'd had her first sexual experience with Luke in the back seat of his parents' Chevy following prom their senior year. "Why would you say that?"

"Because I know you, and I know that, like a lot of girls, you think it's sacred and giving it away ties you to the fella. It's not and it doesn't."

"Says the virgin."

Rhonda laughed. "I love the irony. My reputation is bad girl and yours is saint."

Jessie plucked at a loose thread on the sofa. "I can talk with Royce about flying, and we have a common goal, that's all."

She loved Luke, and yet he wasn't the man she thought about as she lay in bed later trying to go to sleep.

CHAPTER 15

Saturday, June 28, 1941

Mrs. Johnson had finally, finally arranged a dance for the cadets, and Kitty was *forbidden* from going. It didn't matter that she'd helped to transform the austere and boring American Legion Hall into a more festive environment, with streamers hanging down from the rafters. Or that she'd strung white Christmas lights around the windows and draped them across the ceiling. Or that she'd helped Mama bake at least a hundred cookies to be served as refreshments — even though her mother wasn't going either. Or that so many of her friends from school were going. Even Fran had managed somehow to get permission.

But her mother had insisted Kitty was too young, too vulnerable, for boys at war. So here Kitty was, lying on her bed reading *The Clue of the Tapping Heels,* listening to the ticking of her alarm clock, wishing she were as clever and intrepid as Nancy Drew.

The knock sounded just before her mother opened the door and peered in. "I'm going to bed."

"Night." She didn't look up from the page she'd been staring at for the past half hour.

Mama stepped farther into the room. "I know you're upset with me, but there will be other dances and other cadets."

She set her book flat on her stomach. "I just want to dance, have some fun."

"When you're seventeen."

Kitty rolled her eyes, although now at least she wasn't having to wait until graduation. Her mother wanted Jessie to get married but didn't want Kitty to even meet boys.

Mama crossed over and sat on the edge of the bed. "Your father isn't here to put the fear of God into a boy, so he'll behave."

"Luke could do it. Or Royce. He'd make them behave."

"Just be patient." She patted Kitty's leg. "Sweet dreams."

After she left, closing the door on her way out, Kitty eased off the bed, stretched out on the floor, and pressed her ear against the wood. This old house creaked with anyone's movements. Mama's bedroom was right below hers, so she could hear her stirring. She even heard the groaning of the bed when Mama climbed into it. The dance ended at midnight, and it was already ten, but two hours was better than nothing.

Kitty waited until she couldn't hear any creaks at all before quietly getting up and tiptoeing to her closet. She slipped into her favorite green dress and grabbed the heels she wore to church. Barefoot, she crept through the house, avoiding stepping on all the planks and spots that she knew moaned at being disturbed. She'd oiled the hinges on the door and screen door that afternoon, so they didn't make a sound when she slipped through them.

Then she was running toward the Legion Hall. It wasn't that far away. Still, she was gasping for air when she reached it. Leaning against the wall, she slipped on her heels, took a deep breath, and went inside.

She'd convinced Mrs. Johnson that the room shouldn't be brightly lit, although there was enough light to see everyone. The band was at the far end of the room, the refreshment table along one wall.

"You made it," Fran said, grabbing her arm and pulling her into a corner.

"Barely. There's a lot more people here than I expected."

"Mrs. Johnson sent word to the SMU sororities about the dance and the British cadets. Some of the girls came."

Southern Methodist University in Dallas. Sorority girls. Kitty didn't want the competition. The cadets belonged to the town. "Why would she do that?"

"She wanted to make sure there are enough girls to go around."

Kitty didn't like it, but it made sense. Thirty-four students were in their graduating class, a little over half of them girls, hardly enough to ensure all the cadets had dance partners. "Have you been dancing?"

"A lot. You will, too. You'll see."

A cadet wandered over and asked Fran to dance. Left alone, Kitty pressed her back to the wall and fought not to be jealous when Will asked Juliet Barnes to dance. The petite brunette was one of several girls from her high school class who were there tonight. Some of the women of the town — married and unmarried — were presently jitterbugging. She saw Jessie partnered with a cadet. Rhonda was kicking up her heels with the Smythson fella. The way they were holding each other's gaze even as they moved their feet in rhythm to the music — it was like they were secretly passing notes back and forth, only with their eyes.

Kitty needed to be bolder if she wanted to dance. She moved to the edge of the dance floor, waiting for the dance to end so maybe she could gather the courage to approach Will. But as she stood there, it suddenly occurred to her that she'd never really danced. Oh, she'd done a few hops, skips, and waving her arms around at a family gathering or two, but she'd never been out on the floor with a fella. And she'd certainly never engaged in anything as elaborate as what was going on right then. Girls swinging around, being twirled, moving away from their partners, coming back in. Gosh, everyone seemed to know what they were doing, especially those girls from the university. It was disconcerting to realize some of these dances required a knowledge of the steps.

She moved back into the shadows. Mama was right. She wasn't ready for this. What had she been thinking? The song ended and people dispersed, looking for new partners. She didn't want Jessie to see her but hoped Fran would come back.

"Hello, Kitty."

Her heart hammering at the smooth voice, she looked at Will. He'd left his jacket somewhere and was wearing only a shirt and tie. If her mother ever saw him, she'd want to fatten him up, but he took Kitty's breath, and she was afraid he might never return it. She knew she shouldn't like him so much but couldn't seem to help herself. He was so handsome and was always nice to her. "Hi."

"I didn't know you were here."

"I haven't been for long."

"Would you like to dance?"

"I really do, but" — she glanced back at the gyrating dancers — "I realize now I don't really know how."

"I can show you. Just follow my lead." He held out his hand.

"I'm not sure what that means."

"It means I'll guide you." He leaned toward her slightly. "There's no right or wrong. We can just hold on to each other and step quickly over the floor in rhythm to the music. Besides, if you never give it a go, you never will learn, will you?"

"Okay." As she placed her hand in his, she hoped her smile didn't reflect how nervous she was. Not that anyone would probably notice if she did make a fool of herself. They all seemed to be concentrating on their own moves and dance partners. But Will would notice, and she really didn't want to embarrass him.

He kept them on the edge of the dance floor, where it wasn't quite as crowded. Then he took her other hand, pulled her in

221

slightly, pushed her out. Pulled her in closer, placed a hand on her waist, bringing them together before he started guiding her around the area.

"See? Not so hard," he said, smiling.

"Do you know all the fancy moves? I've seen some guys lift girls up."

"I do. When you trust me more, we'll give it a go."

"I trust you now."

He shook his head. "Not enough for that. You have to trust yourself as well."

They'd neared the band, which made it more difficult to talk with him as the music really blared from that side of the room. Once they were edging their way back toward the door, she realized he'd inconspicuously eased them toward the middle. Watching him watching her as though she was truly special, a delight to be with, made her stop wondering about what anyone else might think of her dancing.

The music stopped, and she scrunched up her face, wishing it hadn't. "That was fun."

"Yeah, it was. But we got only a little bit of that song. Shall we do another?"

If she'd embarrassed him, he wouldn't have asked. She was filled with such gladness that she thought she might burst. "I'd like that."

"Hello there, Kitty," Harry said, placing a hand on the small of her back. She'd been so focused on Will that she'd missed Harry approaching. "How about you dance the next one with me?"

"I already promised Will."

"Oh, he won't mind."

"Actually, I would," Will said.

The two stared at each other, and she was left with the impression that they weren't the best of friends. The music started. "Bye, Harrison," she said.

With his brow furrowed, he looked at her as though no one had ever dismissed him before. Still holding one hand, Will grabbed the one he'd released earlier, drew her in close, and began shuffling her backward. Normally, she would have been glancing over her shoulder to make sure she didn't bump into anyone, but she trusted him to ensure she didn't. "You don't like him, do you?"

"As I told you when we met, he flirts with every girl. You deserve a lad who doesn't."

"And you don't."

Releasing his hold on one hand, he swung her out, circling her with his arm going over her head. She twisted around, smiling as he took her hand and brought her back in.

"Not usually," he said.

When he swung her out again, she knew what to do and carried herself under his raised arm before moving back in to face him. "This is fun!"

"You're fun," he said.

She was so glad the cadets were here. They were exciting and different. Nothing ever happened in Terrence, and now something was. She was meeting interesting people who came from far away, learning new things, and being introduced to novel experiences. Everyone seemed happy that the Brits were here. There was such a celebratory atmosphere around town. She thought it would be nice if the cadets never had to leave but could remain part of the community.

When the music ended, Will didn't immediately rush off, but kept his fingers laced through hers. She hoped he'd ask her to dance again, but then the hairs on the nape of her neck prickled. She knew what she was going to discover before she swung around.

Arms crossed, her gaze harsh, her mother stood just inside the doorway. The last thing Kitty wanted was to create a fuss in front of everyone. "I have to go."

Will furrowed his brow. "You just got here."

"I know but . . . thank you for dancing with me."

He looked past her, and she wondered if he could feel the frigid glare. "Is that your mum?"

"Yeah. I'll see you at the drugstore."

"Count on it." He leaned down. "I hope you're not in trouble."

She had a feeling he understood she wasn't supposed to be there. It was embarrassing, but still she spoke the truth. "If I am, it was worth it."

As much as she didn't want to, she left him there to dance with other girls. Her mother didn't say anything until they were outside. "I can't believe you disobeyed me. I'm so disappointed in you, Kitty."

"How did you even know?"

"I couldn't get to sleep, began feeling guilty about making you stay home, and decided I was being unreasonable, so I went upstairs to let you know you could go to the next dance. Obviously, that's not going to happen now. You showed tonight that I can't trust you."

Kitty felt like her entire body was groaning in agony. Mama's unreasonableness was unbelievable. At first, Kitty couldn't go.

Then she could. Now she couldn't because she had. "All I did was dance."

"You snuck out of the house. You betrayed my confidence in you. For the next two weeks you go to work and home. That's it."

She knew that tone, had heard her mother direct it toward Jack countless times. She wouldn't be swayed from delivering the punishment. Kitty was doomed to two boring weeks. Except she'd see Will at the drugstore. She'd just have to make the most of those moments.

CHAPTER 16

Having just finished what had to be her tenth or eleventh dance, Jessie wandered over to the refreshment table, where Mrs. Berg was serving punch and cookies. Picking up a full punch cup, she glanced around and said loudly enough to be heard over the din of conversations, laughter, and music, "It's a wonderful success."

"I'm so pleased everyone is having a grand time. I was talking to Daphne, and I think we're going to plan to have a dance every week."

Daphne — Mrs. Johnson — was mingling among those standing on the sidelines, introducing people who seemed too shy or hesitant to make another's acquaintance. Jessie suspected even more people from the area, from outside Terrence, would attend the next dance because word would spread. It always did. "I think it's terrific. It gives

227

the cadets something to do on Saturday night."

The music was upbeat and lively. The young people — God, when had she started to feel so old; she hadn't been around that much longer than most of these kids — were laughing and dancing.

"You mark my words, a lot of these gals are gonna fall in love with these English fellas," Mrs. Berg said. "Then where will they be when these boys head on back home?"

"They're being discouraged from getting involved with the locals."

"Huh. That'll just make them do it. When have you ever known a fella not to do something 'cuz he was told?"

Mrs. Berg had a point. Jessie's mom had always told her that when it came to the male of the species, you got further by asking instead of telling. "Let them think they have a choice or it's their idea." The wisdom had been shared when Jessie was nine and had begun to realize that she was always told to take a bath while Jack had been asked to take one. After her mom's explanation, Jessie's own stubbornness had kicked in, and her mother had found herself having to ask both her eldest children to do things. Jessie had never wanted to be seen as different from Jack.

She began studying the various gyrating couples. "I thought I saw Kitty dancing earlier."

"You might have. She was here for a bit, and then your mama showed up. Based on her expression, I have a feeling your sister was where she was not supposed to be."

It was so unlike Kitty to be disobedient, but Jessie knew she was infatuated with the cadets, and so she understood her mother's hesitancy to let Kitty attend the dances.

"I'm surprised Luke's not here with you tonight. Never known him to miss a chance to shuffle his boots over a dance floor."

"He's off on some bull buying expedition."

"I'd a thought you'd go with him."

"He wanted to leave at sunup, and I had to work until noon." Luke hadn't been happy. While they hadn't exchanged any heated words, it still felt as though they'd had an argument.

"He's a responsible young man. He's going to be such a wonderful husband to you."

Jessie couldn't seem to escape the hints that it was time she walked down the aisle. She held her tongue and just nodded. He would make a good husband, but she was no longer certain she'd make him a good wife.

"It sure has gotten a lot noisier around here with so many planes flying around all the time," Mrs. Berg said.

She welcomed the topic change. "You haven't heard noisy yet. Just wait until the fall, when we have a full contingent of cadets."

"We'll have to find more girls."

"I don't think that'll be a problem." The girls from SMU were either local or summer students. Once fall arrived, more would no doubt show up for a dance now and then. It would also get more crowded, making it difficult to find people. A lot of room remained tonight, although the people clustered in groups weren't always easily identifiable. She wondered if Royce was in one of them. Earlier, she'd seen him walking around the room, talking with some of the fellas, smiling politely at the girls who approached him.

"Looking for someone?" Mrs. Berg asked.

"I was just wondering where the wing commander got off to."

"I saw him go outside a little while ago."

Deciding a little fresh air would be welcome, she set her empty glass aside. "Appreciate the punch."

After wending her way through the gathering, she slipped out the front door, with the music following her, and took in a breath of the sultry night air before glancing around. A couple was locked in an embrace just beyond the lights. She couldn't make out who they were, didn't want to know.

Walking around the corner of the building, she was met with thicker shadows but spotted a small red glow near an elm tree. Cautiously, she approached until she could see a man leaning with one shoulder against the trunk. As her eyes adjusted, she realized his back was to her and she could more easily determine his shape, his white shirt making him more visible. Strange how she recognized that form. "Hiding out?"

Spinning around, he took another drag on the cigarette, dropped it, ground it out, and blew out the smoke. "Just needed a bit of solitude. It's quite raucous inside."

"The cadets seem to be having a good time."

"They are indeed. They're keeping you fairly busy."

She shouldn't be so pleased that he'd noticed, not that he seemed at all bothered by the attention showered on her. She wasn't altogether certain Luke would have appreciated her many different dance partners, the smiles the cadets flashed her way, or the enthusiasm with which they greeted her. "It's all in good fun. I promise I'm not falling for any of them."

"I'm not certain the same can be said of them not falling for you. A few appeared to be quite smitten."

"I have it on good authority more dances are being planned. Are you going to forbid Rhonda and me from attending?" She kept her tone light, teasing.

"I'd have a mutiny on my hands if I objected to your presence at so public an event. Miss Monroe might very likely quit. And my fellow countrymen would certainly revolt."

She laughed, liking that he was a little more relaxed, wondering if he'd been sipping from the flask that she'd seen Peter sharing with Rhonda. She recognized the tune blasting out through the open windows of the hall. With a smile, she said, "Artie Shaw's 'Non-Stop Flight.' "

"Seems like something a flygirl should dance to. I won't be the smoothest partner you've had all night, but I'm willing to give it a go." He set his cane against the tree and held his hand out to her.

She knew she shouldn't, imagined the rumors that would spread around the airfield and around town if anyone saw them, but there was sanctuary in the shadows here. She slipped her hand into his. He wrapped his fingers around hers and placed his other hand on her waist, while she put hers on his shoulder. His steps weren't even, accented as they were by his slight limp, but she didn't care. They were just preparing for her to twirl beneath his arm when the music ended. Something soft and slow began to play. She'd expected him to release her. Instead, he brought her in closer, the hand holding hers resting against his chest, and she felt the thumping of his heart.

Her own kicked up its tempo as she followed his lead, slow steps, small steps, barely moving from where they were, never taking their gazes from each other. She was grateful for the darkness, that it hid so much that shouldn't be revealed. How much she enjoyed being this close to him, how she liked the rich, earthy scent of him. Even the lingering fragrance of tobacco. She shouldn't be relishing this moment. Nor, when it ended, should she have wished it hadn't.

Slowly, as though he, too, was reluctant to part, he released his hold on her, stepped back, and snatched up his cane. "My fiancée enjoyed dancing. I haven't been able to bring myself to dance since she died."

She felt as though someone had lassoed a

rope around her chest and was pulling it tight. "You had a fiancée?"

"Kate. She was killed last November, when the Germans were relentlessly bombing London night after night."

Ah, God, and she'd asked him that first night if he had anyone special waiting for him at home. "I'm so very sorry. Losing her like that had to be incredibly hard. Were you with her when it happened?"

"No. Sometimes I have to convince myself that being there wouldn't have made a difference. She'd volunteered to be an air raid warden. I told her I didn't like it. She told me she didn't bloody well like me chasing after Jerry. I explained I had no choice. She said neither did she. She had a big heart, my Kate did, always putting others first. It was one of the things I loved about her. When I received word that she'd been killed, it was instantly one of the things I hated about her. I was rather certain she'd been helping others get to the air raid shelters rather than seeing to her own safety." He sighed, shook his head. "My apologies. I've managed to ruin an otherwise lovely evening."

As horrific as the memories were, as much as she ached for what he'd been through, she was grateful he had been comfortable enough to share his agonizing loss with her, that she'd been given the opportunity to know him a little better. "Please don't apologize. She's been gone only slightly longer than Dad, and I still haven't quite adjusted to his absence. I wish I had the power to ease your sorrow."

"You help more than you realize. I should probably go back in now to ensure the lads are behaving properly and remind them they're not to get involved with the locals."

As though the heart ever cared about what it was supposed to do.

CHAPTER 17

"Do you think the Brits will celebrate the fourth?"

Sitting behind the LT controls, Jessie glanced over at Rhonda, who was studying her calf, ensuring the line of her nylons was straight. This was the first morning the cadets had engaged in shooting practice, and she wondered if the continual popping sound had reminded Rhonda of fireworks and prompted her question. "I hadn't given it any thought."

Rhonda looked up. "Would it be awkward if they did? Sour grapes if they didn't? Will Barstow let them know we don't work that day?"

"That's your real worry. You want the day off. You didn't ask Peter during one of your many dances?" Other than the first day, when he'd brought the cadets in, he hadn't returned to the Link building.

236

"I had other things on my mind — like how well he moves. It's a shame Royce's injury stops him from jitterbugging."

Jessie's cheeks warmed with a flush she hoped Rhonda didn't notice. "He's not limping as noticeably. I'm certain he'll be dancing before long."

"I bet he has some moves."

She cleared her throat. "Don't they all?"

The door opened — thank goodness, the cadets had arrived for some LT time — only it was Barstow, looking none too happy. Was he upset with Rhonda and her flirtation?

"Miss Lovelace, we're short a flight instructor this morning. The Brits believe flight hours have precedence over LT time. Would you be willing to take on Emerson's students until he recovers from whatever is ailing him?"

She suspected it was too much drink the evening before. Still, she jumped to her feet. "I'll need half an hour to go home and change."

He nodded. "Then report to Watkins." He was the lead flight instructor. "He'll give you a rundown on what you need to know."

"Thank you, sir. I won't let you down."

A word of reassurance or faith in her abilities would have been nice. Instead, he simply gave another brisk nod, as though it was too much effort to utter anything positive. When he was gone, she looked over at Rhonda and it took everything within her not to squeal like Kitty did whenever she got something she really wanted.

"This is your chance," Rhonda said, beaming.

"It's only for today. I'm sure Emerson is just recovering from a bender. He'll be back tomorrow." She hurried to her locker and grabbed her purse. Once she was no longer taking planes up, she'd stopped bringing her jumpsuit. "But, yeah, I can definitely outfly him."

She made it home and back in record time. Watkins, another former pilot from the Great War, reminded her of someone constantly dealing with a toothache, his jaw jutting out and tense. He didn't seem particularly happy about handing over the maps, routes, and names of her four students for the day. His gruffness didn't dim her enthusiasm for the task ahead.

By the time she arrived at her assigned aircraft, William Wedgeworth was already there, waiting on her. Other planes were being revved up, taxiing, or taking off. The activity was loud and thrilling, filling her with a sense of awe, as she imagined how closely the ground crew rushing around and the pilots heading into the skies mimicked a scramble to confront the enemy. She extended her hand toward the young man with the dark hair and blue-gray eyes. "Good morning, Mr. Wedgeworth."

His grip was firm, solid. "Miss Lovelace, Mr. Emerson doesn't seem to be about. Am I going to have to do the LT then?"

"No, sir. I'll be putting you through your paces in the air this morning."

He grinned. "Jolly good. I don't suppose you'll teach me how to land as perfectly as you did a couple of weeks ago during that contest."

"It's just a matter of concentration and getting to know your aircraft. Do you consider yourself an accomplished dancer, Mr. Wedgeworth?"

"I like to think so. Did your sister complain?"

So he'd danced with Kitty. She could see her sister taking an interest in the exceedingly amiable young man, but she could also see him breaking Kitty's heart. Forcing a smile, she chuckled. "No, no complaints, but I've found good dancers are usually extremely coordinated, which makes for the best pilots. Why don't you take me through your preflight?"

239

She followed as he systematically went around the plane. When they were finished, she handed him a map. "Here's the route we'll be taking today, and the landmarks you'll want to watch for, so you know we're on course. You take the pilot's seat."

She lowered her goggles, hauled herself onto the wing, and clambered over the side into the front seat, while he settled in behind her. After he'd pulled on his leather helmet, she spoke into the funnel of the gosport. "All right, Mr. Wedgeworth, impress me."

One of the ground crew approached and began cranking the propeller. The cadet had already experienced this aspect of flight several times, so she forced herself to wait patiently as he engaged the ignition. It was a bit unnerving not to have flown with him before, not to have a sense of his skill level, but she could easily take over the controls if she sensed that he hadn't yet mastered a needed ability.

As they began taxiing to the area where they would wait for their turn to take off, he wove slightly, as was necessary to gauge their surroundings. It was impossible to see over the nose of the aircraft, so he had to constantly check the sides to make sure they weren't going to hit anything. Once they

240

reached the line of departing aircraft, he crept along until it was their turn. They held still until one of the ground crew with a flag swept it down.

Will gunned the engine and started up the grassy field. Although she wasn't responsible for it, she still experienced the thrill she always did when the wheels began to lift. She hoped to never lose the sense of wonder regarding what had been accomplished. People had the ability to touch the clouds.

"Mr. Wedgeworth, I want to reiterate what I'm certain Mr. Emerson already told you — almost every town has a water tower with its name painted on it, so if you ever have any doubts about where you are, search for the water tower. And if you really feel lost, find the railroad tracks and follow them. They'll usually lead you toward a town. If it's not enough to help you get your bearings, you can always land in a field and find someone in the area to ask."

Once they were past the town, he took the plane higher and headed in the direction of Dallas. Their destination was the Magnolia Petroleum building, the tallest in the area. Atop it sat a red Pegasus sign. When they reached it, he circled it before turning back toward Terrence.

After he brought the Stearman in for a

smooth landing and they were both on the ground, she slapped his shoulder. "That was well done, Mr. Wedgeworth. You shouldn't have any problems with your solo flight later in the week."

"Thank you, ma'am." He grinned broadly, his cheeks turning a little pink.

She'd been impressed and decided he probably was a good dancer. She hoped he'd be dancing until his hair turned gray.

Her next student, Mick Turner, was a little wobbly on the take-off and landing. Rather than following the preplanned route, she took him out to one of the auxiliary fields and had him practice those maneuvers a few times. Although he was doing better, he still had room for improvement. If she were a permanent instructor, she'd give him some extra time for additional drills at the end of the day.

Afterward, she met up with Rhonda in the mess hall, joining her at a table she was sharing with Mrs. Winder. There was definitely no mingling of the sexes here.

"You look happy," Rhonda said.

"I am. It felt incredibly satisfying, but also a bit frustrating, because I'm not doing it every day. They're so eager to learn, to do well. The two this morning were a joy."

"Maybe you need to have another chat

with Barstow before the next class of students and the additional instructors arrive."

Jessie glanced over to where he was sitting with Royce and Peter. "Maybe. I guess it couldn't hurt, and after my performance this morn—"

"See your little secret rendezvous in the darkness with Ballinger paid off," Forester hissed, scooping in low to deliver his message, before carrying on past her. Quickly she twisted around to watch him drop down into a chair at a table with some of the other instructors. Whatever he said to them had them all turning their heads, eyes narrowed, her way. She couldn't tell if they were angry, suspicious, or disgusted, but it was obvious they weren't pleased. Fighting the need to confront Forester, she faced her tablemates.

"What was he talking about?" Rhonda asked.

"Nothing."

"You don't go pale and then red for nothing."

She peered over at Mrs. Winder, who seemed to be engrossed in reading *For Whom the Bell Tolls,* but Jessie was fairly certain she was also capable of listening for any gossip. What she'd done wasn't wrong and certainly wasn't a secret. She wasn't ashamed of it, even if she'd enjoyed the short dance more than she should have. "Remember that morning when I was upset by Forester's attitude?"

Rhonda nodded. "Regarding the war."

"Well, he may have also implied that I was taking advantage of Royce's staying with us to curry favor."

Her friend's jaw dropped. "I think maybe you should have led your rant with that part of the conversation."

"I was a little embarrassed by what he was implying, because it's absolutely not true."

"Of course it's not."

"Saturday night, I needed some fresh air, so I went outside. Royce just happened to be out there, too, and we spoke for a while. I guess Forester saw us and thinks more went on between us than did." Even if he'd seen the dance, how could he make something bad out of that?

Rhonda's eyes narrowed as she looked in the direction Forester was sitting. If a glare could kill, hers would have accomplished the task. "That little —"

"He certainly hinted to Mr. Barstow that more went on."

Jessie jerked her attention to Mrs. Winder, who casually turned a page in the book, her gaze downcast, giving the appearance of her reading. "I'm surprised, then, that Barstow

244

asked me to serve as a substitute instructor."

"I don't know how much choice he had in the matter, since a certain British officer suggested it . . . quite forcefully, as a matter of fact."

Slowly Jessie closed her eyes as the disappointment hit her. She'd stupidly believed that Barstow was beginning to see her value, maybe because of the spot landing contest. Instead, it had come about because of Royce. Why had he suggested her? Because of a slow movement of feet with a song playing in the distance? A motorcycle ride? A heartfelt conversation on her front lawn? Was he trying to do her a favor? Instead, Barstow was going to resent her all the more. As were the other flight instructors.

She studied the secretary, whose nose remained buried in her book. "Thank you, Mrs. W."

With a twinkle in her eye, she peered up from her book. "I think there's a reason Mr. Barstow never married. He continually underestimates women."

Rhonda burst out laughing, while Jessie only chuckled. A few minutes later, when Royce left, even knowing it would probably add fuel to the gossip, she rushed out after him, easily catching up to him. "I wish you

245

hadn't insisted Barstow have me serve as a substitute."

He stopped walking to study her. Then he gave a little nod. "Ah. I thought Mrs. Winder was listening at the door."

"I need to prove myself."

"Which you've done."

To him maybe, but she couldn't help but think he was a bit biased. The struggles, fears, and losses they'd shared had created an intimacy between her and Royce. They'd also ignited confusing feelings within her that made her need to push him away while at the same time she yearned to draw him nearer. "I need Barstow to believe I deserve this. Not only Barstow. The other instructors as well. They . . ." She let her voice trail off.

"They what?"

"It doesn't matter. I've asked you before not to interfere or speak to Barstow on my behalf. I can earn this on my own." Without causing the other instructors to resent her because they thought she was trading favors with Royce.

He gave a curt nod. "Very well, Miss Lovelace. It shan't happen again, but consider this. Perhaps I did it because I wanted the best instructor for my men. And you're letting your pride get in the way."

With that he walked away. His addressing her as "Miss Lovelace" when no one was near to hear their conversation had an ominous ring to it. She was surprised his cane didn't break due to the force with which it was striking the ground. Had she been too sensitive? She wanted Barstow in her corner, believing she deserved this, wanted them all convinced she deserved it.

Maybe she was even striving to convince herself.

In the afternoon, she had another good dancer, Martin Brightwell. As they walked toward the aircraft, he said, "Wish they'd let us carry our pistols with us."

She smiled. "You're not likely to be shot down and have to battle it out with the enemy to escape."

"That's not the only reason we carry the pistol."

"Oh?"

He hesitated and glanced around, before bringing his gaze back to her. His brow was furrowed, and he looked as though he wished he hadn't said anything.

"Mr. Brightwell? You've piqued my curiosity now."

He gnawed on his lip. "I've heard you have a brother in the RAF."

"Yes, I do."

"Well, then, it might bring you some comfort to know . . . we carry the pistol in case we get trapped in a fiery aircraft. To bring a swift end to the agony, as it were."

It brought no comfort at all. Apparently, Jack wasn't telling her everything.

Her final student of the day, Antony Ashby, grumbled about doing the preflight, felt like it was the mechanic's or ground crew's job to make sure the plane was in good working order. He struck her as someone accustomed to others doing for him. He also seemed a bit older than the others, with a Clark Gable–like mustache and a less-than-enthusiastic attitude. She didn't know if he was always so standoffish or simply preferred Emerson to her. She welcomed the challenge of winning him over.

She praised him when he kept the aircraft level, cautioned him when he got too close to the Pegasus sign. He was a little better flying evenly as they headed back to base. While each instructor took their students on a different flight path, so they had plenty of sky in front of them, the time needed to complete the exercise and return was fairly equal, so they arrived nearly simultaneously, requiring they circle the airfield, waiting

248

their turn to land. As Ashby made his final approach, she warned him that he was coming in too fast and too low for the landing. He adjusted and was about to touch down when she heard the rumble of another aircraft, incredibly loud, as though almost on top of them. Looking up and back, she realized it was. "My contr—"

But it was too late. The shuddering jolt slammed them to the ground, just before everything went black.

CHAPTER 18

"Jessie? Jessie? Wake up, sweetheart. Come on now."

She didn't want to. Her head hurt. Christ, everything hurt. The cockpit was at an odd angle, her harness digging into one shoulder. She touched her hand to her forehead. It was wet, with something sticky and thick. Oil? Looking at her fingers, she wondered why it was such a bright red.

"Can you move?"

Gingerly, she turned toward the voice. Royce. With his features tight and furrowed with concern, he was leaning over her. "You have such blue eyes. Like the sky. I could fly into them."

"I think you're done flying for the day. How many fingers am I holding up?"

"Six."

"Can you feel your legs, your feet, your toes?"

She nodded. Her head objected, sending

250

jarring pain ricocheting around it. Jarring. She remembered the sensation of being pushed, jerked, shoved. They'd been hit. Someone had crashed into them. Someone not waiting for their turn. Or maybe he'd had some sort of mechanical trouble, lost control of the plane. "Ashby?"

"Shaken. A little banged up. He's managed to climb out."

"The others?"

"Bumps and bruises. You got the brunt of it, I'm afraid. We have an ambulance on the way."

"Don't need —"

He moved away, and she wished he hadn't. She thought she heard him ordering someone to take care getting her out, but she couldn't be sure. Fog was settling in and then it was night.

People were constantly asking for her name — as though they didn't know it. Was there a single person in Terrence who didn't know who she was, her family, and the details of her life? Bright lights and darkness. A poke, a prod. Cold, then warmth. Finally, they left her alone to sleep on the clouds.

When she awoke, the eyes studying her so carefully were brown.

"Hey, darlin'."

She tried to smile but couldn't be certain she didn't grimace. Everything was hurting again. She wanted to return to the billowy white cumulus. "Luke. What are you doing here? You never come to the airfield." She'd been so disappointed in the beginning that he took no interest in this aspect of her life, while she cared about his cattle and horses. But eventually she'd accepted that they could have separate interests and still get along. Mama never flew. Dad never knitted.

"You're not at the airfield. You're at the hospital." Terrence had a small one, for handling minor surgeries and childbirth. If she was truly hurt, they'd have taken her into Dallas. Gingerly he brushed her hair back from her brow. "You had quite the gash there. Doctor had to stitch it up, bandage it. They think part of a propeller or something else that snapped off hit you. You scared the hell out of us."

"My hard head saved me."

He grinned. "Probably, but you're going to have one hell of a shiner in the morning. Have a sip of this." He placed a straw between her lips. The water was cool and soothing. When she was finished, he said, "I'm gonna let the nurse know you're awake."

He was gone before she could acknowledge his words. When the nurse came in, Jessie went through the whole giving her name, day of the week, year routine. Lights flashed in her eyes.

"Dr. Brown wants to keep you overnight, just for observation," the nurse said. "You can probably go home in the morning."

Then Luke returned, pulled a chair beside the bed, sat, and took her hand, his gaze steady on her. "Didn't think you were actually flying with the students."

"They were short an instructor this morning."

"Next time tell them to find someone else."

How different the two men in her life were. Was Royce even in her life any longer? *Miss Lovelace.* He shouldn't be. He was confusing. Believing in her. Did she really not want him to? She had to focus on Luke, on his worry, his upset. "I don't know what actually happened, but it's not something that normally does."

"You could have been killed, Jess."

"But I wasn't. Do you know how the others are?" Had she asked that of Royce, leaning over her in the cockpit? Had she dreamed it? She felt like her head was stuffed with cotton, and her thoughts were having to hack through it.

He sighed, and she knew he was frustrated, thinking she wasn't taking what happened seriously. She was, but crashes were always a risk. They came with flying. "Heard one fella had a broken arm. The others . . . just minor stuff. You're the only one they're keeping."

"Makes me sound like a good-size catfish you wouldn't throw back."

A corner of his mouth hitched up. "Don't recall something like this happening at the school when your dad ran things."

"We never had a dozen planes in the air at once." She squeezed his hand. "I'm okay. Is Mama here?"

"We're doing it in shifts. She'll come this evening. You go back to sleep now."

"You don't need to watch over me. That's what the nurses are for."

"I'll stay for a while."

She closed her eyes. When she opened them again, Luke was gone, as was the sunlight. Beyond the window was night. Her mother was sitting in the chair, Kitty standing beside her.

"Jack is the one I've been worrying about," her mother said. "Seems I should have been worried about you."

"It was just a little mishap." Now she was sounding like Royce. What surprised her

254

was that she'd had no time to give any thought to what was happening, to be frightened. She'd just thought if she could take over the controls, she could somehow use her skill to divert them, to avoid being hit. She didn't even know who had been flying the other plane. "You wouldn't happen to know who else was involved, in the other aircraft, would you?"

"I don't know who all the cadets are," Mama said.

"Geoffrey Moreland," Kitty said. When Mama gave her a startled look, she added, "I met him at the drugstore."

Jessie was sorry to hear that he'd been the one. Still struggling with the Link and lacking in confidence, this experience was bound to unsettle him even more.

"Rhonda said both planes are pretty smashed up," Kitty added.

"We have a couple in reserve."

"Maybe you should see this as a sign that it's time to settle down, make your home, start your family," Mama said.

Jessie shook her head. "I'm not quitting."

"You're going to turn my hair gray before its time."

Her mother hadn't said those words to Jack. Instead, she'd reiterated her pride in him. Why couldn't she see the value of what

255

Jessie was doing?

The door opened slightly, and Rhonda poked her head into the room. "Am I interrupting anything?"

Jessie was more than grateful for the interruption because, with an audience, Mama wouldn't continue to harp and strive to make her feel guilty. "Tell me you bring details about what happened."

Rhonda stepped in and held up a sack. "I bring burgers."

Jessie smiled. "Even better."

"Hospital food is such a bore," Rhonda said as she set things on a tray while Mama helped Jessie sit up, with a pillow behind her back.

When the tray was on her lap, Jessie grabbed the burger and took a bite, finding herself suddenly starving. "So what do you know about what happened? Who was the other instructor?"

"Your dear friend Doug Forester."

Jessie slammed her eyes closed. She should have known.

"As for exactly what happened, it's still a bit murky, some conflicting stories from what I understand. Royce and Peter are working to get to the bottom of it. Needless to say, they are not happy about losing two aircraft to a situation that probably could

256

have been avoided."

While Jessie ate, Rhonda changed the subject and began talking about July Fourth. Royce was going to let the cadets have the day off, out of respect for the holiday. She wanted to arrange a baseball game between the Brits and the Yanks. By the time Mama and Kitty left, they had been put in charge of hosting a cookout following the game.

"Thank you for that," Jessie said to Rhonda when it was only the two of them remaining in the room.

"Your mom looked very worried and un-happy."

"She and Luke think I need to quit work-ing at the school."

"Get married and have a baby." Rhonda arched a brow. "That ain't gonna happen."

"No, it's not."

Rhonda sat on the edge of the bed. "So here's something interesting. We heard the crash inside the LT building. Rushed out. I don't know how he managed it with his injury, but by the time we got to where we could see the crumpled planes, Royce had somehow climbed up and was leaning in the cockpit."

So she hadn't dreamed it. "He would have done that for anyone who wasn't respond-ing and getting free of the aircraft. From what I gather I was knocked out."

"Yeah, I don't know if he would have had the same reaction. I think you scared him."

"Apparently I scared a lot of people."

"You did me. All that blood, and you were so pale when they finally managed to maneuver you to the ground."

"Head wounds bleed a lot. It wasn't that bad."

"Of course not. That's the reason you have to stay here tonight." Squinting, she slipped a finger beneath Jessie's chin and turned her head. "You've got a lovely black eye."

"I can't decide if this little incident is going to earn me any points or hurt my chances of ever being able to serve as a permanent flight instructor."

"Earned you a lot of worry." She patted her hand. "I'm pretty sure visiting hours are over. I'll let you get some sleep."

The nurse came in shortly after Rhonda left and they went through the same ritual of questions and shining a light in her eyes. She took her temperature, did a few other things, and then lowered the light so Jessie could sleep. In spite of her aches, she did manage to drift off. She awoke to sunlight streaming in and a different nurse checking her over. This one she knew from school.

"How are you feeling this morning?" Eve asked.

"Like I got hit by a truck."

"You're pretty bruised all over. Hopefully, you can take a couple of days of rest before going back to work. The doctor will be in to see you in a bit, and if he approves, you can go home."

"I'm more than ready to leave." She glanced over at the table beside the bed. A small bouquet of purple hydrangea blossoms was nestled in a mason jar. "Where did those come from?"

"Oh, a nice British gentleman brought them by late last night. Said he knew you from the flight school, was worried, and wanted to see for himself that you were doing okay."

"What did he look like?"

"Dark hair, pretty blue eyes. I shouldn't have let him come in after visiting hours, but he was so charming, promised to keep the door open. He stayed for a while. I guess you never woke up."

She remembered now that two hydrangea bushes grew at the front of the house Royce was leasing. She wished he'd woken her. While she tried to reassure everyone that she'd been in no danger, that accidents happened, she was having a difficult time convincing herself that she hadn't come very close to dying. How did she get back in an aircraft when it had suddenly encompassed her worst nightmare?

CHAPTER 19

Tuesday, July 1, 1941

"Thanks, Mama," Jessie said as she climbed out of the car. Her mother had picked her up at the hospital and taken her to the house she shared with Rhonda. Jessie had placed the flowers on the dresser in her bedroom and changed clothes, grimacing at the dark blue bruises on her body, especially the one circling her eye. She really had been fortunate not to lose it. Then her mom had driven her to the airfield, so she could get her motorcycle. Her doctor had advised she take the remainder of the week off and, considering how all the aches and pains intensified with each movement, she'd decided to heed his advice.

"I'm not sure you should ride that thing home."

"I'll be fine."

"Come to the house so I can pamper

you." Which meant chicken soup and hovering.

"I'm going to go to my place and sleep. I'll call you when I get there so you don't have to worry." Closing the door, she waved and waited until her mother drove off to begin her slow, gingerly walk to the administrative building. Some of the ground crew stopped to speak with her.

Billy ambled over. "You scared us, little lady."

"I'm fine. Just a little bruised. I hear the planes were pretty mangled."

"They can be repaired."

"Glad to hear it."

"Good to see you up and about."

She smiled, even though a portion of her face objected. "Good to be up and about." She carried on and went into the administrative building.

Peter was standing just inside, obviously on his way out. "Ah, Jessie, that looks painful."

"Could have been worse."

"Indeed. Always can be, can't it? Hope you're not planning to work today."

"No, I just want to let Barstow know I'll be taking the remainder of the week off."

"Jolly good for you. The others involved in the crash are as well. I'm afraid all the

262

cadets took what happened rather hard, but they'll be more vigilant in the cockpit. I believe we had some not taking matters as seriously as they should."

"Maybe some instructors as well."

He gave a quick nod. "I'll leave you to see to matters." He reached for the door, stopped. "You'll find Royce in the office."

He was gone before she could respond. She hadn't mentioned she was looking for him but supposed people assumed things. She vaguely recalled him calling her *sweetheart* and wondered who might have been near enough to hear, although surely he hadn't meant anything personal by the endearment. His use of the term was probably no different than the waitress at the Cowboy Grill calling each of the customers *hon*.

As she neared his office, she could hear his voice, although she couldn't make out the words. Peering around the doorjamb, she saw he was alone, talking on the telephone. Until that moment, she hadn't realized how badly she needed to see him.

"Right, thank you. Cheerio." After hanging up, he released a long, slow sigh, bowed his head, and began rubbing his temples.

She stepped quietly into the room. "Things not going well?"

Immediately, he grabbed his cane, shoved back his chair —

"You don't have to stand."

— continued following through on his actions until he was. "Miss Lovelace, you should be home resting, not here."

She hated the formality that indicated he was still feeling the sting of her words from yesterday. Yet he'd brought her flowers. She was naive to think things between them had returned to an easy camaraderie. "I needed to get my motorcycle and wanted to let you and Barstow know that I'll be taking the remainder of the week off."

"He's presently working with some students. Just let his secretary know. She'll get word to him."

With a nod, she took a step nearer. "Any idea exactly what happened yesterday? I heard Mr. Moreland was in the other plane."

"He was, but he wasn't at the controls. His instructor was. Mr. Forester."

Her injury protested as she widened her eyes. What in the world was wrong with the man? Let her count the ways. Instead, she decided to give him the benefit of the doubt. "Were they having engine trouble?"

"No, apparently he was simply impatient to land and decided it was his turn. As I understand it, on another occasion" — he gave her a pointed look — "he nearly crashed into an aircraft but the pilot then was able to react swiftly enough to avoid a collision. He's been let go."

Relief swamped her. The man was a menace in more ways than one. "The school is better off. He didn't really believe in the work that was being done here."

"So he made quite clear. Barstow will secure a replacement."

If she hadn't expressed her displeasure with his speaking on her behalf, Royce would have ensured it was her. She knew it as surely as she knew the impact of wind direction on takeoff and landing. "He can probably move up a future instructor's arrival date."

"Probably."

She did wish she hadn't created this awkwardness between them. "Something occurred to me yesterday, while I was floating in and out of sleep. Do you have a minute?"

He hesitated, before saying, "Certainly."

Taking a piece of paper out of her pocket, she wandered over until she stood next to him behind his desk, aware of him stiffening slightly. She unfolded the map she'd carried in her flight suit the day before and

265

spread it out on his desk. "If we drew Great Britain and Europe over this map of Texas and the surrounding states, with Terrence representing London, and mark the approximate location of other critical cities — Paris, Berlin — it might help to orient the cadets so that when they return to England, they'll have a better idea of how to reach their destinations. The terrain will be different, of course, but the direction and distance will be the same, or at least close."

"Bloody brilliant," he said softly.

She looked over to find him studying her, not the map. He was so still, as though any movement would tilt them both precariously. "Thank you for the flowers."

Slowly, so slowly, he lifted his hand and brushed her hair back from the bandage still covering her head. "I wanted to beat him to a bloody pulp."

She knew he was referring to Doug Forester. She'd never considered herself barbaric, but she would have liked to have seen that, not only because he'd placed her in danger but had also put two cadets at risk. "Too bad you didn't have your ancestor's armor with you."

He grinned. She'd like to see more of those smiles.

Gently he placed his thumb on her cheek,

266

just below where she knew the bruise ended. "I didn't expect to have heart-stopping moments of terror over here."

"I'm sorry for what I said yesterday, about your interfering. I know you were just trying to help."

"No, you were right. You were clear from the beginning that you wanted no favoritism shown or perceived. I disregarded your wishes, perhaps in an effort to earn your favor."

She didn't know what to say to that. Suddenly, she was feeling light-headed and had an urge to rest her palm against his cheek and assure him that she cared for him — in ways she shouldn't.

As though he'd confessed too much, he dropped his hand and stepped back. "I'll discuss your suggestion with Smythson and Barstow. I think it has merit."

Just like that, he was the commanding officer and she was the LT operator. "I should go. Mama is probably at my house with a bowl of soup."

He nodded. "Do take care of yourself, fly-girl."

She smiled, grateful not to be Miss Lovelace any longer. Perhaps too grateful, because something was shifting between them, and it made her feel like she was headed for

another crash. Only this one she desperately
wanted.

CHAPTER 20

After she returned to her house, Jessie spent a good bit of the day sleeping off and on. She'd been right: her mother had been waiting on the front porch with a pot of soup in hand. Jessie tried to be patient with all her fussing and worrying, her fluffing up of pillows at her back on the couch and tucking in of a blanket despite the heat. They'd avoided any talk of the airfield or Jessie's future with it.

Luke came over in the late afternoon and shooed away her mom. He tossed the suffocating blanket on the lawn behind the house, and they stretched out on it, holding hands. Warmth filled her because he knew she needed to see the blue sky with its cotton candy–like wisps of white.

"How do you do it?" she asked. "How do you climb back on a bull after it's thrown you off?"

"Very carefully."

Laughing lightly, she turned her head to look at him and discovered him watching her. "That was a serious question."

He grinned. "That was a serious answer." He sobered, held her gaze. "If I don't climb back on, I'm never again going to experience that thrill of pitting myself against nature, against a beast."

For the first time, she felt he had a sense of what flying truly meant to her. She looked back up, knowing if she didn't climb back into a cockpit, she'd only ever have this view.

Wednesday, the aches were still there but beginning to diminish. She still cringed when she looked in a mirror and saw the black around her eye. She removed the bandage covering the stitched-up gash, so she didn't look quite so pitiful. Then she wandered around the house, restless and on edge, wasting precious moments when she could be making a difference, could be doing something worthwhile.

Thursday morning, she was standing in Barstow's office when he walked in, his eyes widening at the sight of her. "I know you need a replacement for Doug Forester. I want that position."

The man who had never smiled at her, whom she'd believed incapable of showing his teeth, actually smiled. "Good morning to you as well." He waved a hand toward a chair in front of his desk. "Please have a seat, Miss Lovelace."

Gingerly she eased down into it. As long as she moved slowly and smoothly, she wasn't likely to groan when her body objected to the abuse of activity.

"That's quite the shiner you have there," he said.

Rhonda had offered to cover it up with gobs of makeup, but Jessie saw it as a badge of honor, a symbol of survival. "It'll fade. About that position of flight —"

He held up a finger. "We'll get to that in a minute. I don't know if you've heard that Mr. Miles has given notice. Apparently, his wife objects to small-town life, so they're returning to Houston. We're in need of a navigation instructor."

"I don't want to teach in a classroom. I want to teach from a cockpit." If she couldn't do that, she'd rather continue as an LT operator.

"Point taken. However, I previously had an application from a Miss Annette Gibson" — he pulled a folder from a stack and set it before him — "who does want to teach in a classroom. I wondered if you knew anything about her."

He was asking her for advice? Was she still in the hospital, in a coma, dreaming? "We've participated in some of the same airshows. We took our instructor certification classes together. She'd be great." And Jessie wondered why in the hell he hadn't selected Annette to begin with.

"Good to know. Smythson and I will be interviewing her this afternoon."

The classroom aspect of the school fell under Peter's domain of ground school instruction. She wondered how much influence he'd had in this decision.

"As for Mr. Forester's replacement, I've asked one of the instructors who was to begin working when the next group of students arrives to report early. He'll begin Monday."

The anger rushed through her like a raging river. Would it have made any difference if she'd come to him Tuesday? If she'd sat here, waiting to catch him when he had a minute? "Damn you." Ignoring the discomfort, she surged to her feet. "I've taught men to fly. I have the skills and the experience." She hated to steal Jack's words but . . . "I'm a damn good pilot. Harness yourself into a cockpit with me and I'll prove it. There isn't a single thing you could ask me to do that I can't do. Test me, Barstow. I dare you."

"You're quite impassioned."

"Because I'm the best one for that job."

"Which is the reason you'll be taking over teaching Emerson's cadets."

Her thundering heart skipped a beat before beginning to slow. "I beg your pardon?"

"Emerson, as it turns out, is a drunkard, so he's been let go. Since you've already worked with his students — and they let it be known they much preferred you to him — I have decided to have you replace him."

"You could have said that from the start."

"To be honest, I only just now made the final decision. I've never had a woman issue a dare to me before. Or exhibit such tenaciousness. But be warned, I will be watching you closely."

"Watch me as closely as you like. You'll discover I'm the best decision you ever made."

CHAPTER 21

Friday, July 4, 1941

Jim Lovelace had been famous for his cookouts, which made glancing out the kitchen window at the large gathering of neighbors, friends, and cadets a little bittersweet. Jessie was grateful people were having a good time, but her father's absence was keenly felt. Turning back to her chore, she began slicing the tomatoes. "How did you talk Luke into manning the grill?"

Until this afternoon, he'd made it a point to avoid anything that involved the Brits.

Her mother looked up from the potato salad she'd just removed from the refrigerator and was setting on the counter. Anything that could be prepared ahead of time, she'd taken care of yesterday. Not that she'd needed to have made anything at all. Everyone who arrived brought some dish. The picnic table outside was already straining beneath the weight of all the food displayed

274

on it. "I simply asked. He's always willing to help out. Unclogged a sink for me last week."

Jessie wasn't certain why she was uncomfortable with her mother's calling on him for help. She heard the front screen door open and close, followed by light footsteps. Wearing flowing, pleated white pants and a sleeveless red shirt that hugged her in all the right places, Rhonda wandered in. Her thick red hair drifted in waves down to her shoulders, the sides swept up and pinned so an abundance of curls rested on top. She held aloft two bottles. "I brought wine! Is it okay if I open one now, Mrs. L.?"

"Absolutely."

Rhonda had spent almost as much time at Jessie's house as she had her own. She made herself at home and retrieved a corkscrew. "The Brits sure gave us a run for our money this morning on the baseball field."

She'd arranged a game between the instructors and cadets. Jessie had sat in the bleachers and watched, her gaze drifting more often than it should to the British dugout, where Royce was coaching. When he'd arrived at the field, he'd greeted her and congratulated her on her new position at the school, adding, "You got it on your own."

275

She wasn't going to doubt his word but also couldn't imagine he hadn't had some influence. "I think cricket is a little like baseball," she said now. "Involves a ball and a bat."

"I guess." After handing Jessie and her mother a glass of wine, Rhonda lifted her own. "To the Brits." She took a sip of the white wine. "I assume they're here."

"Yes," Jessie said. Everyone had gone off to tidy up after the hard-fought game and had arrived only a short time ago.

"Think I'll go say howdy."

"Would you mind carrying out the basket of condiments and set it on the picnic table?" Mama asked.

"Not at all."

"I'll join you for a bit," Jessie told her friend, sliding the sliced tomatoes onto a platter. "I'll take these out, Mama, and then I'll come back to help you."

"No need. I'm almost done."

Holding her glass of wine in one hand, the platter in the other, Jessie followed Rhonda out. "You have a button undone."

"I know. What's a little cleavage on a hot summer day?"

"Is that for Peter's benefit?"

"He's been practically ignoring me since the dance, and I'd like to find out why."

276

"Maybe he thinks you're too brazen."

"He hasn't seen brazen yet."

Jessie laughed. "Were you not listening when Royce said we weren't supposed to fraternize?"

"With the cadets. *He* is not a cadet. And I suspect he'll be teaching me a thing or two."

"You are incorrigible."

"But I provide great fodder for my dad's sermons." They set their items on the table. "Now I'm off to say hello to your guests of honor."

Jessie felt guilty for abandoning her mom, but then she saw three of her mom's dearest friends walking across the portion of the front lawn that was visible from the backyard. The cavalry had arrived and laughter would soon be floating out the window. Crossing with Rhonda to where Royce and Peter stood, beer bottles in hand, she couldn't miss Peter's appreciative gaze wandering down to Rhonda's bare toes — peeking through the tips of her sandals — and then traveling slowly back up to her hair. From an early age, Rhonda had always been able to snag a man's attention. Jessie just hoped in this instance, her friend didn't end up with a bruised heart.

"Miss Monroe," Peter said.

She rolled her eyes. "Oh, please, we don't

have to be so formal here, do we?"

"I don't want to set a bad example for the cadets."

"But, darlin', being bad is so much more fun — and today is for fun."

"The lads are certainly enjoying themselves," Royce said, no doubt hoping to cool down the awareness that was heating up between Rhonda and Peter.

Jessie had never known her friend to show so much interest in only one man. "I imagine Mama will be sending half this food home with y'all."

"Your mum's generosity seems to know no bounds." Royce's voice was filled with warmth, and Jessie suspected every cadet who spent a night here was going to fall in love with her mother.

"She does have a *homely* way about her."

He grinned slightly, and his cheeks pinkened. She did like that he occasionally blushed.

"Excuse me, fellas." Mr. Baker, short and rotund, worked desperately to make it appear his hair wasn't abandoning him by combing what little he had left over the ever-enlarging bald spot. Jessie had always liked him. He exuded the sort of joviality that made him perfect for dressing up as Santa for the Christmas festival held in the town square every December. "I'm Buddy Baker of Baker's Automobile Dealership. You might have noticed it at the opposite end of town, if you've been out that way yet."

He enthusiastically shook the Brits' hands as they introduced themselves.

"He's also the mayor," Jessie offered. "Played a major role in arranging for the airfield to be part of the British training program."

"We appreciate that, sir," Royce said.

"I believe when you help someone else, good comes your way. Which is what brought me over here. I've got a Mercury Eight, secondhand, that's been sitting on my lot for a while, and I'd like to let you fellas use it while you're here. Figure if you can drive a plane, you can drive a car. You ever driven a car?"

"I have, yes," Royce said. "Although I'll have to remember that you lot drive on the wrong side of the road."

Mr. Baker laughed good-naturedly, the big belly laugh that made him such a great Santa. "We drive on the right side, which is the right side, if you catch my meaning."

"I'll concede your point and thank you for the generosity, sir," Royce said.

"No thanks needed." He clapped Royce's

279

shoulder. "My son is serving in the navy on the USS *Arizona*, stationed at Pearl Harbor. I'm hoping he's finding the people near the naval base as friendly."

"How is David?" Jessie asked.

"Seeing the world. Having a grand time doing it. Says the islands are beautiful, like nothing he's ever seen. Bug's got a hankering to go over to Hawaii, maybe at Christmas, and surprise him. She saw an ad in the paper about the joys of vacationing there after traveling over on an ocean liner. She's looking into booking a spot, but we don't need to get into all that. You fellas just mosey on down to the dealership when you're ready, and I'll get you set up with that Mercury."

"We will, Mr. Baker. Thank you," Royce said.

When he was beyond earshot, Peter said in a low voice, "Bug?"

Rhonda shrugged. "It's the name his wife goes by. Have no idea why. Her name is Martha. She taught us English in high school.

"They're good people," Jessie assured them, as her gaze traveled over their guests, stopping at the sight of Luke, who was watching her more than he was the meat on the grill. "If y'all will excuse me."

Stopping by the table, she grabbed a brownie and headed toward the grill. When she reached it, she held up his favorite dessert before slipping it between his lips. A couple of chews later, he was gently tugging her into his arms and kissing her.

When he pulled back, he grinned. "You sure know the way to a fella's heart."

"I just know what you like to eat."

He winked. "You do that."

The heat in his eyes made her blush. It had been so long since they'd had any time alone to be intimate. The tension between them lately certainly hadn't helped the situation, but the incident earlier in the week, reinforcing how life could change in a heartbeat, made her consider that perhaps tonight she'd go home with him. She knew he could be tender enough and would be mindful of her remaining bruises.

"Jessie?"

She swung around. "Annette!" After getting the position yesterday, Annette had returned to Austin to pack up her things. The house Jessie shared with Rhonda had a third bedroom, and they'd offered it to the stunt pilot. "I'm so glad you could come back today and join us."

"I'm anxious to get settled in."

"We're going to have fun." She turned

back to the grill. "Luke, this is another flier. Annette. In the past, we've done airshows together, and she's just been hired to teach navigation to the cadets."

They shook hands.

"Jessie's told me about you," Annette said.

"All good, I hope."

"Pretty much."

"You like teaching?" he asked her.

She smiled brightly. "In a classroom, I love it. Not so much from a cockpit. I'm not comfortable giving the controls over to someone else, especially someone who is untried. Didn't realize it until the first time I did it. My heart was pounding so hard, I thought it might actually burst through my chest. I don't know how Jessie does it. I'm glad she's teaching them from a plane and not me."

"But she's not," Luke said. "That one day earlier in the week was an exception."

Annette was no good at hiding her surprise at his words. "Oh, I thought —"

Jessie had to spare her friend. "I am teaching from a cockpit." Guiltily, she looked at Luke. "Monday I'll start working as a flight instructor."

"Why didn't you say something?"

"I found out only yesterday, and I just haven't had a chance." Even though she'd spoken to him earlier when he'd first arrived and had helped him get set up at the grill, she had avoided telling him because she'd anticipated that he wouldn't be pleased. "Let me introduce Annette around and then I'll come back, and we can talk about it."

"Take these to the table?" He flipped beef patties onto a platter.

"Sure."

Once they were beyond hearing distance, Annette said, "I'm sorry for saying something I shouldn't have."

"You didn't know, and I *was* going to tell him."

"After what happened this week, I can understand his having some apprehension."

"It started long before that. But it's okay. We'll work it out. We always do."

Her mother had meandered outside, so she introduced Annette to her and then to Kitty, who'd begun inviting people to help themselves to the food. Jessie poured Annette a glass of wine and refilled hers before heading over to where Rhonda, Royce, and Peter were still chatting.

"I really appreciate the opportunity to work for the school," Annette said.

"It was a little preemptive planning," Peter said. "When America joins the war, more

283

women will have to take on roles at the school. A good many of the instructors are of fighting age. We decided it would behoove us to begin hiring a few more ladies."

"You think we'll go to war?" Annette asked.

"Don't you?"

"I was hoping this program would prevent it."

"Perhaps I have the wrong of it."

Jessie very much doubted it and suspected he did as well.

"We're not discussing the war today," Rhonda said. "We're just celebrating. Our independence."

They lifted their bottles or glasses and took a sip.

"Jessie surviving."

"Everyone surviving," she amended.

Another round of sips.

"Old friends and new ones," Rhonda said.

That was met with a "Hear! Hear!" followed by a guzzling of beer and long swallows of wine.

"Y'all help yourselves to the food," Jessie said, knowing she needed to pay the piper. "More is coming."

While they wandered off to the tables, she headed back to Luke, aware of his gaze on her the entire trek. She imagined many a gunslinger had taken his stance — feet spread, legs braced, eyes narrowed — before drawing a revolver. She really didn't want to have words with him now but knew she needed to diffuse his anger. When she was near enough, she said, "I was going to tell you. Later, after we weren't hosting so many people."

"Jess, I've been watching your company. Some of them can't be much older than Kitty. They should be in school, not preparing for war."

They were in school. Flight school. Not that he'd appreciate her saying that. "You didn't have a problem when David Baker joined the navy right out of high school. How old is he now? Nineteen?"

"That's different. We're not at war. He's not going to get killed. These boys here are — as soon as they get back to England."

"Some will, yes, and it hurts like hell to think about that, but if I don't train them someone else will."

"Then let someone else do it, so it's not on you."

"What if someone else doesn't train them as well as I do? Or someone dies because I wasn't the one who taught him? What if there's something I can give those I train that nobody else can? More confidence

285

or . . . I don't know . . . the ability to think more clearly in the cockpit or an instinct to know what to do in a tough situation?"

"When you hear that one of them has died, you're gonna wonder what you did wrong, what you didn't teach him. I know you, Jess, it's gonna eat at you."

"I have to do this, Luke. From the moment I learned about the plans for the airfield, I wanted to be a flight instructor. And I've had to prove myself every step of the way. Barstow is finally willing to give me a chance to make a really big difference and I'm not going to walk away from it."

"Because it ensures you're working more closely with *him*?"

As though he'd slapped her, she reeled back a step. "What are you talking about?"

"I don't like seeing my fiancée flirting with a Brit," he ground out.

"I'm not your fiancée."

His jaw clenched. "Jess, everyone in this town knows you're going to marry me. You want me to make it official, get down on one knee right now?"

When he made a move to lower himself, she grabbed his arm, stopping him. "No. Luke, this isn't the way to do it, not when you're angry. Not when we haven't given it a serious discussion or considered all the

286

ramifications."

"Jess, if we're not going to get married, what have we been doing all this time?"

What had they been doing? He'd made no secret of wanting to marry her, and she'd once believed being his wife was what she wanted most in the world. But that was before Jack left, her father died, and training the Brits had filled her life with a purpose beyond herself.

"Hey, Luke, do you have a minute?" Mr. Johnson asked.

Luke studied her for a heartbeat before turning to the banker. "Sure. What do you need?"

As he sought advice on the best pony to purchase for his grandson, Jessie was grateful for the reprieve and glanced around the crowded yard. She spotted Rhonda and Peter standing in a far corner, away from everyone else, eating, talking, laughing. Like butterflies, Kitty and Fran were fluttering from cadet to cadet, no doubt ensuring they had everything they needed. Not until she saw Royce and Annette sitting in separate lounge chairs, seemingly lost in a serious discussion, did she realize she'd been searching for him. Working at the school, training pilots, had nothing at all to do with him. She'd wanted it before she even knew he existed. And she certainly wasn't bothered by him and Annette striking up a friendship. The doubts she was experiencing regarding her relationship with Luke had begun long before — when they'd had their first argument after Jack made his stunning announcement. She'd gone to Luke for comfort and empathy, and instead she'd faced his anger and disappointment over her brother making "such a bone-headed decision."

She nearly jumped out of her skin when a hand landed on her shoulder. Mr. Johnson.

"Glad your accident wasn't any worse than it was," he said.

Accident. Last night she'd dreamed Forester had done it on purpose and the results had been far more catastrophic. She'd followed Royce's habit and gone outside for a while, just to breathe. Had contemplated taking up smoking. "We'll have the occasional mishap." Was Royce influencing her more than she realized? "It's part of training."

"You just be careful. Don't want to lose you. You know more about that airfield than anyone else in the area. Figure you'll help us convert it to an airport when the time comes." After patting her shoulder, he walked off and she turned to Luke, who was studying her intently. Would he want his wife taking on the complicated job of creating an airport?

"We should finish this discussion later when we don't have an audience," she said.

He nodded. "I do love you, Jess."

"I love you, too." But as she wrapped her arms around him, welcomed his coming around her, the words didn't erase her fear that her heart might become the first casualty of her own personal war.

CHAPTER 22

Kitty was beginning to think that if her country did go to war, she could become a spy. She was getting better at subterfuge, at ensuring Mama didn't get suspicious regarding how she truly felt about the cadets.

All afternoon, she wandered around the yard, talking briefly with one cadet after another, never lingering too long with anyone in particular, not even Will Wedgeworth, who was her favorite. Although when she did speak with him, she complimented him on how well he'd played during the baseball game. She and Fran had been in the bleachers, rooting for the Brits. Some of the kids they knew had teasingly called them traitors and turncoats. The game was just for fun after all, and she was pretty sure Rhonda, as pitcher, had gone easy on the competition with the balls she'd thrown their way.

When she crossed paths with Will, she'd

been mortified to admit she was barred from the dances until she was seventeen. Which was so stupid. A few months wasn't going to make much difference. But she didn't argue with Mama, because she was striving to give the appearance of being obedient, so her mom wouldn't watch her as closely.

Most of her mother's friends and their families had wandered home as night approached, although many of the cadets and some of Kitty's classmates had stayed for another round of burgers and to visit. Just before ten, her mother began herding everyone toward the town square. Because so many people were in the group, Kitty was able to slip in beside Will.

With a smile, he wrapped his hand around hers, not that anyone could see, with the shadows weaving in and out around them, the streetlights not able to hold all the darkness at bay. Having never held a boy's hand in so intimate a setting, she'd had no idea a touch could coil itself around her heart. She reminded herself that he would leave in November after he earned his wings, that she was a momentary distraction from war.

The municipal band was set up in the large gazebo, where the mayor was droning on about the country's independence. It seemed particularly profound this year, in light of their visitors, though the townsfolk were doing everything to make them feel welcome. When they'd arrived at the town square, she'd noticed that between the two benches that faced Main Street had been added a sign that read, GIVE A BRIT A RIDE TO DALLAS. Any cadet wanting to go into Dallas during their time off just had to wait on the bench and eventually someone would give them a ride.

"Do you have anything like what we did today in England?" Kitty asked quietly.

Will grinned. He had the best grin. "We don't celebrate giving the Yanks their freedom, but we have fetes and festivals. Jugglers and games, that sort of thing."

"I bet you'd like our state fair. Lots of games there. And rides. And food. So much to see. We always go for my birthday."

His grin grew even brighter. "When in October is your birthday?"

"The ninth. When is your birthday?"

"Not until May."

"Oh, I wish I hadn't missed it." He wouldn't be here next May, but she would send him a card.

They came to a stop beside one of the large oak trees. It was so crowded. Glancing around, she couldn't see her mother.

The mayor finally finished talking and a countdown began.

"What's happening?" Will asked.

"The streetlights will be turned off and the fireworks are going to start."

". . . Three, two, one!"

The town square went dark. A few seconds later, a whistle sounded before a boom cracked through the air, followed by a burst of red, white, and blue streaming light erupting like an unfurling flower. Normally, Kitty loved watching the fireworks, but she couldn't seem to stop looking at Will's shadowy silhouette. His hand closed around her waist, and he drew her nearer to the tree. She wondered if he could tell that her breath was barely coming in and out of her chest. She was afraid if she moved too fast or did anything abruptly, this moment would dissolve like the sparkles in the black sky. Cradling her face, he leaned in slowly, as though afraid of the same thing.

Then his lips were touching hers, and she knew that if she lived to be a hundred, she'd never forget this night, his kiss.

CHAPTER 23

Jessie and Luke started out following the crowd her mother was leading toward the town square, but when they reached her street, she veered off toward the house she was renting. During the late afternoon, she'd helped Annette get settled in before they'd both returned to the backyard for another round of food. Now the place was dark except for the porch light.

"Do you want to come in?" she asked.

"No."

His tone contained a resignation that made her heart hurt and her eyes sting. She was glad they weren't going inside, where the light would be brighter. They'd barely spoken, even when they'd sat together in the early evening. A chasm was developing between them that she didn't know how to bridge without giving up what she wanted.

"I know you don't agree with what I'm doing, Luke." She thought about the times, at the end of a day, when she would visit with a few cadets. Music from the jukebox floated out of the recreation hall windows. Many of the young men sat in rockers or chairs on the screened-in porch, enjoying what little breeze came through. Sometimes, she would stand at the edge of the field and watch them kicking a ball around. Football, they called it. Wasn't like any football she'd ever seen. Often it hurt to watch them. Laughing, playfully shoving one another. Their smiles were bright, as though they hadn't a care in the world. Visiting with them today, she'd felt at a crossroads, on the cusp of abandoning them if she reconciled with Luke. "I can't turn my back on these men, the school, what we can accomplish here. Either be supportive or walk away."

While he studied her, she was surprised to discover she was holding her breath until her chest ached. Partly because she wasn't convinced that she didn't want him to walk away. She was weary of his not understanding, of his not trying to understand. He was set in his ways and beliefs. She was tired of being on edge, of wondering what her stubborn cowboy might find fault with next.

"Damn it, Jess. You're really going to choose them over me?"

"It's not a matter of choosing. Jack told me he didn't choose to go to England. It was something he *had* to do. I didn't truly understand what he was trying to tell me. But now I do. I couldn't live with myself, wouldn't be the person you believe me to be, if I turned away from helping."

"I'd never forgive you if you died doing this, Jess. Because you don't have to do it."

How could she make him fully comprehend that she did? Was he not listening to what she was saying?

"Think we need to take a break for a while," he said. "I need to figure some shit out."

Oh, it hurt, worse than she'd expected. She could barely draw in breath. "That's probably a good idea."

He released a harsh curse beneath his breath, as though he'd been hoping his words would make her see sense. He seemed to be waiting for her to apologize, but she wasn't going to apologize for being who she was or believing in what she was doing.

"Night, Jess."

And yet what she heard was "Goodbye."

He started striding away. She almost ran after him, almost stopped him, but it wasn't fair to him when she couldn't be what he wanted, what he needed.

Then a bang sounded, a bang that came close to shattering her world, because the following display of colorful sparks lightened the shadows around him, this man who had been such a crucial part of her life for so long. No, she'd been part of his. She wasn't certain he'd ever truly been part of hers.

She dropped down on the porch steps, an ache in her chest threatening to crush her, and let the tears fall.

July 22, 1941

Dear Jess,

Days are running together. Another funeral. Another coffin draped in both an American and a British flag. Chuck Robinson of Georgia could make us laugh. I'm going to miss him. Hate how for a few hours afterward I stop thinking I'm invincible.

But then when I'm back in the air, I feel like Dad is up there watching over me. A calm settles in. Maybe you feel it, too. We're not alone up there.

Although maybe I'm just going crazy. Not enough sleep. We're being scrambled at least once a day. After I'm back from a sortie, I'm too jumpy to settle down.

Wish you were here to share a pint. Glad to know you're safeguarding Dad's bourbon. We'll finish it off when I get home. And I will get home.

Love,
Jack

P.S. Hug Trixie extra hard for me.

CHAPTER 24

Friday, August 15, 1941

Waiting for her next student, Jessie stood off to the side, near where the men were huddled, some sitting on a long bench, others crouched or sprawled on the grass. While few instructors had yet to openly accept her, she sensed the distrust or hostility had lessened a bit. But she really didn't care about them. She cared only about her students. Working with them these past six weeks had been the most rewarding experience of her life.

One morning it had been raining. The instructors and cadets had been huddled in one of the hangars watching the light sprinkling of droplets fall, waiting for the weather to clear, because they weren't in the habit of flying when it rained. Royce had walked in and inhaled deeply. "Smells like England. Why are you lot not flying? Waiting for me to bring you your brollies?"

So they'd gone up — after her student had explained that Royce had been referring to umbrellas. It certainly hadn't been one of her more pleasant outings, but based upon what she'd heard of English weather, they didn't have as many dry days as they did in Texas, so it was probably a good idea for the cadets to get a taste of a damper experience. Most of the instructors had grumbled, while the cadets had seemed to take it all in stride.

Now, the laughter and excitement of the cadets reached her before they did. Their enthusiasm was contagious. They'd been so reserved, serious, and quiet when they'd first arrived. Now they were more relaxed.

One of the trainees broke off from the group and headed toward her. He was all freckles, bright red hair, and twinkling hazel eyes. And twenty. Her oldest student. She wanted to make sure he added another sixty years to that number. "Good afternoon, Mr. Brightwell."

"Miss Lovelace."

They began walking toward the plane. "Looking forward to your open post next week?" They were finishing up their ten weeks of primary training. The students would get a week of leave and then they'd move to the Vultee and begin their five weeks of basic training.

"Yes, ma'am. Some mates and I are going to hitch a ride to California."

"Sounds like fun, but that's quite the trek."

"Yes, ma'am, but we're certain we can do it."

She handed him a map. "That's our circuit for today. You'll take her up and fly her. Once we get to this area" — she pointed on the map — "where it's just prairie, we'll practice some aerobatics." They'd been doing rolls for only a few days. They'd get into more advanced maneuvers during their next phase of training.

They reached the Stearman. He began his preflight inspection without her having to tell him. She liked that he possessed confidence and needed minimal instruction. He was a leader and would go far, if he could avoid getting blown out of the sky.

After climbing aboard, with her in the front, he taxied into position and soon they were soaring through the sky, heading toward their destination. He kept the plane level, moving at a stable rate. From the beginning, she'd sensed that he had an affinity for flying and a steady hand.

"All right, Mr. Brightwell. Execute a slow roll." She lowered her gaze to the instrument panel to better judge that he was keeping the plane level, making slight smooth corrections, as it completed a circle that would see it on its side, upside down, and back around until it was once again right side up. But when they were fully inverted, the roll got sloppy and the nose dropped.

"Mr. Brightwell, lift the nose," she ordered briskly. When he failed to comply, she stated calmly but with authority, "My control."

Fighting against the fall he'd placed them in, she leveled out and completed the roll, but once she was upright, the nose unexpectedly dipped toward the ground as though they'd lost some weight in the rear. Reducing power, she pulled back gently on the stick to bring the aircraft out of the dive. When she was once again level, she glanced back over her shoulder and discovered she was alone. Completely alone. Her cadet was gone.

Damn it!

Banking to the right, she caught sight of Brightwell hanging from a parachute as it slowly returned him to earth. Why the hell had he bailed?

She returned to the airfield and sent someone out to pick him up.

"He forgot to secure his harness," Jessie told

the girls that night as they were gathered in the kitchen preparing a meal, "and just tumbled out when we were upside down."

"Bet he won't make that mistake again," Annette said.

"I probably should have checked with him to make sure he was strapped in tight, but after all this time, I really didn't think it was needed."

"It shouldn't have been. What if he'd been flying solo and decided to do some acrobatics on his own? It would have been a disaster." Rummaging through the utensils in the kitchen drawer, she asked, "Do we have a potato peeler?"

Finished checking on the roast, Rhonda closed the oven door. "I don't think so. Add it to the list."

Jessie wrote it on a pad of paper, beneath *whisk*. It seemed every time they cooked a meal, they discovered something that they didn't have on hand. Tonight's meal was a bit more elaborate. They were having a few guests. The official reason behind it was to welcome the two Brits who had arrived this week: the armament sergeant, Bran Finnegan, who would be adding gun cameras to the advanced trainers — so the cadets could grow accustomed to flying and firing a weapon at the same time — and the administrative officer, Mark Powell. The Brits had discovered more than two officers were required to keep everything running smoothly.

"We could just bake the potatoes," Rhonda suggested.

"We're having gravy. They have to be mashed."

"Guess I should have taken homemaking in school," Rhonda said.

Jessie returned to slicing up the tomatoes for the salad. "I can't see you as a home-maker."

Rhonda laughed and picked up her wine-glass. "You have a point. That's the reason I'm in charge of the roast. I just popped it into the oven once we got home from work and I was done. It's almost ready."

Annette stopped peeling the potatoes with a knife and glanced over her shoulder. "Tell me you did season it."

Rhonda simply stared at her.

Annette shook her head. "You're hopeless. I think you only pretend ignorance, so we'll chase you off and not let you help. How are you going to manage when you have your own home? You'll be as useless as that cadet today."

"I intend to marry a rich man and have servants."

"Is Peter rich?"

Rhonda leaned her backside against the counter and took a slow sip of her white wine. "I think he's well off, not that he's ever really mentioned it. Besides, doesn't everyone in England have servants?"

"Well, the servants don't," Jessie said. She furrowed her brow. "But you're not thinking you'll marry him."

"Of course not. We're just having fun. Letting off steam. You know." She dropped her head back. "I'm tired. We probably should have done this tomorrow. Now that we have a hundred students, I'm running that Link all day."

"The next fifty arrive Sunday," Jessie reminded her. "We'll be even busier then."

"Planning anything for Friday night is a mistake," Annette said. "I just want to put my feet up and slowly sip a martini."

"There's another dance tomorrow night," Rhonda said, "and I certainly don't want to miss that."

The Saturday night dances had become a regular event, although Jessie hadn't danced with Royce since that first time. They'd visit at the Legion Hall. A couple of times, she caught up with him outside, while he was smoking his cigarette. Those were her favorite moments, because she felt more

305

uninhibited, less likely to be seen as striving to garner a favor, although what favor could he bestow now that she was a flight instructor? Barstow, much to her shock, had even complimented her recently, assured her she was doing a good job. While Geoffrey Moreland had returned to England after deciding flying wasn't for him, she was relatively certain her four students were going to pass their review tomorrow — even Mr. Brightwell, as long as he remembered to secure his harness. "Salad is done. I'll make some martinis."

"None for me," Rhonda said. "I'm going to stick with wine."

Jessie went into the living room, where Rhonda had set up a table with various liquors. The assortment had grown as her friend spent more time with the RAF officer, who apparently enjoyed a variety of beverages.

She had just dropped olives into the finished martinis when Annette joined her. "I figured you and Luke would be back together by now."

They hadn't seen or spoken to each other since the figurative and literal fireworks. At first, she'd missed him with an almost unbearable ache, but it had begun to dim. While she still loved him, the life he was of-

306

fering her wasn't one she wanted. She wasn't willing to compromise her dreams to create an illusion of a happy marriage. "I guess he's still working things out." She handed Annette one of the martinis.

"Thanks." She took a sip. "Oh, that's good." She licked her lips. "You ever think about what's waiting for these fellas when they get home?"

"I try not to."

"Yes, me, too, but it just seems odd sometimes, to laugh and drink and dance and act like everything is okay."

"Maybe that's how you get through it — you have moments where you can forget what's going on."

A knock sounded on the door. "I'll get it." Annette set her glass down and called out, "They're here!"

Jessie experienced a momentary flash of guilt, because if she was honest with herself, she was anticipating having some time with Royce that didn't involve discussions regarding how to improve the training methods. When they saw each other at the school, they were both incredibly careful not to let conversations stray into any personal territory, and for her, it was becoming more difficult to maintain the distance when she had a desire to know him better. Even when they crossed paths at the dances, they avoided anything intimate.

Rhonda rushed in just as Annette opened the door to their guests. Peter, Bran, and Mark were each holding a different bottle of spirits. As Jessie got close enough to welcome them, she saw gin, rum, and whiskey. Rhonda greeted Peter with a quick kiss on the mouth before starting to collect their contributions to the dinner.

"Isn't Royce coming?" Jessie asked, after the door was closed and everyone was settling in.

Peter's solemn expression of deep sorrow told her bad news was coming before he spoke. "Unfortunately, he received a cable earlier with the devastating news that his brother was killed. We offered to stay with him, but he wanted some time alone. Which I can certainly understand. I don't think we ever grow accustomed to the agony of losing someone we loved. Sometimes we have to come to grips with it in solitude."

Unaware that he even had a brother, Jessie stared at Peter in stunned silence, while Rhonda hugged him as though the loss had been his. "How horrible. Was he a pilot?"

"Yes, followed his older brother's lead. Why don't we open the whiskey and toast him?"

"Y'all go ahead," Jessie said. "I'm going . . . I'm going to check on Royce. If I'm not back when dinner is ready, start without me."

She didn't bother with her key, purse, or anything, simply headed out into the twilight. It was still hot, but she was chilled to the bone and wrapped her arms around herself as tightly as she wanted to wrap them around Royce. How could they have left him in his grief? And yet, she knew him well enough to know he wouldn't have wanted plans changed on his account.

A slight breeze was rustling the leaves in the trees, a sound she usually found calming, but tonight it seemed mournful. She crossed over Walnut and onto Pecan. Lights spilled faintly out of windows. It was nearly eight — they'd decided on a later dinner to allow time to freshen up and prepare the meal. Children had already been called in. Somewhere a cat screeched and a dog barked. Everywhere, everything and everyone carried on with their usual routines as though nothing had changed.

Yet inside her, something had. She knew he'd lost his fiancée to the war, but that had happened before she knew him. While it hadn't lessened the sorrow she'd felt for him, this latest loss felt like it affected her as well, because he had to be hurting, now at this moment, intensely, horribly. She didn't want him to be alone.

When she reached his house, she couldn't see any illumination coming from inside. Only the porch light was on. She wondered if he was even there. Maybe he'd gone out for a drink or to the airfield. The car was in the drive, so wherever he'd gone, he'd walked. Or perhaps he simply preferred to sit in the dark.

She went up the two steps to the porch and knocked on the door. Waited. Glanced around. Knocked again, a little bit louder, wondering if he'd welcome the intrusion. Perhaps she should just leave him alone, and yet she didn't think she was capable of walking away.

A faint glow suddenly appeared in the window, and a few seconds later the door opened. Because the light was behind him, she couldn't see his face clearly but didn't need to in order to know he was ravaged with grief. "May I come in?"

He hesitated before shoving on the screen door and turning his body sideways so she could slip past him. The curtains were drawn, the room lost to shadows. Light was coming from the hallway. He'd probably been in his bedroom. Unlike their living

310

room, which she and her roommates had adorned with an assortment of gewgaws, lamps, shelves, and rugs, this one appeared plain in silhouette, with only a couch and a couple of chairs. She heard the slapping of the screen door as it fell back into place, the click of the door being pushed shut.

Turning, she faced him. She considered saying she was sorry, but the words seemed trite, came nowhere near expressing how much she ached for him. So she simply stepped forward and wrapped Royce in a snug embrace. She felt the shuddering in his chest as his arms came around her and he held on tightly, as though he'd been lost in a turbulent sea and had finally found a life raft. She heard his hard swallow.

"You don't have to be strong," she whispered.

Another harsh shuddering as they just stood there wound around each other. She could feel him trembling, and tears welled in her eyes. After what seemed an eternity, he released his hold on her, took her hand, and led her over to the couch. He didn't have his cane; his limp was less pronounced. She eased down onto the couch. When he sat at the other end, she scooted over and nestled against him. At the moment, she didn't care about impropriety or all his rules about how Brits and Yanks shouldn't get involved with each other. She cared only about offering comfort and was grateful when his arm came around her, signaling he welcomed her nearness. "Tell me about him."

With her head resting in the nook of his shoulder, she was keenly aware of the deep breath he took, felt the rise and fall of his chest, as he prepared to speak about his brother.

"His name is Edward. Four years my junior, but still my ever-faithful shadow. He followed in my footsteps: to Oxford, to the law, to the RAF. He was a flight lieutenant. Flew a Spitfire. He was with a squadron in Kent. I don't know the details other than he had engaged the enemy. I suppose the details don't matter. You're missing your dinner."

She wondered if his mention of dinner had been an attempt to distance himself from the hurt, to remind himself that life went on for others. "I'd rather be here. Do you have other siblings?" It suddenly seemed important to know everything about him.

"No. It'll be hard on my parents. Even when you know the risks, it's still unexpected when it happens. Christ, I hate not being there for them."

"At least they're not having to worry about you."

"I told you that first night, they always worry. I've heard war is hardest on those who keep the home fires burning while waiting for word. Recently I've discovered it's remarkably true. I feel like if I'd been over there . . . I could have saved him. Which is ridiculous. We weren't even in the same squadron. But I'm so damned impotent over here."

Didn't she feel the same about Jack? Hadn't she resented that he'd gone over without her, as though if they'd been together, she could protect him? "It's important, what you're doing. It'll make a difference."

"Will it? Or am I simply helping to add to the carnage?"

Suddenly, he was gone from her, on his feet, standing a short distance away. "I'm not . . . I'm not fit for company tonight. You should leave."

Bringing her knees up, she wrapped her arms around her legs. "I didn't come for polite conversation. You can rant, rave, and throw things around. You're not going to scare me off. If you want to get rid of me, you'll have to pick me up and toss me out."

313

His scoff was harsh, but the slimmest thread of amusement was woven in it. "You're a stubborn wench."

"I tend to be. But I care about you too much to have you go through this alone. If it had been Jack . . . I'd be devastated. I can't help but believe you have to be feeling the same way."

"If one of us had to die in this bloody war, I wish it had been me." His voice was rough and tortured.

She shot up and wound her arms tightly around him. Once again, he held her close, but this time a sob broke free and she felt his tears cooling against her cheek, his bristled jaw scraping her chin. He was so far away from those he loved, and those who loved him. It had to make the moment all the worse.

Then his mouth slid onto hers, and she did what she knew she shouldn't, she welcomed him, tasting the salt of his tears, and something far richer, more seductive. Him.

There was power in the kiss, but also heartbreak. For his loss, for their loss, for what could never be, should never be. They'd been dancing around this attraction, maybe from the beginning, during late-night talks and the occasional unexpected glimpse into the other, a vulnerability revealed and quickly shuttered.

He was heat and fire and hunger. She was kindling ready to burn . . . for him, for this. His hands traveled up and down her back, pressing her closer, flattening her against him. She took pleasure from rubbing his shoulders, brushing her fingers along his neck and into his hair.

He drew back. "I've wanted to do that for far too long. Still, I shouldn't have."

She cradled his strong jaw. "Did you sense me objecting?"

He gave a little huff of a laugh. "No, but I don't know how long I'll be here."

"Until the war is over, you'll be training the cadets." Safe. Out of harm's way. Beyond reach of the Luftwaffe.

"Not necessarily. The future, the world, is all too uncertain. And you . . . well, you have someone else."

Only she didn't. Luke's silence was as profound as his words had been that night. She hadn't advertised their breakup, needing her own time to heal, to make certain she was traveling the right path for her. Right now wasn't the moment to decide what her relationship with Royce should be, or if they even had a future. She was still sorting out her feelings for Luke, and tonight too many raw emotions were battering Royce. Taking his hand, she drew him down beside her on the couch. "You can share memories with me or we'll sit here in silence."

"You would have liked him. He would have liked you." He pressed a kiss to her brow. She snuggled in closer, wishing she'd never have to leave, that the world would never intrude.

August 20, 1941

Dearest Mama, Jess, and Kitty Kat,

I guess all those interviews we did and the stories about the Eagles paid off, because we have so many Americans over here now that they've created another squadron. Yours truly will lead it.

Please don't worry about me. I'm where I want to be, doing exactly what I want to do. What I have to do. I couldn't live with myself if I'd just sat back and watched what was happening over here. I'm proud of what I'm doing.

All my love,
Squadron Leader Jack Lovelace, RAF

P.S. Give Trixie extra treats to celebrate my promotion.

CHAPTER 25

Monday, October 6, 1941

Kitty was in love. Not that she'd told her family. They thought she was too young, but it was only because they viewed her as the *baby*. Her mother had married at nineteen, so how in the heck could a couple of years make a difference?

Every time she saw Will, her heart swelled to bursting. He was so interesting. He had lived a lifetime during his eighteen years, and she desperately wanted to return to England with him when he left in a little over a month. However, her mother would never approve of her leaving before she graduated. And Will wasn't too keen on her going there anyway.

"It's not safe right now, Kitty. It'd break my heart if anything happened to you." He softened the words with a tender kiss, but it didn't seem fair that he had to go where it wasn't safe, and she couldn't follow.

318

They'd agreed to make the most of his time over here. He'd even stayed in town during his open post week and was waiting for her outside the school building each afternoon when she finished with her classes. He'd walk her home. Sometimes along the way he'd pull her behind a tree and kiss her. The other girls thought Will was smashing — she'd begun using some of the words he did because they were more fun — and would blush, giggle, or sigh whenever they saw him. She did wish he could wear his uniform in town, so they could see how truly handsome he was.

Pulling her mother's car into a parking spot at the airfield, she grabbed the satchel dedicated to her journalistic endeavors, got out, and began strolling toward the recreation hall, where several cadets were sitting in the rockers on the screened-in porch.

It was edging toward seven and the sun was slowly disappearing over the horizon. It would be dark soon when Will escorted her back to the car and kissed her.

"Kitty?"

Fighting down her groan, she staggered to a stop, forced a bright smile, and faced the hangar her sister had apparently just come out of. "Hi."

"What are you doing here?"

319

"I'm working on an article for the school paper. 'Our British Friends.' Or something like that, maybe a little catchier."

Jessie crinkled her brow. "Didn't you already write one?"

"That was about the officers. This one will focus on the cadets. I might even do one on the instructors. Would you let me interview you if I did?"

"Sure." Jessie's smile was a little crooked, like maybe she didn't quite trust Kitty's reasons for coming to the airfield. Once school had started in September, Mama had finally relented and allowed Kitty to start attending the dances, but she made certain to dance with several cadets so no one would suspect that she was serious about Will. Especially because Mama had begun going to help at the refreshment table, although Kitty knew the truth: she was there to make sure Kitty didn't get too close to anyone. She was pretty sure Jessie hadn't guessed the truth either. Standing here now, she certainly didn't want her older sister trying to figure things out.

"I'm actually glad I ran into you," Kitty said as innocently as she could. "You know how we always go to the state fair as part of my birthday celebration? I was thinking we could take a busload of cadets. Maybe we could even get some of the girls from my class to go. Make it more fun for our guests."

Her sister's narrowing eyes weren't a good sign. "I thought we were going to go this Saturday. That doesn't give us much time to arrange a field trip."

"It's only Monday. I could post a sign-up sheet before I leave this evening. I could ask the principal to make an announcement at school. We have plenty of time to make it happen."

"You'd have to check with Royce."

"I'll find him. If you think it's a good idea."

She shrugged. "Give them something different to do, I guess. Let me know what you need from me. I'm sure Rhonda and Annette will help out as well."

"Smashing." She grimaced. "I mean great." She held up her satchel. "I need to get my interviews done."

As she neared the recreation hall, she could hear Frank Sinatra crooning "Blue Skies." Will had never seen a jukebox before he came here. She could also hear an occasional clack as balls hit one another on the pool table. As usual, the windows were open and all the sounds, along with some light, escaped into the evening.

Opening the screen door, she stepped

onto the porch. Three cadets stood up from their rockers.

"Good evening, Kitty," they said in unison.

She grinned broadly. "Hi. Does anyone know where I might find the wing commander?"

"He's actually inside the rec," one said.

As though she'd summoned him, he opened the door and came outside. "Hello, Kitty."

"I was wondering if I could talk to you for a minute about an idea I had."

"Certainly. Will here suffice or is more privacy warranted?"

"Here is fine."

He led her to the corner of the porch so they were out of the way of anyone who might want to enter or leave. "What did you need to discuss?"

"I wanted to ask if it would be okay to arrange a field trip for some of the cadets to attend the state fair this Saturday." She explained what she had in mind.

"A couple of the lads attended last Sunday. They were quite impressed. I've no objection to your arranging an outing."

"Wonderful. I'll bring some information out tomorrow."

"I appreciate all your efforts on behalf of

the cadets."

"I like helping out."

He left her then, and she approached the cadet who'd told her where she'd find Royce. "Would you mind if I interviewed you for an article?"

"Not at all."

The other two students had moved elsewhere, so she sat in the rocker beside him. She'd danced with him a couple of times. His name was Mick Turner. "So, Mick —"

"You remembered my name."

She smiled. "I did, yes." She'd never forget a single one of them. Their smiles. The way they laughed. And especially the way they danced. "What do you like most about Texas so far?"

He ducked his head, his grin going up higher on one side. "The girls. They've all been so nice. And they're freer with their kisses here than the birds back home."

She wrote down what he said but wasn't going to put the bit about kissing in her article, because she might get some of the girls in trouble. "What's different than you expected it to be?"

"How big everything is. Your homes, your kitchens especially. Me mum would wear herself out moving about in the ones I've seen when I've stayed with some families.

How kind everyone is. I didn't think we'd be welcomed really, America not coming to fight with us. I thought we'd be ignored, like your daft cousin that you never look at because you don't want him coming over and talking to you. But you've all been first rate."

"Do you think you'll come back after the war?"

"I'd like to. It's sort of me second home now, innit?"

"What do you miss most about England?"

"The tea. Yours is rubbish."

She laughed, because Will had told her the same thing. He was getting used to iced tea, but only if it had a lot of sugar in it. "What will you miss when you return home?"

"The quiet. You can hear the crickets chirping and the breeze blowing. Some nights, I imagine I can hear the stars coming out." Suddenly he leaned toward her. "Won't miss the bloody snakes, though. One was in the cockpit the other morning."

"I heard about that. It was just a garter snake. It's not poisonous. It wouldn't hurt you."

"I didn't know that, did I? Didn't see it until we were about to take off. If I hadn't screamed bloody murder —"

"You shouldn't be embarrassed. Most people scream."

"Your sister just climbed onto the wing, reached down, plucked it up, and tossed it aside like she was Tarzan."

"She's not afraid of much. Besides, she knew what kind it was and that it wasn't dangerous."

"I felt deuced silly. But I do look now . . . everywhere." He leaned back. "Your sister is a good pilot. Good instructor. Has a lot of patience. Based on a few of the stories I've heard, some of the instructors aren't as . . . caring."

"You should tell the wing commander about the ones who aren't as good."

"Not our place to complain. We just need to get the job done and get back."

Wanting to shake off the reminder that they were here temporarily, she closed her notebook. "You've been really helpful. Thank you. Since it's gotten so dark out here, would it be okay if we went inside, and I took a photo of you in your uniform?"

"If you like."

She was very happy to see Will was playing cards with some fellas. After she went around the room taking some candid shots of the cadets engaged in various activities, he helped her arrange some group photos.

They'd make a nice spread for an additional article to run in the *Tribune*. The Brits at play. Perhaps she'd return another time to take photos of them at work: in the classroom and around planes. It somehow seemed important to document their time here.

When she was finished, Will took her hand and walked her outside. It was full-on dark except for the lights from the buildings. When they got nearer to the parking area, Will pulled her around behind the most distant hangar. With her back against the wall, she dropped her satchel and wound her arms around his neck as his mouth landed on hers. Their kisses had changed since that first one beneath the fireworks. They were bolder, hungrier.

He tugged her shirt from her skirt, slipped his hand beneath it, and cradled her breast over her bra. She grew so hot, she thought she'd stepped back into the middle of summer.

He trailed his mouth along her throat, beneath her chin to her ear. "I'm mad about you, Kitty."

"Me, too." She laughed. "Mad about you, I mean."

"Can I put my hand beneath your bra?"

She nodded. It was a tight fit, but she

loved the way his rough palm felt against her skin. She thought her knees might buckle.

"Does that feel nice?" he asked.

"Yes."

"I want to touch all of you, every inch."

She wanted that, too, but if her mother found out, she'd be grounded for life. Besides, it scared her a little, the thought of taking the plunge and not being a good girl anymore. "I'm not ready for that, Will."

He leaned away. She wished some light was here so she could see his eyes. "That's all right." Then he was kissing her again. He was the very best kisser in the entire world.

Sliding his hand out from beneath her shirt, he tucked her shirtwaist back in and picked up her bag. "They'll be calling us to barracks soon."

"We'll be going to the fair Saturday."

He grinned. "Can't wait."

After walking her to the car, he gave her another kiss before racing back to the recreation hall. It hurt knowing that they had only five more weeks together. She wanted to make sure every minute counted.

October 9, 1941

Dear Kitty Kat,

They're keeping us busy over here and we Americans are proving ourselves. Actually impressing a few. The military higher-ups have come by to let us know we're "putting on a jolly good show." Noël Coward even dropped by. He's an actor and playwright who is also working for the war office. I asked him to sign a piece of paper for you. He obliged. I enclosed it for your scrapbook. Maybe someday it'll be worth something.

Thinking of you today. Hope you had a happy birthday.

Love,
Brother

P.S. Give Trixie a slice of cake for me.

CHAPTER 26

State Fair of Texas
Saturday, October 11, 1941

Standing with Rhonda near the fauna-lined rectangular lagoon inside the entrance to Fair Park, Jessie couldn't help but be impressed with the field trip Kitty had arranged, with some assistance. Mrs. Johnson had hired a bus to bring the cadets. Any girls who wanted to escort the cadets around had driven themselves, a long line of cars resembling a parade making the trip to the Dallas fairgrounds. Jessie, Rhonda, Kitty, and Fran had led the way in Rhonda's car.

After organizing several groups and sending them on their way, with about a dozen cadets and girls remaining, Kitty, who'd always enjoyed dressing up in a blouse, vest, boots, and cowgirl hat for the fair, approached Jessie. "We'll meet you back here at eleven."

"Oh, I'm tagging along with you."

Kitty's eyes widened in horror. "Why? You like to look at all the exhibits, and some are so boring."

"They're educational."

Kitty rolled her eyes. "We just want to go to the midway. I'm seventeen now. I don't need a chaperone."

Jessie relented, not that she'd ever planned to accompany them. She'd only been teasing. "So grown up. Go on then."

They were dashing off before she could say another word.

"Kitty sure likes spending time with the cadets," Rhonda said quietly. Like Jessie and most of the women here, she was wearing a skirt and heels.

"I think the girls are intrigued by them."

"Can't blame them for that." She smiled brightly as Peter and Royce joined them. Like the cadets, they were wearing their suits. Most men were despite the warm day, which promised to grow hotter. "Looks like you two are stuck with us."

"I absolutely have no objections," Peter said.

"Let's start with the exhibits, shall we?"

He slipped his arm around her waist. "Lead the way."

With a laugh, she started doing just that. Jessie and Royce fell into step behind them.

He hadn't brought his cane but its absence wasn't slowing him down. He made a point to keep distance between them so they wouldn't touch, but the wide pathways were crowded and sometimes he did accidently bump into her when he tried to avoid ramming into someone else. Since the night they'd kissed, they had avoided being alone, although they'd found opportunities to talk at the airfield. Occasionally he and the other British staff came to her house for dinner or drinks — whichever Rhonda arranged. He'd enjoyed a Sunday dinner at her mother's. Their conversations never got personal, and yet she couldn't help but feel that some intimate communication was taking place in the way she often noticed him studying her. Certainly, for her part, she found it difficult not to take note of the small things: the appreciation he expressed toward her mother, the gentleness he showed Kitty, the attention he gave Trixie. That without anything being said, he'd known they'd tour the fair together.

Rhonda led them into an exhibition of paintings by Texas artists. They wandered slowly along. Jessie stopped in front of a painting of a dappled blue field. "Those are bluebonnets, the state flower. They fill the fields in March and April. You'll see them in

331

the spring."

"You've lost your optimism that we're going to be here only a short while." A touch of sadness laced his words. "There was a time when you would have said 'if you're still here.'"

Perhaps she had become a bit less optimistic, but she also wasn't quite ready for him to leave, wanted to explore whatever was trying to develop between them, what they were striving to push away. "I thought we might avoid discussing the war today."

"That's a jolly good idea. I look forward to a picnic among the bluebonnets."

She wondered if that picnic might include her. She glanced around. "We seem to have lost Rhonda and Peter." She wasn't surprised, had expected it to happen at some point, just not this quickly. "Maybe if we mosey on, we'll run into them."

He arched a brow. "Do you really believe that?"

She laughed. "No. But I am hungry, and since we lost our tour guide, why don't we find something to eat?"

They settled for hot dogs, and she introduced him to Dr Pepper. They walked through the midway, occasionally running across some of the cadets, who were smiling brightly and seeming to have a good time.

They meandered through the livestock area.

"This seems like the sort of place where we'd find Mr. Caldwell," Royce said.

"I don't know if he entered any cattle or horses this year, but even if he didn't, I'm sure he'll come take a gander. Probably a few times. As you can guess, this portion is his favorite part of the fair."

"Let's move on, then, shall we? As you'll no doubt be returning with him."

"Actually, I won't. We're" — she didn't know why it was so hard to say, to confirm, to admit — "uh, no longer seeing each other."

Taking her hand, Royce pulled her off the crowded well-trod path to the side of a building, where they were less likely to be noticed or bumped. His fingers remained laced through hers as he studied her intently. "When did this happen?"

"July Fourth."

She felt his gaze like a steady caress. "I can't imagine he was fool enough to let you go. Was it your decision?"

"It was mutual. We were traveling different roads, finally faced the fact that we had different goals and wanted different things."

He skimmed his knuckles along her cheek. "What do you want?"

You. But even as she thought it, she knew

it wasn't the correct answer. "I'm still figuring out the details."

"I wish you'd said something sooner."

"The timing never seemed right. It wasn't something to simply blurt out. I think I was also adjusting to the change, uncertain as to whether our separation would hold." She'd spent a third of her life with Luke. For a while she'd felt a hollowness, an emptiness. In spite of knowing they'd never be completely happy together, she'd mourned losing him, had felt her heart splinter and crack. She squeezed the hand still holding hers. "I wanted you to know."

He pressed his forehead to hers, then took her mouth softly, gently. "It can't have been easy to go through that, but I'm selfishly glad you did. I'm going to set a rather bad example for the cadets today, I'm afraid."

"You said anything between us was a bad idea."

He touched the scar at her brow. "It is. I need you to understand I won't give you any promises for the future, only for the now."

"I'm not asking for any promises at all."

He took her mouth again, briefly but passionately, as though a boulder had been lifted from his shoulders. Still clinging to her hand, he stepped back and glanced around, looking somewhat relieved that they hadn't drawn a crowd. Then his appreciative gaze landed back on her. "Shall we carry on, Jessica?"

With a nod, she tugged him back toward the path. "No one calls me that."

"Not even Peter? It's his favorite name."

Laughing at the memory that seemed from ages ago, surprised he recalled Peter's words, she glanced up at him. "He was trying to curry favor. He doesn't hide the fact that he's a flirt, which is the reason I worry, because Rhonda is so taken with him. I don't want her to get hurt."

"I'd be more worried about Kitty and Will Wedgeworth."

She staggered to a stop. "What? I've seen her dance with him a couple of times."

"Do you have any notion as to how often she comes out to the airfield?"

"She's doing a series of articles for her school newspaper and the *Tribune*." Recalling that Will was in the group of cadets Kitty had wandered off with earlier, she closed her eyes. "She arranged this outing as an excuse to spend the day with him without Mama objecting. Sneaky." She'd have a chat with Kitty later, in an attempt to spare her any hard lessons, but she doubted it would do any good. Here Jessie was, holding hands with a man her instincts told her she shouldn't.

They began walking again. "I saw something about an ice-skating show. It'll get us out of the heat."

It was crowded. They located seats near the top. "This is much better," she said. "I might spend the remainder of the afternoon here."

"I do miss English weather."

The performers skated onto the ice incredibly gracefully. Her mother had once explained it was all a trick, because the effort was there — it simply wasn't seen. And that was when Jessie had realized she wanted her flying to give the same impression: to be so smooth that spectators would think it was easily accomplished, would be in awe without ever realizing all the hours she'd spent mastering the skill needed to control an aircraft until it was nearly part of her.

With men standing along the edge, a woman came out and performed a solitary routine. Breathtaking jumps, elegant circles. Leaning toward Royce, Jessie said reverently, "Isn't she incredible?"

"Like you in flight."

She was touched by his words, that he shared that aspect of her life. She could so easily fall for him, hard and fast.

Afterward, they were once again immersed in the crowds. She found herself continually monitoring his limp, but it was holding steady, barely noticeable.

A monkey on a leash came up to them and tugged on Jessie's skirt. With a laugh, she started to reach into her purse, but Royce pulled a coin from his pocket and extended it toward the little fellow, who had the audacity to bite on it before tipping his hat at them and racing back to a man playing an accordion.

They walked away, heading in the direction of the midway. They passed a vendor selling hot dogs fried in a corn bread–like batter. Curious, she bought one and they shared it.

"That's different," she said. "I can't decide if I like it."

"It hasn't much of a future, I'm afraid."

She wished the same couldn't be said of them.

CHAPTER 27

Sitting in the back seat of the car, Kitty gazed out the window into the darkness, wondering how it was possible to keep all these emotions inside, if the others returning to Terrence with her could see her glowing with happiness.

She had never had so much fun at the state fair. She and Will had ridden numerous carnival rides. Throwing balls at bottles, he'd won her a stuffed pink bear. He'd held her hand most of the day. Whenever they were anyplace dark, he'd kissed her passionately and thoroughly. But he'd saved the best for the Ferris wheel, their very last ride before it was time to go. Just before they reached the very top, he'd shouted, "I love Kitty Lovelace!" She could have sworn she heard his words echoing through the midway as he put his arm around her shoulders, drew her in, and kissed her as though his very existence depended on it. It was the most romantic moment of her life.

"You're awfully quiet, Kitty," Jessie said from the front seat. "Is everything all right?"

"I'm just knackered."

"You sound more like the Brits than they do," Rhonda said. "The next thing we know you'll start talking with an accent."

"Their words are more fun than ours. The fair has one more week, maybe we can go back next Sunday." For the last day.

"We'll talk about it later," Jessie said, and Kitty had the impression that it wasn't at all what they were going to talk about.

Kitty had been enjoying herself so much that she'd gotten careless and was holding Will's hand when she crossed paths with her sister. Although if Jessie got after her, she had her arguments lined up, since her sister had been holding hands with Royce. It had been odd to see Jessie with someone other than Luke, but it had also seemed right somehow that she was with Royce. Shifting slightly, she rested her head on Fran's shoulder. "Did you have fun with Martin?"

"I did, but he has a girl back home."

"I didn't know that. I would have found someone else to go around the fair with you."

"It's fine. I like getting to know all of them."

"Does Will have a girlfriend back in England?" Jessie asked.

"No. Did you have fun with Royce?"

"I did, yes. I enjoy his company."

"Did he win you that purple bear?" Rhonda asked, which Kitty had been wondering about. It wasn't as large as the one Will had won Kitty.

"He did, playing darts. Did you and Peter play any games?" Jessie asked, but her tone made Kitty think she was asking something else.

"No, we just walked around."

Rhonda and Peter had been snuggling on a bench at the lagoon, when Kitty and Will had gotten there a little after eleven. Once everyone else had arrived at the designated gathering point, the Brits had marched off to their bus and the Yanks had wandered off to their various automobiles.

"Do you love him?" Fran whispered in Kitty's ear.

Kitty just nodded. When she graduated in May, she was going to go to England, war or no war, so she could be with Will.

They dropped Fran at her house, but since they'd known it would be late when they got back to Terrence, they'd arranged for Kitty to spend the night with Jessie. It was the first time she was staying over since her sister moved out, and she'd been looking forward to it, but as she crawled into Jessie's bed, she wished she hadn't gotten caught holding Will's hand. She was fairly certain her sister didn't approve. Kitty had planned to be asleep by the time Jessie finished brushing her teeth and climbed into bed beside her, but a question had been nagging at her and it was easier to ask it in the dark.

"Is Royce the reason you're not seeing Luke anymore?" she whispered.

"No. Luke didn't approve of what I was doing at the school. Not having his support made it harder to do what I needed to do. We'd been growing apart for a while. When I was sixteen, I couldn't imagine my life without him, but we changed as we got older. Not in a bad way, just in a way so we didn't work so well together any longer. That happens sometimes. You think it's forever, but it's just for now. Especially when you're young."

Kitty knew Jessie was trying to suggest the same applied to Kitty, but it didn't. "Do you love Royce?"

The bed wobbled a bit as Jessie rolled onto her side. Kitty made out her silhouette but not much else. "I care for him. I don't know him well enough yet to love him. Do you love Will?"

Kitty gnawed on her bottom lip. She should probably deny it but couldn't. "Yes."

Jessie sighed, sadness woven through the exhale. "Oh, Kitty, it's going to be so hard when he leaves."

"I know, but we're going to write each other. He'll come back when the war is over."

"He might think that now —"

"He will, Jessie. I know him. I know some cadets have girlfriends for just while they're here, but he's not like that. We're not like that. Besides, you had a boyfriend in high school."

"People can change when they're away from each other."

"We won't." They were committed to each other, but if she tried to explain that to Jessie, she'd just say they were too young to understand what that sort of devotion truly meant. "Please don't tell Mama. She'll forbid me from going to the dances again."

"I'll hold your secret, but if you ever need to talk, Kitty, know that I'm here for you. You can confide in me." Scooting closer, Jessie hugged her. "I don't want you to get hurt."

"Will would never do anything to hurt me. I believe that with all my heart."

CHAPTER 28

Monday, November 3, 1941
After glancing anxiously at her watch, Jessie searched the black star-studded sky. Two of the twelve planes that had left a few hours earlier on a cross-country trek had yet to return. One carried two of her students, Cadets Wedgeworth and Turner. In the other were two of Russell Williamson's cadets. He'd been standing with her until a few minutes ago, when he'd been called to the phone.

Even though she knew a thousand reasons existed for them to be the last out there, she couldn't shake off the ominous dread that something had gone terribly wrong. While she knew they had to be able to manage an aircraft without her, she found it a challenge to let them go. She reminded herself that they were experienced. They'd flown solo numerous times. They'd teamed up on a few distant flights. They were at the end of

344

their training. She shouldn't have to worry about them any longer, and yet she did.

"A watched pot never boils."

Glancing over her shoulder at Royce, she forced her mouth into a semblance of a smile. "They're two hours behind schedule."

"They've gotten good marks so far. They know what they're doing."

"That's what worries me." That and the fact that Will enjoyed showboating, going fast, and taking chances. It would make him either an incredible combat pilot or a short-lived one. "They're just a little bit too cocky."

"I like cocky," he said simply, before shifting his attention away from her and to the sky.

At the airfield, they kept things between them professional, but since the fair, they'd gone out a couple of times to dinner and once to a movie, on nights when the cadets didn't have open post and they wouldn't be seen. He was almost fully recovered from his injuries and had even danced with her a couple of times at the Legion Hall. She was incredibly grateful he wasn't one of the cadets who would be leaving in another week. She could already envision Kitty's tearful farewell to Will at the depot. Jessie was pondering how she might make his

345

departure easier for her sister when Russell reappeared at her side.

"That was Montgomery. They encountered low cloud cover with limited visibility. They were forced to land near Jumbo, Oklahoma," Russell said, relief in his voice.

"Both planes?"

"He had no sighting of the other one. Maybe they didn't land close enough to a town or didn't think to call and are just waiting it out. My fellas are spending the night at a farmer's house. They'll head back in the morning."

Surely Wedgeworth and Turner had done the same. They wouldn't be reckless when they were so close to getting their wings, when they would have the opportunity to engage the enemy. "I'm going to fly out at first light," she said quietly, unable to shake off a sense of foreboding. "Just in case they ran into some sort of engine trouble."

What they had done was run into a mountain.

With a pain in her chest that she feared would cause her ribs to collapse, Jessie stood in Kitty's bedroom doorway, knowing her hurt was nothing compared to the agony she was about to inflict on her sister. Royce had offered to do the deed, but Jessie needed to be the one to do it. She'd been their instructor, and while no one had looked at her as though she'd failed, she still felt that she had.

It had taken much of the day to find them and then to retrieve their remains. Jessie had never before been involved in such a grisly task. Several instructors had joined in the search. She had been the one to spot the debris. The best they could determine, based on the wreckage, was that the cadets simply hadn't seen the mountainside until it was too late — if they'd even had a chance to process it was there before they struck it.

"It's the way of the young, to feel invincible," Royce had said. "They'd have been determined to carry on in spite of any hazards facing them. You're not to blame."

But she was. How did she teach caution? How did she explain to Kitty what had happened? Kitty, who now sat on the floor, her scrapbook nearby as she clipped items from the newspaper. Jessie had an absurd thought, wondering why her sister had such an aversion to using furniture. She also knew she was on the verge of breaking her sister's heart. "Kitty?"

Her sister jerked her head toward her and gave Jessie a bright smile. "Hey, there! I didn't know you were here." She rattled the paper. "Did you see the announcement in the paper inviting the entire town to attend the wings ceremony Saturday? I've been talking with people already, telling them how important it is, because we're their family while they're over here. All of us. This is a significant moment for them. We all need to be there."

Jessie was aware of little except the thundering in her ears as she crossed over and crouched next to her sister. "Kitty —"

"What's wrong? You look so sad."

"Kitty, I'm so sorry, sweetheart, but Will's plane crashed."

Her sister let out a bubble of laughter. "Oh, he's not going to be happy about that. He wanted to graduate with no 'mishaps,' as he called them."

The pain in Jessie's chest intensified. She hadn't said it right, didn't know how to say it right as tears began to well and sting her eyes.

Kitty sobered. "That's not going to stop him from getting his wings, is it?"

"Kitty, he's gone."

"Gone? You mean back to England? There was that guy a few weeks ago that crashed his plane and y'all didn't send him away."

"No, he . . ." Closing her eyes, she took a deep breath, slowly exhaled. Opening her eyes, she took her sister's hand and squeezed. "He died. Will died. I'm so sorry."

Kitty slowly blinked, then blinked again. Shook her head. "I don't understand."

"It was a bad crash, into a mountain . . . The visibility was limited. We don't think they saw it."

Jerking her hand free of Jessie's clasp, Kitty scrambled back until she hit the side of her bed. Drawing her legs against her chest, she wrapped her arms around them. "You're wrong. He's a good pilot. You told me so yourself."

"One of the best. But sometimes —"

"How could he not see a mountain?"

"The cloud cover was low, and they were probably flying in it, maybe trying to get above or below it —"

"It wasn't him. It can't be him. I love him."

Jessie scooted up, wrapped her arms around her sister, and began rocking her. "I know you do. But it was him, sweetheart." He'd been the pilot, Turner the navigator.

Kitty's first gut-wrenching sob shook them both and tore through Jessie's heart, and then her sister was clinging to her as though she were barreling into the depths of hell and could find no purchase to halt her descent. "He loved . . . me."

"I know. I could tell just by the way he looked at you." A photograph of Kitty had been wedged in the instruments panel. Jessie imagined Will occasionally glancing over and smiling as he flew. She wondered if it would bring her sister any solace to know that Will had kept her memento close, or if it would serve only to increase her anguish.

"He . . . wanted to come . . . back when the war was over . . . and marry me. He said he'd make sure the war ended soon. It's not fair."

"No, no, it's not."

Jessie held her sister close, feeling inadequate at comforting someone whose girlhood had just been ripped from her. Someone whose innocence was shattered. Someone who would never again be the same.

CHAPTER 29

Thursday, November 6, 1941

Kitty had worn all black only once before — for her dad's funeral. But she'd wanted to wear something special for Will, so she'd gone to Mona's Dress Boutique and spent a good bit of her savings on something suitably somber. As she sat in the front pew between her mother and Jessie, staring at the two caskets with the Union Jack draped over each, she couldn't help but wonder if he'd known — if he'd had a split second of fear before he died. If he'd spared her a thought. If it had been with a sense of loss or a measure of fondness for the time they'd shared.

She hoped he hadn't been scared. Hoped neither of them had been. Him or Mick. That they hadn't known anything. That it had been over before they realized what was going to happen.

The cadets filled one side of the church,

351

the townsfolk the other. Nearly everyone from town was in attendance. She heard sniffles behind her. So many had grown to love these lads, to care about them. They belonged to the community now. Even after they left, they'd still be part of it and hold a special place in everyone's heart. Those who didn't leave were the responsibility of all.

Royce had explained that shortly after he'd first arrived, he'd made arrangements with the Oaklawn Memorial Cemetery to have a portion of land set aside as a British cemetery. "We bury our dead where they fall," he'd told her.

He'd sent telegrams to the families, and they'd responded with the epitaphs they wanted on the headstones. They weren't here, of course. It was too costly and dangerous to come over, but Kitty intended to write them and describe the service. She'd also send them the obituaries she'd clipped from the newspaper, obituaries she'd written with Royce's help.

It all should have eased the hurt, but as Reverend Monroe spoke of being carried on angel's wings and the tears flooded her eyes, her chest threatened to cave in. It felt hollow and empty, but at the same time filled with overwhelming pain. Jessie squeezed her hand, and Kitty wondered

352

how anyone survived this kind of hurt.

The organist began playing "Amazing Grace" as several cadets, Royce, and Peter made their way solemnly to the caskets and hoisted them onto their shoulders. Without thought or hardly any awareness of doing so, Kitty rose to her feet, joining everyone else who did the same, and watched as the fallen began their final journey.

She barely recalled walking behind the caskets to the cemetery at the edge of town. The caskets were set down near two hollowed-out graves. As she took a chair between her mother and Jessie, she couldn't help but think that this part of the cemetery was too barren, too empty — and she wished to God that it had remained so. The reverend spoke a few more words, offered a prayer. Everyone stood as the bugler played last post. It was so forlorn that she would forever carry the echo of it within her. Numb with grief, she retook her seat and watched as the flags were folded. One was handed to Royce. He walked over, knelt, and held it out to her, like she was supposed to take it. She shook her head. "It goes to his family."

"They wanted you to have it. Apparently, he'd told them a good deal about you. His mum is going to send you the letters."

Her eyes flooded as she clutched the flag to her chest. As Mama's arms came around her, she fought not to break into undignified sobs. But it became nearly impossible when four planes flew in from the south over the cemetery in a V shape and one of the silver planes behind the lead aircraft split off and headed toward the setting sun, honoring Will and Mick and signifying their departure.

She somehow managed to hold her grief at bay until she was alone in her room, curled on her bed, and hugging the flag. Then she gave in to the overwhelming anguish and wondered how she'd survive Will's being gone.

A few days later she found the strength to clip his and Mick's obituaries from the paper and slip them into her scrapbook, without gluing them into place.

RAF Leading Aircraftman William Wedgeworth was the son of Gwendolyn and John Wedgeworth and the older brother of Eleanor and Alice. He was born May 15, 1923, in Watford, Hertfordshire, England.

RAF Leading Aircraftman Mick Turner was the only child of Winnifred and Charles Turner. He was born February 8, 1922, in London, England.

Both men returned to their Maker November 3, 1941, a few days shy of receiving their wings. Those wings are now sewn to the left breast of their uniforms as they lie in rest. While they had yet to fly over the skies of Britain, still, they served her with honor and distinction. Godspeed on this final flight to the heavens.

Tribune editor's postscript: The unfortunate reality is that in war, there are casualties beyond the battlefield.

CHAPTER 30

Friday, November 7, 1941
Standing by her plane, waiting for the first cadet to arrive for his review, Jessie could sense the somberness that hung over the airfield like a heavy fog. Invincibility was an illusion. Whether they were in training or battle, death was always a possibility for these young men, and it seemed the truth of that had come home to roost.

Each of the cadets of Class One had a final flight, during which an instructor would grade each of them on various maneuvers. All she would do was call out the task, leave the pilot to accomplish it, and then mark how well he carried it out. Passing meant they'd get their wings. She couldn't seem to move beyond the fact that cadets Wedgeworth and Turner wouldn't receive theirs during the ceremony as well. Every time she envisioned their boyish grins, excitement, and happiness, a hole opened in her chest that threatened to swallow her. She'd been so confident that they were excellent pilots and had learned all they needed to survive what awaited them when they returned home. She'd predetermined she would pass them even before they were to take that last test.

What had she missed? What hadn't she taught them? Had her praise made them misjudge their abilities? Why hadn't they landed? Why hadn't they noted the terrain on their map? Had they gotten lost? The questions circled through her mind like a plane doing continuous loops, until she got dizzy and could make no sense of them.

"Miss Lovelace?"

The eager voice brought her from her morbid musings, and she was relatively certain she'd looked to be daydreaming. Turning, she forced a reassuring smile. "Mr. Brightwell. Feeling confident?"

"Yes, ma'am." He looked down at his boots, back up at her. "Relatively so. A bit nervous, actually. Don't want to muck this up."

"No reason you should. You've passed all the other checks." They reviewed them periodically to ensure they'd mastered what they needed to. "You've been one of my better students." As soon as the words left her mouth, she regretted them and what they might imply, that the two cadets who had recently died hadn't been good students, might have been at fault for what happened. The fault could be hers, if she hadn't trained them properly. She wished she could be certain that it wasn't. "I just mean that you've never been a cowboy . . . You're going to take that literally. Let's just get on with it, shall we?"

He climbed into the front seat — the lead pilot's seat in the AT-6 — and she settled in behind him. After strapping in, she put on the headset that allowed for two-way communication between them. He was already calling out the checks he was making.

After he was finished, she said, "All right, Mr. Brightwell, let's take her up and have some fun. Head toward the north end of Caldwell Field."

He flew level, making adjustments, but she couldn't stop herself from saying, "Keep her steady, Mr. Brightwell. The aircraft should be a part of you."

"Yes, ma'am."

She heard the tension in his voice. He was probably adjusting to her tone. It sounded flat and terse, even to herself. Usually she was more relaxed, friendly, striving to instill the joy of flying. "Okay, Mr. Brightwell, a slow roll to the right."

It was sloppy. No other word for it.

"You can do better than that. Try again."

They hadn't known the weather was going to get bad. She knew that. It had come up unexpectedly. They were probably in it before they realized how bad it was.

"Okay, Mr. Brightwell, show me your barrel roll."

It wasn't bad, and yet she wanted to find fault with it. She didn't want him to graduate. Didn't want him to earn his wings. What if she hadn't taught him enough? What if he was shot down?

After instructing him to perform several other maneuvers, she had him return to the airfield. Once he landed and secured the aircraft, they climbed out. She extended her hand. "Well done, sir."

He seemed surprised, and she wondered if she'd missed something. But he gave her hand a shake. "Thank you, Miss Lovelace. You didn't seem pleased with my performance."

She thought maybe she'd been judging her own more than his. "Don't get yourself killed, Mr. Brightwell."

"I won't, ma'am."

She clapped him on the shoulder before going to get her next and final student, striving not to think about the two she wouldn't test, the two she'd failed.

CHAPTER 31

Saturday, November 8, 1941

Being at the ceremony where the cadets from the first course were receiving their wings was breaking Kitty's heart all over again, because she was so aware of who wasn't there. Who wasn't standing at attention in the group a short distance away from Royce and Peter.

She had considered not coming, but she knew all these cadets, friends of Will's. She'd spoken, danced, and laughed with them. Tomorrow they would leave on the train, and she might never see them again. But she would stay in touch, writing to them as often as possible.

And she was here because it wouldn't have been right not to be when she'd gone around town encouraging people to come, asking them not to let these pilots have no spectators for such a momentous graduation. She couldn't imagine receiving her diploma next May and not having anyone to witness it, to share in her triumph and joy.

This morning, she'd helped retrieve the chairs from the mess and recreation halls and set them out in several parallel lines near the flight line. The abundance of aircraft seemed a fitting backdrop for the ceremony.

Every chair was occupied. Some people stood at the back. The instructors and other staff stood off to the side. Wearing black, she sat between her mother and Fran. These days no other color suited her mood.

As Royce called out each name, the pilot stepped forward. Peter handed him his wings. She knew her mother and some of her friends planned to sew them on all the uniforms this evening so when the graduates reached Canada and changed back into their uniforms, their accomplishment would be visible.

When all the wings had been handed out, the audience stood, and each group of cadets paraded by. After they were again in position, standing at attention, several planes flew over, loud and low. None veering off this time. They would soon return to this airfield to land. Meanwhile, the cadets were dismissed, and people began gathering around the newly minted pilots to offer congratulations and shake hands.

Harry was the first one she approached.

"It was kind of you to come," he said solemnly, with no evidence of the flirtation from their previous encounters. "It can't have been easy."

"Will would have wanted me here."

"He was mad about you. He would have come back."

She merely nodded. It was still too difficult to speak about him. "So y'all leave tomorrow."

"On the ten o'clock train."

She'd known that. The information had appeared in the *Tribune* in a column dedicated to news about the cadets. "I'll be there to see y'all off."

"Will you be at the dance tonight?"

"No, I . . . I can't. I wish you good luck over there." She furrowed her brow. "Or is it bad luck to do that, like performers in a play? You're supposed to tell them to break a leg, which I think is horrid." She pulled a small card from her purse. "When you know where you're assigned, write me with your address and I'll write you back."

He grinned. "I will. Thank you for everything you've done, Kitty. I don't know if we'd have had anyone to applaud for us if

363

you hadn't seen to it."

"I like organizing." She held out her hand, changed her mind, and hugged him. "Do take care and give Jerry what for." Will had told her he was going to do that: give Jerry what for.

She made her way among all of them, giving them her card, trying to find the right words to wish them well. Jessie had warned her about getting attached, about how hard it would be to see them leave, but she couldn't imagine not knowing these fellas. Despite the pain, she had good memories. All the talks, the dances, and the smiles.

She didn't see her sister around, assumed she'd been piloting one of the planes. She doubted keeping them in a tight formation was easy and the cadets who would have been best at it had been receiving their wings.

She would have helped to put the chairs away but the trainees who had arrived last week were already seeing to the task.

Fran came up and hugged her. "I can't believe some are leaving already. Seems like they only just got here."

"It did pass quickly, didn't it?"

"I wish you'd come to the dance with me tonight."

"I can't, Fran."

"I don't have to go. I'll come see you and we can —"

"No, Fran. You go. They need dance partners, especially now that there are so many." At least two hundred.

"I wanted to be like you, Kitty, I wanted to fall in love with one of them, but I'm afraid to now."

"You can't force it, and you can't avoid it. It will just happen when it happens."

"You're going to come back to school on Monday, right?"

She hadn't been to school since Jessie had brought her the news on Tuesday. Her mother would write her an excuse, but she suspected every one of her teachers knew why she wasn't in class. "I will, yes."

"Okay. I'll see you then."

Fran wandered off to speak with one of the cadets, and Kitty began walking toward where her mother had parked the car and would no doubt meet her. How was it that the world managed to carry on?

November 14, 1941

Dearest Kitty,

Imagine we're sitting on the front porch swing, you on my lap, my arms around you, hugging you tightly — like we did when you were younger, when you had a nightmare and we'd sneak out of the house and sway while looking at the stars until you felt safe again. I'm half a world away, but my heart is there with you now. Aching for your loss.

I know Will was a special young man. My little sister wouldn't fall in love with someone who wasn't. I looked forward to meeting him. Instead, Dad will meet him first. I can see him grinning and holding out his hand, one airman to another.

I know you're hurting, and I have no words to ease the hurt. You will cry and you will grieve and you will experience an ache in your chest that you think will kill you, too. But if I've learned anything at all about the British since being over here, it's that Will would want you to be strong and carry on. You are the caretaker of his memory. While he may not have died in battle, still he died for Britain.

All my love,
Jack

CHAPTER 32

Saturday, November 15, 1941

"Are you sure you don't want to come to the club in Dallas with me and Peter?" Rhonda asked. "I bet we could talk Royce into joining us."

Looking up from her place on the couch, with her feet tucked beneath her, Jessie smiled at her friend hovering by the door. "I want to finish this book." Although if Rhonda asked, she couldn't tell her what the story was about. Her eyes skimmed over the words but none of them registered, because her mind couldn't seem to focus on any task.

"At least go to the dance at the Legion Hall."

Annette was already there. "I just want a night in."

Worry wrinkled Rhonda's brow. "Seems to me you've had too many nights in. You need to get out."

"I'm fine, Rhonda. Go on and have fun. Don't worry about me."

A car horn honked.

"That's Peter. I can stay —"

"Go!"

With a quick nod, Rhonda was out the door. Jessie tossed the book onto the low table, brought her legs against her chest, and dropped her forehead to her knees. Lifting her head slightly, she peered at the table with the liquor bottles. She'd begun to have a couple of rum and Cokes before bed, the amount of rum increasing, if she was honest. She'd started the practice, hoping it would help her sleep. But it seldom did. She'd end up eyes wide open, staring at the ceiling, trying to recall every lesson, every instruction, every bit of advice she'd given to Will and Mick. One of the reasons she'd wanted Rhonda out of the house was so she'd be completely alone and could drink to her heart's content with no one seeing her.

She didn't like crawling out of bed with a hangover every morning, and it never lessened the guilt. In some ways, it increased it, because she wasn't her best at the airfield. One morning she'd had to land the plane in a field so she could be sick. That had been embarrassing. Her student hadn't said anything, and she hadn't provided any explanation. She'd just climbed into the cockpit and told him they'd practice rolls another day.

They'd let Emerson go because he was a drunkard. Would they let her go? Had he harbored demons as ghastly as hers?

She couldn't get past the belief that the responsibility for Will's or Mick's error in judgment fell to her. She hadn't been in the cockpit with them for their initial three weeks of training, but she had taken them through the remaining seventeen. Now each class had a different instructor for each phase, so hopefully the training would be more rounded and if one instructor forgot to teach something, another would realize it and fill in the void.

She'd even wondered if she should return to training with the Link or teach in the classroom. Maybe Barstow had been right after all. Maybe she wasn't the educator she thought she was. Maybe he'd seen what was lacking in her that no one else had been able to detect. Maybe she should just quit altogether.

A knock sounded at the door. She ignored it. She didn't want company. She wanted a drink. Unfolding her body, she got up and slowly wandered across the room.

"Jessica?"

She squeezed her eyes shut. Royce. Not tonight. She didn't want him to see her like this. She picked up the bottle of rum, poured some into a glass, and tossed it back straight. Her eyes, nose, throat burned. She wheezed, coughed.

"Jessica, open the door."

Damn him. She stormed across the room and yanked open the door. "What?"

Now her eyes burned for a different reason: the worry and concern etched in his features.

"You weren't at the dance."

"Aren't you observant? Do you want a trophy?"

"I'm not the one you're mad at."

"What the hell do you know about it?" She balled up her fist and hit his chest. "Damn them." Another hit. "Why the hell didn't they land?" Another hit that actually sent him staggering back a step. "How do you miss seeing a goddamned mountain? He broke Kitty's heart. They broke mine. What didn't I teach them? What didn't they learn? Why the hell did you ever tell Barstow to have me substitute that day Emerson was hungover? Why did you have to make him think I knew what I was doing?"

It was only as her hands began to hurt

370

and her arms ache that she realized she was still pounding his chest with each question asked, each doubt, each accusation. She pressed her fists against his chest, held them there, barely able to see him through the well of tears. He closed his arms around her, holding her tightly as he eased her back until he could shut the door.

Great heaving sobs escaped her. She couldn't hold them in any longer. She couldn't pretend she wasn't in agony, that a part of her hadn't died with those boys on that mountain. "God, it hurts."

"I know." He lifted her into his arms. How was he able to support her weight with his injury?

"Your leg —"

"Not to worry. You're my concern right now." He walked through the living room into the hallway. "Which bedroom is yours?"

"The first one on the right." With her arms around his neck, she clung to him as though she'd been tossed from an aircraft, and he was her parachute.

He carried on into her room, set her gently on the bed, stretched out beside her, and once again folded her in his embrace. She didn't know how long she wept, but she became aware of the dampness of his shirt against her cheek, and still he held her, rubbing gentle circles over her back, until the tears became a slow trickle, and she was exhausted. "I'm so tired. If I go to sleep, I dream I'm in the plane with them, they're confused" — afraid, but she couldn't give voice to what haunted her: that they'd known what was about to happen and been terrified — "asking for guidance and I'm telling them the wrong things to do."

"You wouldn't do that. You would know what to do."

"They were good and kind and I liked them. I wanted them to dance until they were old."

He didn't say anything, and she was grateful for that. She was babbling, probably not making much sense to him. "I was so arrogant. I thought if I trained them, they'd survive the war. They'd all survive the war. I didn't give those two the skills to even return home."

"Jessie." His groan was tortured as he held her more firmly. "I know if I say that you can't blame yourself, you're going to tell me to go to the devil, but it is impossible to know why it happened. Perhaps they didn't pay close enough attention during their course in meteorology. Or navigation. Perhaps they didn't spend enough time in the Link in order to master instrumentation. Maybe something was wrong with the aircraft. There are so many factors to be considered."

"They were my responsibility."

"They were mine." Easing her back slightly, he cradled her face, his expression filled with such earnestness, but also pain. "Jessie, I don't know why those lads crashed. We'll probably never know. Bad judgment. Inexperience. Hubris. Maybe they were in the fog before they realized it, didn't expect it to be so thick and to limit visibility. Maybe they got disoriented, lost sight of where they were, didn't realize they were that close to the mountain that would have been on their map. Or they believed they could win against nature. I don't know. What I do know is that there is nothing you did not teach them that would have made a difference. They had more than a hundred and fifty hours of flight time. Their exercise shouldn't have ended as it did, but it wasn't because of anything you did or didn't do. We give them the skills. How they manage them is beyond our control."

She shook her head. "I wish I could believe that, but I let them down. I let you down."

"Do you know I have a list of more than a dozen cadets who have asked to be transferred to you if one of your pupils is determined to be unfit to pilot an aircraft?"

"One of the instructors says it's because I'm female and they just want to . . . ogle."

"He's bloody wrong. In the evenings, the lads sit around and share their day. Their experiences in the plane, what they learned, what they fancy or don't fancy about their instructors. It's how we knew we needed to let Emerson go. They speak of you with the highest regard, and even if they didn't, I've seen you working with them, and I've seen the results of what you've taught them."

The crash.

"The crash aside," he said as though she'd spoken aloud. "It was unfortunate. No, it was more than that. It was devastating. There was a chap in my squadron who downed two Messerschmitts. On his return to base, he crashed and was killed. You certainly can't claim he was a bad pilot or that someone failed to teach him something. We are defying gravity, earthbound creatures taking to the sky. Sometimes, the absolute worst happens.

"I know you're struggling to come to terms with what occurred. I've lost men in my squadron, and I question what I might have done differently to have prevented what happened to them. But we can't af-

374

ford to let the doubts have sway over us. I need you teaching these lads. To be honest, Britain needs you."

"I don't want to be the reason they die."

"You weren't. And you won't be. I believe that with every fiber of my being."

She squeezed her eyes shut and buried her face against his chest. If only she could believe that. "I haven't been able to sleep since it happened."

"Do so now. I'll hold the nightmares at bay."

One corner of her mouth curled up. It felt strange to have even a partial smile. "Are you going to don your ancestor's armor and serve as my knight?"

"I would, but he was rather short actually."

The laugh didn't pass her lips, but it was there, circling in her chest. It felt so much better than the ache. "I never lost a student before," she whispered.

"We'll lose others, I'm sorry to say. It's one of the hazards we face because we envied the birds."

"I always took such joy in flying."

"As well you should." He pressed a kiss to the top of her head. "As did they, sweetheart. Sleep now."

She dreamed of Will and Mick, smiling

375

and happy, soaring through the heavens without the aid of an aircraft.

When she awoke, she was nestled against Royce, his arm around her, his eyes closed, his jaw bristled. At some point during the night, he'd removed his jacket, tie, and shoes. And it suddenly hit her that she was falling for him, hard.

CHAPTER 33

Thursday, November 20, 1941

Kitty awoke to the sound of knocking on her bedroom door.

"Kitty, darling, we have a lot to do to get ready for our guests. I could use your help in the kitchen."

With a groan, Kitty rolled over and shoved her head beneath the pillow. Thanksgiving. It had always been a girls' session of scrambling around the kitchen, gabbing, gossiping, and laughing. Today it would be pure torment. She would be forced to perform, to pretend her heart was more than jagged shards that constantly ached.

"Kitty?"

"Okay!" she called out, wishing Mama would just leave her alone. But she was always asking her to do things. *Take the sign-up sheet to the recreation hall, please, dear. Help decorate the Legion Hall for the Saturday dance. Help me make cookies for the social the War Relief Society is hosting to welcome the newest cadets.* She missed the days when Mama didn't want her to have anything at all to do with the Brits. Maybe like Jessie, she should just move out.

Tossing back the covers, she dragged herself out of bed. It was a chore to make her legs work, but she somehow managed to brush her hair and get dressed.

As she descended the stairs, she could hear voices coming from the kitchen. Jessie was already here. She almost retreated to her room, but she knew they had to cook an awful lot of food, more than usual. Two dozen cadets would be arriving to join them for the feast. Her mother had arranged for additional families to provide places at their tables for the other cadets so none would be eating at the airfield.

At the door, she heard Jessie ask, "Is Kitty coming down to help us?"

"I don't know. She's not doing much these days." Her mother sighed. "I didn't realize she'd fallen for that boy. Lord, I'm worried about her. She's not going to the dances. She's even taking some time from the drugstore. Only leaves the house to go to school."

And to run all those stupid errands. Kitty shoved on the door and stepped into the kitchen. Her mother was at the large wooden table in its center, adding ingredients to a pan of crumbled corn bread for dressing. Jessie was at the counter, crumbling more corn bread into another pan. "What can I do to help?"

She hadn't meant to sound as enthusiastic as someone announcing they were heading to the dentist, but until their company arrived, she saw no need to put on an act.

"The girls are making the mashed potatoes at their place to bring over," her mother said cheerfully. "Did you want to peel the carrots?"

"Sure."

Taking an apron from a peg, she slipped it over her head and tied it, before shuffling to the sink and going to work on the chore.

"Kitty, when you're finished helping, are you going to change into something a little brighter?" Mama asked.

"Did you know that after her husband died, Queen Victoria wore black until the day she died?"

"You're not going to do that, are you?" Jessie asked.

Kitty barely looked at her. "I like black."

Finished with the corn bread, Jessie wiped her hands on a dishcloth, passed the pan to her mother, and joined Kitty at the sink.

"Do you want me to help?"

"I can do it."

Out of the corner of her eye, she saw her sister look helplessly at their mother. Kitty felt a pang of regret at her rudeness, but she couldn't forgive Jessie for what had happened. She'd been Will's instructor, so she was the reason he wasn't on a ship heading back to England now. The reason Kitty would never again see him.

"Kitty, darling, what happened wasn't Jessie's fault."

She stopped herself from screaming, *Then whose fault was it?*

"I just want to take care of it by my lonesome." She'd deliberately used their grandfather's quaint phrase because she wanted to express what she was feeling: alone and lonely.

People began arriving more than an hour before dinner was to be served. Rhonda and Annette hauled in another turkey, mashed potatoes, and gravy. Royce and Peter brought enough beer and ice to fill two tubs in the backyard, along with a couple of bottles of whiskey. It didn't matter that most of the cadets were too young to purchase or drink beer in public — they offered it to them anyway.

380

"They're old enough to die for their country, they're old enough to drink. Besides, they're old enough to drink in England," Royce said.

It was a lovely day, and the Brits preferred to be outside, so chairs were brought out and blankets were spread on the ground. Kitty sat on the swing on the front porch. Jessie and Royce were side by side on a blanket, talking, smiling, occasionally laughing, each sign of joy a stab to her chest. She hated herself for not wanting Jessie to be happy.

A couple of the students settled into the rockers on the porch.

"Does it ever get cold here?" Rupert Tidings asked.

"Sometimes." Kitty knew she needed to be a better hostess. It wasn't his fault she was so incredibly sad. "I'm going to be stuffed when I'm finished eating all this."

The cadets stared at her, blinked, stared at each other. Then Rupert asked, "With both of us?"

That was a strange question, and she wondered if this was another example of miscommunication, something for Royce's list. She held up her plate. "With turkey."

"Oh, right. It's jolly good. Never had a meal like this before. We were sent over at just the right time."

Trixie leapt on the porch and, with tail wagging, stood between the cadets.

"May we feed her from our plates?" Rupert asked.

"Only if you want her to stay with you for the remainder of the afternoon."

By the time they'd finished eating, they and Trixie were the best of friends.

After a while, Rhonda came out and joined her on the swing. She had a glass of wine, but no plate.

"Are you finished eating?" Kitty asked.

"Mm-hmm. Just waiting for dessert. Some of the fellas are talking about playing charades. I'm too full to even think about doing anything but imitating a sloth."

With their plates empty, the cadets went inside.

"I said something" — Kitty kept her voice low — "and the cadets gave me a funny look."

"What did you say?"

"Something about being stuffed after I ate."

Rhonda grinned, leaned toward her, and whispered, "I made that mistake with Peter one night when we were out having dinner. Being stuffed can mean having sex."

"Oh, no." She squeezed her eyes shut,

imagining Will laughing his head off at her mistake, her embarrassment. The poor cadets probably thought she was inviting both of them to have sex with her. Her cheeks felt like they were scalding. One of the things Kitty had always liked about Rhonda was that she'd never talked to Kitty like she was a kid. She was frank, honest, and forthright when it came to things that a lot of people would never say out loud. Certainly no one else would have spoken to Kitty as though she actually knew what sex was. Sometimes, it hurt worst of all that she'd been a good girl and not had sex with Will. She felt the tears leaking out and quickly swept them away.

"Kitty?"

She sniffed. "I'm okay. Today is just hard. Dad's not here. Will."

"I know. I've been thinking about them and Mick a lot today. A day of thanks. And I'm thankful that I knew them, that they were in my life for a while. There will come a time, Kitty, when the good memories will push aside the sad ones."

"Did you learn about handling grief from your father?"

"Hell, no!" Rhonda looked so offended.

Kitty couldn't help it. She laughed.

"In spite of being a preacher, my father

383

never looks for the light at the end of the tunnel. He just wallows in the tunnel. Don't go to him for consolation. He'd just say you did something to deserve the heartache. He'd be wrong."

The door opened and Peter stepped out, holding two small plates. "I couldn't recall which you wanted: apple or pumpkin."

Rhonda's smile was soft and inviting. "I'll have half of each."

With a chuckle, he handed her the pumpkin and leaned against the railing to eat his half of the apple. "It was really nice of your mum to arrange all this."

"I'm pretty sure she's already planning the same for Christmas."

"I think some of the lads are wishing they didn't have to leave." He and Rhonda exchanged plates. It was such a couple's thing to do, and it twinged the ache in Kitty's heart.

She stood up. "Think I'll get some pecan." The screen door hadn't closed behind her before Peter had joined Rhonda on the swing and she was leaning against him.

In the kitchen, Kitty set her plate on the counter with countless others. She turned on the water to fill the sink. Might as well start washing the dishes.

Her mother came up behind her and

placed her hands on her waist, moving her aside and turning off the water. "Just leave everything until our guests have left."

It was near dusk when the cadets lined up and began marching back to the airfield, their whistling reminding Kitty of that first Saturday afternoon. It seemed so long ago, and yet at the same time, it felt like it was only yesterday. She'd been so innocent then, and now she felt as though she'd lived a lifetime.

Going outside, she stopped by the galvanized tub. The ice had all melted, but a couple of bottles remained. After picking one up, she used the opener attached to the tub with a string and popped off the top. Her mother would have a fit if she saw her drinking, but she didn't care. She was almost as old as the cadets, had earned the right through loss to indulge in booze.

It was growing dark. She could hide out here, be alone, until her sister, Rhonda, Annette, Royce, and Peter left. She had a second of wondering if Royce might play a game of checkers with her but decided that would mean Jessie would stay around. She wandered to the tire swing, sat on it, and gently pushed off. Lifting the bottle to her lips, she took a swallow — and gagged. *Ugh. That was dreadful.* Why in the world did anyone drink such rubbish? And Will thought their tea tasted awful?

Lights and laughter spilled from the house. Probably Jessie and her friends helping Mama clean up. She should join them. Rhonda would say something outrageous to make her laugh. Only she didn't want to laugh or have fun or act like everything was all right.

She saw a silhouette meandering toward her. Jessie. Couldn't she just leave her alone?

Kitty gave another little push; the branch groaned. Maybe the tree would topple on top of Kitty, so she wouldn't have to talk to her sister. As Jessie stopped just shy of the swing, Kitty could feel her gaze on her but kept staring ahead. She took another swallow of the beer, forcing down the vile concoction. "You gonna tell Mama I'm drinking?" she asked defiantly.

"I'm not a hypocrite. Had my first sip at seventeen. Thought it was the worst thing I'd ever tasted."

She was not going to feel a connection with her sister but did admit, "It is pretty vile, like medicine."

"Eventually I did grow to like the taste. It's better cold."

Kitty didn't see how that would make a difference. "Why'd you come out here?"

"To see how you're doing. We didn't get much of a chance to talk today."

"I'm all right."

"I don't think you are, Kitty. I don't know what to do for you, how to make it stop hurting. I know you're angry at me, blame me. I want you to know that it's okay. I understand."

Kitty got up off the tire and threw the bottle as hard as she could. She couldn't see where it landed, didn't even hear it hit, so it must have just fallen to the grass. How disappointing. She'd wanted to hear it shatter. "It is your fault, because if it's not, it's his. I don't want it to be his." The scalding tears rained down her face. Dropping to the ground, she wrapped her arms around herself and began to rock. "It can't be his fault."

Jessie's arms came around her, hugging her tightly. "He was a good pilot. They both were. It shouldn't have happened."

"But it did."

"We can't control everything. Like Dad going to sleep and not waking up. Although we don't always know why things happen, it doesn't make it any easier."

Kitty didn't want to admit it, but the words just spilled out. "He worked really hard because he wanted to impress you —

387

but not in a show-offy way. He told me once, 'I want to be as calm and confident as your sister at the controls. She understands everything about the plane and what it's telling her.' He said you'd say, 'Do you feel that, Mr. Wedgeworth?' Then you'd tell him what it was, if it was the plane or him or . . . You just know everything, Jess. You even knew I'd get hurt."

Her sister loosened her hold and eased back. "I didn't know it would be like this, though, Kitty. I wish to God it hadn't been."

"Me, too. I wish a lot of things. That I'd told him I love him one more time. Kissed him once more. Hugged him."

It had grown so dark, but she could feel her sister's gaze boring into her, studying her. Finally, Jessie said, "I always feel closer to Dad when I'm flying. What if I took you up tomorrow evening in Dad's Jenny? You could blow Will a kiss."

She thought she was out of tears, but more surfaced, blurring her vision. It was strange to feel her mouth forming a smile — not a big one, but the corners eased up slightly. "I'd like that."

She didn't know where heaven was, but she knew Will was there. Being among the clouds, maybe the ache would lessen just enough, just long enough, that she could breathe.

CHAPTER 34

Sunday, December 7, 1941

Sitting in a red vinyl chair at the small metal table in the kitchen, Jessie sipped her morning coffee and read the *Tribune.* Her flight with Kitty had seemed to ease some of her sister's anguish. Not enough that she'd yet attended a dance or packed away the black, but she had gone to the recreation hall to visit with the cadets after they'd landed and had returned to work at the drugstore. It was a beginning.

Looking up at the sound of slippers flapping on the floor, she smiled at Rhonda in her robe with her hair still up in curlers.

"Coffee," she lamented. "I need coffee." She went to the pot, poured herself a cup, and inhaled deeply before taking a sip. She closed her eyes as though she'd achieved bliss. "Better, much better."

"I noticed you drinking from a flask last night at the Legion Hall."

Rhonda shrugged. "Peter likes to have a little rum between dances. It would be rude to make him drink alone."

"So you're just being polite?"

"Of course. Besides, my visit with my father yesterday afternoon wasn't one of the better ones. He called me a trollop. I didn't know people even used that word any longer."

Jessie folded the paper and set it aside. "Why would he call you that?"

"I haven't been going to church. He hears I'm gallivanting around with a foreigner. I wear too much makeup. Who knows? I don't think he's ever gotten over Mama running off. When he looks at me, he sees her."

"For a preacher, he's not very Christian."

"Enough about him." Rhonda dropped into a chair, used her foot to nudge another chair away from the table, and placed both feet on the seat. "I heard some interesting gossip last night. Seems Luke took Eve Blessing to the movies."

Jessie was surprised to feel a sense of relief, an easing of the guilt. They'd gone to school with Eve. She was the nurse at the hospital who'd let Royce visit when she shouldn't have. "I always liked Eve."

"You're not bothered?"

"I have some sadness but" — how did she

describe what she was experiencing? — "I'm glad he's not waiting on me."

"In that case, I guess you don't have to keep your relationship with Royce so quiet."

"That's more because of the cadets. He's trying to set a good example for them."

"Well, I doubt that's working. Anyone who sees how intensely he looks at you is going to know something is going on between you two."

"Not as much as you think. We're just . . . friends. He believes you tempt fate if you're more than that."

"I think *you* tempt him — that's his problem. Anyway, he, Peter, and I are going into Dallas to see *Sergeant York* at the Majestic. Come with?"

"Are you playing matchmaker?"

"Three is an odd number. Makes things awkward. Annette is having some cadets over for a home-cooked meal, and I want to get out of her way. Thought you might want to do the same. Besides, you and Royce might be working to deny it, but you're a couple."

Royce drove. Rhonda and Peter were in the back seat, and Jessie didn't want to consider the mischief they might be getting up to. Every now and then, she'd hear the hush of a whisper, but not the words. And there were several soft giggles.

"I hope you don't mind my coming along," Jessie said. "Rhonda hates odd numbers. She had a hard time working with them in school."

Royce chuckled, shook his head, reached over, and took her hand.

"Hey, I heard that," Rhonda said. "I aced math. It was history I didn't much like. I always preferred the present. Speaking of which, we were thinking we'd go out to eat after the movie, someplace nice."

So Rhonda and Peter were a *we* now, expecting it to be understood who was being referred to with that little pronoun. "It's your party. I'm just tagging along."

"Great. Do you have any objections, Royce?"

"None at all."

"We're going to have fun today."

"You're always my fun-time girl," Peter said.

"What is life without fun? Boring."

Once they got into Dallas, Jessie navigated Royce through the various streets until they reached Elm. After they parked, they walked to the baroque five-story building with its striking lighted marquee.

"I've always loved coming here," Jessie

told Royce as they made their way inside, following the crowd of moviegoers. Crossing the black-and-white marble flooring beneath the beautiful crystal chandeliers to the graceful sweeping staircases, she felt like Cinderella arriving at the ball, Prince Charming beside her, his hand resting lightly on the small of her back. Although she hadn't declared Royce her prince, not publicly, not even to him privately. She was more cautious about revealing her sentiments these days, uncertain as to whether it was a result of maturity, lingering guilt over her breakup with Luke, or a desire to avoid Kitty's fate. Or perhaps she was simply following Royce's lead. Yet when she was with him, words came more easily, smiles more often, joy much deeper.

"We'll take the lift, shall we?" Peter asked, guiding them toward the elegantly designed caged elevator.

They rode it to the balcony level and managed to find seats near the front. Jessie sat between Royce and Rhonda.

"Incredibly impressive," Royce said quietly near her ear.

"If a guy brings you here, you know he's serious about you."

He threaded his fingers through hers. "I'll have to keep that in mind."

She glanced over at Rhonda. Peter's arm was draped around her shoulders, and they were nestled close, talking. Jessie leaned nearer to Royce. "Our first official double date. Not that they're noticing that we're here."

"They do seem to have eyes only for each other. At this point, under normal circumstances, I would say I have eyes only for you, but I don't want to give you hope there can be more between us than there is."

"Because of the cadets?"

"Because in war the only certainty is loss."

Did he truly believe that if something happened to him, she would grieve any less because he'd held his feelings for her secret? "It's so beautiful here. Let's not allow the war to intrude."

He studied her briefly before nodding and saying, "All right." He slipped his arm around her, and she snuggled against his shoulder, inhaling his spicy scent, relishing his warmth.

The lights dimmed. Neither of them spoke nor moved during the newsreels. She was grateful when the movie started, although she wondered if he might have preferred something along the lines of *The Wizard of Oz* to a story about a hero from the last war. At one point, she whispered, "Are the battle scenes upsetting?"

"I'm watching you."

She peered up at him. He looked as though he wanted to say more. Instead, he shifted his attention to the images on the screen. Did he need to be so cautious regarding the cadets or uncertainty? Peter wasn't hiding his feelings for Rhonda. The cadets' situation was different. They were leaving. Although it hadn't stopped one of them from getting engaged. The announcement had been in the *Tribune* last week. Jessie wanted people to know how much Royce meant to her. It was something they needed to discuss, maybe this evening.

When the movie ended, before the closing credits had even begun to roll, the flickering on the screen suddenly stopped and lights came on. "Ladies and gentlemen."

A man with a microphone, probably left over from the days when the theater had been a venue for vaudeville acts and live performances, stood before the screen. "It is with shock and horror that we have just learned that the Japanese attacked by air with overwhelming force the naval base at Pearl Harbor this morning. Hundreds, if not thousands, are feared dead."

Jessie sat in stunned disbelief. With his arm still around her, Royce hugged her tightly. Without even realizing how it happened, she discovered she was clutching Rhonda's hand. After a brief, heavy silence while everyone processed the announcement, a cacophony of sound suddenly erupted around them as some in the audience wept while others cheered and clapped.

"We'll go to war now!" a man shouted.

"About damned time!" someone else yelled back.

"I'm heading to a recruiting office," a man near them said.

"We'll have this war over with before the end of the year," another voice responded.

No, you won't, Jessie wanted to tell them. How many times had men marched off to war thinking it would be over in a matter of weeks? She looked at Royce. He reflected no joy that America would be joining the fight. Instead, he looked as devastated as she felt.

"I'm so terribly sorry," he said quietly.

All around them, people were getting up, rushing out. How was it possible that they had the ability to move? "They're right," Jessie said. "We'll have to get involved now. We can't stay on the sidelines after this."

Releasing Rhonda's hand, she managed to get to her feet, and immediately Royce was there, his arms, strong and comforting, encircling her. Pressing her face to his chest, she squeezed him hard, never wanting to let go, to face the awful reality of what waited for them.

"I don't understand." Rhonda's trembling voice reflected a mystified tone. "They said Hawaii was too far away from Japan to be attacked. How did this happen? We need to get back to Terrence."

It was doubtful they'd find any other answers there, but it was where you went when you were frightened, confused, and devastated: home.

A little over an hour later, they entered the house on Pecan desperate for more news. The radio in the car didn't work — the joy of being gifted with a previously owned vehicle. It was fine for the short drive to the airfield, but it left a lot to be desired when their country had just been attacked.

Annette and several cadets were gathered before the radio like they were sitting in front of an open campfire. A symphony of music was filling the room. How could there be music at a time like this? Everyone turned, eyes round with fear and worry, to stare at them.

"The Japanese bombed Pearl Harbor," Annette said.

"We heard. They made the announcement at the theater." Jessie set her purse on a small table and lowered herself onto an arm of the couch. "Have there been any details?"

"Not much. They'll interrupt every now and then when they have more to report. It's bad. We were totally unprepared. Battleships were sunk, aircraft and airfields destroyed. They say the casualties will be catastrophic."

"Anything about the *Arizona*?"

She shook her head. "No, why?"

"That's the ship David Baker, the mayor's son, is serving on."

"Shit," Annette whispered.

Jessie stood up. "I have to go see Mama."

She was out the door before she realized Royce was with her. Reaching over, she took his hand, and he pulled her in close. "How did you deal with this day after day?"

"You just take it a minute at a time."

"In an instant everything changed." Two weeks ago, they'd been feasting, and today Japanese ships could be headed their way to wage war. "How could we be so blindsided?"

It didn't matter. Eventually, questions would be answered. Still clutching his hand, she broke away and they began walking. "I have so many different emotions roiling through me right now. Anger, shock, terror, worry, heartbreak. All those people who died. I thought I could empathize with what you were going through in England, but it was only sympathy. I have an entire gamut of emotions and don't know what to do with them."

"You pour them into determination and resolve."

She could do that. She would do that. They would get through this. The country wouldn't fall. It might take a while, but they would be victorious.

When they walked into the house, she found her mom and Kitty in the living room, just as the others had been, sitting near the radio as though they needed to do that to hear it properly. Her mother got up and embraced her tightly. "You're all right."

As though she'd truly been in danger. Jessie decided when the unexpected happened, people experienced a sense of relief and hope when the expected arrived. "Has there been any word about David?"

Her mother reached out and squeezed Royce's arm as though to assure herself that he was solid and real. "No. I called Bug" — with her brow deeply furrowed, she shook her head — "but they haven't heard anything."

"It's not looking good," Kitty said, coming across as far too mature for her age. "Sounds like they just came in and wiped everything out."

Jessie eased down onto the couch, making room for Royce to sit beside her. It was incredibly comforting to have him near, a source of strength, someone who could guide them through this. "We'll declare war now, won't we?"

"I don't see how you can't," Royce said.

They would get more involved. They would send men off to fight. They'd have to ration. They'd have to . . . She could think of a thousand things they'd have to do. She was terrified at the thought of what the future would bring.

The following day a somberness hovered over the town and the airfield. While Jessie stood in the canteen holding Rhonda's hand, Royce by her side and Peter next to Rhonda, with instructors, staff, and cadets still and silent, she listened to Roosevelt's speech on the radio as he declared war on Japan. Three days later, her country was at war with Germany.

CHAPTER 35

Jessie crawled out of bed near dawn. She hadn't slept well all week, although she wasn't certain anyone else had either. An anxious pall had settled in as everyone struggled to determine how to move forward. It seemed wrong to laugh, tell jokes, or smile as the reports on the casualties continued to roll in. Hundreds, possibly thousands — military and civilian souls — had perished only a week ago. They'd arisen to enjoy a beautiful, picturesque morning and instead had experienced horror. She couldn't shake off a sense of doom, and it seemed many around her were experiencing the same.

The dance scheduled for the evening before had been canceled on Tuesday, the decision reversed on Thursday, canceled again on Friday. No one could decide if it would be appropriate to have a festive night.

In the end, they had gathered — without a band — simply to visit and talk, drink punch, and eat cookies. Conversations centered around what to expect, what they should do. Everyone wanted advice from those who already had been entrenched in a war that looked to be far different from the last one.

The advantage to getting up so early was that she was able to take her time in the bathroom getting ready for the day without constantly being interrupted with knocks on the door from one of her housemates who needed in. Afterward, she went into the kitchen and sighed at all the groceries stacked on the counter. Aware of the rationing in England, Annette and Rhonda had almost personally cleared the grocery shelves of flour, sugar, and canned goods. They didn't have enough room in the cabinets to store everything. It was inconceivable to Jessie that food supplies would get that bad here, but her mother had done the same thing. So had others in town, creating the shortage they'd feared.

Once the coffee stopped percolating, Jessie poured herself a cup, went into the living room, curled up in the corner on the couch, and took a slow sip, wondering if coffee might become rationed. She had no idea how imports would be affected. So many unknowns. So many aspects of war she feared they were ill prepared for.

A few instructors had already given their notice. As had a couple of the mechanics. Barstow had approached her to see if she knew any women who might be interested in working at the airfield — in any capacity. She'd given him a list of potential instructors. Odd how quickly his attitude had changed. She wondered if it was because she, Rhonda, and Annette had proven themselves as capable as men.

She was so lost in her thoughts that the knock on the door nearly made her jump out of her skin. Like everyone, she was on edge. An article in the paper had reported on a group of ranchers who'd formed an armed coalition to guard the Rio Grande and ensure the enemy didn't try to enter the state through that border.

Setting her now-cold coffee aside, she went to the door, aware of no stirring sounds coming from the hallway. It was nearly eight, but she was still the only one moving about. Opening the door, she welcomed the cool morning breeze, a little surprised to see Luke standing there. "Hi." She shoved on the screen. "Come on in."

"No time. I've got a train to catch. Just

wanted to stop by and say goodbye before I left."

Only then did she notice the small brown suitcase resting at his feet. Dread pierced her chest. "Where are you going?"

"It's our war now, Jess. Enlisted with the marines. Off to Parris Island for training."

The marines. She knew no branch of the service was safe but wished he had let her teach him how to fly. She tried to see around him. "Are your parents with you?"

He shook his head. "Ma started crying during breakfast. Thought it best to say my goodbyes at the house. Didn't need her bawling at the depot. Leaving is hard enough without that."

"Would it be all right if I waited with you?"

He gave her the lopsided grin that had so charmed her in high school. "I'd like that."

"Let me grab a sweater." Suddenly chilled to the bone, she snatched one from her closet and jerkily pulled it on before hurrying out to the porch and closing the door behind her. Slipping her hand into his, she held on tightly as they walked to the depot.

"Heard you took Eve to the movies," she said quietly.

"Just the once. She was nice, but I couldn't see things working between us. I hear rumors about you and that Brit. You gonna marry him?"

"I like him, but he's not the reason things didn't work with us."

"I know. I did a lot of thinking, finally came to the conclusion that deep down, I knew what I was offering wasn't the life for you. You've always been more ambitious than me. You wouldn't have been happy as a rancher's wife, Jess. I wouldn't have been happy if you weren't." He gave her a wink. "Get this war behind us, and I'll find the right woman."

She blinked back the tears stinging her eyes. "She's going to be so damn lucky."

They reached the depot. Several young men she knew were waiting on the platform, some alone, some with family. No one shouted enthusiastic greetings. A few nodded in acknowledgment. The mood was somber, a heavy shroud hanging over the travelers.

"Dad would be disappointed you didn't join the U.S. Army Air Forces."

"I considered it, but the marines seemed a better fit. I like to keep my feet on the ground and with all the hunting I do, I'm a crack shot with a rifle."

He'd wanted to teach her to hunt, but she couldn't bring herself to shoot an animal that had never done her any harm. They'd really never had the same interests. Still, she couldn't stop studying all the lines in his face, afraid she might never see it again. "I wish you weren't so tall. Please remember to duck."

He gave her an odd look before glancing off in the distance, and she knew he wouldn't hide, wouldn't cower, and he damned sure wouldn't run away from the fight.

The whistle of an approaching train reverberated through her. "Would you mind if I wrote to you? Jack says letters from home help to keep him going."

"I'd like that. Don't know if I'll have much time for writing back."

"That's all right. You'll know we're thinking of you."

The train pulled into the station with a screeching of brakes that shattered the quiet of the morning and echoed ominously. Before the Brits had come here, Jessie had always found the arrival and departure of trains a romantic thing, a symbol of people going places, a sign of adventure. Now it represented the start of a journey into danger.

"Don't suppose you'd send me off with a kiss, for old times' sake," he said.

Her nod was barely perceptible as she rose

up on her toes, wound her arms around his neck, and planted her mouth on his, pouring all the love she'd felt for him in her youth and all the affection she still held for him into the kiss. He'd been her first in all things. Her first date, her first kiss, her first boyfriend, her first love.

When he pulled away, she hugged him more tightly and whispered, "Promise me you won't take any risks, you'll stay safe, and you'll come back."

"You know me, Jess. I don't make promises I'm not a hundred percent sure I can keep." Offering her a small smile, he tucked a finger beneath her chin. "But I'll try my damnedest to come home."

Abruptly he broke free of her hold and, with long, loose-jointed strides, made his way to the train. She waited until he appeared in a window to move up to the car. People around her were shouting their goodbyes, women were crying. Even though she saw him through a misty haze, she refused to let the tears fall where he could see them. "I'll send you some brownies."

His smile bright with bravado, he laughed. "You do that!"

The whistle shrieked and the train began chugging away from the station. She waved until she couldn't see him. Waved until she

could no longer see the train.
Then she let the tears fall.

CHAPTER 36

Sunday, December 21, 1941
After another week of restless nights, an hour or so before dawn, Jessie rode her bicycle — purchased three days earlier because they were being told to conserve gasoline — to her mom's house, in need of the comfort provided by the porch swing and Trixie's head resting over her feet. Things were still changing at a rapid click, and it was taking some adjusting. The town council had met and set a date in January for a blackout dress rehearsal. People were periodically stopping by the school to ask Royce for advice on how they should pre-pare in case the enemy attacked here. They wanted to know the best way to help the war effort. Everyone seemed nervous and on edge. Fifteen more men had enlisted. The *Terrence Tribune* had begun recording their names and the military branches in which they'd serve.

Now that America was embroiled in the war and "we are all in this hash together," the cadets had been given permission to wear their uniforms when they left the airfield. It was impossible now to mistake them for anything other than what they were: the boys in blue.

Regretfully, three of the cadets from the first class had been killed in action. A column in the newspaper titled "News on Our British Boys" had included the information along with cheerier news about promotions and commendations. Jessie assumed Kitty provided most of the details, because she was keeping in touch with all the cadets as much as possible, writing letters weekly. Staying in contact was helping her to heal, but Jessie couldn't help but believe it also served as a reminder of her loss. She still wasn't attending the dances and continued to wear black.

Jessie was brought out of her reverie by the distant roar of an AT-6 coming from the direction of the airfield.

Fingers of sunlight had only just eased over the horizon. Rushing to the edge of the porch, she saw the silhouette of the airplane flying away from Terrence, no doubt its pilot striving not to disturb anyone who was still abed or cause a panic at the unexpected sound of an aircraft overhead. But why was anyone manning a cockpit at this time of morning on a day when the airfield should be quiet?

After giving Trixie a final pat, Jessie climbed onto her bicycle and hightailed it to the airfield, various scenarios circling through her mind, keeping pace with her peddling. A rogue student? A thief? A saboteur? Or maybe it wasn't a plane from the airfield. Could it be an enemy fighter?

She swept onto the dirt road and could see no one standing about. Many of the cadets spent their open-post night else-where, traveling to another city for a bit of adventure or staying in someone's home to enjoy a break from the barracks. Obviously, none of the remaining students had been bothered by the noise of a plane taking off, preferring instead to take advantage of the one morning a week when they could stay in bed late.

After bringing her bike to a halt and lean-ing it against the side of the hangar, she hur-ried inside, retrieved her binoculars, and rushed outside. Scouring the sky, all she could see were glorious streaks of orange, pink, and blue as the sun eased farther over the horizon. Running to the flight line for AT-6s, she raced along one length of planes

412

and then the other, counting as she went. One was definitely missing.

She hoped it was one of the instructors, and not a student, who had taken it up. On occasion, when she needed to escape her cares, she flew the Jenny. Among the heavens, all the troubles of the world could fall away for a while. Unfortunately, they always returned once the wheels touched down. She hadn't taken any time for herself up there since the attack at Pearl Harbor. It seemed so much needed to be done. Redoubling her efforts to train the cadets, keeping up with the news that inundated the papers and airwaves now that the United States was officially at war. Honoring her obligation to assist her country in whatever capacity she could by learning to live with rationing, providing comfort, and helping where needed.

The Bakers had only yesterday received a Western Union telegram from the navy, informing them that their son was "missing following action in performance of his duties and in service to his country." More information would be forthcoming when it was received, but not a soul in Terrence didn't think he was dead, killed when the *Arizona* sank. She had visited with the family yesterday evening to offer condolences.

413

In low whispers, women murmured their opinions on whether a memorial service should be held now or if they should wait for confirmation of what they all believed to be true. What if his remains were never found?

She fought not to wonder how many families in various parts of the world had gone through the same uncertainty since a madman had first taken action to dominate the world.

With a sigh, she began walking toward the hangar. Since she was here, and it was such a lovely morning, perhaps she would take the Jenny up, escape the realities for a while. Just soar unfettered and free . . . but gasoline was so precious now that she couldn't justify what was essentially a joyride. Then it struck her hard that whoever had taken the plane up better not be using it for that sort of purpose. So if it wasn't a student wanting to hone his skills by getting in some flight hours —

Catching sight of a speck on the horizon, she lifted her binoculars, bringing the shadow into focus. It was an AT-6. The wind sock showed the wind blowing in from the east. The pilot flew once over the airfield and then banked to come in for a landing from the necessary direction.

The wheels touched down with precision and rolled to a stop a short distance away. Surprised, she watched as Royce climbed out of the cockpit and hit the ground. She didn't waste any time in marching over and stating quite succinctly, "Well, good morning."

As he dragged off his leather helmet, he looked over at her. "What are you doing here?"

"I could ask the same of you."

He looked guilty as sin as he glanced around before bringing his attention back to her. "I needed the practice, wanted to get in some hours."

"When did you start flying again?"

"About a month ago."

Why hadn't he told her? Why did ominous dread slither through her because he hadn't? "We're supposed to conserve gasoline."

"Yes, I'm aware. How did you know I was here?"

"I didn't know it was you specifically. I was sitting on Mama's porch when I heard a plane taking off and saw it leaving this airfield. I came to check it out. I certainly didn't expect it to be you. Why would you need the practice? Are you going to start teaching the cadets?"

Slowly, he shook his head, lifted a hand,

415

and tucked some curls behind her ear, his thumb grazing over her scar as it always did. "I was going to wait until after Christmas to tell you, but I'll be returning to England in January, with the next course of students who earn their wings."

Her stomach lurched, like she was in the cockpit of a plane that had suddenly lost all power and gone into a dive. "Are you going to be training cadets for combat?" She knew they received some additional training when they returned.

"No, Jessica, I'm getting back in the fight. I hope to fly Spitfires, although I'll happily take a Hurricane."

"You're going into combat." She wished she'd been able to say it with more enthusiasm, more support, but she hated the thought of his putting his life at risk.

"Yes." His hand had never left her, and now he trailed his fingers along her chin, as though striving to map out her features. "I've been testing my leg when no one is about, and it no longer hampers my ability to control the plane. I can do more good there than here."

"But overseeing the training of pilots is important."

"It is, yes. Incredibly so, which is the reason I'm glad they have you. Our replacements —"

"Our?"

He grimaced. "Peter is returning as well, but keep that between us for now."

If Peter had told Rhonda, she would have told Jessie. Lord, Jessie would have heard her crying if nothing else. "When did you decide this?"

"After my brother was killed. The guilt of being here and not there . . . Rationally, I know it would not have changed the outcome, but I have to go back. I need to be in the thick of things."

She rubbed her hands up and down her arms. The sun was out fully now. She should have felt warmer, but instead she felt chilled, like she did when Jack had shoved the rare snowball inside the back of her shirt. She wished Royce had involved her in the decision, but he'd always been intent on keeping some distance between them, and perhaps this was the reason: he'd known he wasn't going to stay. Hurt, angry, and terrified, she wanted to weep, to rant, to hold him close so he couldn't leave. "You really think you're up for a dogfight?"

He hesitated, studying her for a full minute before finally nodding. "I believe so, yes."

"Prove it." She started marching toward

the hangar.

"Where are you going?" he called out.

"To get my gear," she tossed over her shoulder. "Let's see if you can stop me from kicking your butt."

They flipped a coin to see who took off first. She won, so went last, giving her the advantage. But his calculating gaze as he studied her during those few heartbeats while the coin was in the air told her that he was already relegating her to the role of enemy. If she beat him, she suspected their relationship would stall and whatever feelings he might hold for her would sour. But she didn't care. She was determined to win, to convince him that it was foolish to even contemplate going back into the skies over Britain and Europe. The thought of his dying was more terrifying than the possibility of his coming to hate her.

They were using the AT-6s because the gun cameras would provide proof that they'd hit their target and eliminate any doubt that one of them was claiming a victory not earned. For her part, cheating would have been tempting. Anything to keep him out of harm's way. Even though she knew it wasn't fair to him when he wanted to go so desperately, when guilt was

418

gnawing at him.

She understood guilt, had experienced it. But had also learned it could lead to a lack of judgment. She imagined his viewing every enemy combatant as the one who'd shot down his brother, taking unnecessary risks to get even, to get revenge. That in his quest for vengeance he might misjudge an opponent's ability to outmaneuver him.

She'd feel the same if Jack were killed, desperate to wreak havoc on every Messerschmitt pilot. None would be safe from her fury.

Even now, as she followed Royce into the sky, she was feeling it, going into combat mode, determination building within her soul, her heart pumping, blood rushing through her, creating a roaring in her ears like the waves crashing against the shore. Yet she also experienced a calmness and steady resolve. She knew this aircraft. It was her armor, her weapon. It could save and it could destroy. She was its master, and it followed her commands.

Royce was before her, his aircraft weaving widely and frantically, on purpose, preventing her from getting a bead on him, biding his time, waiting for her, for the contest to begin. Then he made a hard turn to the right. She followed.

419

Unexpectedly, he cut to the left, and she cursed, already committed to her turn. Gunning it, she pulled back on the stick and climbed, glancing back over her shoulder, spotting him coming up at her six.

She began to roll as she reached the apex of her loop, leveled out — now above him, heading toward him. She was willing to play chicken but unwilling to place herself clearly within his sights, so she flipped the plane onto its side, making it a small target.

He again cut to the right, and she followed, ready to adjust if he should take another sharp turn.

He pitched down, slicing toward the horizon. A series of loops and twists followed. She fought to keep up, cursed when she momentarily lost sight of him in a bank of clouds, and cursed more loudly when she realized he was coming in from behind her.

She needed to get into position to come at him from out of the sun, so the blinding light would make her more difficult to see. Weaving, she increased her speed. He followed suit. She was grateful to be wearing gloves to absorb the dampness on her palms. Her breaths were calm and even, although she was now not only fighting him but her own survival instincts that were screaming for her to run.

Abruptly, she pulled up and reduced power. He flew under her, the roar of his engines drowning out her own thoughts. Once again the pursuer, she increased speed, lined up her shot —

He climbed, she followed. Higher, faster, spinning, rotating. Then he made a sharp loop and was suddenly behind her again.

"You're going into the Channel, Jessica." The radio that allowed them to communicate between the two planes crackled. His voice came across steady, almost regretful.

He banked left, heading back to the airfield. He was good, she'd give him that. She took several wide, slow turns just to calm her racing heart. She supposed when actually fighting for survival, one learned tricks, mastered reading an opponent, conquered how to stay focused.

After shaking off the disappointment, she returned to the airfield. A crowd had gathered. Apparently, they'd had an audience.

She taxied to a stop, shoved back the canopy, unhooked herself from the harness, removed her helmet and goggles, and climbed out. He was waiting for her. Jack would have been grinning, rocking back and forth on his heels, crowing. Royce actually looked as though he'd lost.

"You're good," she said.

"So are you."

"Not good enough."

"I'd say one out of three times you'd beat me."

She scowled at him. "Surely one out of two."

He grinned. "Possibly."

"Want to go back up and find out?"

He shook his head. "No. But I could do with some breakfast. Join me at the café."

"Winner pays."

"Absolutely."

She licked her lips and swallowed. "If I'd won, would you have stayed?"

Slowly he shook his head. "It's frightfully hard to leave you, Jessica, but I have to do this in order to remain a man I can live with. A man you'd . . . welcome spending time with now and then."

"If anything should happen to you . . ."

"I wish I could say it won't, but we both know it probably will."

Yet still he was going. They all continued to go.

"I've changed my mind," she said. "It'll be my treat."

He smiled. "You're a remarkable woman, Jessica Lovelace."

Not so remarkable. Simply trying not to let on that she was scared to death for him.

CHAPTER 37

Christmas morning, the scent of pine greeted Jessie in her mother's foyer, carrying her through memories of so many other Christmases, but this one had a very different feel to it. Uncertainty. Innocence lost. But as she stepped into the living room, the large tree with its ornaments, sparkling lights, and tinsel reflected hope. It seemed particularly poignant because it had been almost a year since her father had died. If not for the war, she suspected they would have felt his loss more keenly — but knowing more loss was to come, they all seemed determined to celebrate, hold the fear at bay, and make wonderful memories to be taken with those who would be leaving and held close by those who were staying.

Yesterday evening, more gifts than usual had rested under the branches: gifts for the two cadets sleeping over, the RAF officers and staff, Rhonda, and Annette. Her mother had knitted everyone scarves. She'd also arranged for every cadet to spend Christmas Eve and Christmas Day in someone's home. It had been a monumental task but "Christmas is a time for family," she'd told people as she encouraged them to open their hearts and their doors.

"You're here!" Her mom gave her a huge hug. "Want some eggnog with a little bourbon?"

"It's not even noon."

"Your dad never bothered with a clock on Christmas."

Jessie smiled. "In his memory, yes, I'll definitely have a glass." She followed that with greetings to the two cadets — Larry, who was playing checkers with Kitty, and Walter, who was watching as though enthralled with the movements of the pieces, but she suspected was more interested in her sister — the administrative officer, Mark Powell; the armament instructor, Bran Finnegan; and finally to Royce, who stood beside him. They each held a glass of eggnog. Rhonda was spending the day with only Peter. Annette had left that morning for Austin to be with her family.

Moving away from the others, Royce kissed her on the cheek. "You look lovely."

424

She was wearing emerald green, which brought out the shade in her eyes. He was in his uniform, and so damned gorgeous in it. "So do you."

He grinned. "Handsome, surely."

"Very."

"Here you are, Jess," her mom said.

She took the glass and held it up. "Cheers."

All the Brits followed suit, and she took a sip, grateful to discover only a hint of bourbon. Her mother's pour was much lighter than her father's had been. "Was Santa good to you fellas?"

"Indeed," Powell said. "Received a telegram this morning. My wife gave birth to a little lass in the wee hours."

Joy swept through her. Even in the worst of times, happiness could be found, life went on. Although how difficult it must be for him to be here while his wife was there. How long would it be before they saw each other again? How long before Jessie's countrymen would be shipping off to foreign shores and might go months or years without seeing family? Still, she smiled brightly. "Congratulations. They're both doing well?"

"She wouldn't have it any other way, my wife."

"Please let her know we wish her the best."

"I will. When she sends a photograph, I'll share it."

"I'd like that. I'm sure the baby is beautiful."

"If she takes after my wife, she is. Not so much if she takes after me."

She looked at Royce. "Did you find coal in your stocking?"

He chuckled low. "No. My mum sent a cardigan she knitted. I'm not certain I'll use it while I'm over here. Does it ever get cold? We're rather used to snow at Christmas."

The day was sunny and warm. Children were running around in shorts. "Our weather is part of the reason your government wanted a school here. We do have cold days, but they seldom last and usually arrive out of the blue."

"I shan't hold my breath for one then. She also sent some crackers."

Jessie furrowed her brow. "Are they better tasting than what we have here?"

He grinned. "I'm not even certain you have them here."

The crackers, as it turned out, weren't crackers after all — at least not the kind Polly the parrot might want. Sneakily, he'd set a wrapped tube, with paper gathered at each end, beside every dinner plate at the table. When they sat to eat and discovered

426

them, he insisted they couldn't be opened until after they'd finished their feast.

The gathering was small enough that they all sat around the table, her mother encouraging Royce to sit at its head. It was a bittersweet moment with him at her dad's place, a reminder that life carried on. He looked as though he belonged there, and she wondered if someday he might return for a visit . . . or maybe more. For her.

By unspoken agreement, no one brought the war into the room. As they enjoyed turkey and ham, they discussed families, fishing, movies, and books. After plates were cleared away and clean saucers set down, her mother walked in carrying what looked to be a domed cake.

"I've never made one of these before." She set it down at her place. "Wait."

She rushed back into the kitchen and returned holding a shot glass. "Brandy," she said, before pouring it over the dome, striking a match, and setting it alight.

Jessie and Kitty gasped in surprise. The Brits clapped.

"It's a Christmas pudding," her mother announced, beaming. "For our guests. I do hope it's tasty."

After the fire extinguished itself, her mother served the dessert until everyone had some in front of them, although no one made a move to eat. As though in anticipation of something grander happening, they were all looking at Royce. He spooned up a portion and slowly savored it, before smiling. "A triumph, Mrs. Lovelace."

Jessie had never seen her mother blush so much. "I'm so pleased." She waved her hands as she retook her seat. "Everyone, dig in."

It was a mixture of sweetness and spice with a hint of the brandy. Around the table, murmurs of satisfaction echoed. When they were finished, Royce announced it was time for the crackers. The Brits needed no instruction as they grabbed the ends of the tubes and jerked hard. Pops burst through the air along with an assortment of items. Kitty asked for help and one of the cadets took hold of one end of hers, both of them pulling. When it came apart with a pop, she laughed lightly. Jessie thought it was incredibly wonderful to hear her sister laugh at long last.

"What is this?" Kitty asked, unfolding paper. "A hat." Glancing around, she saw that their guests had already put theirs on. "Y'all look so silly."

"Be a good sport, Kitty," Royce said. "Crackers are a serious business. Don't make us the only ones looking silly."

She put hers on with a burst of laughter before reaching for what looked to be a wrapped candy.

"Do you need some help?" Royce asked, noticing that hers hadn't yet been opened.

Jessie could probably do it alone, but instead of trying, she held it so the other end was pointing his way. They pulled hard and when it broke apart, her items went flying all over the place. They both laughed and she knew she'd never forget that sound of their joy mingling.

After helping with the cleaning up of the table and kitchen, Jessie followed her mother into the living room. Royce was standing near the fireplace, watching the others, who were engaged in a card game with Kitty at the small table where she usually played checkers.

With a smile, her mother sighed contentedly and settled onto the couch. "I'm taking the remainder of the day off. You fellas just fix yourselves sandwiches if you get hungry later."

Jessie edged closer to Royce. "Christmas is Trixie's favorite day. She gets a heap of leftover scraps. You two have a rapport. I wondered if you might like to do the honors."

"Yes, I would, very much." He set his glass on a nearby table, followed her into the kitchen, and picked up the large bowl full of a dog's idea of heaven.

Jessie opened the door, and they went out into the backyard. Trixie dashed over and stopped before them, her tail wagging furiously. Jack had taught her to wait for her food, but it was obvious she was straining to do that. "You can just set it down," she told Royce.

Trixie dug in, and he laughed at her enthusiasm. She loved his laugh, hadn't heard it nearly enough.

"The crackers were fun, just what we needed today," she said quietly.

"They're just a bit of silliness, but I'm glad my mum sent them. We always had them at Christmas, even after we were grown. And plum pudding. Your mum did an excellent job with that."

"I couldn't believe when she set it afire."

"That was always my favorite part." He studied her. "I was hoping to find a moment alone. I have something for you. It's just a little —"

He reached inside his jacket, removed a small velvet box, and extended it toward

430

her. "I should have wrapped it."

"No, that's fine. I just wasn't expecting . . ." She took it and carefully lifted the lid to see a set of silver angel wings attached to a silver chain. Tears were welling and burning her eyes.

"It was the closest thing I could find to anything that resembled flight. And to a lot of these lads, you're a bit of an angel, I think."

"It's beautiful. Perfect. Much nicer than the Sheaffer fountain pen I bought for you." She'd presented it to him last night when they'd all exchanged gifts in the living room. He'd given her a lace handkerchief then, probably because they'd had an audience and the necklace was more personal, a sign of what their relationship had been becoming, one with feelings that seemed too big to hold.

"I value that pen. They're hard to come by in England. I suspect pens will be as rare and precious here before long. I'll use it to write you . . . if you like."

It was the reason she'd given it to him. As a hint. Fighting back the tears — she couldn't cry in front of him — she nodded. "I was hoping you would. Will you put your gift on me?"

He draped the silver chain around her

neck and fastened it, taking his time, his fingers warm against her nape. She touched the wings where they rested just below the dip in her collarbone. She was never going to take it off.

"There," he said succinctly, as though dismissing a group of cadets, and she wondered if the moment was as hard for him as it was for her.

"I was thinking . . . and I realize this is probably bold of me . . . but I was thinking maybe we could drive into Dallas for New Year's Eve. Go to a club for a couple of dances, dinner, champagne at midnight, get rooms — separate, of course — in a hotel, and stay the night."

"You think your mum is going to approve of us going off?"

"I'm not in high school." She'd be twenty-five at the end of January. "I do what I want. Nothing happens here on New Year's Eve. They shoot off some fireworks, but I don't even know if they'll do that with the somber mood everyone is in now. It might be the same in Dallas, but where's the harm in finding out? We're not going off to get married."

"I'd like very much to spend the evening with you. I just don't want your expectations to end in disappointment."

"They won't." How could they when she'd have him to herself for a while?

433

CHAPTER 38

Wednesday, December 31, 1941

Royce and Jessie drove to Dallas in the mercury that Mr. Baker had loaned the British officers, the automobile they'd pass on to their replacements. The weather had cooled considerably since Christmas, with forecasts of snow. Royce had mentioned that perhaps they should delay their "outing," but Jessie was willing to risk the worst blizzard in Texas history for a couple of days alone with him. He would be leaving in two weeks, and any delay carried the risk of them possibly never having this time together, these memories. Texas weather was too unpredictable.

They spoke about the school, how Royce's replacement — Squadron Leader Michael Hollingsworth — who had arrived two days earlier seemed "the capable sort, a good chap." Jessie admitted to liking him but would have said the same even if she hadn't.

434

Royce didn't need to be taking any worries with him when he left. She wanted him solely concentrating on engaging with the enemy and evading death. For the next two days, though, she intended to push everything out of her mind except for the moments in which they were together.

No fears, no worries, no predictions, no what-ifs. It would be the ending of one year marked by changes, the beginning of another that promised only more drastic changes. He'd already reminded her several times, "No promises, no commitments."

Her head was acknowledging the words, but her heart wasn't listening.

She suspected Rhonda was going through the same thing. She was with Peter as much as possible. Sometimes late at night, she'd hear her friend weeping. But that was something else she didn't want to think about at the moment.

They'd left straight from the airfield as soon as their responsibilities for the day were over and had arrived at the Adolphus a little before seven. Any other time, she would have been impressed by the twenty-two-story building that more closely resembled a castle than any hotel she'd ever seen. The lobby was grand and glorious, with sweeping stairs. They each checked in for their respective room, although she did boldly ask the man behind the desk if they might be able to get rooms on the same floor. A bellboy was available to help them with their luggage, but Royce declined the offer. He had the kit bag he'd arrived with in June and was carrying the small suitcase she'd packed. For one night, they didn't need much.

Anticipation was thrumming through her by the time the elevator stopped at their floor. Although it was awkward with him carting their baggage, she wound her arm around his as they strolled down the hallway until they reached her room.

"Looks like mine is just down there," he said.

Using her key, she unlocked the door, and he held her case out to her. "Would you bring it in?" she asked.

He stepped over the threshold and switched on the light. She followed and closed the door. He turned slowly, as though uncertain as to what he might find when he was finally facing her. But she'd been contemplating how she wanted to handle this moment ever since they'd made the decision to welcome in 1942 at a club in Dallas. They'd lined up things to do tomorrow to create memories, but it was all designed to keep them busy, to prevent them from thinking about what the next year or two or three might bring.

She took a deep breath. "I reserved two rooms only for propriety's sake. I know it's a waste of money not to use one of them, but I want to spend whatever time we have together actually being together."

He had yet to lower the bags, simply stood there studying her. She came a little nearer, grateful he didn't retreat. "Would you happen to have packed any *erasers* in that bag you're clutching?"

His puff of laughter was almost sad. "Sweetheart, I can make no promises to you. The odds of . . ." His words trailed off as though he had no desire to give voice to the reality of what his future might hold.

"I don't want promises. I want memories."

"Jessie, your country has been plunged into war. Everything suddenly becomes immediate. I've been there, I've seen it, I know what happens. We lose the ability to think rationally, because we fear death will soon rob us of the ability to think at all. There's going to be a rash of weddings, of people striving to feel some sense of normalcy. Bad decisions are going to be made in the heat of the moment. The regrets are going to last a lifetime."

"Am I wrong then in thinking you care for me . . . at all?"

"If I didn't care for you, I'd already have you in that bed."

Those might have been the sweetest words she'd ever heard, and the accompanying smile she gave him must have signaled that he was losing this argument.

"I don't want to be responsible for you being hurt," he said.

Stepping up to him, she flattened her palms against his chest, against his blue uniform. He'd probably worn it in an effort to remind her that he was returning to the battlefront and would immediately see action, because he already had the training, knowledge, and experience. "There are no guarantees of going through life without pain. Which is why I think it's important we grab every ounce of happiness while we can."

He released a long exhale that sounded like surrender. "Would you think me a cad if I did pack rubbers?"

She gave him an impish smile. "Would you think me a harlot if I packed some in my luggage in case you didn't?"

The bags hit the floor just before his mouth latched onto hers with passionate purpose. His arms were around her, bring-

438

ing her in close, while she relished the feel of his muscles beneath her hands. There was slightly more to him now than when he'd arrived, not so much that his uniform no longer fit, but it was filled out, probably as it had been the first time he'd worn it. She didn't want to think about his going back to a shortage of food, but they'd begun rationing things here. Sugar was already incredibly precious. More rationing would come in the months ahead. No guarantees, nothing stayed the same.

But this would, what she felt at this moment, all the love pouring out of her to encompass him. If she had only the ending of one year, the beginning of another with him, it would be enough, she would make it be enough. If he came back to her, she'd be waiting for him. Meanwhile, she would take each day as it came, doing her part to bring this god-awful war to an end.

She slid her hands over his back, around his sides, and settled them at the buttons of his jacket and went to work. He unbuckled the belt, finished her task, shrugged out of the jacket, and tossed it onto a nearby chair. Her buttons were next, followed by the buttons on his shirt. Other buttons and zippers were undone, until they were standing bared before each other. He looked more powerful than she'd expected — firm muscles, lean, but sturdy.

"You're so beautiful," he whispered reverently.

"So are you."

He lifted her into his arms, and she almost cursed his leg and hip that had healed to the point that they could support her weight, could take him away from her.

After carefully setting her on the bed as though she were fine china, he followed her down, and once more he took possession of her mouth. Desire, heated and frantic, swept through her. She would never have enough of touching him, of him touching her. As they became lost in the throes of passion, she realized she'd lied. The memories weren't going to be enough.

CHAPTER 39

Jessie woke up, still naked and in his arms. His dark hair askew, he was watching her.

"I didn't mean to fall asleep. What time is it?" she asked.

"Nearly nine. We should probably get dressed if we're going to the club."

Like a contented cat, she stretched, making sure as much of her touched as much of him as possible. She skimmed her fingers over his chest. "I wish I weren't, but I am hungry."

He pressed a kiss to the top of her head. "I am, too."

But she didn't think he was talking about food. He'd be returning to this room with her.

They moved about as though they'd been together for years, sharing the bathroom, washing up, straightening hair, and putting on clothes. He was clad in his uniform again, while she was wearing a red long-sleeved evening gown with an enticing V in the front that was more risqué than anything she'd ever worn.

He trailed a finger along the dip in her dress. "I'm looking forward to taking this off you later."

She was fairly certain she was blushing. Rhonda had painted her fingernails a red to match the gown, and Jessie wasn't feeling quite herself. Her friend had also given her a slew of makeup and tips, but she had decided not to use any of them. She'd never mastered putting on makeup, and her attempts always left her looking like a two-bit trollop. That wasn't a memory of her that she wanted him to have.

They arrived late at the club Rhonda had recommended, their reserved table already given to someone else, and no more tables were to be had — until the manager stepped in and insisted a table would be made available for a man in uniform.

They were seated away from the dance floor. The lighting around them was dim, romantic. The music provided by the jazz band seemed rather muffled, and the gorgeous Black singer, dressed in a golden evening gown, crooned more slow, heartfelt songs than upbeat ones. People didn't seem to be dancing with as much enthusiasm as in the past, as though they were expecting a bomb to fall through the roof at any moment. A couple holding each other barely moved from their spot on the dance floor. She saw one girl, weeping, clinging to her dance partner. Jessie wondered if he'd already enlisted or had been one of the men recently called up.

While waiting for their meal to arrive, Royce scooted his chair around until it was touching hers, until his leg was against hers, his hand wrapped around hers. Tonight, in this place, it didn't seem forward or unwarranted. Everyone appeared to be needing a little more comfort. He leaned toward her. "I like the way your eyes sparkle in the candlelight."

"I'm happy tonight." She wanted him to have a memory of her happy, and the champagne was certainly helping. He'd ordered a bottle, and she'd enjoyed a glass with nothing in her stomach to absorb any of it. She was feeling a little light-headed and giddy. "I'm glad we're here, although I suppose I expected it to be a little more festive."

"Everyone is adjusting to reality, I suspect."

"You must have thought we were incredibly insensitive when we celebrated your arrival in town with dances, socials, and invitations to speak at lunches."

"It was a bit jarring to go from rationing to abundance, from cautious optimism to such unfettered exuberance, but we hold dances in England and still go to the cinema and theaters. You can't let the enemy take away your joy for living. Otherwise, they've won. I predict next New Year's it'll be a bit more lively here and Terrence won't cancel its fireworks show."

The town council had worried that filling the night sky with exploding lights would make them a target for any nearby unseen enemy.

As though he'd been listening in, their waiter stopped by, leaned down, and said quietly, "At midnight, we won't be shouting 'Happy New Year' or releasing streamers — since we don't know if the next year will be happy. A more moderate welcoming in of the New Year is planned."

She and Royce nodded as though it was expected, and perhaps in a way it had been. After the waiter walked off, she admitted, "I don't know if I really could have shouted 'Happy New Year' with any real conviction."

He stayed where he was when their steaks arrived. They took their time savoring what would probably become a rarity for her and most certainly one for him. So many times, she was tempted to say, "Don't go." But she knew if she tried to hold him back, he would come to resent it. Part of the reason things had stopped working with her and Luke was because he wanted a homemaker and she wanted to be an aviator — and he hadn't been willing to accept her choices. The truth was that Royce's choice was part of the reason she loved him: his willingness to put himself in harm's way no matter the cost.

When they finished the meal, he ordered another bottle of champagne.

"Are you trying to get me drunk, Mr. Ballinger?" she asked, giving him a seductive look that she hoped was as intriguing as the ones Bette Davis delivered on-screen.

He laughed. "No, Miss Lovelace. I just want to ensure you have a good time."

"Then dance with me."

He escorted her onto the dance floor. People were a little more relaxed, probably a result of too much champagne or too many cocktails. People often swayed into them, but no one seemed to mind. The jitterbug and Lindy Hop weren't danced as enthusiastically as in the past but did help to lift some of the melancholy.

Then the band began playing "Tonight We Love" and everyone moved closer.

Royce circled an arm around her waist, drew her nearer, the one hand holding hers coming to rest on his chest as he slowed their movements, their eyes locked. He was so handsome in his uniform that her heart ached. Her airman, her love. "Royce —"

"I know."

Did he? Did he know how big and all-encompassing what she felt for him was? "You're going to share England with me someday."

His smile was soft, wistful. "Every inch of it. We actually have seasons there, you know."

"I look forward to experiencing them."

His gaze grew more intense. "I didn't want to come here. Now I don't want to leave, but if I don't, I fear I'll become someone neither of us would like. However, no matter where I am, Jessica, I'm going to remember how wonderful it was to have you dancing in my arms."

In spite of her eyes stinging, she wasn't going to cry, wasn't going to give him tears to remember. "I love you. I know you don't want me to say it, but I do."

Before he could respond, the music stopped, and the singer began calling out the countdown. "Three, two, one." She lifted a flute of champagne and smiled, but

446

it seemed forced. "Happy New Year, everyone."

A few people called out "Happy New Year" in return. The clinking of glasses echoed around them.

"Happy New Year, flygirl," Royce said, and she knew in his kiss he was pouring the words he wouldn't say — couldn't say. Words he feared might be a burden to them both. He knew the agony of losing a love senselessly.

While people began singing "Auld Lang Syne," he gathered her close and escorted her back to their table. After paying the check, they returned to the hotel.

To her room. To her bed. Where they finished welcoming in 1942 by making tender love.

CHAPTER 40

January 1942

The first week of January it snowed, and the temperatures dipped into single digits. Miserable weather. And yet, Royce insisted the flying lessons continue. Weather in England wasn't always ideal.

It was brutally cold in the cockpit, and Jessie was grateful the AT-6 had a closed canopy, so they could avoid being hit directly by the wind. She had to take over a couple of times from her students when the pitch got too bad and they were in danger of losing control, but for the most part they handled things well. Which was good, because at the end of the following week they'd receive their wings, and on Sunday they'd board the train to start their journey back to England.

Royce would be leaving with them. She fought not to think about that, but it was with her always.

Since they'd returned from Dallas, they'd spent time in each other's company in the evenings, but not in each other's beds. They had housemates, and Royce wanted to protect her reputation. As though she really cared about that. She considered suggesting that they go into Dallas on Saturday night and check into a hotel, but it reeked of desperation — yet she was desperate to be with him. Kisses simply weren't enough.

The days before he'd be leaving seemed to be rushing by. She had this insane notion that with America now taking an active role in the war, maybe the Axis powers would simply surrender. But here they were more than a month into it, and no one seemed willing to give up.

Just like Royce had planned to wait until after Christmas to tell her he was leaving, it seemed the town had been biding its time until the holidays passed. Seventeen more of the town's men had enlisted. The announcement was made that no more new tires would be sold. A civilian air patrol was established. The blackout rehearsal scheduled for the seventh was postponed a week because of the below-freezing temperatures. "If you don't like the weather, wait a few minutes," the mayor chuckled at the town hall meeting, although no one chuckled back. It was as though the seriousness of the situation had finally hit home.

The following Friday, January 16, the weather was a lovely sixty degrees, and it was agreed the blackout would happen that night. The new moon would make it easier to detect anything that needed to be corrected. They'd asked Royce, with his experience, to fly over the town to make sure no light could be seen. Everyone was worried that Germany or Japan might start doing bombing runs in the area, although Jessie wasn't exactly sure how they'd manage to travel such a great distance — but then, they'd misjudged the Hawaii situation, certain the islands were beyond reach of any enemies.

They also asked Royce for suggestions regarding the best material to use for blackout curtains. Annette had sewn sequins on the side facing away from the window to bring some cheer into the rooms. None of the homes had basements, because the ground was so hard to dig into, but the town council was discussing the need for an air raid shelter.

A little before ten, she and Royce drove to the airfield. A ground crew was on hand to light the runway for their takeoff and landing. The plane was waiting on the flight line.

She and Royce walked around it, doing their preflight check. When they were finished, he said, "If you don't mind, I'll pilot."

"I don't mind. As a matter of fact, I'm looking forward to a closer inspection of your flying skills."

The warmth in his eyes, his small smile, told her that he wanted to kiss her, but too many of the crew were around — not that it should matter any longer. In two days, he'd be leaving. She climbed into the rear cockpit, did her interior check, and put on the headgear that would allow them to communicate.

"Everything okay back there?" he asked.

"Perfect."

"Righto then. Let's see if we can detect any lights in the town."

The propellers began to spin, and they were soon taxiing toward the lighted path set for them. When in position, he waited for permission from the control tower, and then he was racing along the ground, the plane began to lift —

Up it went into the dark, moonless sky. Then he banked left, heading toward the town. She thought it was eerie to see the black void where she knew there should be some illumination. All the store lights, signs, and streetlights had gone dark. Any glow inside homes wasn't escaping into the night. People had done a good job of covering their windows. They'd taken the task seriously.

"Impressive," Royce said. "Do you see any lights at all?"

"No. It's like this every night in London, isn't it?"

"Yes."

"How do you even get around?"

"Very carefully."

"We're over the town, and I can see some building silhouettes, but I think it's only because I know to look for them."

"They've done incredibly well."

"Don't you think it's unlikely, though, that we'll ever be attacked?"

"It's best to be prepared." He spoke into his radio, alerting the tower to inform the mayor that no lights were seen and that the staff and crew could go home.

"Why are you sending them home before we land?"

"Because we're landing somewhere else."

A while later he was touching down at Love Field. After ensuring the aircraft was secure and that it would be refueled and ready for takeoff at dawn, he slipped his arm around her waist and led her out of the airport. She was determined to let the happiness and joy she was feeling drown the sorrow that hovered. It could come forth after he left, when she no longer felt the need to display a stiff upper lip for his benefit. She understood his need to return to the action and was going to support him in every way possible. No guilt, worry, doubt, or second guesses. They were in this together. A team.

They took a cab to a nearby hotel. She paid no attention to its name or lobby. She concentrated on him, the confidence with which he approached the desk and secured them a room, the wink he gave her as they headed for the elevator, his purposeful and perfect stride as they went down the hallway. After he unlocked the door, he lifted her into his arms and carried her over the threshold with tenderness.

There was no pretense from either of them as to the reason they were here. One more night, possibly one last night alone, when they could indulge in eliciting pleasure. He sat her on the edge of the bed, knelt before her, and began removing her boots as she shrugged out of her fur-lined leather jacket and set it aside. She combed her fingers through his dark hair. It was the longest she'd ever seen it. He looked rather unkempt, but she liked it.

With her boots gone, he went to work on the buttons of her flight suit, leaning in, trailing kisses over the skin no longer hidden from him. It seemed important to go slow, to make the memory longer. Wherever he touched, he branded her. "After you leave, I'll still feel the heat of your mouth on me."

He groaned low. "Only fair. I can recall each one of your touches."

He eased the material aside, slid it off her shoulders, removing everything that prevented him from seeing all of her. Then she did the same for him, taking her time, relishing that she had the opportunity to know every inch of him once more, to bask in the sight of him, while he stood patiently before her, watching her with hunger in his eyes that sometimes caused her to struggle with a button or a buckle. His desire for her was something she'd always wanted, and she hadn't even realized it until it had become hers.

The seconds were ticking by, and a shudder ran through her. They were moving too slowly while time was moving too fast. He'd be gone for months, maybe years. These last hours had to fill the well of longing, had to be enough to get her through the lonely nights that were certain to follow. It didn't matter that she had family and friends to comfort her. Somehow, he'd managed to take up residence in her heart. When he was completely nude, she cupped her hands around his shoulders and leapt up, wrapping her legs around his waist as his hands settled beneath her to offer support. Their mouths came together with a fury of passion, as though they'd only been gliding along and now were going full throttle. His groans, her moans, echoed around them as need took over.

They fell on the bed, starved for what the other could give, equally desperate to gift the other with pleasure. Within his arms she flew beyond any realm she'd ever known.

When she returned to earth, sprawled on top of him, she desperately hoped the tears she'd been unable to hold back didn't touch him.

They didn't sleep. He described places he'd take her to when England was once again safe and she visited. She told him about the bluebonnets that would blossom and blanket the land in blue in spring. How much she wanted him to see them. But she knew it probably wouldn't be this spring. Maybe the next.

They made no other future plans, as

though to do so would jinx things for them. He wasn't the only one in danger of dying. Earlier that week, they'd lost an instructor and a cadet when a plane had crashed coming in for a landing. They didn't know what had gone wrong, but it had served as a reminder that every time a pilot went up, risks were faced.

They made love whenever they grew too quiet, when thoughts seemed to grow too heavy. Each time, Jessie wondered if it would be the last, didn't want it to be. So they'd make love again, until dawn began edging over the horizon.

They ate breakfast at a nearby diner, before returning to Love Field. The AT-6 was waiting for them. She piloted them home.

CHAPTER 41

Saturday, January 17, 1942

Jessie was glad that they were again holding a dance on Saturday night, because it gave people an excuse to be happy, to smile and laugh without guilt. The wing parade had been held that afternoon. Royce had taken the graduating cadets into Dallas for dinner.

They'd only just arrived at the Legion Hall. People were greeting them, wishing them well, even though most of the townsfolk would be at the train depot in the morning to see the officers and newly minted pilots off.

She didn't wait for Royce to find her but made her way to him. He brought her in and gave her a quick kiss. Then he glanced around. "Kitty?"

She shook her head. "I couldn't get her to come." Out of respect for the cadets, her sister had attended the wing ceremony.

"There's a part of me that thinks she's too young to have felt so deeply but I don't know that the heart really cares much about age. I just hate that she's still hurting so badly."

"I doubt Hollingsworth is going to have any better luck than I did at getting the cadets not to date while they're over here."

"I think it's good that they go out with girls, that they enjoy any moments they can. Even their commanding officers." She flattened her palm against his chest. "I'm interested in dancing with this commanding officer."

He grinned. "I've officially turned everything over to Hollingsworth, but I'll dance with you anyway."

She'd planned to give him all her dances tonight but didn't have the heart to turn down any of her students when they invited her to dance.

She was taking a break by the refreshment table, watching Royce jitterbugging with Annette, when Lisa, Russell's wife, approached.

"Hi," Lisa said somewhat shyly.

"I wasn't expecting to see you here." Russell had left right after the New Year to fly planes for the navy.

"I wanted to make sure there were enough

dance partners to go around — and I have to fill my time with something. I feel like I'm spending my days just waiting."

"You have a pilot's license, don't you?"

"Only a private license. Before he left, Russell mentioned y'all were in need of more instructors, but I'm not qualified to teach."

"Do you have any interest in working as a control tower operator? I think the training takes only a month or two."

Lisa perked up. "Is that something y'all need?"

"Desperately. Two of our operators will be reporting for service in a couple of weeks. Why don't you come to the airfield Monday, and we'll see what information they can share? You could even watch them for a while, see if it's something you might want to do."

"I'd appreciate that. Thank you."

"With men being called to serve, people are going to have to become more accepting of women filling in where we can. We need to keep training these pilots, if we have any hope at all of winning this war."

"They should have you out talking about the war efforts."

Jessie smiled. "I've never been as comfortable on the ground as I am in the air. Talking publicly" — she shook her head — "maybe if I could do it from a cockpit."

Lisa laughed. "I know what you mean. I've always felt most at home in one, but for me, it was only recreational." She glanced to the side. "Oh, I think your man is waiting for a dance. I won't keep you."

Her man. As she watched Lisa walk away, she supposed her feelings for Royce were no longer a secret in this town. She wore her heart on her sleeve. But then, based on the warmth in his eyes as he joined her, so did he.

Her mother approached. "Everyone is beside themselves that they got a passing grade on the blackout. I do hope it doesn't become a regular thing. I don't know how you manage in England."

"It's preferable to being a target. Even the trains that run at night are blacked out."

Her mother glanced around. "I think some people are rather relieved that we're finally at war. It was a bit nerve-racking wondering if or when it might happen. Now at least we can all be on the same side." She gave him a soft smile. "We're going to miss you. I don't suppose you'd like to come by early in the morning for one last breakfast."

He looked helplessly at Jessie.

"Actually, Mama, I was going to prepare

him breakfast."

"Of course. You need a little time together before he goes. We'll see you at the depot then."

Leaning down, he kissed her mother's cheek. "Thank you for everything, Mrs. Lovelace."

There were tears in her mother's eyes when she said in a rough voice, "Dot."

She gave Jessie a quick hug before walking off.

"One last dance," Royce said, "and then perhaps we'll slip out. I don't have a house-mate tonight." Rhonda and Peter had gone into Dallas.

She nodded. "One last dance, but it has to be a slow song so you can hold me close."

When one started to play, she went into his arms as though she had a thousand times before and would again. She wasn't going to think about tomorrow. Only this moment. The fragrance of him, dark and spicy. The way her head fit in the nook of his shoulder. How small her hand felt nestled in his larger one. How they moved in a rhythm that was theirs more than the music's. How attuned they were to each other. How she'd never feel this way with anyone else ever again.

When the dance ended, while they'd

461

planned to slip out, people kept catching them, shaking Royce's hand, wishing him luck, saying goodbye. He was one of theirs now, just like the cadets. It seemed to take forever to go through the phalanx, but she didn't resent a single second of it, because it was gratifying to see that people appreciated him as much as she did. Those who'd been suspicious of the foreigners no longer were.

As they finally stepped out into the cool night air, he said, "I'd like to stop by your mother's house to see Kitty."

The first one to greet him was Trixie, her tail wagging wildly as he crouched and gave her an affectionate scratch behind the ears. "You be a good girl."

Once they entered the house, Royce went into the living room, while Jessie went up the stairs and knocked on Kitty's door.

"Come in."

She shoved it open and peered in at her sister curled on the bed, reading. "Royce is downstairs. He'd like to say goodbye in case he doesn't see you at the depot in the morning."

"I don't know if I can say goodbye without sobbing."

Jessie walked in and sat on the edge of the bed. "It's all right if you cry."

462

"We didn't shed a tear when Jack left, not where he could see."

Her heart ached because she thought her sister was struggling with more than worry about her tears. Jessie's last year in high school had involved football games, going steady, wearing Luke's football jacket, and prom. Kitty's final year involved heartbreak and now war. "Maybe we should have. I don't know. We were trying to put on a brave front so he wouldn't know how scared we were, how worried. We didn't want to make his leaving hard on him."

"Do you love Royce?"

"Very much."

"Are you going to cry tomorrow?"

She brushed Kitty's hair back from her face. "Not where he can see."

"Are you scared he won't come back?"

"Yes, I am."

"It hurts so much, Jessie. It still hurts so much."

With tenderness and care, she wrapped her arms around her sister, felt the shudders running through her with her sobs. "I know." And she knew she wasn't talking about Royce's leaving. "But Will wouldn't want you to be sad forever. And what you have to think about are all the times you made him smile and he made you smile.

The laughs and the talks and the just being together." Which was so easy to advise when her own heart hadn't been shattered.

"I try not to get to know them, the cadets. At the drugstore. But they flirt and talk and ask me questions. I've thought about quitting but then I start to get curious about them and it's a chance to visit with them a little bit. But I don't want to ever fall in love again. It hurts too much."

Jessie's own chest was in danger of collapsing with the tightness taking hold. She began rocking her sister. "Oh, Kitty, don't say that. Will wouldn't want that. You're young. You don't have to love right away, but someday . . . someday you'll be able to think of Will without crying. You'll remember him without hurting."

Leaning away, Kitty sniffled and wiped at her eyes. "Sometimes I don't want it to stop hurting. I'm afraid if it does, I'll forget him."

"You'll never forget him. Neither will I. He was one of my very first students. And a little cocky, but he learned fast. He was a natural pilot."

"Then why did he crash?"

"Even the best pilots can't control the weather or certain conditions that make flying hazardous. But he wouldn't want you dwelling on it, Kitty."

Nodding, she slid off the bed. "I want to wash my face before saying goodbye to Royce."

Waiting in the hallway, afraid if she went downstairs, her sister might retreat to her room, Jessie didn't want to contemplate how much it would devastate her if she received word that Royce had been killed. She'd been unwise to fall in love with him, but neither did she believe war was a time for putting love on hold. If anything, it should be embraced and experienced to the fullest. What was the point in fighting valiantly if there was no love to be had, if it was being rationed as stingily as eggs?

When Kitty came out of the bathroom, they descended the stairs arm in arm, but once they stepped into the living room, Kitty broke free, rushed to Royce, and flung her arms around him. He'd come to his feet, and Jessie was surprised the force of Kitty slamming into him didn't send him staggering backward.

"Please come back," Kitty pleaded.

He squeezed his eyes shut, and Jessie wished she hadn't seen the anguish in his face, because it brought home how hard he was striving not to have her worry. Rather than make her sister a promise he might not be able to keep, he said, "I was hoping

465

we'd play one more game of draughts before I leave."

Kitty giggled and fell out of his embrace. "Maybe I'll let you win this time."

When they started playing, Jessie sat on the sofa and watched. So many in town had said goodbye to loved ones over the past few weeks, but at the airfield there had been a good many hellos as replacements, most of them women, had arrived. Now they had female mechanics, parachute riggers, and additional Link Trainer operators.

Kitty's laughter rang out. "I always beat you."

"I'm simply not skilled at strategy," Royce said as he stood.

"In the spring I'm going to plant trees at the British portion of the cemetery. And I'm going to make sure that it always looks nice."

"That's very kind and thoughtful of you, Kitty. It'll bring a great deal of comfort to the families to know their lads are being looked after. But you mustn't forget to look after yourself. We need to mourn the loss of those we love, but eventually we must rejoin the living."

"Some people make fun of me. They don't think I could have really loved Will as much as I did because I'm so young."

"They sound rather foolish to me. And

they've probably not read *Romeo and Juliet.*"

Jessie thought it was wonderful to see Kitty smiling — a true, relaxed smile.

"I'll write to you," Kitty said.

"I'd like that very much." He cupped his hand over her shoulder. "I have to go now, walk your sister home."

"I'll see you at the train depot."

"Very good."

Placing his hand on the small of Jessie's back, he guided her out into the night. Bundled in her coat, she snuggled against him as they walked to his house for their very last night together.

CHAPTER 42

Sunday, January 18, 1942

Jessie had begun to loathe the train depot. The platform was crowded with those who'd come to see off the Brits or their own sons who had recently enlisted. She stood beside Royce as people came over to shake his hand and wish him well. The War Relief Society was handing out sack lunches to everyone preparing to board the train — Brit and Yank. She was glad the pilots were wearing their uniforms, their wings clearly visible. Earlier she'd made her way to each one, letting him know what a privilege it had been to work with him. While she didn't voice her worries aloud, she prayed each would remain safe.

From a distance, the train whistle sounded. She'd once thought it the most wonderful sound in the world. Now it simply echoed loneliness and sent dread cascading through her. Dread for what awaited these young men. For what awaited Royce.

With a loud clanging and hissing, the train rolled into the station and came to a stop. Only a few people disembarked, and the conductor was soon shouting, "All aboard!"

Stiff upper lip. Chin up. She tried to recall all the British expressions she needed to emulate so Royce wouldn't see how her heart was breaking, how terrified she was for him. She looked up at him. "I'll write."

"I will understand if someone else catches your fancy."

"Don't be daft. Isn't that how you'd say it?"

"Christ, I'm going to miss you."

His arm quickly snaked around her waist as he drew her up against him and blanketed his mouth over hers. Hungry. Desperate. Decisive. A last kiss. A hope for another.

Her arms wound around his neck like the wild vines on trees by the creek. To secure. To hold. To never let go.

Two short whistles of the train indicated she had to. Now. Before she was ready, before she wanted to. They broke apart.

"Keep training them well," he said.

"I will. Watch for Jerry."

"I will. I love you." Ducking in, he kissed her once more, quickly, before running for the train that had started to roll forward.

That wasn't fair. She sprinted after him. He jumped onto the train, hung on to the railing, and looked back. She raced alongside. "I love you!"

He grinned broadly. "I know." He blew her a kiss.

She stopped abruptly, just in time to avoid tumbling off the platform. Waving frantically, she watched until he was little more than a shadowed silhouette still hanging from the train, until he wasn't visible at all, until even the train disappeared.

Only then did arms come around her. She turned into her mother, inhaled her comforting lavender fragrance, and wept against her shoulder, the pain in her chest threatening to overwhelm her.

Originally, she'd wanted to teach flying because she'd thought she might make a difference, might help to save her brother's life. Now she wanted to save them all.

FROM THE *TERRENCE TRIBUNE*

January 19, 1942

To the good people of Terrence,
  When we arrived here seven months
ago, I had no idea that I would come to
care so much about the residents of your
fair town. You welcomed us into your
homes and hearts, and treated strangers
as long-lost friends.
  I haven't the words to express our appreciation for your hospitality, and more,
for your genuine interest in the lads. It is
with a measure of profound sadness that I
leave you now but know that I carry memories of you with me.
  I pray the war will come to a hasty end,
and your losses will be few. And may we
all lift a pint together again.

Sincerely,
Royce Ballinger
Wing Commander, His Majesty's
Royal Air Force

CHAPTER 43

Sunday, January 25, 1942
Curled on the couch before anyone else was awake, Jessie felt she'd moved through the week as though on an elevator, getting from one point to the next, without doing much of anything, in spite of the fact she was now the chief advanced flight instructor and had overseen the arrival of five new flight instructors — two men who were too old to enlist and three women. Barstow had contacted some of the men he'd flown with during the last war and pressed them into coming to help. She'd taken them through an orientation. All the continuing changes in personnel had occurred without a hiccup and with the cadets barely noticing. Unfortunately, however, two students on their first solo flights crashed into each other as they were landing. One walked away without so much as a scratch while the other broke his nose. The planes were sent away for repairs.

She missed Royce with an ache that left a huge hole in her chest. He'd phoned her just before boarding his ship. "I love you, Jessie — but don't wait for me. If you meet someone else . . ."

He hadn't finished the thought, and she hadn't responded specifically to what he was saying because the choice was either to lie and say she wouldn't wait or to admit she would wait and cause him to worry. She suspected he'd just wanted to hear her voice, to give her a chance to hear his one last time, in the event a German U-boat attacked Royce's ship while crossing the Atlantic. She'd simply said, "I know. I love you, too, a love that's as big as the Texas sky."

Since then, she'd been scouring the newspapers for any reports of ships being hit or sunk. Whenever possible, she was listening to the radio. The news was grim. They didn't seem to be making any headway in winning the war. But then, it seemed they were still in the preparation phase.

Retching echoed from the bathroom. Slipping off the couch, she padded barefoot down the hallway and rapped on the door. "Are you okay?"

"I'm fine," Rhonda muttered, sounding anything but okay.

473

"I'll make you some hot tea if you think you'll be up for it."

"That would be great."

After the tea finished brewing, she added an abundance of sugar and set a couple of crackers on the saucer. When she carried it into the living room, she saw Rhonda huddled in the corner of the couch, incredibly pale. Jessie handed her the tea.

"Thanks. Never really liked hot tea but don't think I can handle coffee. Peter is going to send me some proper English tea." Rhonda nodded toward the newspaper resting on the coffee table. "Nothing in there to make me think he won't, is there?"

"So far the ship they're on hasn't made the news."

"How much longer do we need to worry? Two weeks?"

"About that. But I'm more concerned about you."

"Just something I ate."

"It was something you ate a couple of days ago. And last week."

Rhonda set the cup and saucer on the low table, kept a cracker, and nibbled on it. Jessie couldn't remember her friend ever looking so miserable.

"I'm in trouble."

The words were a punch in the gut, even

474

though Jessie had suspected it was not spoiled food causing her friend to begin her mornings hunched over the toilet. Moving up, she wrapped her arms around her. "Oh, Rhonda."

"It was the state fair, I think."

She leaned back slightly. "The fair?"

She nodded. "We didn't stay. We snuck off and went to a motel. After that he'd sometimes climb in through my bedroom window — like we were in high school. But I'm pretty sure it was the fair day when *this* happened."

"Does he know?"

Tears welled in Rhonda's eyes. "That's the reason he went back. Jess, he's married."

That punch almost knocked her out. "Oh, Rhonda. Shit. The bastard —"

"No, he told me in the beginning. Before anything happened between us. Remember at your cookout, I told you he'd been avoiding me after the dance? He knew he was developing feelings for me, knew that he shouldn't, didn't want me to get hurt. But I didn't care. It was just supposed to be a harmless flirtation. He isn't happy in his marriage. Neither is she. Their families are in politics, and it was more of a political alliance."

"Like it was during medieval times?"

"Something like that. He was pretty sure she was having an affair even before he came here. He's going to get a divorce. But who knows how long that will take or when he'll have the opportunity to return so we can get married? It's not as if he's only a couple of hours away. And the journey is dangerous as hell."

"Did Royce know?"

"I doubt it. They hadn't known each other before they got this assignment. The situation regarding his marriage was so strained already, he never wanted to talk about it. If I hadn't been so nuts about him and pushed, he probably never would have said anything to me either. Ironic, isn't it? I was so certain he wasn't the marrying kind and Royce was."

"Royce did have a fiancée, but she was killed during the Blitz."

"Damn. All this uncertainty." She took the tiniest of nibbles on her cracker. "My dad will disown me. Barstow will fire me."

Jessie was afraid Rhonda was correct on both counts. Some of the people in the town would think what her friend had done was horrible, would consider her a tramp. She was in for a rough time. "Maybe Barstow won't."

"Once I start to show, he won't have a

choice. He can't have someone with loose morals teaching. I'm preparing for it. Peter is going to make arrangements for funds to be sent to me each month. He's going to set up a trust or something, so I'll be okay. Except for the ostracized part."

"I'll stand by you, Rhonda, help out any way I can. We'll get through this together."

"I want to wait to tell Annette, in case she doesn't want me living here. I've got nowhere else to go."

"I'm a little insulted you thought that I'd kick you out," Annette said, as she wandered in and perched on the coffee table, carefully avoiding the tea that had no doubt gone cold. "I wasn't eavesdropping but caught enough to figure out what was being discussed, something I'd already guessed had little to do with rotten food. I know what it is to face disapproval because of my career choices. We shouldn't have to go through it with our personal choices."

"But what I did is a sin."

"Is there anyone in this room who hasn't enjoyed a bite from the apple?"

"I got caught. People are going to know I did it."

"I don't think the normal rules apply during war," Annette said kindly. "And if the townspeople get too judgmental, I think we

477

can be a formidable trio."

With that, Rhonda burst into tears. Hugs and reassurances followed. Jessie knew she had the very best of housemates. They would get through any of the challenges that faced them.

When tears were dried and smiles were visible, Jessie said, "Mama's cooking a roast for Sunday dinner, and you're all invited."

A couple of hours later, while her friends visited with Kitty in the living room, Jessie was in the kitchen placing rolls on a baking sheet. Her family had always been there for the rough times, and this week, she needed them to help shore up her strength so she could focus on training the cadets, rather than worrying about every detail of a war that was too vast and complex to be reduced to news snippets here and there.

"Bug — Mrs. Baker — said they're going to have a memorial service for David," her mom said quietly. "There won't be a body, of course, but it'll bring them some peace."

They'd finally received word that he'd perished on the *Arizona*. "It's hard to believe he's not coming home."

"I know, but there are going to be so many more. Have you heard from Luke lately?"

"I got a letter this week, actually. He's received a sharpshooter badge."

"I'm not surprised. All the hunting that boy did."

Jessie smiled. Luke could be an old man, and her mother would still refer to him as a boy. Still, she wished he wasn't so good with a rifle. It made it more likely that he would see action. "He'll finish his training in February. He thinks he'll probably be sent somewhere in the Pacific."

"Hope he gets to come home first. His mama misses him something fierce."

Jessie missed him as well, but it was closer to the way she missed Jack or a dear friend. Opening the oven door, she slid in the rolls. "How did you manage not to worry when Dad went to fight in the last war?"

"Oh, sweetie, I worried. But I had you and Jack to keep me busy. It was hectic, but I was so grateful to have twins. You gave me purpose and focus. Just like these cadets are giving you."

"Half our staff are women now."

"I read in the paper about some girls going off to work in factories. Every day, it seems boys are leaving. Some of Kitty's classmates aren't even waiting until graduation because they're so afraid the war will be over before they get a chance to fight. They're quitting school and getting their mothers to sign letters giving them permission to join. Of course, some will need that even after they graduate — so damned young, too damned young."

Jessie wasn't accustomed to hearing her mother use profanity, but it was being spouted everywhere lately, interjected into nearly every conversation, as though no other words were strong enough to carry the weight of emotions felt.

When they were all seated around the table, an abundance of food spread before them, her mother said, "With rationing, this will probably be our last large meal for a while, so I want you all to eat up and enjoy. Let none of it go to waste."

As food was passed around, Rhonda asked, "Kitty, are you going to go off to college when you graduate?"

"No. I've spoken with Mr. Morris at the *Tribune.* One of his reporters left to work as a war correspondent for another news organization, so he's hired me as a part-time reporter. If I do well, he'll hire me full-time after I graduate."

"That's wonderful. You always liked writing and cataloging the town's history."

"I'm looking forward to it."

"Are you going to stop working at the drugstore?" Annette asked.

"No, I'll keep doing that. I enjoy meeting

480

and talking with the cadets. So many hang out around the soda fountain. I think it's one of their favorite places. And I like slipping them a free fountain drink when Mr. Delaney's not looking."

Jessie was grateful to hear she visited with the cadets, even if she was still wearing black. "With two jobs, when will you find time to do your schoolwork?"

"I'll find time. I have nothing else to do."

"Are you going to start coming to the dances on Saturday night?"

"No, I don't want to dance. But I'm glad they're doing that for the cadets. They need to find fun where they can. I write to those who have left and to the families of those who will never leave. It helps to have someplace to put sorrow and fear."

The burdens her sister carried at seventeen that Jessie hadn't. She couldn't help but hope her sister would again find joy.

On the eighth of February, Jessie received a telegram.

Arrived.
Love you deeply.
Royce

She smiled, assuming it was his having

481

gotten across the Atlantic safely that had him being so unguarded with his sentiments. His letter, whenever it arrived, would no doubt encourage her not to wait for his return.

Rhonda had also received a telegram, and while she hadn't revealed its contents, Jessie was certain it had filled her with the same sense of unheralded relief. She felt as though for the first time in three weeks, she could actually breathe again. It was with renewed vigor that she went to the airfield to train her students.

March 9, 1942

My dear flygirl,

I'm a cad for writing you, and in so doing, offering any encouragement to wait
for me. Yet I find incredible comfort in having this small connection with you, and I
smile as I write these words with the
fountain pen you gave me.

I've been assigned to Squadron ——
located in ——. I'll send you a telegram
with directions on where to send any letters you may write. I suspect the censors
will simply mark it out here.

I have already engaged a couple of
times with the enemy. They don't offer up
half the fight you did. I think we might be
well served having women in the cockpit
going into battle. If only it could be done
without loss of life. I don't think it is your
ability that is questioned, but the impact of
the loss. Even though women have been
warriors since the dawn of time.

On the way back over here, Peter shared
some unexpected news with me, which I
suspect you now know as well. We are
serving in the same squadron. Our time in
Texas has forged a bond we'd not shared
before. We both miss the warmer climes
and the warmth of the people.

I miss you dreadfully.

My love,
Royce

July 17, 1942

My dearest darling,

I received your cable. A little girl. With your red hair, I hope. I so regret that I was not able to be there with you, my brave darling. I know these months have not been easy, and I am incredibly grateful to the Lovelace family for surrounding you with their love in my stead.

My wife has been fighting me on a divorce, more concerned with ensuring she receives a pension should I perish, rather than my perishing. But I have finally obtained proof of her infidelity and am moving forward with obtaining my freedom. Acquiring open post to return to marry you will be a bit tricky because of the length of time the journey will require, but I shall see it happens. In your last letter, you mentioned coming over here. I actually began to shake. It is too dangerous, sweetheart. I could never live with myself if you — and now our precious babe — were permanently taken from me.

Please be patient. I will get this matter sorted, and hopefully, we will be wed before the year is out.

Give our darling girl a kiss for me. Prepare yourself for the one I intend to

deliver to you once we are together again.
It shall go on for days.

Always,
Your Peter

September 20, 1942

Dear Mama, Jess, and Kitty Kat,

As of today, I wear the uniform of the U.S. Army Air Forces. After months of rumors that my Eagle Squadron would be transferred to the American forces, it happened.

I have mixed emotions. The Americans are not yet battle-tested and still lack the experience and grit of the Brits, and I find myself losing patience with their arrogance and ignorance. To be honest, I'm also a little resentful that two years ago, the country I'm now fighting for was willing to imprison me for coming across the pond to defend against tyranny — and will now benefit from all I've learned during that time when it didn't want me here.

However, we were promised — if we fought for America now — we wouldn't face any consequences when we return home. We were assigned our rank based on the one we held in the RAF. After making a fuss, we were given permission to wear RAF wings sewn over our left breast pocket. By God, we earned them and wanted recognition for our time serving in the RAF. The U.S. silver wings we wear over our right pocket.

It's strange being around so many Americans again. I've grown accustomed to the British ways. But suspect I'll adjust fairly quickly to my new circumstances. A common enemy makes for strange bedfellows. However, at least it's now clear that we're all on the same side. And we have a war to win. I'll be home before you know it.

Love,
Major Jack Lovelace, USAAF

P.S. Give Trixie a scratch behind the ears and a treat from me.

CHAPTER 44

Saturday, October 24, 1942

Wiping the counter at Delaney's ten minutes before closing, Kitty glanced down at the other end, where a cadet was slowly sipping his Coca-Cola and reading a book. His name was Alec McTavish, he hailed from Scotland, and he came in every Saturday afternoon and did the same thing until closing. Only today he was wearing his wings. There had been a ceremony earlier in the afternoon, and she'd noticed when he stepped up to receive his wings. She still attended the ceremonies, welcomed the cadets, and saw the pilots off at the depot. Periodically, she'd interview one for the *Tribune.*

After graduation, she'd begun working at the newspaper full-time. Fran had left to attend nursing school with plans to join the Army Nurse Corps when she finished her training in three years. Kitty desperately

489

hoped the war would be over long before that. Fran had tried to convince Kitty to go with her, but Kitty wasn't yet ready to leave Will.

A little over two weeks earlier, she'd turned eighteen. It was the first year she hadn't gone to the state fair, but then, there'd been no state fair held. Although she probably wouldn't have gone anyway. She still wasn't attending the dances, couldn't shake off the sense of guilt that she was certain to experience if she had any sort of fun. When she wasn't working, she was tending to the British cemetery. Five more cadets had lost their lives while training. As had an instructor who was in one of the planes when it crashed. While Jessie had told her Will had been a good pilot, she hadn't truly believed it until that moment, when someone with so much experience had been unable to stop an aircraft from crashing in a field on a clear day. The danger of flight had truly struck her then. She didn't understand why anyone would continue to go up.

She made her way to the other end of the counter. "One more before we close up?"

"Aye, if you dinnae mind."

Because of the scarcity of fountain drinks, she was supposed to limit customers to one but often made exceptions for the cadets.

After setting his glass in front of him, she wiped at an invisible spot close to where his elbow rested on the counter. "I don't understand."

A corner of his mouth lifted slightly. "What do you not ken, Kitty Lovelace?"

She smiled. They'd chatted a few times over the months, and he had a habit of addressing her by her full name. He was dark-haired, handsome, and broad shouldered. "You keep spending your Saturday afternoons here. Why aren't you out having a picnic with a pretty girl? Or taking a stroll with one? The girls in this area are mad for the cadets. They'd like listening to you talk, if nothing else. Why aren't you out doing things?"

"Ah. Well, you see, Kitty Lovelace, I actually have my eye on a pretty lass. But she's in mourning, and I thought if I sat here often enough and long enough, I might have a chance to see her in red, or another bright color. But, alas, I leave tomorrow, and I've only ever seen her in black."

As though his reasons pushed against her, she took a step back. She hadn't wanted to hear those words. She couldn't decide if he was mean for saying them or she was for being the reason they were true.

"Don't look as though I've kicked a

puppy, Kitty Lovelace. I envy the lad who earned your love. It's a powerful thing, and he had to be very special. Because of that, I'm knowing he wouldnae want you mourning him and wearing black forever."

"You don't know anything about it," she whispered.

" 'Tis true enough. So tell me about him."

She hadn't spoken about Will in months and certainly had never spoken about him to a cadet — or pilot now — who had never met him. "He had a wonderful laugh."

"He enjoyed life, then?"

She nodded.

"Would he not want you to do the same, to carry on so his life has more meaning? Donnae think he'd want you in the grave with him."

"I'm not . . . I'm . . ." She glanced around. "We're closing now. You have to leave."

"Will I see you at the dance tonight?"

"No."

" 'Tis a shame." He set a nickel on the counter and slid off the stool. "Find a way to laugh again, Kitty Lovelace. He'd want that for you."

Wrapping her arms around herself, she watched him stride out of the drugstore. The arrogance, to tell her what Will would have wanted. To judge her and the manner in which she mourned. He simply didn't understand how deeply her love ran. And who was he to judge how she lived her life, when he spent hours sitting at the drugstore counter, reading a book, and drinking Coca-Cola? It was absurd.

But that night as she sat on her bed, her legs crossed beneath her, looking through her scrapbooks, she couldn't help but think she had sleepwalked through her last year of high school, through this last year of her life. Her friendships had narrowed to Fran, and now she was away, preparing for a fulfilling occupation helping others. Through her articles for the *Tribune*, Kitty was documenting the sadness of war — yet Will had laughed. All the cadets found ways to laugh, smile, and have fun. In spite of loss and fear and uncertainty. She concentrated on Will's death rather than his life, something she'd never expected of herself. It was unsettling; perhaps Alec was right, and she was wrong.

Suddenly no longer in the mood to be alone, she rolled off her bed and headed downstairs. Her mother was at the dance, helping to serve refreshments. Kitty left her a note, although she suspected she'd be back before Mama returned.

As she walked through the night, she

remembered how everyone in town had worried they'd be attacked, how they'd prepared. After passing that blackout test, they'd gone through a time when they'd blacked out every night and then they'd become lax, feeling safe and secure. But the rationing and the rubber drives reminded them they were at war. And the lists of casualties. Thirty of the pilots who had trained here were prisoners of war, missing, or dead. Yet every five weeks, another batch of cadets arrived.

When she reached Jessie's house, she jaunted up the steps and rapped on the door. It was a few minutes before Rhonda opened it, her daughter nestled in her arm. "I was just feeding Molly. Come on in."

Kitty stepped over the threshold, closed the door, and followed Rhonda into the living room, where her sister's housemate sat in a rocker. Kitty curled up on the corner of the couch, her favorite spot. For a minute, she simply watched as the red-haired baby suckled on a bottle. When it had become obvious Rhonda was pregnant, she'd been let go from the school. After Molly was born, however, Rhonda had managed to get her job back at the airfield, and Kitty's mother took care of the baby during the day. Some people had been scandalized by the unwed mother, but Kitty had seen how much Rhonda and Peter loved each other. She suspected things like this happened during war.

"Did you come by for a reason?" Rhonda asked.

"Just needed to get out of the house."

"You could have gone to the dance."

Jessie still went to the dances, in spite of her love for Royce. Kitty had actually considered going — for all of a heartbeat. She wondered if the Scot would be there. "I'm not ready yet, but maybe soon. Do you know a cadet named Alec McTavish?"

Rhonda smiled. "Oh, yeah. Gave him a few turns in the Link Trainer. Always did well. Serious fella, though. Seemed a lot older than his nineteen years. But then, I'm feeling a lot older than my twenty-five. Feel more like fifty some days."

"You don't look it."

She laughed. "You're sweet to say so, but this little one isn't sleeping through the night yet. I'm surprised your sister doesn't kick us out."

"She wouldn't do that. When is Peter going to return?"

"Don't know yet. He's trying to get reassigned back over here. There are five other schools, so if he can't get a position in Terrence, maybe he can oversee training at one of them. Then it would just be one trip across the Atlantic for him. I'd feel better about that. I told him not to come over just to get married. There's no reason now. I've suffered through the worst of being the town tramp. People have accepted me and our daughter. For the most part."

Kitty knew Rhonda's father had scorned her and transferred to another town to preach. She actually liked the new preacher better. His sermons revolved more around heaven than hell.

"So has Mr. McTavish caught your eye?" Rhonda asked.

She shook her head. "I was just curious about him. He'll be leaving tomorrow. It's not good to fall for these guys. Royce told me that. But I didn't listen."

"The heart's not good at following advice. It wants what it wants. Emily Dickinson said something along those lines. That's about all I remember from English class." She rested her daughter on her shoulder and began rubbing her back. "After she burps, would you like to hold her?"

Smiling brightly, Kitty nodded. "I should bring my camera over and take a picture of you both to send Peter."

"That would be nice."

Kitty stayed only until she'd rocked Molly to sleep and helped to put her to bed. But after she put her own self to bed, she couldn't stop thinking about Alec McTavish.

The next morning, a little self-consciously, she walked to the depot and, once there, slowly began wending her way among the cadets, shaking hands, and wishing them the best. Then she saw Alec, tall and broad, with a smile that put the brightness of the sun to shame.

"Why, Kitty Lovelace, I knew you'd look bonny in red."

It had felt strange to stand in front of the mirror and stare at her reflection in something other than black, but it had seemed the right thing to do as well. "You be careful, Alec McTavish. Don't make me put on black again."

"Wouldn't dream of it, my wee lass."

"Write me with where I can send letters, and I'll write you back. Just put my name, the city, and state on the envelope. The postman knows where to find me." He'd once told her she received more letters than anyone else in town.

"I look forward to hearing from you."

The high-pitched shriek of the train whistle echoed around them.

His grin was the most beautiful thing she'd ever seen. "Farewell, Kitty Lovelace. Thank you for sending me on my way with such a fine memory."

Then he was dashing for the train, and she wanted to grab him, hold him back, and not let him go.

An arm reassuringly circled around her shoulders. "I didn't know you knew Alec," Jessie said.

"He came into the drugstore. We talked." He'd given her a lot to think about. "I want to work at the school."

"What about the newspaper?"

"I can keep doing my 'British Boys' column and let the rest go. I wasn't doing that much anyway." She looked up. "I want to help make a difference. I know I'm not a pilot, but there has to be something I can do."

"Over the summer, the Brits began increasing the number of cadets for each course. Soon they'll be a hundred each."

"I thought more were coming into the drugstore."

"Next week, the army will start sending us American pilots to train. There's a lot of record-keeping. Mr. Curtiss, who handles the dispatch duties and keeps track of the training and flight hours for each of the cadets, has mentioned he is going to need an assistant. You'd be perfect for it. I can't hire you, but you might go talk with him."

"I like gathering information. I'll do that."

Jessie smiled. "Good."

People had wandered off, leaving only the two of them standing on the platform. "Do you think they'll run out of men to send here?" she asked.

"No, someone somewhere is always growing up."

She couldn't help but feel that maybe her sister was referring to Kitty as well. "I was afraid if I was happy, it wouldn't be fair to Will."

"I know. War leaves behind a slew of widows and broken hearts. But these men, and in some cases women, are fighting — and dying — so we can again find happiness. Everyone living with rationing and collecting rubber and knitting socks — everyone doing without and doing what they can — is contributing in some small way so we can put this tragic time behind us. Don't we honor their sacrifices by finding joy where we can?"

"I don't want to forget the losses."

"You won't. And neither will I. But what we're doing will hopefully mean fewer."

Kitty wanted to be part of it now. Maybe

she always had. Maybe that was the reason she hadn't left with Fran. Her destiny was here, and she could make a difference.

November 17, 1942

Dearest Jessie:

I'm writing with tragic news. Peter was shot down near —— and was captured by the Germans. Presently, he is being held in a prisoner of war camp, Stalag Luft III. Since they are not wed, I'm not certain Rhonda will be notified so have taken it upon myself to provide what information I can so you may share it with her. Better to come from you in person than in a letter from me. Unfortunately, I know little more than what I've already written.

I believe he will be allowed to write two letters, although God knows how long it will take for them to be delivered. Rhonda should contact the International Committee of the Red Cross in Geneva to find out how to get letters to Peter. As I understand it, there are all sorts of rules regarding what is forbidden, so it is best she check with them.

For what little consolation it will bring, he is out of the fray — although being in a German prison camp is no jolly good time.

I shall end this here but will write soon with more uplifting news.

Yours,
Royce

CHAPTER 45

Saturday, March 13, 1943

Jessie stood with Rhonda, the other link trainer operators, and the ground and flight instructors as the latest group of cadets received their wings. The ceremony was a bit more elaborate than the first few they'd provided for the graduates. An army band played. The Army Air Forces Flying Training Command and the RAF delegation in Washington had sent speakers and representatives. The audience now included people from Dallas and the towns surrounding Terrence. Jessie suspected some of the younger women in the audience were either girlfriends of or at least dating cadets. Articles about "our British friends" had appeared in the *Dallas Morning News* and the *Dallas Times Herald. Look* magazine had even had a piece about the school that included interviews with a few of the cadets and photos of them at a social put on by the

502

War Relief Society.

Glancing over at Rhonda, she thought her friend had aged considerably since she'd received news of Peter's capture. While she wrote him every day, she had yet to receive any word from him.

Between the British and American cadets, the school had more than four hundred students now. They'd built two more barracks. Another hangar had been erected to house the additional aircraft needed. They were short on ground school instructors. Flight instructors were filling in where they could. Everyone recognized the urgency, the dire need for pilots. They'd all worked through Thanksgiving. No holiday lights had adorned the town in December. No one had uttered the words *Happy New Year.* Jessie was beginning to doubt there would ever again be another year of happiness — then cursed herself for her lack of faith.

As part of the staff, Kitty was standing nearby, dressed in her khaki skirt, shirt, and tie. She enjoyed her role at the school, keeping track of flight hours and checking logbooks. She was attending the dances again. She smiled more, even laughed with the cadets. But the young men all seemed to realize she'd never be more than a friend, and many looked upon her as they would a sister.

She was corresponding with the young man she'd seen off at the depot, and Jessie prayed he wouldn't bring her heartbreak. Although all their hearts cracked a little every day as the casualties were listed in the newspaper. Cadets they'd trained. Boys they'd grown up with or dated. Killed. Missing. Prisoner.

She'd begun to dread opening the paper, but it seemed wrong not to acknowledge the losses. And then there were the ones during training. A crash in a lake, a field, some woods. Straying from a course. Unexpected weather. Disorientation. Sometimes they could determine it had been the result of an issue with the aircraft. Sometimes they could only guess.

But these ceremonies always brought her a short-lived sense of relief, because these cadets would no longer be under their care, her care. These had made it through.

The ceremony came to an end.

"Any idea how many this is now?" Rhonda asked.

"You'd think I'd know but it's a bit of a blur. Six or seven hundred. We can ask Kitty to start posting the number somewhere."

"She has certainly settled in."

"She looks around this place and sees the potential for gathering and organizing a lot of different scrapbooks." Kitty had begun creating memory books for each class.

"She's quickly made herself indispensable. Even helped me get some things organized with the Link Trainer." Rhonda was in charge of six other operators now. "Oh, hey, Mrs. L. I'll take Molly."

Jessie's mother passed the nearly eight-month-old over and Rhonda settled her on her hip. "Was she good?"

"Mine were never so little trouble."

"Thanks, Mama," Jessie said with a touch of sarcasm. "Jack, maybe, was a handful, but I was an angel." Then she nudged her friend's shoulder. "I'm going to make the rounds."

"Sure. Go on."

She started by shaking the hands of those who had earned their wings. While she had nothing at all against the American students, she planned to ensure she was always training the Brits. They were the ones she'd begun with, and she intended to end with them, when things finally came to a close. Although they were the same age as the cadets who had first arrived that long-ago June, the ones graduating seemed younger to her now. Maybe because she felt so much

505

older, not as cocksure as she'd once been, but her determination to teach these young men remained as strong.

She spoke briefly with the U.S. Army and RAF representatives. When those from the RAF expressed an interest in visiting the graves of the fallen, she introduced them to Kitty, so her sister could take them to the cemetery. She periodically placed flowers on the graves and had planted the trees she'd promised Royce she would.

Jessie made her way to Hollingsworth. She liked him, and they got along well, both striving to ensure everything ran smoothly. "This has grown into quite the ceremony. We didn't have such distinguished guests in the beginning."

"I think those in authority have come to recognize how important these programs are. You and your fellow instructors have done a remarkable job ensuring that our lads are all well trained," he said.

"With the rare exception, we've always had good instructors. Although I'll be honest, I don't think I ever really expected the war to go on this long."

"It does sometime seem it'll never end."

"But it will." She had to believe that.

CHAPTER 46

Saturday, December 25, 1943

Although Kitty smiled and laughed with the cadets whom they'd welcomed into their home for Christmas dinner, although she played checkers with them and ensured they had their fill of the pies that were baked with a little less sugar this year, she struggled to comprehend what was truly happening in the world.

Because she continued to write her column sharing news on the cadets who had returned to England, she had access to all the major newspapers to which the *Tribune* publisher subscribed, and the articles filling the pages for much of the year had been horrifying. The Nazis were executing thousands upon thousands of Jewish men, women, and children. As part of a plan that they were calling the "final solution." They were determined to annihilate the Jewish people.

Kitty couldn't comprehend such an atrocity. She'd become more dedicated to her job of recording the training of each cadet, of keeping track of their flight hours, of ensuring they were prepared for the job that awaited them when they returned to England. Their task was bigger than preventing Hitler from invading their country. They needed to see the entire Nazi regime destroyed. She was determined to do her part to ensure that accomplishment happened.

As Jessie and Rhonda began to lead the Brits in caroling, Kitty quietly slipped away and began walking toward the cemetery. Earlier in the week, she'd placed potted poinsettias in front of each headstone, and the sight of them as she approached lifted her spirits a little.

When she reached the first grave, she knelt before it and then stretched out across it. It was the closest she could come to hugging Will. So many of his classmates had died. She sometimes wondered if it would have been harder on her if he'd been killed far away from her, and she'd received the news via cable. At least here, she could visit.

"Merry Christmas, my love." Fewer tears fell, but they burned all the same and her heart still clutched with the memories. "Oh, I miss you." She sighed. "But I also feel a little guilty."

After sitting up, she traced her fingers over his name. "I've been writing to a fella. His name is Alec McTavish. He writes back. Our correspondence isn't like all the others. We write about personal things, our feelings, and maybe . . . seeing each other after the war. I wouldn't say that I love him . . . but I think that I could. He tells me about his home, and his family, and the things he likes to do. He thinks you'd want me to find someone to love me, to marry me, to ensure I had a good life and happiness and 'bairns.' " She laughed. "At first, I thought he was referring to barns, and I couldn't figure out why he'd think you wanted me to have barns. But he meant babies. I have to read his letters with a dictionary nearby. But they always make me smile. Just like you did."

She glanced around. "I don't even know if you'd recognize me now, Will. I was so innocent, naive, when you knew me. Not so much now. Such horrible things are going on in the world, and I don't know if I'm doing enough. Jessie assures me that keeping track of the paperwork is an important job. And someone has to do it, or the cadets won't get their wings. They need pilots desperately. The war is taking an awful toll

— on everyone. I knew Hitler was bad, but he's downright evil. He has to be stopped. He will be stopped. I believe that with all my heart. Germany, Italy, Japan — they'll all be defeated."

She pressed her fingers to her lips, then to the headstone. "In the spring, I'm going to plant flowers around the edge of this area. Daffodils. Your mother told me they were your favorite. Your family is doing well. They're going to visit when the war is over." She looked across at the increasing number of graves. Seventeen now. "I suspect the families of all who rest with you will. I wish you didn't have so much company. All right. I have to go back home now. I have a few more games of draughts to play."

Before leaving, she stopped at each headstone, delivering words of cheer from their families. She supposed some in town thought she'd gone a little mad spending so much time here, but she intended to ensure these brave souls were never forgotten.

CHAPTER 47

Saturday, May 6, 1944

On Saturday afternoon, Jessie was curled on the corner of the couch, her feet tucked beneath her, a sidecar in hand, and Kitty was similarly posed on the other end. Her sister often came over to relax after work and had given up her position at the drugstore. Rhonda sat on the floor, arranging wooden blocks, which Molly took great delight in knocking down. When the child's laughter rang out, everyone smiled. It was a wonderful way to end the week.

"I think she's going to be tall, like her mother," Jessie said. She'd be two in July. They'd all breathed a huge sigh of relief once she'd begun sleeping through the night. She had more godmothers than any other child in town. She was spoiled. More people had begun to accept her, especially because fewer babies were around since the men had gone off to fight.

"And tall like her father. She definitely has his eyes," Rhonda said. "I hate that the bastards won't let me send a photo or a drawing of her to Peter so he can at least see what she looks like as she's growing up."

"They probably worry you'll include some hidden message in the background," Kitty said. "If I were a spy, I'd find a way to communicate using any means possible."

"If you were a spy, who'd keep us organized and ensure everything ran smoothly at the airfield?" Jessie asked.

"If you're saying I'm irreplaceable, then maybe I need a raise."

"Talk to the Brits."

Kitty laughed. "I don't have Jack's persuasive skills, so I don't see more money in my future, but that's okay. I enjoy the work, especially when I get to tell you what to do."

The door opened. Annette walked in and announced, "Mail. Is it just me or is Royce writing you more often?"

Jessie held out her hand and took the envelope, thicker than usual. He *was* writing more often and had apparently given up on convincing her not to wait for him. He often mentioned things they would do and places they would visit after the war. "Thank you."

"Read it to us," Rhonda said.

Setting her glass aside, Jessie slipped a nail beneath the flap. "I'm not going to read it to you."

"You don't have to share the sexy parts, but I've had only one letter from Peter during all this time since he was taken prisoner, and he just reassured me he was all right. I could do with hearing some words from one sweetheart to another."

She started to get up. "Think I'll go read this in private."

"No," Rhonda said. "Stay here. You don't have to read it aloud, but it'll be fun to watch you blush."

"I'm not going to blush," she muttered as she settled back down. Although there had been an occasional letter when he'd mentioned their more intimate moments together and she'd wondered if the censor had grown as warm reading the words as Jessie had. She pulled out the letter and along with it a smaller envelope with Rhonda's name written on it. Her immediate thought was to hand it over to her friend, but a sense of foreboding had her unfolding her own letter and reading it.

The words jumbled around, made no sense, caused her chest to feel like a great weight had landed on it.

"Why have you gone so white?" Rhonda

asked. "Has he been wounded? Captured? Don't tell me it's a Dear Jane letter and he's met someone else?"

Jessie lifted her gaze, and Rhonda reared back as though she'd been slapped. "Don't look at me like you're not my best friend anymore."

How could she remain her best friend when she was going to destroy her? Getting up, she walked over and dropped onto the floor. She swallowed hard, fighting back the tears, searching for the right words, words even Royce had written that he lacked. *Better to come from you in person than through a letter.* "Rhonda, I wish . . . Oh, God, I'm so sorry. I don't know how to tell you, but it's Peter. He —"

"Do not tell me he's dead. He did not die in that damn prison camp."

"No, sweetie, he didn't. He was one of more than seventy men who escaped . . . but then most were recaptured. Hitler was furious. He ordered fifty executed. Peter —"

"No." Rhonda held up a hand, shook her head. "Don't you tell me . . . Peter wouldn't try to escape. He'd just wait out the war. He'd —" Tears rolled down her cheeks.

"I'm so incredibly sorry."

Rhonda's wailing sob echoed through the room, and Jessie enfolded her in her embrace, rocking her gently, rubbing her back. Annette lifted Molly, who'd also begun to cry, into her arms and carried her from the room. Jessie's heart was breaking for her friend, could only imagine that Rhonda's had shattered into a thousand shards.

"It has to be a mistake."

"I wish it was." But Royce had written with certainty. The escape had happened March 24. Peter had been executed April 6. It had taken time for word to get back to Britain, for Royce to get word to her. "Royce said Peter had given him a letter to send to you if the worst happened. It's here, when you want to read it."

Rhonda eased away. "I loved him so much."

"I know."

"I wasn't supposed to. He was supposed to be like all the others, just a good time for a while."

"I could tell he fell for you, just by the way he looked at you."

"Why didn't he just stay put?"

Now wasn't the time to remind her that a prisoner of war camp was no country club. They had no guarantee the prisoners wouldn't at some point be killed or fall ill and die. She pressed the envelope into Rhonda's hand. "I wish I could offer you more. Hopefully his words will bring you some comfort. But I'm here for you, whatever you need."

Taking the letter, Rhonda flattened it against her breast, where her heart beat for a man who would never return to her.

My dearest darling,

If you're reading this letter, it's because fortune was not on my side. No, that's not true. Fortune was incredibly kind to me. It took me to Texas, gave me you. In spite of the horrors of war and my mission to get lads ready to face them, those months with you were the absolute happiest of my life. I regret not a single moment spent with you.

I do, however, regret I was unable to keep my promise to make you my beloved wife. Please take care of our little girl and my big girl — I love you both more than life. I hope only that with my death, I have helped to ensure a better world for you both.

I love you, sweetheart.

Always,
Your Peter

June 10, 1944

My dear Miss Lovelace,

Never in my life have I found a letter so difficult to pen or not known exactly where to begin. My son has spoken of you with such affection, and so the unenviable task of being the bearer of cruel tidings falls to me.

As you are no doubt aware, the RAF and the USAAF were critically involved in the events surrounding D-Day. This morning my husband and I were the recipients of a devastating cable. Royce has failed to return from one of his missions and has been listed as missing. Details are presently scarce, yet I cling tenaciously to the hope that the worst has not befallen him.

I have enclosed a letter he left with me to be delivered to you upon his death. I remain ever optimistic you shall have no cause to read it. However, I wanted to send it along because as soon as we receive any further notification regarding his well-being, I shall immediately send you a cable. I thought, depending upon the news, you might find some comfort having the letter already in hand.

This is a hell of a way to introduce myself, I must say. I apologize for not writ-

ing sooner. It would have no doubt softened the blow of receiving such dreadful
news if it had come from someone with
whom you were a bit more familiar. But I
foolishly believed that, having sacrificed
one son, I would not be forced to suffer
through the loss of another.

I wish to express my heartfelt appreciation to you for your efforts in seeing our
young men take to the skies so they may
meet with success in this righteous endeavor that has brought such despair to
so many.

Regardless of what the future holds,
thank you, Miss Lovelace, for loving my
son.

Most sincerely,
Victoria Ballinger

CHAPTER 48

Saturday, June 17, 1944

It was difficult to believe that eleven days ago, Jessie had been filled with such optimism and hope. Although the news had been scant to begin with, they'd heard reports that the liberation of Europe had begun. As more reports came in, it became apparent that victory was going to come at a heavy cost.

Now, sitting on the porch swing, she clutched a portion of the price. It had taken the letter from Royce's mother a week to reach her. No cable had come during that time. She didn't know if it would have made sense had it arrived before the letter. But with all the present chaos in Europe, his *mum* had probably anticipated that news wouldn't come straightaway.

"Are you going to read it?" Kitty asked, sitting beside her.

"No." It was only to be read if he was

520

dead, and she wasn't ready to give up hope that he was still alive. She thought it would be months, years, before they had a true understanding of the scale of the operation that had taken place on June 6. "Yet I can't seem to set it aside. It's like holding part of him." She desperately didn't want it to be the last thing she ever received from him.

She glanced over at her sister. "I don't know if I truly understood how badly you hurt when you lost Will. Sometimes I feel like I can't even breathe, that there's just no air to be had."

Kitty gave her a soft, understanding smile. "Well, you haven't lost Royce yet. There's still hope."

She nodded. It was more than many had. He could have been taken prisoner. She didn't want to consider that if he'd survived a crash, he might have had to fight off the enemy with the pistol he carried or that the Germans, in their fury over the invasion, might have executed him solely for being a British pilot. Not knowing his fate or what he was facing was an agony unto itself.

"I'm glad we received a cable from Jack letting us know he was okay," Kitty said.

It had come two days earlier, short and to the point: *I am well. Getting the job done.*

"It has to be so hectic right now. I doubt

he'll have much time for writing. If he's not flying, he's probably sleeping," Jessie told her.

"Casualty lists should start arriving soon. I wonder how many who trained here, danced and laughed with us, perished."

"Too many, but then, I think one is too many. Did you read that article by Ernie Pyle, about the landings on the beaches?" Jessie asked.

"Yes. It had to be so terrifying. But it should all come to an end soon now, shouldn't it?"

"I don't see how it can't. And I don't see how we can't win."

On August 10, the promised cable finally arrived.

Royce is alive. Recovering from his ordeal. Sends his love.

August 24, 1944

My darling Jessica,

You are never far from my thoughts, even if I am slow in writing. This mishap was slightly more troublesome than the first. Going down in enemy territory meant a good bit of hiding out and relying on the kindness of strangers. But I am home now, well on the way to recovery, and will soon be back in the fight.

I'm sorry for all the worry I must have caused you. But you were always with me. I had moments when giving up would have been the easier course but doing so would have prevented me from ever again seeing your smile or hearing your laugh or gazing upon the stubborn set of your chin when you were determined to have your way.

When next we meet, after all this time, know that I don't expect you to still love me. Nor do I wish to put any pressure on you to retain your feelings for me. But know that you shall always hold my heart. I am alive today because of you.

Yours,
Royce

CHAPTER 49

Thursday, May 10, 1945

"All right, Mr. Collins, there's no rest for the wicked. Let's see if you've finally mastered that Immelmann turn," Jessie said, a bit of teasing along with the seriousness in her tone. Like everyone else in town and at the airfield, the young cadet was distracted, gleeful that the war in Europe had finally come to an end on Tuesday. Wednesday, the cadets had been granted open post to celebrate the hard-earned victory — even if a tremendous amount of work remained to be done.

This morning they'd all gotten back to the tasks at hand, but with renewed energy and determination. The war was still raging in the Pacific and pilots were desperately needed there.

Jack had sent a telegram that he was to be transferred to the Pacific. Dread had filled her. Earlier in the year, Luke had been killed at Iwo Jima. While Jessie had been mourning with and comforting his family, his mother had shared the letter she'd received from Luke's commanding officer, commending her son for his bravery, and informing her that he had nominated Luke for a Medal of Honor. Jessie hadn't been surprised. Although Luke would have hated dying on a piece of land that meant nothing at all to him, she knew without a single doubt that as soon as his boots had landed on the shore, he would have given the fight all he had.

Collins flew up into the loop and, once inverted, righted the plane and leveled out.

"You handled that well, Mr. Collins. You're behind the enemy now. He's at your mercy."

"I hope so, ma'am."

"Take her home."

"Yes, ma'am."

A few months after Peter's death, Rhonda had received a letter from his parents. They hadn't quite known what to make of the Texan who had ruined his marriage, even though he'd assured them it had been ruined long before he'd ever left for America — was one of the reasons he'd volunteered to go to the States. When the war was over, they planned to send her money so she and their granddaughter could travel to England. They wanted to make a home for them, to maintain their last connection to the son they'd lost.

When they'd been celebrating — laughing, joking, dancing, drinking — the end of the war in Europe, Rhonda had said quietly to Jessie, "I'll stay for a few more months, but by fall, I'll give my notice. I want to take Molly to England, so she'll have grandparents at last and will know people who can tell her stories about her father." Her own father had never acknowledged that he had a grandchild.

Jessie had hugged her tightly. "I'm going to miss you."

But she understood why she wanted — needed — to go. She thought Peter would have wanted her to be with his parents, to find love and acceptance where she could.

After his letter last August, Royce had seldom written, and when he did his letters were brief. He never mentioned the future or missing her. Jessie tried not to worry, but she sensed that something drastic had changed between them. What had he experienced while he was missing? Had he fallen for someone else? A nurse who had cared for him or . . . whoever had harbored him behind enemy lines?

They neared the airfield. This was the one time when she wasn't particularly thrilled to be sitting in the rear of the cockpit, because she didn't have a clear view of what was before them. But she concentrated on the instrument readings, not worried about her pilot's skills. Collins was in his final phase of training and was, well, he was a very good dancer. They touched down lightly, bounced a couple of times, and slowed. He taxied forward, coming to a stop along the flight line.

When he shut off the engine, she said, "Nice landing, Mr. Collins."

"Thank you, ma'am."

Getting out of her seat, she swung a leg over onto the wing and froze as her gaze fell on the hangar and the two figures standing there. Her mind raced back four years. Barstow's hair had gone grayer, but he hadn't changed much. The man standing beside him wasn't in a gray wool suit but in a blue RAF uniform. She'd recognize his build anywhere. Royce.

She jumped off the wing, tossed aside her helmet and goggles, and started running, somehow managing to unharness her parachute as she went and discarding it along the way. She'd never run so fast in her life, didn't even realize her legs had the ability to fly, but that's how she felt as she flung herself at him — not having to travel far because he'd been rushing toward her. His arm came around her and she took his mouth — not passionately, just gratefully, joyfully. He was back. He was here, alive and well, and hugging her —

With only that one arm.

It was then that she pulled back slightly and realized the other sleeve of his jacket was empty. Because she was almost melded to him, she felt him stiffen. She searched his beloved face. "Did this happen when you crashed?"

He nodded. "I was in enemy territory and had to hide out. By the time a farmer found me, infection had set in and my arm was beyond saving. He sawed it off himself, brave man."

She was horrified. "You were the brave man."

"I wanted to die from the agony of the ordeal and what followed but doing so would have meant never seeing you again."

In the first letter he sent her after he was back in England, she'd thought he'd been referring to surrendering to the Germans, not death.

"Why didn't you let me know? In one of your letters?"

"Because I was afraid you'd try to come over, and I didn't want you put at risk. And then . . . I selfishly wanted you to tell me in person if it makes a difference, if it changes your feelings toward me. I will understand, Jessica. I'm not the man who left —"

"Don't be daft," she said, cutting him off, using a word she'd picked up from the Brits. "You're here, you're alive, and I love you more now than I did four years ago. If absence makes the heart grow fonder, I'm near to bursting."

With a laugh, he buried his face in the curve of her neck. "I didn't think it would matter, not to you, but I knew chaps with sweethearts who . . . well, they weren't you. God, I missed you, flygirl."

CHAPTER 50

Sunday, September 23, 1945

In her mother's kitchen, Jessie rolled out the pastry for the apple pie that would be cooking while they all ate their Sunday afternoon dinner so they could enjoy it afterward fresh from the oven. On September 2, the war with Japan had finally come to an end. A week later, the British Flying Training School closed. The cadets were already on their way back to England. Royce was assisting with the dismantling of the school and seeing the equipment turned over to the army. Once his responsibilities ended, he and Jessie would travel to England, where he would return to civilian life and she would teach flying. They'd been married in August.

Earlier in the week, Rhonda had begun her journey to England. It had been hard to say goodbye, but they'd see each other soon and if all went as planned, Rhonda would

530

live near Jessie and Royce.

Annette was staying on to teach at the civilian flight school that would become part of the new airport. Kitty had been hired to help oversee the conversion and to take over all the administrative aspects of the school.

"I saw in the newspaper there would be no state fair again this year," Jessie said.

"Probably wouldn't have gone anyway," Kitty said as she mashed potatoes. "I have special memories from the last time we went. I was different then, so innocent. I don't know if I'll ever feel quite the same about the fair."

It was difficult to believe her sister was going to be twenty-one. But then, it was difficult to believe she'd be twenty-nine in January. In some ways, she felt like she and her sister had grown up during the war.

"Once we get these army guys out of the way," Kitty said, "we're going to be busy at the school. The war brought a lot of interest in flying. The school and the new airport will provide jobs for those returning from the war, although I'm hoping a lot of the women will remain."

"Before you know it, you're going to be a pilot," Jessie said.

"Nah, flying's not for me. But I like helping those who do want to fly."

Jessie opened the oven door and started to slide the pie in. "I imagine —"

Barking interrupted her, barking right outside the house.

"Is that Trixie?" her mother asked. The dog seldom barked.

"I think so."

"Whatever is wrong with her?"

"I don't know. I'll check on her."

Holding a newspaper, Royce had come into the hallway about the same time she did. "What is troubling Trixie?" he asked.

"Maybe some critter is out there."

"I should see to it then."

"I've got it." She took the time to kiss him before opening the door. A man wearing a U.S. Army Air Forces uniform was kneeling on the front lawn. Trixie was alternately jumping on him, snuggling against him, and excitedly running around him. Then the man looked up and grinned. "Oh, my God. It's Jack!"

She rushed outside. He stood just as she leapt into his arms, and he swung her around. "You idiot, why didn't you tell us you were coming home?"

"Wanted to surprise you."

"Oh my Lord, oh my Lord," her mother was calling out between sobs.

Jack released Jessie. "Hey, Mama." He

embraced her tightly. "Don't cry, now."

Jessie swiped at her own tears as Royce started making his way down the porch steps, but Kitty flew through the door and raced up to Jack. Without releasing his hold on their mother, he brought an arm around his younger sister and hugged her. "Boy, you grew up while I was gone."

Kitty stepped away, but their mother stayed close. Jessie wasn't certain she was ever going to leave her son's side.

"My word, but you've gotten skinny," Mama lamented.

"That's why I came home. So you can fatten me up."

Reaching out, Jessie took hold of Royce's hand. He'd joined them quietly, obviously not wanting to impose on the reunion, and she wished that he'd been able to have a similar one with his brother.

Jack looked over and smiled. "You must be Royce."

Her husband released his hold on her and extended his hand. "You'd be Jack."

Pumping Royce's hand, he said, "Guilty. I've heard a lot about you."

"And I you."

"I don't know if you got my letter, but he's my husband now," Jessie said proudly, the joy at being able to say those words radiating through her voice.

"I didn't, but congratulations." Jack beamed. "I'd say this good news calls for a shot of bourbon." He winked at Jessie. "I assume you still have some of Dad's bottle lying around."

"I saved it just for this moment."

After a round of toasts, they sat down to eat. Conversation and laughter flowed, and for the first time, Jessie felt like the war really was finally over.

CHAPTER 51

Kitty stood on the platform, anxious, nervous, relieved — too many emotions bombarding her. She didn't know if it was possible to actually fall in love with someone through letters, but she certainly felt as though she had. Alec had a poetic way of writing, and he seldom mentioned the war. Instead, he'd shared stories from his childhood, painted a portrait of Scotland, and wrote about his family. She'd followed suit, describing areas he hadn't seen, enticing him with places they'd visit someday. Always, they referred to someday. He had a way of filling her with hope of better things.

In a few minutes, his train would be arriving. Still in the RAF, he'd managed to get a lengthy enough leave to come spend a few days with her. Apparently, he was something of a hero . . . according to Royce anyway, who told her Alec had been awarded the

535

Distinguished Flying Cross. Alec had certainly never boasted of his exploits or his commendations. He was more her gentle giant.

A train whistle echoed in the distance, and she resisted the urge to gnaw at her bottom lip and ruin the look of the vermilion lipstick she'd reapplied only minutes earlier. Nearly three years had passed. Would he even recognize her after all that time? Would she him?

She'd sent him a few photographs, but there were times she was so far removed from the girl who had served fountain drinks to young cadets that she could hardly believe she was the same person.

Large and majestic, the train lumbered into view. The stories it could tell of those it had brought here and those it had taken away. It would soon be the start of Jessie's journey to England. It was hard to envision the town without her sister close by. Jack had mentioned that he wasn't certain he would stay. For him, after having crossed an ocean, the town suddenly seemed too small, suffocating. She couldn't imagine the wide world that awaited her siblings or being part of it.

Hissing and bellowing, the train screeched to a stop. Not as many people were disembarking these days. Not as many were waiting on the platform.

So when Alec McTavish stepped out of the car, she laughed. It wouldn't have mattered if a thousand people had scrambled off, if a thousand had been rushing forward to board or greet those they'd been waiting for — she would have known him. Her heart knew him with as much certainty as her eyes.

She didn't remember running to him, but her feet were suddenly lifted off the ground, her arms wound around his neck, his around her waist, as he swung her in a wide arc.

"Just as bonny as I remember in your red," he sang out in his Scottish brogue.

Drawing back, she cradled his face, familiar in spite of the deeper lines. "Thank you for not making me dress in black."

He grinned. "My pleasure, my wee lass."

"Now you're home."

"Aye. In your arms, I'm home."

EPILOGUE

Having finished with her tales, Kitty watched as her granddaughters placed crimson poppy wreaths against the headstones. It was the second Sunday in November, Remembrance Day in Britain, and these British boys were to be remembered as well.

"I'm going to take a little stroll," she said to the eldest of her three daughters, who stood beside her.

"People will be arriving for the ceremony soon."

Few from that time were still here, but their children and grandchildren and great-grandchildren — like hers — still came to honor the fallen.

"I won't be long. Just want to visit with your father for a bit."

Slowly, she made her way along the path, past where her parents were at rest, until she reached the red granite headstone of her beloved. For thirty years, Alec had worked as a pilot for a commercial airline that flew out of Dallas. After he retired, he'd served as mayor of Terrence for a time. While she, as odd as it sometimes seemed when she looked back, had managed the local flight school, despite never learning to fly. Alec had often offered to teach her. "One of us has to keep our feet on the ground," she'd teased him.

Jack had returned to the country and people he'd fallen in love with during the war. Jessie and Royce had remained in England. Jessie had eventually realized her dream and for a few years had flown as a commercial airline pilot. Rhonda had never married.

But they were all gone now, and Kitty missed them with a fierceness that was impossible to put into words.

Yet she still smiled as memories came floating back, and she saw Alec as the young man he'd been. "I'm so glad you didn't give up on me, that you sat at that counter waiting for me to be ready. What a glorious life we had, my love." She kissed her fingertips before pressing them to his headstone. "Soon," she whispered.

She meandered back to the special portion of the cemetery. The wreaths were all in place. More people had arrived.

Several broke away from the group. "Auntie Kitty." The eldest of her nieces wrapped her arms around her. Jessie's daughter. Jessie's son was also there, embracing her next. Jack's two sons and his daughter followed. And finally leaving her husband's side to hug Kitty tightly was Molly, who had so resembled her mother in her youth, and had named her son after her father. They all had their families with them. It was a tradition to come together every few years, to remember, to reminisce, to recall how it all had started. A war that had destroyed and torn apart had also brought together.

With her family surrounding her, Kitty welcomed all the others who had gathered. The townsfolk. A few relatives of those who rested here. One year, Will's family had visited. It had been a bittersweet reunion.

At eleven o'clock, one of the two RAF officers in attendance asked that they observe two minutes of silence. Afterward, a British dignitary spoke about sacrifice. A prayer followed. Then a rumble sounded, and just as four silver jets became visible, racing across the sky, one veered off. The missing man formation always caused Kitty to tear up, tears that thickened as the bugler sounded last post.

She thought fondly of Jessie. Her sister had had England. While Kitty had tended with loving care this small bit of Britain.

ACKNOWLEDGMENTS

It took a village to bring this story to life and I am forever thankful to those who traveled on this journey alongside me: First and foremost, my amazing editor, May Chen, whose patience and guidance went above and beyond, while I was writing my first book where the main focus was not the romance. She always manages to make me reach deeper to create characters that readers will care about. I so appreciate her willingness to take a chance on this story.

My agent, Robin Rue, for her encouragement and support when I first approached her with the idea of writing a story set in Texas during World War II.

The team at HarperCollins/William Morrow, for their enthusiasm and efforts on behalf of this story.

Fellow author and friend Barbara Dunlop, for loaning me her bush pilot husband, Gord, who has flown a Stearman and patiently guided me in portraying the intricacies of flight as accurately as possible. Any errors related to aviation are mine.

Kristi Nedderman, assistant city archivist, City of Dallas, who provided invaluable information on the State Fair of Texas. Of minor note, my research indicated corn dogs were introduced at the State Fair of Texas in 1942. However, after 1941, the state fair was not held again until 1947, so it seemed they had to be there in 1941.

Linda Winder, my high school journalism teacher, who helped to create an Angleton School History Center and was able to share archived information regarding the number of students who might have been enrolled in a small-town school in 1941. She also provided information on enlistments as well as the deaths of past alumni who served during World War II.

My in-laws, who answered my questions regarding details relating to small-town life and Texas schools before and during the war. My father-in-law, for sharing his experiences with the U.S. Marines as a seventeen-year-old recruit, just before the war ended. While recruits west of the Mississippi are generally sent to San Diego for boot camp, he was sent to Parris Island to accommodate the large number of enlistments. I found it plausible Luke might have gone to Parris Island as well.

Tom Killebrew, who wrote *The Royal Air Force in Texas* and *The Royal Air Force in American Skies,* documenting the British Flying Training School programs.

I also want to express my appreciation to Bill Huthmaker and the volunteers of the BFTS Museum in Terrell, Texas, for answering my questions. If you're in the area, I highly recommend taking a tour of the museum, with its displays of uniforms, logbooks, a Link Trainer, photographs, and memorabilia. Afterward, visit Oakland Memorial Park. The main road that takes you inside branches off into two forks. Take the one to your right and follow it until you see a small monument and twenty gray headstones lined up evenly, surrounded by hedges and protected by the shade of towering trees.

Every November, a ceremony is held to remember the young men at rest there. RAF officers and other British dignitaries attend, to ensure these men are not forgotten. To this day, their resting places are lovingly tended by the Terrell War Relief Society. The names of the fallen in the order in which they took their final flight:

Richard Mollett, age 24 (November 30,

1941); William Ibbs, age 21 (January 18, 1942); George Hanson, age 20 (January 21, 1942); Raymond Berry, age 19 (February 7, 1942); Leonard Blower, age 21 (February 7, 1942); Aubrey Atkins, age 24 (February 14, 1942); James Craig, age 19 (May 28, 1942); Geoffrey Harris, age 21 (September 17, 1942); Allan Gadd, age 31 (October 27, 1942); Thomas Travers, age 21 (October 27, 1942); Alan Langston, age 19 (February 1, 1943); Vincent Cockman, age 20 (February 20, 1943); Frank Frostick, age 22 (February 20, 1943); Michael Hosier, age 20 (February 20, 1943); Maurice Jensen, age 19 (February 20, 1943); Kenneth Coaster, age 19 (September 17, 1943); Maurice Williamson, age 20 (November 27, 1943); Harold Slocock, age 19 (February 7, 1945); Thomas Beedie, age 26 (September 3, 1945); Raymond Botcher, age 21 (September 3, 1945).

P.S.
INSIGHTS, INTERVIEWS &
MORE . . .

■ ■ ■ ■

ABOUT THE BOOK

■ ■ ■ ■

AUTHOR'S NOTE

On January 17, 1991, an article written by Dan Shine appeared in the *Dallas Morning News* titled "The Air Unites Us" and told the story of Virginia Brewer, sixty-eight at the time, who looked after the twenty graves of fallen British pilots in Terrell, Texas. It was my introduction to the No. 1 British Flying Training School and sparked the idea for a story that haunted me through the years.

In 1940, as Great Britain was drawn further into war with Germany, the government realized it needed many more Royal Air Force pilots than could be trained in a small island country in danger of attacks from enemy aircraft. Initially, schools to train RAF pilots were established in a number of Commonwealth countries, but more schools were needed. Therefore, Prime Minister Winston Churchill approached President Franklin Roosevelt for assistance.

Because the United States had adopted an isolationist policy, a great deal of strategizing occurred to find a way to help Britain without the United States appearing to be actively involved in the war effort. In 1941, civilian pilot training schools were converted to British Flying Training Schools. The first BFTS was established in Terrell, Texas. Two more would be located in Oklahoma and then one in California, Arizona, and Florida. For the span of a few months, a seventh school was opened in Sweetwater, Texas. (It was later used to train women pilots.) The first British cadets arrived in June 1941, the last in early 1945. During those years more than 6,600 pilots earned their wings at these civilian schools.

Terrell, Texas, and the airmen who protected the skies over Great Britain hold a special place in my heart, because my father graduated from Terrell High School and my mother was a young girl growing up just outside of London as bombs fell.

Although this story takes place in Texas, the fictional flight school and town are meant to be a representation of all the BFTS's and neighboring towns. While I have tried to be as factually accurate as possible, I have taken some literary license. I was unable to find a specific example of a woman serving as a flying instructor at a BFTS, but women were training pilots for the U.S. military, so I feel that somewhere they may have also trained British pilots. I did find examples of women teaching navigation and meteorology as ground instructors in the classroom. They also served as Link Trainer operators, mechanics, administrative staff, parachute riggers, and control tower operators.

Will's crash into a mountain was based on a February 20, 1943, incident that involved two AT-6's crashing into the Kiamichi Mountains in Oklahoma. On February 20, 2000, the students of a small school in Rattan, Oklahoma, erected a marker at one of the crash sites to commemorate those lost and to ensure that aspect of the war was never forgotten.

The student falling out of the cockpit during a roll is based on a documented account of a cadet who forgot to harness himself in. As is the incident of one plane landing on top of the other, with minor injuries suffered and the aircraft severely damaged.

This story also incorporates other aspects of World War II history. American fliers joined the RAF before the United States declared war on Germany. Because of the

Neutrality Acts, they were at risk of losing their American citizenship. The exact number who joined up is unclear because not all admitted to being Americans — hoping to avoid having their involvement confirmed so they could return to the U.S. after the war. Unable to use their passports or obtain visas, they had to sneak out of the United States via Canada to travel to England to join the RAF. *Yanks in the RAF* by David Alan Johnson is a fascinating account of those who began their service before December 7, 1941.

British Squadron 601 *was* nicknamed the Millionaire's Squadron because its fliers were members of White's, an exclusive gentlemen's club. Sons of the aristocracy, the wealthy, and the elite, they proved themselves during the Battle of Britain.

Peter's escape from Stalag Luft III was based on an actual escape from the prison camp that housed captured airmen. On the night of March 24, 1944, seventy-six prisoners escaped through a tunnel. Seventy-three were recaptured. Furious by the embarrassment, Hitler ordered fifty executed. The movie *The Great Escape* was based on the escape from this camp.

*British plot within Oakland Memorial Park, Terrell,
Texas.*

All photos by Lorraine Heath.

Monument dedicated by Lord Halifax, British ambassador to the United States, on April 16, 1942.

A peek inside a Link Trainer. This is an older model, not the blue box originally used at the school in 1941.

The Link Trainer crab that marked the pilot's course.

Link Trainer controls managed by the Link operator.

Flight sergeant jacket with wings.

READING GROUP GUIDE

1. Prior to reading *Girls of Flight City* were you familiar with the various jobs American women took on in helping to train British Royal Air Force pilots?

2. Jessie, Rhonda, and Kitty each have very distinct personalities. Which of the three women resonated with you the most?

3. Despite aviation being a heavily male dominated space, Jessie fights fiercely to become an instructor to train British pilots for the RAF. What were some of the challenges that came along with being a woman in this space? What were the rewards?

4. The girls of flight city played a big role in preparing the young British cadets for flight, sacrificing a great deal in the process. Would you have taken on the girls'

role if you were placed in their shoes?

5. What did you make of Rhonda and Peter's relationship? Were you surprised by how their relationship unfolded?

6. At sixteen, Kitty was excited about all the young men coming to her town and was hoping to experience her first taste of love. How did she change throughout the story?

7. How do you think Jessie's, Rhonda's, and Kitty's lives might have evolved or been different if the British had never come to Terrence?

8. Were you satisfied with the ending of the novel? Is there anything you would change?

ABOUT THE AUTHOR

When multiple *New York Times* bestselling author **Lorraine Heath** received her BA degree in psychology from the University of Texas, she had no idea she had gained a foundation that would help her create believable characters — characters often described as "real people." Her most recent novels include *The Duchess Hunt, Scoundrel of My Heart, Beauty Tempts the Beast,* and *The Earl Takes a Fancy.* The daughter of a British beauty and a Texan stationed at RAF Bovingdon, Lorraine was born in England but soon after moved to Texas. Her dual nationality has given her a love for all things British and Texan, and she enjoys weaving both heritages through her stories.